THE
DEADLY
MYSTERY
OF THE
MISSING
DIAMONDS

T0025826

ALSO BY T E KINSEY

Lady Hardcastle Mysteries:

A Quiet Life in the Country

In the Market for Murder

Death Around the Bend

Christmas at the Grange

A Picture of Murder

The Burning Issue of the Day

Death Beside the Seaside

The Fatal Flying Affair

THE
DEADLY
MYSTERY
OF THE
MISSING
DIAMONDS

T E KINSEY

THOMAS & MERCER

This is a work of fiction. Names, characters, organizations, places, events, and incidents are either products of the author's imagination or are used fictitiously. Any resemblance to actual persons, living or dead, or actual events is purely coincidental.

Text copyright 2021 by T E Kinsey
All rights reserved.

No part of this book may be reproduced, or stored in a retrieval system, or transmitted in any form or by any means, electronic, mechanical, photocopying, recording, or otherwise, without express written permission of the publisher.

Published by Thomas & Mercer, Seattle

www.apub.com

Amazon, the Amazon logo, and Thomas & Mercer are trademarks of Amazon.com, Inc., or its affiliates.

ISBN-13: 9781542020787
ISBN-10: 1542020786

Cover design by Emma Rogers

Cover illustration by Jelly London

Printed in the United States of America

THE
DEADLY
MYSTERY
OF THE
MISSING
DIAMONDS

France,
July 16, 1917

Dearest Flo,
I don't know when, or even if, you're going to get this – the mail has been taking an age to get across the Channel lately. I'll go ahead and write it anyway, and hope for the best.

Thank you for your last. I loved the story about Gertie Farley-Stroud and her new dog. Won't it get confusing if they call the dog Gertie, too? Maybe she shouldn't have let her granddaughter name it. Anyway, I'd love to see them again when I next get some leave – both the lady and the dog. She's my third favourite Englishwoman. (And look at that – I've been so long among you all that I've forgotten how to spell. There's no 'u' in favorite. I'm going native.)

I know I complain, but life behind the front lines isn't so bad, really. Obviously I can't say much about what we see, but among the, let's say, 'unpleasantness' (I wonder if that's mild enough for the censor – you'll have to let me know) there are always moments of joy and hope, no matter how small or fleeting. The boys can be so funny and charming, even in their darkest moments. I wonder if that's an English thing. You seem to cope with adversity with defiant resignation. Except that you're not English, are you? But you're only half Welsh, surely? (I await your scathing response to that one.)

My fellow nurses are all absolute darlings. Well, most of them. I can't name names in a letter that might be intercepted by the Bosch (they might attempt to undermine our morale by exploiting our dissatisfaction, or some such bunkum) but if she uses my hairbrush without asking one more time, she'll learn not to mess with this 'Yank'. I know where we keep the senna, and no one wants to spend any extra time in these latrines, let me tell you.

Have you heard from Ivor? (I still can't bring myself to call him Skins – it really doesn't suit him.) Or even Barty? It's so frustrating. I only joined the Fannies to get closer to him – to keep him safe, maybe? I don't know how I thought that would work, but it made sense when I left Maryland. I knew I could do nothing at all from three thousand miles away so I simply had to get closer. I just can't seem to actually get to him, though. I put in a request to be moved nearer to him every time I find out where his regiment is, but by the time I get there they've moved on, or he's performing in a concert party in Paris, or . . .

You get the picture. I don't think the Powers That Be in the First Aid Nursing Yeomanry are going to indulge me many more times.

I was wondering if he might have written to you or Emily, thinking the letter would be more likely to reach you than me. He's an idiot, but he's my idiot and it's frustrating to know I'm never more than a hundred miles from him and I still can't see him.

But I'm getting maudlin now, and I have to stop that. No one wants a sad-eyed nurse at their bedside and I have to be on duty in a moment.

So how about something a little lighter? There was an incident nearby that made me think of you and it was sufficiently exciting that it was reported in the local newspaper (clipping enclosed). There was an old-fashioned hold-up on the road to Calais. I wanted to imagine men with bandanas over their faces, armed with Colt six-shooters, riding palominos and holding up the stagecoach, but the newspaper tells a more mundane story (the French press can be very stodgy and strait-laced sometimes). If my French is as good as I think it is, it was a man in an old coat with a muffler over his face. But he did have a six-shooter, even if it was a French army pistol, and he held up a small van on its way to the port.

But that's not the interesting part. Well, it's quite interesting, but it's not what made me think of you and Emily. The newspaper reported the theft of 'some cash' and 'the driver's lunch', but there's a rumour going around the aid station that the courier was carrying diamonds. Can you imagine it? An actual diamond thief. Right here in France, just like one of your cases back home. I thought of you two roaring into town in your beautiful motor car and solving it all, like one of your mysteries. Wouldn't that be fun?

But the clock has beaten me. There's a messenger waiting in the office to take the mail and I have to go and change some dressings.

Give my love to Emily. I promise to visit on my next leave.

Your friend
Ellie

Chapter One

Singer Mickey Kent announced the Charleston, and the gentle-men of the Aristippus Club and their lady guests whooped their approval. As the band struck up the familiar tune, a startlingly beautiful young thing, her face aglow and her headdress askew, loudly proclaimed the dance to be 'the capybara's spats', earning her a cheer of her own.

Skins Maloney looked out from behind his drum set at the wildly flailing dancers and smiled. He caught the eye of his old friend Barty Dunn and nodded towards a particularly uncoordi-nated gentleman dancing near the front of the low stage. He was half a beat behind the band, and his swivelling feet seemed in con-stant danger of tripping him up, but such was the look of unself-conscious pleasure on his doughy face that it was impossible to do anything but share his glee.

Dunn grinned round the neck of his double bass and inclined his head towards another candidate. This one had no chin, and a neck so thin that his shirt collar appeared to be floating freely in mid-air, but he, too, was lost in the joy of the dance. His delight was equally infectious.

His dance partner was less impressed. Twice now she had been jabbed in the ribs by an errant elbow, and she was trying to put some empty air between them to save herself from further injury.

It had been, as always, quite a night. The Dizzy Heights had been the club's resident band for some months, and it was the club, not the band, who thought themselves the lucky ones. Aspiring bands fought eagerly for even the sniff of a chance of a 'residency', no matter where, but the Dizzy Heights had long since passed 'aspiring' and were well on the way to 'highly respected'. Their reputation among jazz aficionados in London was such that clubs were chasing them rather than the other way round.

They had regular spots at a couple of the more fashionable jazz clubs on weeknights and kept Saturdays open for 'special' bookings (of which there was never a shortage). But Friday nights were spent at the Aristippus Club, a gentleman's club in Mayfair that was experimenting with providing regular entertainment for its younger members. The older members had a more traditional view of what a gentlemen's club should be and still tutted impatiently if anyone so much as breathed too loudly in the reading room, but there was a new generation coming through and they wanted some fun. A delegation had approached the band and a deal had been struck, not least because Skins was so amused by the club's nickname: 'Tipsy Harry's'.

It was always a lively crowd, who made up for in enthusiasm what they lacked in dancing talent and musical knowledge, and the band always had a splendid time. This evening's crowd — many of whom were there to celebrate the birthday of one of the members — had been among the most enthusiastic they had played for, and this, the third Charleston of the night, was the raucous climax to an already-exuberant affair.

There were cheers and applause as the band brought the song to a close.

'Thank you, ladies and gentlemen,' said Mickey through his tin speaking trumpet. 'You've been a wonderful audience and we've been the Dizzy Heights. Enjoy the rest of your evening. Goodnight.'

More cheers and applause followed, mingled with a few shouts of 'Shame!' and 'Just one more song!'

'Black Bottom!' called the capybara's-spats woman.

'I told you to be careful where you sat,' was the inevitable reply from her friend.

Laughter. More cheering. The band left the stage and retired to the back room that had been reserved for them. Bottles of beer and a heaped plate of sandwiches awaited.

'This is better than working for a living – eh, lads?' said Skins as he put his drumsticks in his old army pack and helped himself to a cheese sandwich.

Dunn was looking for a bottle opener. 'How would you know?' he said. 'You've never done a day's work in your life.'

'Well, no,' conceded Skins. 'But I've got a cracking good imagination. And my old man worked on the railways. I saw what proper work did to a bloke. And all I'm saying is I'd rather play a couple of hours for a bunch of "bright young things" than break my back laying track like my dad.'

Eustace Taylor, the band's trumpet player, had come into the room behind him.

'Well, you'd do better to put a bit of effort into it, if you don't want to find out first-hand what it's like laying track,' he said. 'Your timing was out in the middle eight of "Fascinating Rhythm". And do try to keep that blasted cymbal under control during my solo in "Dippermouth Blues", there's a good chap.'

Skins rolled his eyes and shook his head, but said, 'Right you are, Eustace. Always happy to receive your notes.'

Eustace frowned. 'Yes, well,' he said. 'Just you be careful.'

Skins had been playing ragtime since before the war and had been one of the first to bring proper American jazz to the London clubs as soon as he'd been demobbed. Eustace, meanwhile, had spent the years before his call-up playing second trumpet in the Dorsetshire Philharmonic. But his claim to a formal musical education (he was always suspiciously vague about where and with whom he had studied) gave him an all-too-apparent feeling of superiority over the lesser mortals in the band, despite having come to jazz comparatively late in life.

'How is it that you've never decked him?' asked Dunn once Eustace had retired to a corner of the room to annotate his trumpet score.

'Well, he's about six inches taller than me, for a start,' said Skins. 'I'm not sure I could reach. But you reckon I'm a good drummer, right?'

'Best in London.'

'That's what it says on the posters,' said Skins. 'But I'm all right. And the audiences? What do you think they reckon?'

'I don't think most of them would know a decent drummer from a coalman, but they don't complain.'

'Right,' said Skins. 'So, if you think I'm all right, and I think I'm all right, and the buck-and-wing and Charleston brigade think I'm all right, what do I care what the second trumpet in the Seaside Philharmonia thinks? Let him have his moment.'

'You're a better man than I am,' said Dunn.

'Never been in question, old son, never been in question. Hello, ladies.'

The band's saxophonists, Blanche Adams and Isabella 'Puddle' Puddephatt, always stuck together.

'How the devil are you, Skins?' said Blanche. 'Nice work in "Fascinating Rhythm" tonight. Well done. Loved that syncopation in the middle eight. Gave it a lovely feel.'

'Why thank you, ma'am,' said Skins, doffing an imaginary hat. 'What about you, Puddle? Did my humble efforts please you?'

'Everything about you pleases me, sweetie, you know that,' said Puddle. 'Is there any gin?'

'Just beer,' said Skins. 'But there's plenty of it.'

'That'll have to do,' she said. 'Pour me one, would you?'

Skins opened another bottle of beer and poured two glasses. He handed them to the woodwind section.

'This happens week after week,' said Blanche, pointing at the bottle. 'It's a bit much asking a girl to swill beer when there's gallons of champagne out in the other room. You got us this gig, Skins dear – do something about it, would you?'

'I sorted out the regular booking,' said Skins. 'But I didn't get involved in the catering.'

'Well, then, who did?'

'Elk, I think,' said Dunn. 'He served with the club's wine steward at Ypres. Or something. I forget the details.'

'We need a manager to sort these things out. Someone who can get us something other than beer to drink, at least. We can't leave it to the banjo player.'

Elk turned round. 'Did someone mention the banjo player?' he said.

'They did, mate,' said Skins. 'Blanche thinks you did a rubbish job sorting out the catering.'

Blanche scowled. 'I said nothing of the sort. I merely suggested that it shouldn't be up to the banjo player to have to arrange everything like this. We need a manager.'

'You'd get no complaints from me,' said Elk. 'It was a nightmare. You have no idea how much trouble I had to go to just to get them to put beer back here. They thought champagne would do. I mean, I ask you.'

Blanche shook her head.

'Not a bad night, though,' continued Elk, obliviously. 'Cool new bit in "Fascinating Rhythm", Skins. Nice one.'

Skins raised his glass. 'And that, my old mate,' he said to Dunn, 'is why I've never taken the trouble to lamp our trumpeter.'

◆ ◆ ◆

The Dizzy Heights had been formed in 1923 by Ivor 'Skins' Maloney and Bartholomew 'Barty' Dunn. The two men had made a name for themselves in the years before the war, performing the new ragtime music that had made its way over from America in the 1900s. They had played in several bands of varying degrees of competence and popularity before striking out on their own as musical mercenaries, billing themselves as 'The Greatest Rhythm Section in London'.

Skins had been a lively boy, always quick with a joke and quicker to dodge out of the way of the cuff round the ear that inevitably followed his cheeky remarks. His grandmother had delighted in telling him, 'You should be on the stage, little Ivy.'

Indulgently, he had always said, 'You reckon, Nan?'

And she would say, 'Yes, son. Sweepin' it.' She would cackle wheezily at her own comic brilliance, and little Ivor would smile kindly and scamper off to find fresh mischief.

But he'd loved the music hall, and he actually did want to be on the stage. He was so often seen hanging around the stage door that the stagehands came to know him, and occasionally enlisted his help fetching and carrying for them. As a reward, they would let him in from time to time, to watch a show from the wings. He learned the comic routines and knew all the songs, and dreamed that one day, just as his nan had said, he really would be on the stage where he belonged.

In 1900, at the age of ten, his first proper job in the theatre – also exactly in accordance with his nan's predictions – involved sweeping the stage.

He was cleaning up one morning while the band were running through some new numbers. The percussionist, hemmed in by a big bass drum, a snare drum, a pair of cymbals, and assorted whatnots and thingummies that Ivor was unable to identify, missed his cue and completely fluffed the snare drum flourish that was supposed to end the song. The band fell silent apart from a few impatient tuts from the piano player, so that the only sound in the theatre was little Ivor's boyish laugh.

This induced the rest of the band, who weren't known for their serious outlook on life, to laugh, too. They liked Ivor the Errand Boy and were inclined to indulge him. Even the percussionist's frustrated embarrassment at his own mistake evaporated once he realized who had been mocking him.

'You reckon you can do any better, you little chimp?' he said. 'Get down here and try it. Go on. Shilling says you can't.'

Never one to pass up the possibility of extra cash, Ivor clambered into the orchestra pit and wormed his way into the percussionist's corner. He watched carefully as the tall drummer demonstrated the figure but then stood unmoving as the man handed him the sticks.

'Go on then, little man. Show us what you've got.'

'I can't,' said Ivor with uncharacteristic meekness.

'You seemed a good deal more cocky up there on the stage,' said the drummer. 'Not so easy now you're down here, is it?'

He reached out for the sticks but Ivor held on to them.

'No, I mean I can't reach the drum,' he said. 'You must be about nine bleedin' foot tall. How am I supposed to reach the drum from down here where the normal people live?'

The band laughed again, and a few moments later they had found an old beer crate for the boy to stand on. He held out the sticks.

'Like this?' he said.

The drummer adjusted his grip slightly and Ivor smiled. That felt right.

He tentatively tapped the snare drum. It was loud. Much louder than he had expected. He tapped it again. He had the feel of it now.

'Want me to show you again?' said the drummer.

'No, I've got it.'

He tried the figure slowly. The sticks bounced off the taut drum skin faster than he could control them, and the little flourish ended in a chaotic, rattling jumble.

To Ivor's surprise – and immense relief – no one laughed.

'Give it another go,' said the drummer.

Ivor tried another four times, each time getting a little better but each time ending in a clattering mess.

He took a deep breath. Steadied himself. And had one last try.

He rattled through the little drum figure at full pace and finally got it dead on. The band applauded.

'You want to watch out, mate,' said one of them. 'The sweeper-upper's after your job.'

From then on, Ivor spent all his spare time in the orchestra pit, watching, learning, and asking endless questions. The percussionist gave him an old pair of sticks to practise with, and he drove his family mad, tapping out rhythms on any available surface. But it paid off. Later that year when the percussionist was ill, Ivor stood in. His proficiency earned him the nickname 'Skins'. The name also suited his skinny – though he preferred 'wiry' – frame, but people seldom commented on that, nor his short stature. What struck almost everyone who saw him was the smile. Few had ever said he was handsome, but the warm, cheeky smile, so freely offered to almost everyone he met, guaranteed that a fair proportion of them would later declare him 'oddly attractive' or 'weirdly good-looking'. His personal favourite had been a girl from Tottenham who had said, 'I don't know what it is . . . there's something about you . . . is it your hair?' He was very proud of his hair. By the time he was eighteen, he had left the theatre and was working as the drummer in a ragtime band with his old mate Barty.

Barty Dunn had known Ivor since they had played together on the streets of Hornsey, where they grew up. Unlike his diminutive pal, no one was ever in any doubt as to why they found Dunn attractive – he was most definitely the good-looking one of the pair. Tall, athletic, and with the darkest blue eyes anyone had ever seen (or so he had been told, many, many times), he was everyone's idea of handsome. He was generally genial and charming, but was given to bouts of melancholy brooding which, to Skins's perpetual bafflement, seemed to make him even more attractive. While Skins was bouncing around, larking and joking, trying to charm the girls, Dunn just had to, as Skins put it, 'stand there looking sullen' and the girls would 'throw themselves at him'.

Although Dunn's family had been no better off than their neighbours, they had aspirations for their children (more often characterized as 'ideas above their station') and the young Dunns were all encouraged to learn musical instruments. Barty was given piano and violin lessons and worked hard at both, but the first time he saw a double bass he knew that was the instrument for him.

His parents couldn't properly afford the battered second-hand violin they'd bought him from the pawn shop, and they certainly couldn't stretch to something as exotic – and inconveniently huge – as a double bass, so he admired the instrument from afar. But he put a few pennies away each week from his job at the Barratt's sweet factory in Wood Green, and by the time Skins was ready to join a ragtime band, Barty had his own double bass and nothing could stop him following his old pal on the path to fame and fortune.

Black American soldiers had introduced the boys to the new 'jazz' music while they were serving in France, and as soon as they were demobbed, they had set about assembling a group of like-minded musicians to take London by storm.

It had taken them four years and many changes of personnel to get what they were after, but eventually they had the band they wanted. Gigs were hard to come by at first – clubs were still a little suspicious of the new music – but slowly the doors started to open to them as the 'bright young things' demanded the music they were listening to on their gramophones. The Dizzy Heights had arrived.

◆　◆　◆

When the party had finally wound down and the last of the guests had tottered tipsily on to the streets, the band retrieved their instruments and cleared the makeshift stage. Eustace Taylor packed up his trumpet, Benny Charles his trombone. Blanche and Puddle had a saxophone and a clarinet each. Elk Elkington put away his banjo and Mickey Kent tied a length of string to his speaking trumpet and slung it over his shoulder.

It was getting on towards dawn and the buses and trams were already running, taking the early starters to work, but they served just as well to take the late finishers in the band home. All except Skins and Dunn.

Skins and his drum set had been turned away from more buses and trams than he could count ('You can't bring all that tat on here, mate – what do you think this is, a bleedin' totter's cart?'), and the one time he'd tried to get it down the escalator at a tube station had ended in disaster. Dunn and his double bass had fewer problems by comparison, but it was still like travelling with a drunk friend, and he, too, had been turned away from many a bus with a weary 'Only room for one more, mate, sorry.'

They had the use of a storeroom at Tipsy Harry's if they wanted it, but it wasn't always convenient and they often needed somewhere else to store their bulky instruments. Fortunately, Barty Dunn 'knew a bloke' who ran a shop on New Row, near Covent Garden. In return for free admission to any club the boys happened to be playing, and the occasional complimentary drink, he let them store their instruments in the shop's stockroom. The only problem that remained was how to get them there.

To this end, they had invested in a large handcart which would carry Skins's drums and Dunn's double bass and still leave room for any extras – their best suits if they'd been playing somewhere posh, or a crate of beer left over from the show, perhaps. Most often the space was occupied by Dunn's romantic conquest of the evening, who would giggle her way round town before he whisked her back to his digs in Wood Green.

Tonight, though, Dunn had left the party with only Skins, his bass, and a few bottles of champagne liberated from the party on his way out.

'Unusual for you to be bird-less after a gig,' said Skins as they wound through the deserted West End streets, pushing their clattering cart. 'Although it's been happening a lot lately, hasn't it?'

'A worrying trend, mate,' said Dunn. 'That one with the massive feather on her headband kept giving me the glad eye, but by the time we came off she was canoodling in the corner with some chinless twit with a monocle. A bleedin' monocle.'

'Losing your touch, then?'

'Do you know, I think I might be. It's been weeks since I've had so much as a chaste peck on the cheek. What if I'm getting too old?'

'You've only just turned thirty.'

'Five years ago,' said Dunn. 'I'm ancient now. No one wants to go to bed with an ancient bass player.'

'Look on the bright side, though. There were times not so long ago when we didn't think we'd live to see thirty. But we got through it. And you'll get through this little drought. And you're a jazz musician. We're cool. The kids love a musician.'

They had arrived at the shop by now. Skins let them in and Dunn helped him lug his drums and traps case through to the back. With the gear safely stowed, they locked up and leaned the cart against the wall. They said their goodbyes on St Martin's Lane and Dunn strolled off towards the bus stop, whistling a tune they'd been trying to learn after hearing it on a gramophone record brought over by some visiting American musicians. Skins carried on up past Seven Dials and on towards Bloomsbury.

By the time Dunn got to Finsbury Park, the sun was up and people were already making their way to work. He couldn't face the two-and-a-half-mile walk home, so he opted to wait for a tram to take him to Wood Green.

◆ ◆ ◆

Barty Dunn made his way round the corner from the tram stop at Wood Green, to the little terraced house on Coburg Road where he rented a room from Mrs Phyllis Cordell. She had lost her husband and both her sons in the Great War, and had welcomed Dunn into her home. She was grateful for the much-needed rent, and for the company of the rakish musician who added a bit of glamour to the otherwise perfectly ordinary, working-class street. Although, by Dunn's reckoning, she was not much more than ten years his senior, Mrs Cordell doted on him like an indulgent mother, chuckling over his tales from the clubs and clucking over his hangovers and minor ailments.

She didn't mind the strange hours he kept, nor did she bat an eyelid at the seemingly endless succession of pretty young ladies who emerged from his room just after lunch several times a week. She made them a cup of tea and offered them a sandwich, chattering away as though she was delighted to have them in her home. Which she was. But she didn't expect to see them again. She knew it would be a different face that came blushing into her parlour next time.

This was the sole source of friction between tenant and landlady.

'I don't mind who you spend the night with,' she had said one afternoon as she handed him yet another cup of tea. 'And I don't mind what you get up to when you do. Lord knows I'd enjoy a bit of that meself if I ever got the chance. Not that I ever will. Woman of my age.' She laughed at the very idea of such a thing. 'But I don't want to see you ending up lonely. You need to find a nice young woman. A war widow, maybe. Settle down. Make a life for yourself. A family. You need a family around you. Everybody needs that.'

'But what would you do then, Mrs C?' he'd asked with a smile. 'I can't leave you on your own.'

'I'll have Gallipoli,' she said, and patted the gormless mongrel's friendly head.

She had adopted the dopey dog a few years earlier and had named him after the disastrous campaign that had taken both her boys from her. The neighbours had tutted.

'You don't want to be calling him that,' one had said. 'It'll be like dwelling on it. You should put it all behind you. No good'll come from reminding yourself of it every time you call the dog in.'

But she had insisted that it would be a comfort. The name of her new canine companion would take the sting out of it.

'It might have took my boys,' she had said, 'but now I can hear the name and think of this little fella instead. I can remember my

17

boys as the two handsome lads who went off to war, and Gallipoli as the silly little mutt who keeps me company now they've gone.'

It didn't make sense to anyone but her and Dunn.

He let himself into the darkened house with his latchkey. Mrs C always left him a glass of milk and a tongue sandwich on a shelf in the larder – 'just in case you're hungry when you get in' – and he sat at the kitchen table and ate it while he waited for tiredness to tell him to take himself off to bed.

Gallipoli had heard him come in and stirred himself from his basket by the stove to see if there might be any food on offer. Dunn peeled a slice of tongue from the generously filled sandwich and shared it with the dog, who ate it greedily. He lolled sleepily against Dunn's leg for a few moments more, but when it became evident that there was to be no more to eat, he padded back to his basket and settled down again.

'Room in there for an old soldier?' said Dunn, but the dog was already asleep. 'Better get myself upstairs, then. See you tomorrow, old mate.'

After a quick visit to the toilet in the tiny backyard, Dunn trod lightly up the stairs and into his room. Mrs Cordell had taken the wartime blackout restrictions more seriously than most and had run up thick, heavy curtains to try to stop light from spilling out on to the street.

'What you doing that for?' her neighbour had asked. 'We've got the streetlights half covered up.'

'And when the zeppelins come,' said Mrs C, 'they'll see your house, not mine. You can come and sleep in my parlour when they bomb you out.'

'What are they going to bomb us for, all the way out here?'

'The sweet factory. Good for morale – sweets. They want to break us, them Germans.'

'Liquorice Allsorts,' laughed her neighbour. 'Vital war supplies.'

Mrs Cordell had blacked out her windows nevertheless, and her neighbours had nervously followed suit. Now, nearly seven years after the end of the war, the blackout curtains served to supply semi-nocturnal Barty Dunn with the darkness he needed to sleep his way through the morning.

He threw his clothes over the back of the chair and all but fell into his bed. Sleep came almost immediately.

◆　◆　◆

It only took Skins about twenty minutes to walk home from the shop. He and his wife, Ellie, lived in a Georgian town house on a leafy street not far from the British Museum. The house was part of a row of similarly impressive dwellings, each fronted with white-painted stone at the ground floor, with dun-coloured bricks on the three upper floors. A gate in the black-painted railings opened to give access to the 'area' below street level – the servants' and tradesmen's entrance to the house – while the front door was reached by climbing a flight of six stone steps. The tall windows on the first floor gave on to narrow balconies which none of the street's residents ever used. It was rather more house than anyone expected a jazz drummer to live in, and they were right to think so – it was Ellie who had bought it for them using money from her inheritance.

Under the terms of her father's will, the entire – quite substantial – family fortune should have become hers when she married. When the trustees in America had learned that her husband-to-be was a musician, however, they had invoked 'the gold-digger clause'. It had been inserted by her father's lawyers to protect her from such undesirable ne'er-do-wells and had frozen the bulk of the money until the tenth anniversary of their marriage.

Under pressure from her Aunt Adelia, they had grudgingly released enough to enable her to buy a property in London suitable for a member of the Wilson family of Annapolis. There was an annual allowance, too, sufficient to keep her comfortable. But the trustees handled the household bills and servants' wages themselves and were unwilling to allow her control of the full amount until they knew that this Maloney fella meant business.

Skins let himself in. It was half past four in the morning so there was no one about. Even the housemaid – who, it seemed to Skins, was always working – was still fast asleep. He knew he should be, too, and that if he got his head down as quickly as possible, he'd be able to spend some time with Ellie and the children before he had to go out to work again.

Like Dunn, though, he found himself too wide awake to go straight up and instead went to the kitchen to make himself a cup of cocoa. He took it through to the drawing room, where he planned to sit in his favourite armchair and read yesterday's paper.

When he arrived he found Ellie lightly snoring in her own favourite chair, her dark hair strewn across the winged back and the paper resting on her delicate nose. He gently touched her arm and she stirred.

'Hello, love,' he said. 'What are you doing down here?'

She folded the paper and sat up. 'Catherine had a nightmare so I went to try to comfort her. By the time she was settled I was so wide awake I thought I might as well come down here and wait for you.'

'Poor kid. Is she all right?'

'She's fine. But how are you? You must be done in.'

'I'm fine, too. And all the better for seeing you. I wish I'd known you were down here, though – I'd have made you some cocoa.'

She smiled. 'I was hoping to be able to welcome you home, but I nodded off. Sorry.'

'Don't be daft,' he said as he sat down. 'Anything good in the paper?'

'Not a thing.'

'There never is,' he said. 'I don't know why we bother with it. We hardly get time to read it, and when we do, we just complain it wasn't worth reading.'

'We need to keep up with current affairs,' she said.

'And why's that?'

'I come from a very political family. We like to keep our fingers on the pulse.'

'Which is why you used to be a nurse, obviously. It all makes sense now.'

'The metaphorical pulse, goofus.'

They had met in Weston-super-Mare in 1910 when Ellie was touring Europe with her aunt. That trip got 'a little out of hand' and the two women were spirited home by the American embassy after a series of unpleasant incidents at their hotel. But the encounter at the Arundel Hotel where Skins and Dunn had been playing with Robinson's Ragtime Roisterers had changed their lives forever.

Skins had managed to hand her his calling card before she was whisked away, and the two youngsters struck up a transatlantic correspondence that carried on uninterrupted until the war. Their letters became more sporadic as the mail ships began to face attacks in 1915. The last letter Ellie received from him told her that Skins and Dunn had volunteered together for the Middlesex Regiment and were certain to be in France by the end of the year. Ellie had no intention of leaving it at that. She had a plan, and it only took three years of working her way round the local aid stations in France to get it to work perfectly.

Skins had thought himself lucky to get all the way to the summer of 1918 with only minor scratches and a bruised ankle to show for it. Then, one bright, sunny day in August 1918, a stray shell landed directly in front of his company's trench. Skins was leaning against the wall telling a joke about a talking dog when the shell exploded. The sturdy construction of the trench had protected him and all his friends from the blast, but the signpost on the trench's lip, pointing westwards and indicating that Tipperary was 'a long, long way', did not fare so well. It was knocked over by the force of the explosion and landed on Skins's unprotected head, knocking him unconscious.

The official record showed simply that he had been wounded in combat, but the unofficial record kept by one of the junior officers said that he had been 'rendered unconscious by a sign of dubious comic value while telling a joke of equally dubious comic value and being, in direct contravention of Standing Orders, sans tin hat'.

He regained consciousness quickly, but the sign had opened a gash in his head that required stitches. He was taken to the local aid station where he was seen by an excitingly familiar American nurse. She stitched his head wound and demanded that he spend at least two hours of his next leave taking her to dinner.

They married as soon as he was demobbed in 1919.

And now, to the intense irritation of her extended family, she was a musician's wife and living in London. Her uncles and cousins were completely unable to understand why she didn't want to marry a member of the Maryland senate and settle down where she belonged. Only her Aunt Adelia supported her decision to lead an independent, modern life.

'You probably ought to get back up to bed,' said Skins. 'I'll not be long.'

'I probably should,' she said. 'I've got things to do tomorrow.'

'Today.'

'Today, then, pedant. Can I have a sip of your cocoa?'

'Always.'

Ellie stood and took the cup from him, kissing the top of his head as she did so. She took an enormous gulp of the hot chocolate and set off upstairs.

Skins looked at the tiny dribble of cocoa she'd left him and settled down to read. In spite of his fervent belief that he wasn't anywhere near tired enough to go to bed, it wasn't long before he found his eyes swimming out of focus. It was time for bed after all.

Chapter Two

Sunday had been a day of rest, but the band had another late night on Monday in their regular slot at the Augmented Ninth. It was a new club that advertised itself as providing 'the hottest jazz and the coolest cocktails', and its clientele could listen to the latest tunes while getting themselves one more than one over the eight if they so chose. Skins had tried to tell the owners that if they had to explain the club's name it probably didn't work, but they were adamant. And he was right. None of the club-goers got it, but they knew it had something to do with music and they didn't care as long as the music and the booze were good.

Dunn had arrived home in the early hours of the morning and was fast asleep, dreaming about the band. Things were going well, but Skins seemed to have a broken bass drum. Every time he kicked the pedal it gave a rattling thud, not a satisfying boom. The more he kicked, the worse it got. He hit over and over again, getting faster and more urgent, while Dunn and the band marvelled at the speed and skill of their drummer's right foot. Perhaps he should consider taking tap-dancing lessons. But the sound just wasn't right. Maybe the skin was split.

A voice accompanied his drumming. 'Mr Dunn!' it yelled.

Very few people called him Mr Dunn.

'Mr Dunn! Open up. It's the police.'

Dunn struggled to consciousness.

The policeman was still hammering on the door.

Dunn got up and went to the window. He opened it and leaned out over the street.

'What,' he said groggily. 'The bleedin' hell. Do you want?'

The constable stepped back from the door and looked up. 'Mr Dunn?' he said. 'Mr Bartholomew Dunn?'

'The very same,' said Dunn. 'And you are?'

'Constable Grine, sir. I've been asked to take you to Scotland Yard.'

'What for?'

'No idea, sir. "Take a vehicle and pick up Bartholomew Dunn of 76 Coburg Road in Wood Green," they said. And here I am.'

Dunn sighed. 'Give me a couple of minutes to put some trousers and boots on,' he said. 'You can come in and wait – the door's open.'

He closed the window and looked around for his clothes.

Finally dressed, he made his way downstairs and found Constable Grine sitting in the front parlour reading one of Mrs Cordell's magazines.

'Will I be long?' he said.

'Long, sir?'

'This business at the Yard. Will it take long?'

'I couldn't say, sir. Depends what you've done.'

'I haven't done anything.'

'Then it shouldn't take long at all.'

'Am I under arrest?'

'You'd know if you was under arrest, sir,' said Grine. 'I'd have said, "You're under arrest." I have a whole spiel to go with it about taking things down and using them against you at your trial. You'd definitely have noticed. But I haven't said that, so you're fine.'

25

Dunn hunted round for a piece of paper and a pencil. 'I need to leave a note for my landlady,' he said. 'She'll wonder where I've gone.'

'Your landlady, sir?'

'She must have nipped out for a paper or something. She worries about me.'

'Right you are, sir.'

They left the house and Grine led the way to a Black Maria parked a short distance up the road.

'You're joking,' said Dunn. 'A prison wagon?'

'It's all that was available, sir.'

''Ere,' said a shrill voice from the front door of number 74. 'What do you mean by makin' all that racket this time of the mornin'? Ain't you got better things to do?' She caught sight of Dunn. 'Oh,' she said, 'they've finally come for you, 'ave they? I knew it wouldn't be long. No good ever come of havin' musicians on the street.' She leaned into the word 'musicians' to emphasize her contempt.

'It was bound to happen sooner or later, Mrs M,' said Dunn cheerfully. 'They were always going to catch up with me.'

'I knew it,' she said triumphantly. 'Well, good riddance to ya.'

'See you later, Mrs M,' he said. 'Let Mrs C know where I've gone.'

'Oh, I will,' she said. 'Don't you worry about that. That poor woman deserves a better lodger than you after all she's been through.'

Grine opened the door at the back of the van and Dunn started to clamber inside.

'Lovely woman,' said Grine.

'It's a cheerful and friendly neighbourhood, Constable. Cheerful and friendly.'

'It very much seems that way, sir. Make yourself as comfortable as you can. We've got one more stop to make, then we'll go to the Yard.'

◆　◆　◆

The next stop, though Dunn was initially unable to work out where they were from inside the windowless van, turned out to be in Bloomsbury. He sat alone for about ten minutes in the motionless vehicle with only the ticking of the cooling engine to keep him company before the door opened and Skins clambered in to join him.

Constable Grine slammed the door and a few moments later they were off.

'Morning, mate,' said Skins. 'Nice day for an outing.'

'Any idea what's going on?' asked Dunn as the van rattled along.

'Not a clue,' said Skins. 'I was fast asleep, dreaming sweet dreams, and suddenly there's Ellie shaking me awake and telling me that the police want to speak to me. I thought of legging it out the window before I remembered I hadn't done anything.'

'And your bedroom's on the second floor.'

'That, too. So I pulled on some trousers and went down to see what was what.'

'And what was what? Grimes was in your morning room?'

'Grine,' said Skins.

'Really? Poor bloke.'

'Really. He was there, though, like you say. Although he was in the drawing room. The housekeeper had made him a cup of rosy and he was sitting there reading a magazine—'

'Good old Mrs Dalrymple.'

'Salt of the earth. Wouldn't be without her. Always happy to supply visiting rozzers with tea, our Mrs Dalrymple.'

'The boys in blue do like a cup of char. He's quite a one for the magazines as well, that lad. He was reading one of Mrs C's when I found him.'

'It's important to keep up to date. So anyway, he says, "Would you mind accompanying me to Scotland Yard, please, sir?" And I said—'

'You said you were only a drummer, but if he hummed a few bars your wife would probably be able to pick it up on the piano.'

'He wasn't impressed,' said Skins. 'Usually goes down all right, that one. So into the deafening silence that followed one of my best gags, I just said, "Why?"'

'And he didn't know.'

'Apparently not. Just doing his job . . . they don't tell him nothing . . . All the usual rubbish. So here I am with my best mate in the back of a Black Maria when I should be fast akip in my comfy bed.'

'Still, like you said, it's an outing, isn't it?' said Dunn. 'Nice trip down to the river. Do us good.'

'Not exactly sightseeing, though, is it? Why don't they put windows in these things?'

'To shield the alleged miscreants from the vulgar gaze of the populace, me old mate. You can't have every Tom, Dick, and Harry gawping in at the prisoners. Wouldn't be right.'

'You're much more thoughtful and considerate than people give you credit for,' said Skins, stifling a yawn. 'This better be worth missing my kip for. Have we got another gig tonight?'

'Yup. It's the dance lesson at Tipsy Harry's.'

'Oh, that one. That's going to be a bore. Can't they use a gramophone? I don't mind playing for their posh dances, but a lesson?'

'Apparently they tried a gramophone but it wasn't loud enough. They need a band.'

'And they chose us,' said Skins.

'They chose the Finchley Foot-Tappers first, apparently – they didn't reckon a band of our calibre would be interested. The Foot-Tappers did one or two, I think, but they let them down at the last minute last week. One of the blokes had a word with Mickey and here we are.'

'So I've got to play for dance lessons for people who are too good for a gramophone after . . . What time is it?'

'It was showing five past eight on the clock on Mrs C's mantelpiece when I left.'

'After less than three hours' kip, then. This better be over quick so I can get my head down this afternoon or I'll end up face down in my traps tray.'

The two men lapsed into silence as the van chugged through the London streets. The journey to Victoria Embankment only took another ten minutes, but by the time they arrived at Scotland Yard, they were both asleep.

The door opened and slammed against the side of the van.

'Wakey, wakey,' said Constable Grine. 'We're 'ere.'

They struggled out on to the street and followed Grine into the turreted red-brick building.

'Yes?' said the bored sergeant behind the counter in the entrance hall.

'It's me, Sarge,' said Grine.

The sergeant looked up. 'So it is, lad, so it is. I thought you was out on a job for the Super.'

'I was,' said Grine, proudly. 'I've got 'em.'

The sergeant looked the two musicians up and down.

'They don't look like bank robbers to me,' he said.

Grine frowned in puzzlement. 'They're not. Not so far as I know, anyway.'

'Then what did you bring 'em in here for? Superintendent Nicholls wants the two suspects for the Midland Bank job. I wondered why they wasn't in handcuffs.'

'I fetched these two for Superintendent Sunderland,' said Grine. 'Not Nicholls.' This conversation wasn't going at all the way he had expected.

'Sunderland?' It wasn't going the way the sergeant had expected, either. 'Sunderland up on the third floor?'

'That's right, Sarge. Sent me out first thing.'

'But he's on secondment to the War Office. What does he want with these two loafers?'

'Oi,' said Skins. 'Less of the loafer.'

'You look like you was dragged out of bed,' said the sergeant.

'I was.'

'There you are, then. Loafer. The rest of us was at work.'

'And where were you at four this morning while I was at work?' said Skins. The conversation definitely wasn't conforming to his own modest expectations, either.

'Four in the morning, eh? What are you, then?'

'A musician.'

'Jazz?' said the sergeant, suspiciously.

Skins nodded.

The sergeant sneered. 'Even worse. Bleedin' racket. I liked you better when you was a loafer.'

'Now, Sergeant,' said Dunn in his silkiest tones. 'Let's not all get off on the wrong foot here. You don't like musicians, my colleague here doesn't like being called a loafer, poor Constable Grimes here—'

'Grine,' said the other three men in unison.

'Poor Constable Grine here,' continued Dunn, 'has been sent on an errand for a senior officer. Why don't you sign us in or whatever it is you do, and we can go and see this Superintendent Sunderland. You and my colleague can stop getting on each other's wick, Grine can complete his task, Sunderland can tell us what it is he wants us for, and then I can get back to my bed. I've had three hours' sleep and I'm due back at work at seven this evening. It might be a "bleedin' racket", but they only pay us if we're awake to make it.'

The sergeant looked him up and down again. He didn't like being told what to do, especially by civilians, but he was forced to concede that the tall man was talking sense, even if he was a musician wanted for questioning by a superintendent seconded to the War Office.

He recorded their details in the logbook and sent them with Grine to the third floor.

◆ ◆ ◆

Grine led them up more flights of stairs than Skins thought acceptable for first thing in the morning, and along a long, linoleum-floored corridor. He stopped at a door whose sign proclaimed it to be the entrance to the office of 'Detective Superintendent O N Sunderland.' He knocked smartly on the glass panel.

'Yes,' called a voice from inside.

Grine opened the door a fraction and leaned in.

'I've got the two men you wanted to see, sir,' he said.

'Have you, indeed?' said the unseen voice. 'Thank you very much. Send them in, please, Constable.'

Grine threw open the door and ushered the two musicians into the office.

Sitting behind the desk was a slim man who appeared to be in his late fifties. His thinning grey hair was neatly trimmed and his eyes were bright behind his round, wire-framed spectacles. His dark grey lounge suit was well cut and immaculately pressed, his silk tie perfectly knotted. He took off his glasses and stood to greet his visitors.

'Skins,' he said warmly. 'Dunn. Do come in. How marvellous to see you.'

Slightly puzzled, Skins and Dunn entered the room and shook the superintendent's hand.

'Sit down, please. Tea? Bring a tea tray, Constable, would you. And see if you can scare up any biscuits.'

Grine closed the door behind him.

'We've met before, haven't we?' said Skins. 'Before the war. Down in Gloucestershire. When Wally Holloway copped it at that party. You were Inspector Sunderland then.'

'That's it,' said Sunderland. 'Must be, what, seventeen years ago now? I'm glad you remembered.'

'I'm not likely to forget our trumpeter being bumped off. I mean, we've had some savage reviews over the years, but no one else has been so disappointed that they killed one of us.'

Sunderland laughed. 'I should think it sticks in the mind, yes.'

'Oh,' said Dunn, who had been struggling to recall. 'Littleton Cotterell. You're Lady Hardcastle's pal. I remember now.'

'That's it. I used to be with Bristol CID, but I moved up here after the war. You've . . . you've changed a lot.'

'Seventeen years, a world war, and being married to an American heiress will do that to a man,' said Skins. 'We were just kids when you met us.'

'I suppose you were, yes. You always seemed so self-assured.'

'Cocky.'

'A little,' said Sunderland with a smile. 'I confess I assumed you were older than you were.'

'We used to get that a lot,' said Skins. 'But you can hardly blame us for being a bit lippy. One of our mates had just copped it. That was a bit of a "rum do", as the officers used to say.'

'Wasn't it just? Rum do's seem to follow Lady Hardcastle around, though. Do you see much of her these days?'

'Her mate Flo and my wife are best pals. Have been for years. You know how it is when someone saves your life.'

'Really?' said Sunderland.

'Long story. But they write every week. Phone calls, too. Expensive blimmin' phone calls. So we see her and Lady H whenever they're in town – Lady H's brother and his family live in London. She claims she's getting too old for nightclubs. Makes a great show of how Flo has to drag her along, but they always have a great time. They're good company. The band loves them. How about you?'

'I love them, too,' said Sunderland.

'No, I mean, do you see them?'

'Not as often as I'd like, but we keep in touch. You know how it is.'

Dunn was beginning to get the tiniest bit impatient.

'No offence, Superintendent,' he said, 'but I'm assuming you didn't drag us both from our beds for some misty-eyed reminiscences about the olden days. How can we help you?'

'Dragged from your beds?' said Sunderland with some dismay.

'It was before eight in the morning,' said Dunn.

'Which seems like a perfectly reasonable—'

'We're musicians, Superintendent,' said Skins. 'We work nights.'

'Oh my lord, I really am sorry,' said Sunderland. 'I honestly didn't think. I just sent Grine off in a car—'

'In a Black Maria,' interrupted Dunn.

'In a what?'

'He said it was the only vehicle available,' said Skins.

'Good lord,' said Sunderland. 'It's not exactly the best way to get someone in to ask them a favour, is it? I'm really very sorry.'

Grine knocked and entered with the tea tray, then left without saying a word.

'You want a favour?' said Skins as Sunderland poured the tea.

'From us?' said Dunn.

'I do, indeed,' said Sunderland. 'It's a bit of an imposition – a bit of a damned cheek, if I'm brutally honest – but I think it'll be "right up your alley", as they say nowadays.'

'How's that, then?' said Skins. 'You need a band for the Met Police Summer Ball?'

'As a matter of fact I think we probably do, but that's not it, no. This is altogether more interesting. More intriguing. More the sort of thing you used to get involved in with our mutual pal.'

'Lady H?' said Dunn. 'Not sure it's fair to say we were ever "involved" in any of her cases. We just happened to be nearby a couple of times.'

Sunderland smiled. 'Even so, I imagine you'll find this one a – how did she put it? – "a bit of a lark".'

'Lady Hardcastle said that?' said Skins.

'Sounds like the sort of thing she'd say,' said Dunn.

'It does,' agreed Skins, 'but why did our names come up in a conversation between you and Lady H?'

'I'm sorry,' said Sunderland. 'I'm getting ahead of myself. Sugar?'

Skins grinned. 'Six lumps for me.'

Dunn tutted. 'Just two, please.'

'I burn a lot of energy,' said Skins.

'I'm sure you do,' said Sunderland. 'It's not really my thing, I'm afraid, but I imagine this new jazz music is quite energetic.'

'It can be if you're doing it right. Oh, ta.'

Sunderland handed him his cup of tea.

'Lady H,' said Dunn as he accepted his own tea with a nod of thanks. 'Favour. Bit of a lark.'

'Yes, quite right,' said Sunderland. 'My apologies. So easy to get sidetracked by tea. Let me see . . . How to begin . . . ? I suppose it's simplest to say a couple of my cases seem to have merged into one and I need a hand with some surveillance. And possibly a bit of discreet snooping.'

'From us?' said Skins.

'From you, yes. I have a squad of men of my own here, but only a small one – we're not at the top of the pecking order, crime-wise, so I have to make do.'

'And what is it you do?' said Skins. 'You and your team, I mean.'

'We deal with . . . older cases. Quite specific older cases,' said Sunderland.

'Burglaries? Fraud? Murder?'

'No, not quite. Although sometimes. Let's take a step back . . . How was your war?'

'I beg your pardon?' said Skins. 'My war?'

'Yes. How did you get on? You served?'

'Middlesex Regiment. Both of us. Joined up together.'

'Right,' said Sunderland. 'You got through it unscathed, I trust?'

'I got walloped on the head near the end,' said Skins. 'But Barty here didn't get so much as a hangnail.'

'To be fair, we spent a lot of time behind the lines entertaining the troops,' said Dunn. 'Concert parties and the like. We did our time in the trenches, obviously. A few assaults. But nothing like what a lot of the boys went through.'

'Quite. Takes guts,' said Sunderland.

'Don't know about that,' said Skins. 'Stubbornness and ignorance'll get you through most of it.'

Sunderland laughed. 'I'm sure you're making light of a terrible time. You know there were deserters, of course. Men who weren't blessed with your . . . stubbornness and ignorance, who took it upon themselves to bugger off and leave their mates to it.'

'We lost a few, yes,' said Dunn. 'Saw a couple shot "for cowardice". Not sure that was right, if I'm honest.'

Skins shook his head. 'Not young Bernie Butcher, at any rate. He was in a right state, that poor lad. He didn't know if he was coming, going, or been by the time they court-martialled him. Shell shock. Lost his mind. Terrible thing.'

Sunderland sipped his tea. 'There were some . . . Look, between these four walls, there were some appalling miscarriages of justice. But there were some among them whose minds hadn't been messed up, who just took off. And some of those used the whole thing as an opportunity to get away with some pretty serious crimes. And I've been given the unenviable task of trying to find them.'

'Rather you than me,' said Skins.

Sunderland smiled. 'It's not the glamorous end of policing, I grant you – very few dawn raids and pavement arrests. But I like to think I'm doing important work and it comes with occasional glimmers of excitement. Like now, for instance. I've got a lead on a missing deserter who could well be hiding out under your very noses. And his is a very interesting case indeed.'

'Under our noses?' said Dunn. 'One of the band?'

'Oh, good lord, no,' said Sunderland, quickly. 'My sources tell me you've been booked to play for dance lessons at the Aristippus Club in Mayfair. Is that right?'

'That's right,' said Dunn.

'That is right,' said Skins. 'You're better-informed than I am. I thought we were just Tipsy Harry's regular dance band. But like you say, we're booked to play for their dance lessons, an' all.'

'Who's Tipsy Harry?' asked Sunderland.

'It's what the members call the Aristippus Club,' said Skins. 'Don't ask me why.'

'Tipsy Harry . . .' said Dunn. 'Arri-stippus . . . ? Surely you can hear it.'

They looked blankly at him.

Dunn sighed. 'So, anyway, Aristippus was a Greek philosopher. He believed in taking pleasure, but not being controlled by it. He was very keen on control in general, actually. He liked the idea of adapting circumstances to suit himself, not adapting himself to his circumstances. Pupil of Socrates. Liked a drink. So "Tipsy Harry" seems like a good name for him. A Good Time Charlie if ever there was one. Or a Good Time Harry, in this case.'

The other two men simply stared at him.

'What?' he said. 'I live alone. I read.'

'Well, that explains the club's nickname, then,' said Sunderland. 'But anyway. There's a rumour of an inkling of a suspicion of a possibility that someone might have reported overhearing something that led us to surmise that it might just be imaginable that one of the men on our list, one Arthur Grant, is living it up in London.'

'Good solid lead, then,' said Dunn.

'It's the sort of flimsy gossip and hearsay I work with all the time, I'm afraid,' said Sunderland. 'The thing is, the name "Aristippus" has come up a couple of times, both as part of a missing deserter case and something altogether more baffling, and I can't ignore it. But neither do I have the manpower to investigate it properly. My little group redefines the notion of being "spread a bit thin". So I need a couple of likely lads on the inside who can do a bit of snooping on the QT and report back. And when I mentioned the case to Lady Hardcastle she suggested you two at once. Said you'd be perfect for the job.'

'Did she now?' said Skins. 'I can't say I'm not a bit disappointed she didn't come to us direct. You'd have thought Flo would have told Ellie, at least.'

'I'm so sorry, I assumed she had. Your wife's name came up in conversation, actually. It seems she already knows about the case.'

'Ellie knows about the case? The deserter?'

'Well, part of the case, anyway,' said Sunderland. 'It was in the papers when she was in France during the war. She told Flo about it. But I'm getting ahead of myself.'

'So it's more than just rounding up a deserter,' said Dunn. 'What, exactly, is it you want us to do?'

'As I said, just a bit of snooping. Eyes and ears open around the club, and let me know if anyone strikes you as a bit dodgy. Nothing dangerous.'

'What's this bloke Grant supposed to have done,' asked Skins, 'if he's not just your common or garden deserter?'

Sunderland took a moment to compose his thoughts. 'In 1917, around the time he disappeared, so did about twenty-five thousand pounds' worth of rough diamonds that had been smuggled out of Antwerp and across the German lines. They were on their way to Calais but they never made it.'

Skins whistled. 'Oh, so that's it. I do remember Ellie talking about that one. The whole area was buzzing with it, she said. She thought it was probably just a rumour, though. But it was real? And you reckon Grant pinched them?'

'It was and we do.'

'Whose were they?' said Dunn.

'Not his, that's for certain,' said Sunderland. 'To be honest, I've never managed to find out the full details. Obviously some well-to-do Belgian trying to get his wealth out of the country in case the Germans were there to stay after all – probably had it in mind to follow the gems to safety at a later date – but it's all been very hush-hush.'

'What happens when you catch him?'

'Grant? He goes on trial for desertion and theft.'

'How will we know him if we see him?' asked Skins. 'Presumably he's not calling himself Grant any more or you'd have him already.'

'His army record says he's five foot seven, brown hair, brown eyes, and wears a size eight boot,' said Sunderland. 'He was born in '95, so he's thirty years old.'

'So if we see someone who looks exactly like every other bloke who served in the war, he's our man.'

'In a nutshell, yes. But I'm hoping you'll spot someone who doesn't fit in. This man was a private, conscripted in 1916. Norfolk Regiment. He was a near-penniless farm labourer when he was called up, but now he's palling about with the toffs at "Tipsy Harry's". Or so the rumour goes. He must be pretty good to have gone unnoticed so far, but I doubt anyone's been looking too hard as long as he wears the right jacket to dinner and settles his bar bill.'

'It's quite a big club, Tipsy Harry's,' said Dunn. 'Lots of members. Lots and lots.'

'The official register says there are two hundred and thirty-six. We had a word with the secretary – very helpful chap. But there are fewer than four dozen of what he called "active members" – the sort who are there more than a few times a year – and just a handful of real regulars. And of them, just one small group of about the right age, all of whom joined within the past twelve months. Now we've linked Grant to the club, we're assuming he's one of this core of new regulars. It makes sense to me, at least, for reasons I'll come to in a minute.'

'Why now?' said Skins. 'If you know where he is – or where you think he is – why not just keep an eye on the place and take a closer look yourselves when you've got the manpower? Why do you need us at all?'

'I knew you were the men for the job,' said Sunderland. 'Straight to the heart of it. There's another side to all this, and time is very much not on my side. Our source first came to us – well, came to my colleagues in the Flying Squad, in fact – because he'd got word of a possible theft from the club. The Flying Squad passed it on to C Division CID, saying it was nothing to do with them. Not a robbery, you see? The Sweeney are only interested in armed blags, not burglaries. C Division smiled politely and filed it away, but a pal of mine there passed me the file when I sent round a memo asking if anyone had any intelligence on Arthur Grant and the Aristippus Club.'

'How is time against you, then?' asked Dunn.

'There's a dance contest coming up on the twelfth of June – a little over three weeks from now.'

'Which must be why they want us for their lessons,' said Skins. 'Getting ready for the big day.'

'That's my assumption,' said Sunderland. 'But that's not the interesting part. Not from a criminal point of view, at least.'

'You've not seen them dancing,' said Skins. 'We've played their Friday Night Bash – some of them ought to be locked up for crimes against the goddess Terpsichore.'

'She was a Muse,' said Dunn.

'What?'

'Terpsichore wasn't just any old goddess, she was one of the nine Muses.'

'I live and learn,' said Skins. 'But what's interesting about it, then?'

Sunderland chuckled. 'This is a Lady Hardcastle kind of inter-esting. There's a rumour . . . Actually, to be fair, this one is more of a legend. Or perhaps a myth. What do you know of the Treasure of the Mayfair Murderer?'

'Not a thing,' said Skins. 'Barty? Sounds like the sort of thing you'd have read about in your lonely Wood Green garret.'

'Doesn't ring a bell,' said Dunn.

'Shame,' said Sunderland. 'I hoped it might fire your imagina-tions. In 1805, the president of the Aristippus Club – one of its founder members – was hanged for the murder of a Hatton Garden diamond merchant. He had tunnelled into the merchant's premises from the cellar of the house next door and was helping himself to the contents of the safe when the merchant interrupted him. A scuffle ensued and the merchant was stabbed through the heart with an ornamental dagger—'

'Ornamental dagger?' interrupted Dunn. 'You're making this up, surely.'

'You'd think so, wouldn't you? No, it was an actual engraved ceremonial dagger – part of the official regalia of the Master at Arms of the Aristippus Club. That's how they caught him and how Sir Dionisius Fitzwarren-Garvie became known as "the Mayfair Murderer" – a lot more romantic than "the Hatton Garden Stabber". His trial was the talk of the town, partly because the robber was a toff from a posh club who turned out to be the most notorious jewel thief of his day, obviously. But what really got peo-ple gossiping and speculating was that the gems he stole from the merchant's safe were never recovered. His London home, his coun-try estate, his accomplices' homes . . . even his beloved Aristippus Club were all turned upside down. They never found a trace. And so began the legend of the Treasure of the Mayfair Murderer. Now, the smart money was always on one of his associates passing it to some unknown party – it was probably smuggled out of the country never to be seen again.'

'But?' said Skins.

'But legend has it that it's concealed in a secret vault at the Aristippus Club.'

'Now I know you're making it up,' said Dunn. 'Ornamental daggers *and* secret vaults? Pull the other one.'

Sunderland chuckled again. 'You're going to love the next part. For a hundred and twenty years people have searched the club looking for the treasure. Members, staff, private detectives, adventurers – they've all explored every corner of the club looking for the secret entrance to the vault. After Howard Carter found Tutankhamun's tomb, they even had a couple of Egyptologists poking around using "techniques learned from exploring the ancient pyramids". They've never found it.'

'Because it's not there,' said Dunn.

'So you'd think. But the legend persists. And it draws out all the chancers—'

'And loonies.'

'Them, too. But they all come sniffing round the Aristippus sooner or later. More so now there's a new rumour for them to work on. The latest scuttlebutt is that the clue to the treasure vault's location is in the club regalia. Some item in the garb or paraphernalia of the club officials holds the key, so they say, to the secret. The trouble is that the regalia itself is locked in its own impenetrable vault – actually, it's a rather ordinary safe in the club president's room, but they like to say "vault". Anyway, it's locked up tight and only brought out on high days and holidays.'

'Like, say, annual dance competitions?' suggested Skins.

'Exactly like that, yes, Skins old lad. The secretary has confirmed that the dance contest most definitely warrants a formal club ritual. So on go the robes, out come the daggers and the sceptres and the orbs and who knows what else, and they parade around at the opening ceremony like it was a coronation or the investiture of an archbishop.'

Skins was shaking his head. 'Let me see if I've understood. A bloke who deserted in France eight years ago, in 1917, might or might not have broken his cover to join a gentlemen's club in Mayfair, because he's worked out what a hundred and twenty years of detectives and archaeologists couldn't fathom.'

'And he needs access to the club regalia,' said Dunn, 'so he's joined in with the dance contest because that event guarantees all the club bigwigs will be out in their . . . in their big wigs, and that means he'll finally get access to the secret vault and the Mayfair treasure—'

'Which he doesn't need because he's got thousands of pounds' worth of uncut diamonds of his own already,' interrupted Skins.

'Exciting, isn't it?' said Sunderland.

'Why not just put a few of your blokes in the club on the night?' said Skins.

'I could have a dozen men on duty at the dance and they'd never spot our man – we've no idea who we're looking for. That's why we need you two to go in and see if you can find out a little more about these new chaps so we can narrow it down. And I couldn't afford it, anyway – I'd need a wheelbarrow-load of cash to pay the overtime. My little squad doesn't get handed that sort of money except on a dead cert. And probably not even then.'

Skins and Dunn laughed.

'Well, we're certainly cheap,' said Skins.

'But will you do it?' said Sunderland. 'You'll be there anyway, so it'll not cost you anything. And there's no danger. All I need is eyes and ears.'

'So you want us to look out from the stage and . . . and do what, exactly?' said Skins.

'Well, your view from the stage would be a good place to start. But then, just, you know, chat to them. Get to know them a little. See what's what.'

'And report back to you.'

'Just so,' said Sunderland. 'We'll nab the chap if needs be – there'll be no danger. Like I say, I just need eyes and ears inside the club.'

Skins and Dunn looked at each other, and Dunn shrugged. They and Ellie had talked often over the years about the exploits of their friends Lady Hardcastle and Flo Armstrong, wondering if they'd have been able to crack the cases those two worked on. None of them had ever truly thought they'd be any good at 'all that detective stuff', but the imagined glamour of it had always held some appeal. It certainly had for Skins. He loved the idea that Ellie had an actual spy in her family. He raised his eyebrows and looked imploringly at Dunn.

Dunn laughed. 'Go on, then. Why not?' He turned to Sunderland. 'He's always fancied himself as a bit of a Richard Hannay on the quiet.'

Skins sneered sarcastically at his old friend and raised two fingers.

'I don't mind if you don't want to do it,' said Sunderland. 'I've got nothing to offer but the unspoken thanks of a grateful nation, after all. But it'll take the pair of you, I think, so if you don't want to do it, Dunn, just say.'

'Course I do,' said Dunn. 'Truth is, Lady H used to speak very highly of you, too – though she still calls you "Inspector" Sunderland—'

'To my face, usually. I like to think of it as affectionate teasing.'

'Sounds like her. But the point is that she used to say you were one of the only coppers she'd trust in a pinch. I reckon she'd do it for you if she could. So I reckon we should, too.'

'That's marvellous,' said Sunderland. 'Simply marvellous. Thank you. Do help yourself to biscuits.'

◆ ◆ ◆

Sunderland had spent some time giving the boys as much information as he had about Arthur Grant's war record. It wasn't much, but at least they knew where he had served, and where and when he had last been seen. The superintendent had also asked for regular reports.

'Don't go to too much trouble over it – a brief note of what you saw, who you spoke to, that sort of thing. A phone call will do. Or a telegram. Just so I know how things are going.'

Then he had wished them well and sent them on their way, but not before he managed to find a car for Grine to take them home in.

'Let's send them back in something a bit more dignified, eh, Grine?' he said. 'Lord knows what their neighbours must have thought with you turning up in a blessed Black Maria. Do your best to restore their reputations, won't you?'

So they had set off from Victoria Embankment with Skins and Dunn in the back of the police car like visiting dignitaries.

'You reckon we can do this, then?' Dunn asked as they headed round Parliament Square.

'Like I keep telling you,' said Skins, 'I'm a dab hand at under-hand and stealthy. It's in my blood. If he really is a member at Tipsy Harry's, we can winkle this Grant bloke out no problem.'

'In your blood? You do talk tosh sometimes, mate.'

'Course I do,' said Skins. 'Part of my roguish charm, ain't it.'

'I suppose it is. But we've got to be careful.'

'I don't reckon there's no risk to us. No one knows we're working for the rozzers. And even if Grant starts to think we're asking too many questions, he's not going to do anything – he'll just clam up.'

'You're talking like you think we'll know him from the off,' said Dunn. 'He's been one step ahead of the army and the police for eight years and you reckon we'll swan in, take one look at the membership as they line up for their dancing lesson, and know who it is straight away? Then all we have to do is ask him a few clever questions and he'll fall into our cunning trap?'

'Well, no. Not when you put it like that. But it's got to be worth a go, hasn't it?'

'It has.'

'And there's bound to be a reward if we find this missing treasure.'

'You don't seriously believe all that guff, do you?' said Dunn. 'Secret treasure vaults in gentlemen's clubs? It's a bit much.'

'Yeah,' said Skins. 'It probably is a bit hard to swallow. But it would buy the band a van.'

They watched the daily life of London pass by as their journey took them northwards. Jazz took them all round the country – they even dreamed it would take them abroad one day – but neither of them could imagine anywhere else being anything like as lively, mundane, filthy, sparkling, friendly, hateful, or just plain wonderful as London. It was home, and they both loved it.

Skins was dropped off first and he opened the front door with his latchkey. Even after six years of it, he still couldn't get used to the idea of waiting on his own doorstep for one of his servants to let him in. He hung his hat in the hall and set off to find Ellie.

A short while later, Dunn was relieved to see his own road empty, but his luck didn't last long. As they drew up outside his house, Mrs McGuffie from number 74 was out of her door before the police car had come to a complete stop.

'I've told her, you know,' she said as Dunn got out. 'Don't you think I haven't.'

'Thank you, Mrs M,' he said. 'That was very kind of you.' He leaned back in. 'Thank you, too, Constable Grine. Hope we haven't kept you from anything.'

'Don't you worry about me, sir,' said Grine. 'Always happy to be kept away from things. Mind how you go.'

Dunn slammed the door and banged on the roof of the car. Grine drove away.

'I told her,' said Mrs McGuffie.

'I know, Mrs M. You said.'

'I told her you was hauled away by the police. In a van. Like a common criminal. I told her she should sling you out. Can't have lodgers bein' hauled off by the police.'

'I'm sure she'll consider your advice most carefully, Mrs M. Thank you.'

He went in to number 76 and closed the door behind him. Mrs Cordell didn't throw him out; she gave him a cup of tea.

Meanwhile, Skins had tracked Ellie down in the study, where she was writing a letter.

'Hello, love,' he said from the doorway. 'Fancy a cuppa?'

'Oh – hi, honey,' she said. 'How was the Big House? Did the cops rough you up any?' She looked up. 'Oh, no, you look fine.'

'It was touch-and-go for a minute,' he said, 'but we made them see reason.'

'Of course you did. That boy Grine looked like a lovely fellow. I'm sure he'd not have let you come to any harm. Although I over-heard Mrs Dalrymple talking to Cook. From the way our beloved housekeeper told it, you'd been dragged off by a whole squad of burly bulls. She didn't expect to see you till the hanging.'

Skins laughed. 'He took us down to Scotland Yard to see an old mate of Lady H's.'

'Did he, indeed? And what did this "old mate" want with you?'

'As if you didn't already know,' he said as he kissed the top of her head. 'I'll get Cook to put the kettle on, and I'll tell you all about it.'

Littleton Cotterell
19 May 1925

Darling Ellie,
Hello, old sport. What's new in the Great
Metrollops? I trust you're all well.

Herself and I went into Bristol for a concert performed by . . . well, now that's a tale in
itself. I'd been told it was going to be the Vienna
Philharmonic – one of the finest symphony
orchestras in the world, don'tcha know – who
would be playing something from the Romantic
repertoire.

'It'll be Tchaikovsky, I expect,' Lady
Hardcastle had said, breezily. 'You'll love it.'

It turns out there had been what she now
describes as 'tactical exaggeration' in order to
secure my compliance. They were, indeed,
Austrian, but they were an amateur orchestra
from Innsbruck. Such was their devotion to their
Tyrolean home that they eschewed evening dress
and were instead bedecked in lederhosen and

dirndls. And it was an evening of Strauss waltzes and, to my horror, Franz Léhar's *Merry Flippin' Widow*.

Still, it was a night out and we were invited to the reception afterwards – Lady Hardcastle knows the conductor. But she would, wouldn't she? He owns a score signed by . . . I want to say Gustav Mahler, but it could have been anyone. Ravel? Elgar? Charlie Chaplin? Anyway, it was stolen a few years ago when he was working for a more upmarket orchestra in Vienna. We tracked it down and returned it to him, and he's been her best pal ever since. At least, that's how she likes to paint it. He was grateful enough to invite her 'backstage' for a glass of warm champagne and some cold vol-au-vents, at any rate.

She sends her love, by the way, and says to remind you that we're in London at the end of the month (not this weekend coming, but the next – we arrive at her brother's on the twenty-ninth). She wonders if we might meet for lunch at the Ritz on the first (Monday). And I wonder that, too. Do let me know.

Has Supt Sunderland been in touch? I told him how intrigued you were by the deserter and the missing treasure thing. I still have that letter you sent during the war – it's astonishing to think the diamond robber you told me about in '17 has turned up on your doorstep again. Well, on Skins's doorstep at any rate, but you know what I mean.

I hope the boys decide to help him – he's such a sweetheart. We miss his friendly, professional presence in the Bristol CID. It was good to have such a dependable ally there, but when his wife died in the Spanish flu epidemic (I told you about that, didn't I?) there wasn't much to keep him here. Apart from us – and we couldn't compete with the offer of promotion and his own department in London.

We are 'between jobs' at the moment. There's a Soviet agent we need to keep an eye on, and a couple of Germans and an Austrian who need to be warned off, but mostly it's quiet (you might wish to take this opportunity to read between the lines and work out why Lady Hardcastle was so keen to get us to the Innsbruck Sinfonia's performance at the Colston Hall, and why the second chair trombonist now has such a haunted look in his eye). All of which means that I should welcome the opportunity to get stuck into a proper mystery again. It's been a while since we had to find any lost treasure. There was a case in Warsaw before the war that involved a diamond diadem – that was a hoot. And, of course, there was a stolen emerald in Littleton Cotterell where I first met darling Skins. But treasure maps and concealed vaults? I'm ever so slightly jealous, so please keep me up to date with any progress. If there's a puzzle to be solved, I'd love to have a go.

I'm sure you don't need any guidance but I've been working for Herself for too long and her habit of offering unsolicited advice has rather rubbed off on me. I'm not sure there's a secret to it, though, to be honest. I gather Supt Sunderland was planning to ask them just to keep their eyes and ears open for him. Vague and seemingly unhelpful though that may be, it's pretty much all they need to do. They need to get to know their 'targets'. Find out who they are, watch what they get up to . . . We'd do nothing much more.

I suppose I might poke around the club if I thought I could get away with it – see if the building could reveal any of its secrets. I know many have tried and failed over the years, but it never hurts to have a look for yourself. Lady Hardcastle, meanwhile, would charm all and sundry into being horribly indiscreet – people do love to talk. But we're not possessed of magical powers so there's nothing we could do that 'the boys' can't. Apart from some skilled breaking and entering – I still haven't lost my skill with a picklock – but Skins always seemed like someone who could pick a lock. I'd wager there are a few tales from his past he hasn't told either of us.

Meanwhile, though, don't forget to see if you can adjust your plans so we might meet for lunch on the first.

Your friend
Flo

Chapter Three

The Aristippus Club occupied a large – yet oddly discreet – building almost hidden away in the backstreets of Mayfair. It had taken Skins and Dunn about half an hour to push the handcart the mile or so from New Row, and Dunn was not in a cheerful mood.

'How long till your missus gets her hands on her inheritance?' he said as they heaved the recalcitrant cart round to the yard at the rear of the club.

'Four more years yet,' said Skins.

Dunn grunted. 'Do us a favour when the time comes? Tenth anniversary is tin, right? Ask her for a car – they're made of tin. A nice big one with plenty of room for drums and basses.'

'You could always buy one yourself if it's that important to you.'

'On our wages?'

'We've just had another fantastic month. What else do you spend your money on?'

'Not birds, that's for sure. Not these past couple of months, anyway.'

'There you go, then. Treat yourself to a nice new motor. Or a second-hand one.'

'I'd much sooner moan at you to get one if I'm honest, mate.' Skins knocked on the back door. 'That's what I thought.'

The door was opened by a liveried flunkey.

'Yes?' he said.

Skins was impressed that the man had made such an apparently short and simple word last almost two seconds.

'We're with the band,' he said. 'We need to bring our gear in.'

'Your gear?' Another two syllables; another three seconds.

Skins indicated the handcart and its musical burden.

'Ah,' said the flunkey. 'Your . . . gear. You must be from the Finchley Foot-Tappers.'

'No, they couldn't make it. We're the Dizzy Heights.'

'Are you? I thought you played at the club on Fridays.'

'We do.'

'But today is Tuesday.'

'We're early.'

'Wait here, please.'

He closed the door.

'I could have stayed in bed,' said Dunn.

'I could be with Ellie and the kids,' said Skins.

The flunkey returned.

'This way,' he said. 'You may leave your . . . cart there.'

They grabbed as much as they could carry but that still left a fair amount to be fetched in.

'You couldn't lend a hand, could you, mate?' said Dunn, nodding towards the snare drum and traps case still on the cart.

The man frowned. Clearly this idea had never occurred to him and he was struggling with the novelty of it. 'A hand?' he said at length. 'I shall get one of the boys to bring your remaining . . . "gear" to the ballroom.'

'You're most kind,' said Skins.

They followed the flunkey through the familiar maze of servants' corridors, up a flight of stone steps to the main part of the building and along another, this time marble-floored corridor that ended at a set of double doors. The flunkey threw them open to reveal the spacious ballroom. The walls were hung with portraits of notable former club members, the ceiling with extraordinarily elaborate chandeliers.

'Looks even better in the daylight,' said Skins. 'Very elegant.'

'Is it?' said the flunkey. 'I'm sure I wouldn't know.'

'Definitely elegant,' said Skins. 'Ballrooms are always "elegant". Mountains are always "majestic". And barmaids are always "buxom". It's the law. You can look it up.'

The flunkey seemed impervious to badinage. 'They'll want you down at that end.'

'On the stage?' said Dunn. 'Where the band usually goes? I'm not sure I like the idea of that.'

'The boy will be here presently with the rest of your impedimenta.'

'You're a diamond,' said Skins. 'Oh, before you go . . . Don't suppose you know anything about the Treasure of the Mayfair Murderer? You know, what with you being a long-standing loyal servant of the club and all that.'

'I'm afraid I cannot say, sir.'

'Can't say, or don't know?' said Dunn.

'Yes, sir,' said the flunkey. 'There are rumours, of course, but nothing more than that.'

'So you don't know where the vault is?' asked Skins.

'I should be living it up in the south of France if I knew that, sir.'

'You and me both, mate. Do you reckon the rumours are true?'

'There are so many. Some say the entrance is concealed in plain sight along one of the corridors. Some say it is hidden in the darkest depths of the most inaccessible parts of the cellars. Some say it opens with a simple key. Some say there are puzzles to be solved.

I even heard – you'll love this one, sir – I even heard that the door can only be opened by satanic ritual.' The flunkey laughed.

'And no one knows where the key is,' said Dunn.

'Nor even if there is a key, sir. All we have are stories.'

'Ah well,' said Skins. 'Have to stick to earning an honest living, I suppose.'

The flunkey looked as though he believed being a musician was a far from honest way to earn a living, but he bowed politely and went on his way.

Skins clapped and listened to the sound reverberating around the room.

'We always sound good and lively in here,' he said. 'It's like playing in a church.'

'When was the last time you played in a church?' said Dunn.

'Tell the truth, I haven't even been inside a church since me and Ellie got spliced. It's what I *imagine* it must be like to play in a church. Are we expecting many eager dance students? That'll deaden the sound a bit.'

'Not a clue, mate. All done through Mickey, like I said. All I know is we're playing at seven for a dance lesson and we'll be done by nine. Refreshment, I've been promised, will be provided.'

'That's a turn-up. They usually have good nosh here.'

There were some chairs stacked in a corner of the stage, so Dunn arranged five of them for the band. Skins had a little stool of his own, while Dunn and Mickey stood throughout. During instrumental numbers Mickey would leave the stage and find a bar stool to perch on, preferably where he could be easily approached by his many adoring female fans. Dunn often grumbled that he was the only one who stood up all night.

The rest of Skins's drum set arrived and he set everything up in his usual spot, stage left. He gave everything a quick tap to make sure it was all in order, adjusted the snare drum head a little, and went to sit on one of the chairs next to Dunn.

'What time is everyone here?' he said.

Dunn looked at his watch. 'About now, I reckon.'

Nothing happened.

'It would have been fantastic if they'd all walked in just then, wouldn't it?' said Skins.

'I'd change my bill matter to "Mystic Barty, prognosticator and bass player to the aristocracy". We'd be swamped with bookings. We'd—'

The door opened and a fresh flunkey entered, followed by Blanche and Puddle. Benny and Elk weren't far behind.

'It's all in the timing, mate,' said Skins. 'It's always about the timing.' He stood up. 'Welcome, one and all. The Dizzy Heights rhythm section is proud to welcome you to our humble whatsaname. Please, come in. Make yourselves at home. We have laid out chairs for you, fashioned from the finest . . . wood. Cushions available on request.' He turned to the flunkey. 'Cushions?'

The flunkey looked at him blankly.

'Are there cushions, old mate?'

'Cushions?' said the flunkey, who was clearly unused to receiving requests from anyone other than club members.

'Cushions, yes. For the comfort of the band's delicate posteriors.'

'I shall have to enquire.'

'You do that, me old china. Pot of tea wouldn't go amiss if the kettle's on.'

The flunkey flunked off.

'I've taken a liking to playing this gaff,' said Puddle. 'I could definitely get used to places like this.'

'Some of us have played the Royal Albert Hall.' Eustace had entered unseen while Skins was asking about the soft furnishings.

'Meanwhile, some of us have to make do with cushy little jobs playing for dance lessons for a handful of toffs.' Mickey had been close behind him. 'You take what you can get in our line of work. And this'll do nicely, thank you very much.'

'If you'd rather play second trumpet in a provincial symphony orchestra, darling, I'm sure they'd be delighted to have you back,' said Blanche. 'We'd get by without you somehow.'

'Now then, now then,' said Skins. 'Let's not fall out. Mickey's right – this is a cushy number. Think of it as a paid rehearsal. Half a crown says we don't get to play even one number all the way through before the dance teacher stops us to correct someone's entrechat.'

'That's a ballet jump, you nit,' said Blanche. 'But I apologize, Eustace. I should love to play the Royal Albert Hall. You have every right to be proud.'

Eustace harrumphed and stalked to his usual seat, where he took his trumpet from its case and fitted the mouthpiece.

'Who's the dance teacher?' asked Puddle. 'Anyone know him?'

'It's a her,' said a voice from the door. 'Millie Mitchell, at your service.'

A tall, slender woman with her jet-black hair cut in a boyish bob strode into the room. She spotted Mickey, who had turned to greet her. They walked together towards the corner of the room to discuss the arrangements for the evening.

At first glance her elegant movement seemed almost impossibly perfect, but after a few steps across the room Skins spotted the tiniest limp. An old injury, perhaps, but it might explain why this graceful beauty was eking out a living teaching moneyed oafs to dance instead of knocking them dead on the West End stage. Or even the ballet. She moved like a ballet dancer, he thought. Although maybe she was a little too tall. Then again, loads of people seemed tall compared with him. Maybe she—

His thoughts were interrupted by a nudge in the ribs from an amused Puddle.

'Don't drool, darling, you're a married man,' she said.

'No drooling here,' said Skins. 'Barty's your boy if you want drool. I was just exercising the old detective skills. The lady has a limp.'

'A limp what?' said Dunn.

'You'll have to forgive him,' said Skins. 'He can't help himself.'

'He's right, though,' said Dunn. 'I was drooling slightly.'

'As well you might,' said Puddle. 'I'd not kick her out of bed.'

Skins looked at her quizzically. 'I didn't know you were—'

'I'm not, darling, but look at her. A goddess made flesh. What mortal wouldn't sell their soul for just a glance from those perfect blue eyes? And those legs. My god, if I had legs like that . . .'

Blanche had joined them on the stage. 'What would you do if you had legs like that?'

'What wouldn't I do, darling? With every eligible male in the place drooling on their shoes' – she indicated Dunn, who had returned to his own contemplation of the living incarnation of Terpsichore standing at the other end of the ballroom – 'the world would be mine and everything that's in it.'

Blanche was less impressed. 'You see girls like that everywhere. We had one in the Fannies in the war. All legs and . . .' She held up her cupped hands in front of her chest. 'She was a so-so nurse, but the boys adored her. They used to joke about getting shot again just so they could come and see her.'

'You see?' said Puddle. 'Who wouldn't want power like that?'

'Yes, but she wasn't happy. Takes more than a shower of drooling Tommies to make you happy.'

'Well, if my fairy godmother turns up and offers me the chance to look like that, I'll not be turning her down.'

The confab on the dance floor was finally over and Mickey was approaching the stage. It seemed they had a plan.

◆ ◆ ◆

Once the band members had settled into their customary places, instruments were unpacked, assembled, tuned and warmed up. They trotted through Puddle's new arrangement of the old music-hall song 'Where Did You Get That Hat?', which was about to go into the regular set list after a couple of trial runs at private parties.

Unlike Eustace, Puddle tended to play down her classical training. She didn't mention her time at the Royal College of Music, nor her time playing clarinet in several of Europe's more prestigious symphony orchestras, but she wasn't shy about her skill as an arranger. The band had no formal leader, with Mickey Kent serving as public spokesman when the need arose, but Puddle and Benny Charles, the Antiguan trombonist, split the arranging duties between them, with occasional contributions from Barty Dunn, who 'had a good ear'.

As the number drew to a close, a man's head appeared round the door. His hair was so smooth and shiny with pomade that it looked as though it had been varnished. Skins and Dunn exchanged amused glances. The gleaming head withdrew but the door remained open. They could hear his voice shouting, 'Come on, you chaps, they're here.'

A few seconds later, five men in their early thirties tumbled into the ballroom. They were in high spirits and had obviously had a livener or two to give themselves a little Dutch courage for the dancing ordeal to come.

Dunn leaned down to talk to Skins. 'Is that it?' he asked quietly. 'Where's the birds?'

'Gentlemen's club, ain't it?' said Skins. 'No birds allowed. I'm surprised they let Blanche and Puddle in, to be truthful. And Millie

Whatsit over there must have some special hold over someone . . .
Oh, there you go.'

One of the five newcomers approached Millie Mitchell and
swept her into his arms to deliver a theatrical kiss.

'My darling,' he said. 'Thank you. How absolutely divine of
you to give up your time for us like this. Allow me to introduce
you to the Alphabet Gang.'

His four pals made a great show of arranging themselves in a
line with a gap in the middle. Skins looked closely and was disappointed to note that they were all about the same height – probably
something close to five foot seven, just like every other bloke they'd
ever met.

'We have Alfie, Bertie, Danny and Ernie,' he said, indicating
each man in turn.

'Where's C?' said Millie.

'That's me, you silly goose,' he said.

'But you're Bob.'

'Bob Chandler, see? C.'

'Everyone else uses their first name, sweetie. Do they call you
Chandler?'

'No, they call me Charlie.'

'But—'

'It's quite simple, old thing,' he said. 'Ernie here' – he indicated
the bespectacled man at the end of the line – 'is really called Edwin
Cashmore.'

'So you should call him Eddie,' said Millie.

'Cashmore . . . more cash? Earn-y? Get it?'

Millie groaned.

'Then Dudley Daniels becomes Danny.'

The long-nosed man, next in line, bowed.

'I've become Charlie,' continued Charlie. 'Then Jimmy Albert
here is Bertie.'

The man with the varnished head smiled and nodded.

'And Cornelius Rawson here is Alfie.'

'Why?' said Millie.

'So we can be the Alphabet Gang.'

'But why aren't you Bobby? Then Jimmy Albert could be Albie, and Cornelius Rawson here could be . . . oh, I don't know . . . Corny.'

The men shrugged and, as one, pointed at Alfie.

The smiling, buck-toothed man at the end of the line frowned for a moment and then erupted with a loud 'Hah!' A penny had finally dropped. 'Well, I'll be blowed,' he said. 'That would be much simpler. Where were you when we needed you, old girl? Takes me an absolute age to explain why all my chums call me Alfie.'

'It was your blessed idea,' said Danny. 'We tried to tell you at the time but you just looked vacant and told us you didn't understand what we were on about.'

'Should have been more . . . how do you say it? Forceful,' said Alfie. 'Chap needs to have things explained to him two or three times. Pictures help.'

The other men shook their heads.

'Well, that's the gang, anyway,' said Charlie. 'And this lovely lady is my darling fiancée, Millie Mitchell. After you lot saw off poor Georgina, she's the poor soul who'll be teaching you duffers all the new steps so we can beat the boys from the Wags Club in the dance contest. Let's see if we can impress her a little more than we did Georgina. Poor girl had never seen anything like it.'

The Alphabets gave a ragged cheer.

'And, ah, who are those chaps over there?' said Alfie, pointing to the band.

'That'll be the band, Alfie,' said Charlie.

'I can see that, old horse. I mean, who are they? I thought old Thingy Doo-dah's band played for the lessons. Did last week. You know, the chaps from Highgate with that knockout filly on the horn thing and whatnot.'

'They're from East Finchley,' said Charlie. 'They're called the Finchley Foot-Tappers and they couldn't make it because "old Thingy Doo-Dah" – who prefers to go by the name of Henry Bignell, by the way, should you ever chance to meet him again – had double-booked us with a twenty-first birthday party in Belgravia. And they were paying more. Sir Freddie Thompson's youngest girl. Lovely family. And the horn thing is a saxophone. These nice people have two. Anyway, luckily for us, Millie happened to know Mickey there . . .'

Mickey gave a small wave of acknowledgement.

'. . . and he was able to step into the breach.'

'All well and good, old boy,' said Alfie. 'But who are they?'

'The Dizzy Heights,' said Charlie. 'They play for the dance here every Friday night.'

'Do they, by George? Are they any good? Can they play a Charleston? I've got to work on m'Charleston.'

'Mickey?' said Charlie. 'I hate to be a bore, old thing, but would you mind playing a few bars to set poor Alfie's addled mind at rest?'

Mickey looked to the band, who picked up their instruments. '"The Charleston", then?' he suggested.

Skins counted them in and they gave the assembled dance students the first verse of the popular tune.

'Will that do you, Alfie?' said Charlie.

'Very nicely, old bean. Very nicely indeed. Ready when you are, Miss Mitchell.' He shuffled a few clumsy steps.

'I think we'd better start with the basics,' said Millie. 'The most basic of basics.'

The Alphabet Gang, it turned out, were truly terrible dancers. Charlie had a slight grasp on the basics, no doubt taught to him by his talented fiancée, but the others were an utter shambles.

Amiable Alfie, of the buck teeth and cheerful demeanour, was quite a mover. He was surprisingly graceful for a chubby chap, and managed to move all his limbs in time with the music. His problem was that he couldn't for the life of him remember exactly how and where to move them – remembering the individual steps and the order in which they came was completely beyond him. The result was a chaotic mess, but one that was entirely in time with the band.

Bertie's varnished head stayed completely still while the rest of him writhed about underneath as though head and body were under the control of two entirely separate people. He was able to remember the steps, but executed them with a peculiar loose-limbed fluidity that failed to match the jolly precision intended by the dance's creators.

Danny was shy and awkward. In an apparent attempt not to draw too much attention to himself, he kept his movements small and jerky. It suited him, thought Skins. He was all pointy elbows, pointy knees, pointy nose – his little pointy dance steps fitted him perfectly.

Ernie seemed to have the worst of it. He had Alfie's poor memory for the steps combined with Danny's jerky self-consciousness, and, worst of all, no feel for the music whatsoever. He looked like he was dancing to the beat of an altogether-different drummer. One who was playing at a different tempo. In a different time signature. In another world, where the Charleston had never been invented. Over the years, Skins had learned to spot the stragglers and had always tried to play a little louder, a little simpler, a little more pre-cisely, to give them a clue as to where the beat was, but Ernie was beyond the help of even the most obvious percussive hints.

Only Charlie seemed to know what he was doing. Clearly, he had the advantage of having had some private tuition from his fiancée, but he had a modicum of natural ability, too.

Skins was disappointed that no one had taken his bet – he'd have cleaned up. The record for shortest performance so far was three bars before Millie shouted for them all to stop.

'Gentlemen, please,' she said, clearly struggling not to lose her temper. 'How have you been dancing a Charleston all this time without being able to do this? Come on. One-and-two-and-three-and-four. Remember? Step-and-tap-and-step-and-tap. Swivel those heels inwards on the step. Stay up on your toes, Alfie – keep your heels up. From the top, please, Dizzies.'

Skins counted them in and laughed to himself as he watched the dance students nodding their heads along with him, trying to fix the tempo in their heads, readying themselves for that first step.

They made it all the way to the chorus this time before Millie called a halt.

'Bobby, darling – I mean "Charlie" – would you be an absolute sweetheart and get someone to bring us some refreshment. I think it's time we took a break.'

'Right you are,' said Charlie. 'Beers all round?'

The other four cheered.

'What about you chaps?' he called to the band. 'You lot deserve a drink and a sandwich after all that. A drink, a sandwich, and our humble apologies.'

The band cheered.

Charlie set off to find one of the club's flunkeys while the four remaining Alphabets formed a conspiratorial huddle at the other end of the ballroom. Finding herself suddenly alone, Millie joined the band on stage. Mickey found her a chair.

'You don't mind if I sit up here for a moment, do you? I feel a bit exposed down there.'

The band offered a cheerful collective welcome.

'I'm so sorry, where are my manners. Millicent Mitchell. Although everyone calls me Millie, obviously.'

Blanche gave her a friendly smile. 'Millie Mitchell?' she said, still smiling. 'How lovely to meet you. I'd introduce everyone but we're not as conveniently named as the Alphabet Gang. I'm Blanche. Blanche Adams.'

They shook hands.

'You have the patience of saints,' said Millie. 'I had no idea what we were all letting ourselves in for when I agreed to this. Bobby . . . Charlie – I'll never get the hang of that . . . Charlie said his pals wanted a bit of tuition before this stupid contest they've organized. "You know the sort of thing, old girl. Polish up the old skills." He failed to mention that they couldn't dance a step between them. They go to clubs. They go to dances. They go to parties. They even had a few lessons with another teacher before she ran off. Presumably screaming and vowing to give up dance teaching and become a nun. What on earth have they been doing all these years? They dance the Charleston like they've never even seen it before. It's been about for a couple of years now. Surely everyone can Charleston.'

Skins put up his hand. 'I can't,' he said. 'I'm always sitting down when it's on.'

'Well, at least you've got an excuse, darling,' she said. 'And I bet you could make a better fist of it than these duffers.'

'Don't get your hopes up,' said Dunn. 'I've seen him dance.'

'That's a shame. Drummers often make such good dancers. Have you heard of that American chap Fred Astaire? He was on Broadway last year in *Lady, Be Good*. The papers say he's a terrific dancer. And quite the drummer, too, apparently.'

Skins attempted a seated tap dance behind his drum set.

'I'd stick to drumming if I were you, son,' said Dunn.

Blanche smiled. 'Do you teach full-time?'

'Have to now,' said Millie. She pointed to her leg. 'Went over on the ankle a while back. Tore the ATFL quite badly and it never healed quite right. I was never destined for greatness – always the tall one in the chorus, me – but with a dodgy ankle I can't even get a job as Third Hoofer from the Right. Teaching is all I have these days.'

Blanche frowned a little. 'That's a shame. But you're terribly good at it. You think we've got the patience of saints, but all we have to do is start and stop at the right time. You've got to bite your tongue every time that Alfie character taps when he should step, and then swivels on his heel.'

'I'm beginning to wish I'd brought a stick. Or one of those long whip things they use for training horses.'

'A lunging whip,' said Puddle.

'Is that what it's called? Alfie would be black and blue by the end, but he'd bloody well know how to Charleston. Ah, here comes my beloved and his booze-bearing . . . butler? He's not a butler, is he? Ah well. Seconds out. Round two. I'll make sure they tip you handsomely.'

She got up and returned to the side of the room where the flunkey had placed jugs of beer, several plates of sandwiches, and a large number of clean glasses.

◆　◆　◆

The Alphabets improved only slightly as the evening wore on, but by the end of the lesson they were at least approaching a basic level of competence. Millie was able to congratulate them on their progress with genuine sincerity, which provoked a certain amount of embarrassed shuffling and 'Well, I don't know about that'-ing. She implored them to practise what they had learned before they met again, and they agreed enthusiastically when they realized that meant she would be returning the following week.

'Thought we might have put you off,' said Alfie.

'Nothing of the sort, darling,' she said. 'You've come along in leaps and bounds in just one evening. Imagine what you could do after a few lessons more.'

'It's the leaping and bounding that'll be our undoing,' said Bertie.

'We'll knock that out of you,' she replied. 'The band suggested I bring a lunging whip next time. Keep you in order.'

The Alphabets laughed.

'Not a bad idea, that,' said Ernie. 'I had an aunt who used to train horses. Never had any trouble once she had a whip in her hand.'

'I knew a chap in the army who liked it when a girl had a whip in her hand,' said Alfie. 'I remember there was a bordello in Paris where—'

'Alfie?' interrupted Charlie. 'Do shut up, there's a good chap.'

'Right you are, old boy. Right you are. Time and a place for bordello stories. Understood.'

Charlie shook his head.

Still laughing, Millie kissed Charlie goodbye and left the ballroom. The rest of the Alphabets left a few moments later, telling Charlie they'd see him in the bar. He beckoned Mickey over and handed over an envelope. They exchanged a few words before Charlie waved to the band and called, 'Thank you so very much, ladies and gentlemen. Same time next week if you can bear it?'

They agreed they would, and he left to join his pals.

The Dizzy Heights began to pack up.

'Fancy a pint?' said Dunn, as he bent to pick up his bass case.

'Don't mind if I do,' said Skins. 'Somewhere near the shop, though – let's get this gear put away first.'

'Do you mind if I tag along?' asked Puddle.

'The more the merrier,' said Skins. 'Anyone else? Lamb and Flag for a swift one before last orders?'

They were quite a sociable group, and often went out together when they weren't working, but at such short notice a couple of them had places to be. There were families to get back to and – in Elk's case – another gig to play, but Benny and Blanche said they'd love to join them.

'Delighted to have your company,' said Skins. 'You can help push the cart.'

'There's always a catch,' said Benny.

'You can put your trombone on it, though, mate. Save you carrying it all that way.'

'I wouldn't be going all that way if I weren't going for a drink with you.'

'You make an excellent point,' said Skins. 'Now give us a hand with these temple blocks and we might make it over there before closing time.'

◆　◆　◆

The four of them made short work of the journey back to New Row, and they were in the pub with a drink in front of them in less than three-quarters of an hour.

'Good health,' said Benny, raising his rum.

'Here's mud in your eye,' said Dunn.

'Here's what in my where?' said Puddle. 'Where do you pick up this rubbish?'

'I'm hip to all the new lingo. I keep my ear to the ground.'

'Well, quite. That's where everyone throws their rubbish.'

Glasses were clinked and sips taken.

'What did you make of that lot, then?' asked Skins.

'The Alphabet Gang?' said Benny with a throaty chuckle. 'Usual crowd of moneyed fools, if you ask me.'

'They were, weren't they. Did . . . did any of them strike you as a bit . . . odd?'

'They were all plenty odd,' said Benny. 'You got any specific oddness in mind?'

Skins gave Dunn an enquiring look.

Dunn shrugged. 'Don't look at me, mate. Your call.'

Skins paused a moment in thought. 'All right,' he said at length. 'I'm not betraying any confidences. See, Barty and I know this bloke. Well, know *of*, is more like it. He's a copper. We met him years ago out Gloucestershire way, but now he's working at Scotland Yard. He's asked us to help him out with something.'

Puddle laughed. 'You two?' she said. 'He must be desperate.'

Skins grinned. 'I can't argue with you there, Pudds. He must be.'

'But why did you agree?'

Skins shrugged.

'I just went along with it because Skins did,' said Dunn.

'And I just went along with it because he did,' said Skins. 'Well, that and the fact that another mate of ours seemed keen on the idea.'

'You two have a lot of mates,' said Puddle.

'We've been around a while,' said Skins. 'But this one is special. She introduced me to my wife.'

'Very special indeed, then,' said Benny. 'What exactly does he want you to help him with?'

Benny Charles spoke slowly and deliberately. His deep voice always seemed to have a smile in it, but there was often a sadness in his eyes as though they had seen more than they wanted to. Which they had. He had served in the British West Indies Regiment and had seen terrible fighting in the Middle East, about which he never spoke. In truth, none of the band spoke of their wartime experiences, bar the odd humorous anecdote, but Benny seemed to his bandmates to have been more deeply affected than the rest of them. Unlike many they knew of, though, it hadn't driven him to bitterness and anger, but to patience and compassion. He was only twenty-nine years old, but he was known to many as Uncle Benny, a man whose cheerful kindness could make any problem seem trivial.

'He's hunting for a deserter. He reckons he's a member at Tipsy Harry's and he's asked us – me and Barty – to keep an eye out for anyone who might fit the bill.'

'They must have hundreds of members,' said Puddle. 'How does he expect you to find one bloke among all those?'

'Miss Puddle is right,' said Benny. 'They must have a hundred or more members at that club. We know what them places is like. How do you expect to find this one man? It's like trying to find a needle in a big pile of needles, if you ask me.'

'Our police mate has his reasons for thinking it's one of the dance class lot,' said Dunn. 'Wants us to look for anything odd.'

'Like I said, I reckon they were all pretty odd. But I always find the English upper classes a bit peculiar. No offence, Miss Puddle.'

Puddle touched his arm. 'Oh, I'm not upper-class, sweetie. More of a middle-class girl made good. A bit of musical talent opened the doors, and the accent is put on. At least I think it is. I can't seem to stop doing it now.'

'Why they looking for a deserter after all this time?' asked Benny. 'It all ended nearly seven years ago. We should be putting it behind us now.'

'Probably should,' said Skins. 'But this geezer half-inched twenty-five grand's worth of sparkle.'

Jaws dropped.

'Jewellery?' asked Puddle.

'Uncut diamonds,' said Dunn. 'Smuggled out of Antwerp and on their way to Blighty. Only they never got here because this bloke Grant pinched them en route.'

'Wait till you hear the next bit, though,' said Skins. 'The superintendent reckons there's secret treasure hidden at Tipsy Harry's, and that old Granty joined up to nick it.'

'Secret treasure as well?' said Puddle.

'The Treasure, if you please, of the Mayfair Murderer,' said Dunn. 'Some Georgian bloke – founder member of the club – killed a diamond merchant, nicked his stock, and hid it at the club. No one's been able to find it for a hundred and twenty years, but now there's a rumour that someone – they're assuming Grant – has worked out it has something to do with the club regalia that comes out for special events like the dance contest.'

'How?' said Benny.

'How is it connected?' said Skins. 'No one knows. No one even knows if it really exists, but the police reckon Grant's at the club and that's why the superintendent wants us to be there – to try to flush him out. He's convinced something's going to happen on the night of the contest and that's why he wants us to keep our peepers on the Alphabet Gang.'

'If he's so certain something's going to happen at the dance contest, why involve you?' asked Puddle. 'Surely he could just get his men to infiltrate the place on the night and keep an eye on things.'

'He could fill the place with coppers,' said Skins, 'but they wouldn't know who they were looking for. If they knew that they'd have nicked him already. They need us in there to sniff him out beforehand.'

'I doubt he could even do that,' said Dunn. 'Lack of manpower, see? He's only got a small team and they can't be everywhere at once.'

'Good point. And you know the place by now – absolute labyrinth. Imagine a load of hairy-ar— a load of big old coppers stomping about the place getting under each other's feet. Grant would have it away on his toes while they were still trying to get from the front hall to the ballroom.'

'And no one's even certain he's there,' said Dunn. 'It's only a tip-off from . . . Actually, where did it come from? He didn't say, did he?'

'He didn't,' said Skins. 'The whole thing was very vague as far as I could make out. You could see why he wouldn't want to put his own men on it.'

'I see,' said Puddle. 'So you're on the lookout for someone who doesn't fit in. Someone odd.'

'In a nutshell,' said Skins. 'So who do you reckon?'

Puddle frowned in thought. 'It was a strong field. Alfie was the fat one?'

'With the buck teeth. "He could eat an apple through a tennis racket," as my gran used to say.'

'He was utterly charming. Quite the mover, but as gormless as anything.'

'Could he be a wrong'un?'

'Oh, I don't know,' she said. 'He can't dance, that's all I saw.'

'Well, unless he's a cracking good actor,' said Puddle, 'it can't be him. I imagine he has trouble finding a matching pair of socks in the morning, let alone nicking gemstones and disappearing for all these years. Who's next? Bertie? Was he the one with the gleaming hair?'

'That was him,' said Benny. 'There must have been a whole jar of pomade on that boy's head.'

'Well, he wasn't so goofy,' said Puddle. 'He was the one who led them all in, wasn't he?'

'He was,' said Skins. 'Strangest dancing I've ever seen, but he didn't say much.'

'Could be him,' she said. 'Quiet and unassuming, but sneaky and organized.'

'Sneaky?' said Dunn. 'How do you work that out?'

'Well . . .' she said. 'You know. Sneaking about the club, opening doors, finding the dance class.'

Skins and Dunn laughed. Benny shook his head and took a sip of his rum.

'You may well laugh,' she said. 'But I have a nose for these things. Who's next. Oh, Charlie. Oh, my goodness. Charlie. He was a dish, darling. Taken, though. But so charming. Every inch the officer and gentleman. Was he an officer, this deserter?'

'OR,' said Dunn.

Puddle looked blank.

'Other Ranks,' explained Skins. 'He was a private.'

'Well, it's unlikely to be him, then – he's the real thing. You can't fake that sort of poise.'

'If he's been hiding out all this time,' said Benny, 'he's got to be good. You just said it couldn't be Alfie because there's been people after him for years and he's still on the loose. Whoever it is has got to be sharp.'

'Well, I shan't hear of it,' said Puddle. 'Charlie is an absolute honey pie. Who was D in their little alphabet?'

'Danny,' said Benny. 'Skinny fellow. Big nose. Shy, like he had something to hide.'

'There's your man, then,' said Puddle, proudly. 'Trying to stay out of the limelight. Doesn't want to draw attention to himself. Struggling to keep up the pretence among all those officers. I bet the others were all officers, weren't they?'

'No idea,' said Dunn. 'We'll find out soon enough, I'm sure.'

'And E . . .' she said. 'Oh, Ernie. Spectacles. Never could trust a man in spectacles. I had an uncle who wore spectacles. He did time for embezzling from the company accounts. Ernie's definitely your man.'

'And everyone else except Alfie,' said Skins. 'Because he's too stupid.'

'Could be a bluff,' said Benny with a wicked twinkle. 'He might just be pretending to be a ha'penny short of a shilling. He could be a criminal mastermind.'

Skins sighed. 'You're no help at all, you two. I wish I hadn't bothered.'

'Oh, darling,' said Puddle. 'Don't be like that. We'll help, won't we, Benjamin? I've always wanted to be a sleuth.'

'We just need to get to know them all a bit better,' said Skins. 'Are you really keen to help?'

'Of course,' said Puddle.

'Sure,' said Benny.

'Fantastic,' said Skins. 'We need another drink and a plan.'

Dunn finished off his pint. 'I'll get them,' he said. 'Same again?'

Bloomsbury
May 21, 1925

Dearest Flo,
I'm sorry to hear about the concert. Or perhaps I'm not. I'm very much of the opinion that an evening of lederhosen, dirndls, and threatening trombonists in the corridors of a concert hall is right up your alley. The lady doth protest too much, methinks. And it must be true because Queen Gertrude said it, and we know what a reliable character she was.

We're all jogging along nicely here in Bloomsbury. The children are as mischievous as ever (which I love), as is Ivor (which I also love, if I'm honest). He's showing no signs of growing old, nor even of growing up.

I've been gadding about with my pals as usual. Our bridge night at Caroline Weaving's house descended into bawdy chaos when Betty Jackson shared a filthy joke her husband had told her and we had to spend five minutes explaining it to Audrey Redder. I swear, some of these women have led the most sheltered lives. As the conversation went on, though, it became clear that others are aware of wild things I've never even thought of. I am, it seems, distinctly average.

The charity committee continues to take up much of my time, of course. Do you remember I told you about our plan to take a party of children to Margate for the day? We're getting closer to making that a reality, though we're still short of a few adult volunteers to act as chaperones/shepherds/guards. Individually the children are little darlings, but once in a herd they can become a bit unruly. I'm sure it will all work out.

Oh, and I went to the Chelsea Flower Show yesterday with my friend Lilian where we entirely failed to see the King and Queen. According to the newspapers they arrived at ten and stayed for an hour and a half. We arrived at twelve so we didn't even spot their entourage. I'm sure you're used to hanging around with royalty, but it would have been rather glamorous and fun to see them. Heigh ho.

To my slight surprise, Ivor and Barty have agreed to help Superintendent Sunderland. I know you said you thought they were ideal for the job, but I wasn't completely convinced they'd go along with it. I can't believe it's the same case I wrote you about all those years ago. And I can't believe it was true. I thought I'd had a whole lifetime's worth of excitement after our adventures in Weston, and with an actual war going on a few miles away there was no chance of anything as glamorous as a diamond robbery happening on the road outside our little aid station.

But it was true, and the boys have decided to help. They have absolutely no idea how to go about things, mind you. Since meeting you (when was that – seventeen years ago?) Ivor has always fancied himself as a crime-solving adventurer, but the poor dear really doesn't have a clue.

They know the 'new' members of the club they're supposed to be looking at from this 'Alphabet Gang' they're playing for, but beyond that, they're drawing a blank. Ivor is convinced every one of them is far too stupid to be a diamond thief who has evaded the authorities for eight years. But that can't be right, can it? He likes to believe he treats everyone the same. 'I just take people as I find 'em, Ells-Bells. Prince or pauper. No prejudice here.' But I still think he has a bit of a blind spot when it comes to the upper classes – he assumes they're all idiots. To be fair, he might have a point in a lot of cases, but not all of them.

They need . . . I don't know how to say it . . . filtering? Sifting? We need some systematic way of working out who's who. Who's a genuine idiot and who's a cunning criminal on the run. Any tips from the experts?

And then there's this mystery treasure story. The boys are enormously skeptical but I think there might be something in it. There's no smoke without fire, as they say. Any tips there on finding out more about it? You must have contacts at the newspapers. Can you get someone to look in the archives and see if they can find out more about this Hatton Garden robbery and the Aristippus Club member who was hanged for it?

I'm going to try to work out a way of gaining access to the club on my own account to see what I can find out. I'm not going to ask Ivor if he can pick locks quite yet, but it might come to that.

But I must dash – I hear Edward exhorting Catherine to 'put your hands up on your head like horns', and I fear another bullfighting incident and its attendant injuries, breakages and recriminations.

Give my love to Emily.

Your friend

Ellie

P.S. Lunch on the first would be swell. Thank you.

Chapter Four

It was Ellie Maloney's strict rule that if the band wasn't working and Dunn didn't have a date, he should come round to the house in Bloomsbury for dinner on Thursday evening. In previous years, they had struggled to get together because although the Dizzy Heights tried hard to keep the diary clear on Thursday nights – even musicians needed a little time off – Barty Dunn's kaleidoscopic love life had meant that he was seldom available. But in recent months he had been a regular visitor, and was, he freely admitted, glad of the company.

He arrived at seven sharp and Mrs Dalrymple let him in.

'Good evening, Mr Dunn,' she said as she took his hat. 'Come on through, won't you? Mr and Mrs Maloney are in the drawing room.'

'Evening, Mrs D,' said Dunn, brightly. 'How's your knee?'

'Oh, mustn't grumble. Thank you for asking, though. Everyone's been so concerned. But it was just a wee tumble. I'll be right as rain in no time.'

'I'm sure you will. And what about your nephew? Did he get that apprenticeship he was after?'

'Aye, he did. My sister and her husband are so proud of him. Lucky to have a job in this day and age. Third generation of the family working at the shipyards, mind you.'

'Good for him.'

'I see you have your hands full there. Would you like me to take those?'

'No, ta, Mrs D. They're for the lady of the house.'

'Right you are, dear. Just go on through. They're expecting you.'

Dunn nudged the drawing room door open with his foot.

'Hello!' he called. 'Burglar here. Just come to do a little light burgling. Carry on about your business. I'll try not to get in the way.'

Skins hopped up from the floor where he had been playing with the couple's two small children. The gramophone was playing 'The Teddy Bears' Picnic'. Any other doting father might have arranged the children's menagerie of soft toys around a picnic blanket, where they could enjoy an imaginary pork pie and a glass of ginger beer. Skins, though, had opted to furnish them with cardboard instruments and stand them in a line so they could perform for the delighted toddlers.

'Hello, mate,' he said. 'Come on in. We've got nothing worth nicking, I'm afraid. But we can do you a nice plate of nosh if you're hungry.'

Ellie put down her trumpet-playing teddy bear and stood to kiss Dunn's cheek. 'Hi, honey,' she said. 'Ooh, what you got behind your back?'

Dunn brought out his right hand to reveal that it held a bottle of champagne.

'Oh, you absolute peach,' she said. 'I love champagne.' She turned to Skins. 'You never bring me champagne. I knew I married the wrong one.'

'Don't be fooled by his apparent generosity,' said Skins. 'It's not like he bought it. He half-inched it from Tipsy Harry's at the weekend.'

'Well, it's very thoughtful, darling, thank you. Pity there's just one, mind you – I could do with a couple of drinks after the day I've had.'

Dunn's left hand appeared, holding a second bottle.

'Ivor, darling, I want a divorce,' said Ellie. 'I want to marry the man with all the champagne.'

Ellie was the only person in the world allowed to call Skins 'Ivor'.

'I'll pack my things and be out by morning,' he said.

'Sorry it's not chilled,' said Dunn, handing her the two bottles. 'I should have nicked some ice while I was at it.'

'Where would you have put it?' said Ellie.

'In Mrs C's larder.'

'Cold in there, is it?' asked Skins.

'It would be with a load of ice on the shelf.'

Ellie laughed. 'Did I ever tell you that the first time I had champagne I was in—'

'Weston-super-Mare,' said Skins and Dunn together.

Ellie harrumphed. 'Well, if you're not going to indulge me and let me regale you with my tales of youthful derring-do, perhaps you'll be good enough to help me round up the monsters so we can get them into bed before dinner.'

'Leave it to me,' said Dunn. He scooped up the giggling Maloney children, one under each arm. 'Where do you want them? I could put them in the bin, but they'd probably get out. If you can get me a cab, I can have them dumped in the lake at Regent's Park before anyone knows they've gone. Although if I'm taking them that far, I might as well feed them to the lions.' He roared and the two youngsters giggled and wriggled.

'Feed Catherine to the lions,' said little Edward. 'She's stinky.'

'I'm not,' said Catherine indignantly. 'You are.'

'If they're both stinky,' said Ellie, 'we'd better not feed them to the lions – we might make them sick. I think we should bathe them and get them into bed.'

'Story!' shouted both children together. 'Uncle Barty. Story.'

'If you run upstairs and ask Nanny nicely to get you ready for bed, I'll send Uncle Barty up in a moment. Off you go.'

Dunn put the children down and they scampered from the room.

'You don't mind, do you, dear?' said Ellie as their footsteps thundered on the stairs.

'Not at all. I'll tell them the one about the musician and the Parisian waitress.'

'Teddy bears and toy soldiers will be fine,' said Ellie. 'But thank you for the offer.'

She pressed the servants' bell, and a few moments later Lottie the housemaid hurried in.

'Yes, ma'am?' she said, breathlessly.

'I keep telling you, you don't have to run, dear,' said Ellie. 'Nothing's ever that urgent. Could you get us a big ice bucket and three glasses for the champagne, please. We'll have it in the dining room. And could you tell Mrs Ponton we'll be ready for dinner in about half an hour.'

'Right you are, ma'am. Thank you, ma'am.'

Lottie hurried away.

◆ ◆ ◆

Half an hour later, the three old friends sat down to dinner.

'Delicious nosh as always,' said Dunn as he tucked in. 'Love this fishy tomato soup.'

'It's Maryland Clam Chowder, you uncultured oaf,' said Ellie. 'It's taken me a little while, but I finally persuaded Mrs Ponton to try making some dishes from the old country. Our last cook wouldn't countenance it. "I'll not be cookin' none of that foreign muck if you don't mind, Mrs Maloney," she said, and served us boiled beef, boiled mutton, and steak and kidney pudding – which was at least steamed rather than boiled. The only thing she was prepared to put in the oven was shepherd's pie, but only because she'd been free to boil the life out of the mince and potatoes first. We had to let her go.'

'This is boiled, though, this soup.'

'Chowder.'

'This chowder.'

'It is, but it reminds me of home. And the next course is to die for. Maryland Chicken. You'll love it.'

'Is it boiled?'

'Fried. Then steamed. Cream gravy. Mashed potatoes. I asked Cook to get corn on the cob but apparently the greengrocer looked at her like she was asking for mermaid tears collected in a unicorn horn.'

'I've never heard of it,' said Dunn.

'You're all peasants.'

'I keep telling you that, love,' said Skins. 'But you had some fancy, romantic notion about improving us. Something about taming the musical savages.'

'And look how far you've come,' she said, pouring everyone more champagne.

'I owe it all to you.'

'Yes,' she said. 'Yes, you do. Now, tell us, Barty dear, what's happening in your world? How's the romantic drought?'

Dunn looked accusingly at Skins. 'Do you have to tell her everything?'

'I don't have to, mate,' said Skins. 'I just like to.'

'Why don't you try to find a nice girl you have something in common with?' said Ellie. 'Someone you could – oh, I don't know – stay with for more than a night? Someone to love.'

'You sound like my landlady,' said Dunn.

'It's only because we care about you, sweetie. We want you to be happy. What about Blanche? Is she still single? I've not spoken to her for simply ages.'

'I'm not dating Blanche Adams. She's . . . It would be like going out with my sister.'

'I like her.'

'I like her, too.'

'Is she well?'

'My sister?'

'No, you goofus. Blanche.'

'As far as I know. Come along tomorrow night and you can ask her yourself.'

'Where are you playing tomorrow?' she asked.

'It's the regular one at Tipsy Harry's,' said Skins.

'Oh, yes – sorry, I keep thinking that's Saturdays. Sure, I'd love to. I can scope out the regulars and see if Superintendent Thingummy's deserter is there. Maybe take a look around for the secret vault. Then I can ask Blanche why she's not dating Barty.'

'Don't you bloody dare,' said Dunn.

'Well, one of us has to do something and it doesn't seem as if it's going to be you.'

Lottie arrived bearing a platter of chicken and a bowl of mashed potatoes. 'There's carrots and peas on the way, ma'am. I couldn't carry it all at once.' She hurried out.

'She explains that every time, bless her,' said Ellie. 'She must think me a frightful ogre.'

'You can be quite terrifying,' said Dunn.

'Me? How on earth do you make that out?'

'You know how to use a gun, for one thing.'

'Where I come from, everyone knows how to use a gun.'

'Yes, but I saw you shoot a tin can off a fence at about a hundred and fifty yards. There were blokes in our platoon couldn't hit a bus at ten feet. I'd not mess you about – you might shoot me.'

'But *she* doesn't know I could shoot her dead before she got to the corner of the street,' said Ellie. 'And I've been nothing but charming and polite. Kind, even.'

'Some people are just nervous and eager to please.'

'Well, I hope she's not unhappy here. I like her. But anyway, what's it like, this Tipsy Harry's place?' she said.

'Typical posh blokes' club,' said Skins. 'All marble and plummy accents.'

'Liveried servants,' said Dunn.

'How the other half live, eh?' said Ellie.

'You are the other half,' said Dunn. 'Look at this place.'

'Sure, we're comfortable,' she said. 'But not liveried-servants-in-a-private-gentlemen's-club comfortable.'

'Well, I think you'd fit right in,' said Dunn.

'And I think I really could help you find your deserter. And the treasure.'

'You'd better come with us, then,' said Skins.

The band arrived at the club early the next evening and set up as usual in the ballroom.

'We seem to be spending a lot of time here these days, what with the lessons and all,' said Blanche. 'Did we ever find out why the East Finchley mob couldn't do the rest of them? They were double-booked for that first one we did, but what about the others?'

'Not completely sure,' said Mickey. 'Rumour is that they might be splitting up. Something to do with a dispute over their shares of the takings, I heard. But I also heard their sax player was ill, so I don't know what to make of it. Probably that, to be honest – if I had half a crown for every time someone told me a band was splitting up, I'd be a member at a place like this instead of the hired help.'

'But what would you do with yourself all day?' said Puddle. 'You live for the thrill of the performance.'

'I could do without all the whatchamacallit, though. The admin. I'm a singer, not an office clerk.'

'We need a manager, sweetie,' said Blanche. 'I keep saying so.'

'Not sure we can afford it. They'd want their ten per cent.'

'My sister would do it for less,' said Puddle.

Mickey laughed. 'Your sister?'

'Capable girl, my sister. She'd have the whole thing licked into shape in no time. She loves a bit of admin, does our Katy.'

'We have enough trouble persuading some venues that it's all right to have two women in the band, without having one doing the bookings.'

'Well, if you change your mind, just let me know.'

'Do we know what's wrong with her?' asked Blanche.

'Puddle's sister?' said Mickey.

'No, you simp, the Foot-Tappers' sax player. Nice girl. Vera.'

'You know her?'

'There's not many of us granted the great honour and privilege of being allowed to play *men's* music. We stick close, us musical girls. I'll take her some flowers.'

Mickey untied the string from his speaking trumpet and walked off, shaking his head.

The room filled rapidly with excitable revellers. Some sat at the tables around the edge of the room, sipping their cocktails and champagne, but many more had already taken up their places on the dance floor. All were chattering excitedly.

Club rules dictated that gentlemen must be dressed in dinner suits (black tie was just about acceptable) or mess dress uniforms as appropriate. For the lady guests, though, the sky was the only limit. Some still preferred long evening gowns, but the more daring, younger women were in knee-length cocktail dresses. One young flapper, gleaming in a gold-sequinned affair, neatly complemented the newly installed 'mirror ball' that glinted over the dance floor. Headdresses abounded, ranging from elegantly simple jewelled bands to elaborate constructions topped with enormous ostrich feathers.

But no matter how any of them were dressed, they were all itching to get started.

At precisely the appointed hour, Skins counted the Dizzy Heights in and the dancing began. As always, the dancers' enthusiasm was woefully unmatched by their dancing skills, but nobody seemed to care. And why should they?

Dunn caught sight of the Alphabet Gang and leaned down to point them out to Skins.

'That dancing lesson doesn't seem to have done them any good,' he said.

'Leave them alone,' said Skins with a grin. 'They're having a good time.'

'Where's your missus?'

'Over there with . . . I want to say Dudley?'

'That's his real name,' said Dunn. 'Danny, they call him.'

'Ah, yes. Well, she's over there with him. Probably tapping him for all the gen on the secret treasure. She's quite excited by it all.'

'As long as she doesn't scare him off.'

'She's a canny one, our Ellie. She knows what she's doing. Unlike Danny. Blimey, but he's rubbish.'

Dunn laughed. His attention turned to Millie Mitchell. She wasn't the sort of woman he usually went out with – and she was obviously very much in love with Charlie anyway – but there was something about her. She was a beauty, it was true, but there must be more to it than that. Perhaps it was her self-assurance, he thought. Or her grace on the dance floor? Most likely her utter unavailability, he decided, and turned his attention back to the complex bassline of the current tune.

He smiled to himself as he hit every note spot on. This, he was forced to admit, was what it was really all about. Women came and went – well, they did in his life, at any rate – but the thrill of making music with his friends never left him. By their collective, coordinated efforts, he and the other seven Dizzy Heights were making people want to dance. Dispensing joy, one bar at a time. What could possibly beat that?

After an hour, everyone – dancers and musicians alike – was ready for a break. The band retired to the back room that had been set aside for them, while the dancers settled at tables and waited for the liveried staff to bring more cocktails and champagne.

The back room was quite a few cuts above the usual shabby green rooms in the other clubs and theatres they regularly played. The decor was classy, the chairs comfy, and the food and drink luxurious and plentiful. Dunn had had a quiet word with one of the committee members and there were now several bottles of champagne chilling in ice buckets on the table.

'I could get used to this,' said Elk, tucking in to something he thought might be called a vol-au-vent but wasn't completely sure.

'Now we're the resident dance band, you might be able to,' said Mickey.

There was a sudden commotion at the door.

Mickey and Elk looked over to see Millie Mitchell, her arm dripping blood, being helped by Barty Dunn. Everyone fell silent.

'Come on in and sit down, love,' he said.

'Blimey,' said Mickey. 'Look at the state of you. What happened?'

'Nothing dreadful,' she said. 'One of the Alphabet Oafs blundered into me and knocked me on to a table. Broke a glass and gashed my arm. Ernie said there might be a first aid kit in here.'

'Whereabouts?' called Blanche from the other side of the room.

'He didn't say. Charlie would know. He tried to come with me but he . . . well, he passed out. He's a bit of a cissy when it comes to blood.'

Blanche had searched the sideboard on her side of the room and had found an old army first aid haversack. She brought it over to where Dunn and Puddle were tending to the wounded dance teacher.

'Blanche will take care of you – she was a Fanny,' said Puddle. 'Shut up, Skins.'

Despite being married to a former member of the First Aid Nursing Yeomanry, Skins still took childish delight in their nickname. 'I didn't say nothing.'

'But you were thinking it. I could see your silly smirk from here.'

'You know me too well. I get in trouble with Ellie all the time when she talks about the Fannies. Where is my lovely wife, by the way? I thought she'd be helping. This is just her sort of thing.'

'She had to see to Charlie,' said Millie. 'The fainting.'

Blanche removed the napkin that had been inexpertly wrapped around Millie's arm and began to examine the wound. 'Can someone get me a bowl of water and some more clean napkins, please? Or tea towels?' She looked more closely before re-covering the gash and pressing the napkin tight. 'I think this is going to need stitches,

Millie dear. If there's a suture kit in the bag, do you mind me doing it? Or would you rather we get you to a hospital?'

Millie smiled. 'You were a nurse in the war, they said?'

'I was.'

'Then by all means, go ahead.'

The water and napkins arrived and Blanche set about making running repairs to Millie's arm.

'Where did you serve?' asked Millie. Her arm was beginning to feel extremely sore and she wanted to take her mind off it.

'Oh, all over France,' said Blanche as she worked. 'Wherever they needed us.'

'You must have some stories to tell. Was it dangerous?'

'Not so much. We were always a fair way behind the lines.'

'But you had to be close by. I'm not sure I could ever have done anything like that.'

'The Advanced Dressing Stations were a little further up, it's true, but we were never in any real danger from the fighting. Well, I say that. We weren't completely safe but the closest I ever came to proper danger happened when I was at home on leave. I got back to find myself posted to another station because ours had been destroyed.'

'My goodness,' said Millie. 'What on earth happened? Was it shelled? One heard about atrocities like that. Shelling hospitals. Barbaric.'

'No, nothing like that,' said Blanche. 'It was an aeroplane. A German Albatros, they said. It had been shot down. The story was that the pilot could have bailed out, but he stayed in the plane try- ing to steer it away from the dressing station. He didn't manage it. Everyone was killed.'

Millie said nothing; she just sat there, looking up at the former nurse.

'Sorry, darling,' said Blanche. 'Didn't mean to bring the mood down. There we are. All done.' She pinned the end of the bandage in place. 'I'd see your doctor in a day or two to get the dressing changed and the wound checked, but you shouldn't have any trouble. I've seen people get better from much worse. You'll have a scar, but I've made a neat job of sewing it all up – even if I do say so myself – so it should only be a tiny one.'

'What with that and the limp, I'm beginning to look like an old soldier myself,' said Millie. 'Thank you so very much. If there's ever anything I can do for you . . . anything at all.'

'Think nothing of it,' said Blanche. 'All in a day's work for the Dizzy Heights. Songs, jokes, and emergency medical attention. That's us.'

'Jokes? I didn't know you did jokes.'

'We try not to let them do it very often, but Skins and Dunn fancy themselves as a comic turn. They think it adds a little extra zing to the proceedings.'

'We have them rolling in the aisles some nights,' said Skins.

Puddle had brought a glass of brandy for the casualty. 'Some nights. Most nights they just stare blankly at you before telling you to shut up and play another song.'

'Early days yet,' said Dunn. 'Early days.'

Charlie's head appeared round the door. 'Hello, all. What news from the dressing station?'

'All stitched up and ready to return to the front,' said Millie. 'Are you all right now?'

'What? Oh, yes, that. Right as rain. Come back and join us. Will you chaps be ready to play again soon? The natives are getting restless.'

'We'll be on in a little while,' said Blanche. 'Give us a few minutes to tidy this lot up.' She indicated the bowl of bloody water and the even bloodier napkins.

Charlie whitened and wobbled slightly. 'Don't worry about that – I'll get the staff to see to it. If you're all fit, we'd rather you played. We've dancing to be getting on with.'

The Dizzy Heights gathered themselves together for the second set.

◆　◆　◆

The dance ended without further incident and the next few days were similarly excitement-free. Barty Dunn had once again entirely failed to find a date and was giving serious consideration to Ellie's suggestion that he look closer to home, to someone with whom he actually had something in common. To Blanche Adams.

She was clever and funny. She was talented and capable – watching the businesslike way she had tended to Millie's injury had been something of a revelation. And obviously they shared a taste in music. Now he came to think about it, she was quite good-looking, too. She was a few years younger than him, he reckoned, but that shouldn't be an obstacle. It couldn't be more than, what, eight years? Nine at the absolute outside. And it might be much less. She might be older than she looked. And age didn't always matter, did it? He was a catch, after all. Well, sort of. He didn't have a steady job, as such, but he'd not been out of work for nearly twenty years. That had to count for something.

He would ask her to dinner after the dance lesson. Probably. Or the pictures. Everyone loved going to the pictures. There was a new Clara Bow film, he was sure. Or Buster Keaton. There must be a Buster Keaton film on somewhere. There always had been in the past.

The Augmented Ninth had been closed on Monday night for decoration, so they had left their instruments at the Aristippus Club. This meant that their journey to Mayfair on Tuesday evening should have been easier than usual. Except that it was raining. Dunn had hopped off the tube at Russell Square and together they walked the half an hour to the Aristippus Club, with Dunn complaining even more energetically than usual about not having a van.

'Or even a car,' said Dunn. 'Couldn't you afford a car? You could do without at least one of your servants.'

'I offered to pay for a cab,' said Skins, 'but you were having none of it. You're fine with me blowing all my cash on a car, but a few bob for a taxi is beyond the pale, apparently.'

'Well, the next time I suggest walking a mile and a half in the rain, tell me I'm an idiot.'

'You're an idiot.'

'The *next* time. This time I'm a man of principle and honour.'

'And waterlogged boots.'

'Them, too.'

They finally arrived, moistened and bad-tempered, and set about lugging the instruments out of the storeroom and into the ballroom.

'You know how Puddle and Blanche keep on about us getting a manager?' said Dunn.

'They've got a point, don't you think?' said Skins.

'Definitely. I reckon it would be worth taking a drop in our share of the takings just to have everything properly organized – someone to make sure there are clean towels in the dressing room, a few bottles of beer for after. That would be more than worth it, come to think of it. But I was wondering if managers help lug things about.'

'I'd pay extra for one who'd do that. Or for a porter. Could we hire a porter between us?'

'That would be swanky, wouldn't it?' said Dunn as he heaved a couple of instrument cases on to the stage. 'Would he bring us drinks? Press our clothes?'

'Like a batman? I like the way you're thinking, old son.'

It took several trips, but they finally had everyone's gear on the stage, with the chairs in their usual places. There was still three-quarters of an hour to go before things were due to kick off, so they set off in search of someone who might be able to supply them with a couple of towels and a warming drink.

The club bar was the place to be, it seemed, and it was there that they met Charlie and the rest of the Alphabet Gang. Alfie, Bertie, Danny, and Ernie were engaged in some sort of indoor version of croquet, using the club's leather chairs and the older members sitting in them as natural obstacles. Charlie was umpire.

Once he saw the state the two musicians were in, Charlie kindly arranged for them to be supplied with the necessary hot toddies and towels.

'I'm pretty sure we can get those clothes a bit drier for you, too,' he said. 'At least get them pressed – that should make a difference.'

'It's all right to sit about the club in our underwear, then?' said Skins. 'I mean, I'm game, but I didn't think it was that sort of place.'

Charlie laughed. 'We keep a supply of bags and shirts for just such occasions. Accidents will happen, and all that. I'm sure we'll have something in your size till your own things are a bit drier.'

They allowed themselves to be led off to another room to change. On the way out, they met Millie.

'Oh, hello, you two,' she said. 'You look like a couple of drowned rats. Are they looking after you?'

'Just off to get our clothes dried,' said Dunn. 'See you later?'

'If you can bear it. You're quite the best band I've worked with. You're all set up?'

'Everything's ready to go. We just need the rest of the band and some dry clothes, then we're all yours.'

'Good-o,' she said. 'See you in half an hour.'

They left her waiting for an escort to take her into the bar.

❖ ❖ ❖

Skins and Dunn were in a small side room in the club where one of the servants had laid out clean, dry clothes for them. They were still in their underwear and trying to decide if it would be funny for them each to spend the rest of the evening in the trousers intended for the other.

'We could just put them on and not say anything,' suggested Skins. 'It would be a scream.'

'It's all right for you, short-arse, but how would I even fit in yours?'

'Oh, go on,' insisted Skins. 'Just try it.'

There was a knock at the door.

'We're not decent,' said Skins in a falsetto.

The door opened and Blanche popped her head round. 'Are you two idiots nearly ready? Eustace wants to warm up.'

Skins giggled, still in falsetto. 'But we're still in our unmentionables.'

'I can see that. Hurry up and get some bloody trousers on.'

'Aye-aye, Captain.'

'Oh, Blanche,' said Dunn. 'Umm . . . before you go . . . can I . . . can I have a quick word?'

'Only if you're wearing trousers,' she said.

'Right you are.'

He struggled into the nearest pair, which happened to be the ones intended for Skins. Before he could complain, Skins had pulled on the other pair and was heading out the door.

'I'll leave you to it, mate,' he said. 'Got to check the drums.'

He waddled off in his oversized trousers.

'What can I do for you?' said Blanche. She raised an eyebrow as Dunn attempted to button up the much smaller trousers.

'Skins's idea,' he said. 'He thought it would be funny if we were wearing each other's kecks.'

'Hilarious,' she said, dryly.

'I'll get him back so we can swap. So . . . well, now . . . the thing is . . .'

'Spit it out, darling. It's not like you to be tongue-tied.'

'It isn't, is it? But . . . you see . . . what I was wondering . . . Do you fancy dinner one night?'

She looked at him quizzically. 'A tryst? An . . . assignation?' She paused. 'A date?'

'Well, dinner, at any rate. Do you fancy it? Just the two of us? Somewhere up West? Nice bottle of plonk? Bit of a chat? See how things go?'

She thought for a moment. 'All right, then. Why not?'

'Really?'

'I was wondering when you'd ask, to be honest.'

'Wizard.'

'But it's all off if you ever say "wizard" again.'

'Right you are,' he said. 'Thursday evening? Pick you up at eight?'

'That would be lovely.'

He smiled broadly. 'Could you do me a favour now, though, please? Could you go and get our idiot drummer? I'm not playing for the Alphabet Chumps in these.' He indicated the ill-fitting trousers.

'I don't know,' she said. 'I think you look rather dashing.'

But she set off in search of the puckish percussionist nevertheless.

To the surprise of no one in the band, the dance lesson was another hilarious mess. In fairness, the participants clearly didn't expect much else, either, so the whole thing was extremely good-natured. Millie gave her instructions, the band played a few phrases of an appropriate song, the Alphabet Gang galumphed about, Millie shouted, the band stopped. Repeat until exhausted.

Millie called for the halftime break just as the beer and sandwiches arrived. She excused herself and left by the door at the other end of the room as the trays were being brought in through the main door. The Alphabets descended on the drinks table and helped themselves. Danny, the awkwardly angular, shy Alphabet, brought one of the trays over to the band.

'We were a bit remiss last time,' he said timidly. 'We only supplied beer. The other chaps – the Muswell Hill Mugwumps or whatever they're called – had a young lady playing the horn thing—'

'Saxophone?' suggested Dunn.

'That's the chap. Anyway, she preferred a Sidecar. One week it was a Gin Rickey. So I brought one of each for the ladies.'

'That's very thoughtful, sweetie, thank you,' said Blanche. 'What do you think, Pudds? Gin or cognac?'

'I'm a gin girl all the way,' said Puddle. 'You know me.'

They took the proffered glasses, clinked them, and raised them in a toast to the Alphabet Gang.

'Here's mud in all your eyes,' said Puddle.

Danny smiled and handed out beer to the rest of the band.

'What did you say to him?' asked Blanche once he had returned to his pals.

'Here's mud in your eye. Barty said it the other day. It's the latest thing, apparently.'

'From America,' Dunn confirmed. 'Got to stay hip in our game, doll.'

Blanche gave an exasperated shake of the head and took a sip of her cocktail.

'That's very tasty,' she said, smacking her lips. 'The members can't dance, but someone on their staff makes a damn fine Sidecar.'

The break lasted just long enough for the drinks to be drunk and the sandwiches to be eaten – the Alphabet Gang were itching to get back to their lesson. Millie had promised that if they showed her they'd made some progress with the basic Charleston steps, she'd show them something new to wow everyone at the next Friday night dance, even though they might not use it in the contest. They hadn't actually made much progress, but she cheerfully agreed that they'd been working hard, and assured them that the secrets of the new steps would be vouchsafed them after the break. To a man, they agreed that 'impressing fillies on the dance floor' was more important than drinking beer, and pressed eagerly for a return to work.

Of course, it was a slog. The usual suspects – Alfie and Ernie – made a complete dog's dinner of it, failing entirely to marshal any of their limbs to follow the instructions given them by the ever-patient Millie. Bertie, his hair so thickly coated with Brilliantine that it now looked as though it had been replaced with a Bakelite wig, made a half-decent fist of it but still seemed unable to introduce his head and neck into the action. Danny's interpretation was more or less accurate, but still hampered by his tendency to jerky angularity. Only Charlie looked as though he actually belonged anywhere near a dance floor, and he was soon being ribbed by his pals who accused him of cheating.

'Cheating how?' he asked.

'Well, you've got Millie here giving you all the inside information,' said Alfie. 'Tips and whatnot. Bet you've been practising this in secret all week.'

'I've been here all week with you, you idiot. When would I have . . . Oh, never mind. You just concentrate on trying to remember which is your left foot and which is the right. How did you ever manage to march in the army?'

'Colour sergeant took pity on me. Used to tap the old left leg with his stick. "Don't you worry, Lieutenant," he'd say. "I'll see you right." And I'd say, "So that's the right, then?" And he'd say, "No, sir, that's the left." Not much call for parade drill in the trenches, though, so it turned out not to matter much, what?'

'I suppose not, no,' said Charlie.

'Can we try it one more time, please, gentlemen,' called Millie, sounding not entirely unlike a colour sergeant herself. 'From the top, please, Dizzies.'

Skins counted them in. The band played. The Alphabet Gang stomped and stumbled. And then the music stopped. The Alphabets were confused – they thought they'd been doing well. They looked to Millie, but it was nothing to do with her. They turned to remonstrate with the band for ruining their most successful effort so far. And that was when they saw why the band had stopped playing and were out of their seats and yelling for help.

Lying on the floor, her saxophone beneath her, was Blanche Adams.

'Someone call a doctor,' shouted Puddle.

Benny had already set down his trombone and was kneeling beside his stricken colleague, trying to find a pulse.

'I think it might be too late for that,' he said calmly. 'I think she's dead.'

Chapter Five

One of the senior members of the club was a doctor. Danny found him in the reading room and he hurried to the ballroom but there was, as everyone already knew, nothing he could do. He called the police to report the sudden death and made arrangements for Blanche's body to be taken to the local public mortuary.

'Has to be done, I'm afraid,' he said when Puddle tearfully protested. 'Sudden death like this with no obvious explanation has to be reported to the coroner. There'll have to be a post-mortem to determine the cause. Was she in good health?'

The band had been in a shocked huddle since Benny's pronouncement. No one answered for a few moments.

Finally, Elk looked over. 'Fit as a flea,' he said. 'Never took so much as a day off work sick. We've all been on the crocked list at one time or another, but not Blanche.'

'You have my deepest sympathies,' said the doctor, kindly. 'I know how terrible it is when one loses a comrade.'

The ambulance came and went, followed by a police constable from Bow Street who took witness statements.

'Why are the police involved?' asked Eustace.

'Nothing to worry about, sir,' said the constable. 'Just routine. We just need to make sure the coroner has all the information he needs. There'll almost certainly have to be an inquest. Sudden death, you see.'

He spoke to everyone in turn, but they all told him the same thing. One minute Blanche was playing, the next minute she was lying on the floor on top of her saxophone. He offered them all his sympathies, thanked them for their time, and returned to Bow Street, leaving everyone very much at a loss as to what to do next.

Millie and most of the Alphabet Gang retired to the bar, leaving only the band and Danny in the now rather bleak ballroom.

Danny approached the stage. 'Is everyone all right?' he asked.

'Thanks, mate,' said Skins. 'It's all a horrible shock. But we'll look after each other.'

'If there's anything I, or the club, can do, you've only to say. You've met a few of the gang. Bunch of misfits, the lot of us. But we look after each other, too. And we've rather taken to you all. Had a word with the other chaps. You've done us proud these past couple of weeks and they like the cut of your collective jib. So . . . well, as I say – anything you need. We'll find someone else to play for these stupid classes, of course.'

The Dizzy Heights looked at each other.

'Well,' said Dunn after a moment. 'The thing about Blanche is she's – she was – a grafter. Like Elk said earlier, she never missed a day. The band always came first, and she took our responsibilities seriously. We promised we'd play, and we'll play. Right?'

The band nodded and muttered agreement.

'It'll be a difficult time – we all loved her – but she wouldn't want us to let anyone down.'

'She wouldn't,' said Puddle. 'She'd be angry with us if we did.'

'So we owe it to Blanche to see it through,' said Dunn. 'We'll get you through your dance contest with the . . .'

'The Wags Club,' said Danny.

'We'll play for you, get you ready. You beat them for Blanche.'

'When you put it like that,' said Danny, 'it does sound like a fitting tribute. But don't make any hasty decisions. We'll understand completely if you wish to back out. And bear in mind that we'll want to train a bit harder. We're going to need more than one lesson a week if we're to be ready in time. Just think about it, but don't make any rash commitments. We'd certainly appreciate your help, but we'd understand.'

He left them to continue packing up.

'Did she have any family?' asked Benny.

'A brother in Wimbledon,' said Puddle. 'I should tell him.'

'The police will do it,' said Benny.

'But it would be better coming from one of us. No one wants a policeman standing on their doorstep telling them their sister has died. It should be a friend.'

'You got the address?'

'Yes,' she said.

'I'll come with you,' he said. 'You shouldn't have to do it alone.'

The rest of the band agreed, and Benny and Puddle set off to take the District Railway to Wimbledon.

'They've left her sax and clarinet,' said Skins. 'We ought to look after them in case her brother wants them. We'll put them in the shop.'

Mickey, Elk, and Eustace helped Skins and Dunn to take their instruments out to the cart and then they all went their separate ways. The rain had stopped, but that meant the streets were crowded with all the people who had delayed their journeys to avoid the deluge. It took Skins and Dunn slightly longer than usual to get back to the shop and on to Bloomsbury, where Skins invited Dunn in for a nightcap. The bassist declined. He wanted to be alone.

Dunn kept to his room for the next couple of days and made no effort to go out, not even to his regular dinner with Skins and Ellie. The band had nothing in the diary and he just didn't feel up to the idea of seeing people.

By Friday morning, though, he felt the need to do something, so he set off for a walk through the north London streets. He still wasn't at all certain how he felt. Blanche's sudden death had been a terrible blow, to be sure, but he was unsure why it had affected him so badly. Friends had died before – under more gruesome circumstances – and he had felt the same combination of shock and loss, but there was an added dimension this time. This time it was someone he . . . Someone he what, exactly? Fancied? Cared about? Wanted? Had decided to settle for? They didn't have any sort of relationship beyond the friendly comradeship of the band and the promise of a date that could now never happen, so why had this hit him so hard?

She had been a remarkable woman, to be sure. Funny, talented, excellent company. Was it regret at what might have been? Had he left it too late? Had happiness been right under his nose all this time? Had she felt the same? Had she just been coolly waiting for him to do something about it? Waiting for him to realize that his philandering wasn't ever going to get him what he wanted?

He wandered for quite some time until he found himself outside a station, where he decided to hop on the tube to Russell Square to see Skins and Ellie. It hadn't been a conscious decision, but now he thought about it, that was probably where he'd been heading all along.

Mrs Dalrymple showed him in to the drawing room and said she'd let the Maloneys know he was there. He sat at Ellie's piano and began to play a few melancholy chords. A melody suggested itself almost at once and he picked out a few phrases before improvising around the new tune.

Ellie had been standing in the doorway listening for a few minutes.

'That's pretty,' she said. 'You should play more often.' She walked over and hugged him warmly. 'Hi, sweetheart. How are you? I'm so sorry about Blanche.'

He stood and hugged her back. 'I'm all right. How's our boy?'

'He's putting a brave face on it,' she said. 'You know what he's like. If there's a choice between showing his feelings and making a dumb joke, he'd always rather make the dumb joke. Is that an English thing? Is that your stiff upper lip?'

'Something like that,' said Dunn. 'We just find emotions a bit . . . you know . . . embarrassing.'

'Well, it gets my nanny, I can tell you. Just say how you feel.'

'I feel fine.'

She pulled back and hit his chest. 'You're as bad as Ivor.' She stood on tiptoes and kissed his cheek.

Skins appeared at the door. 'Who's as bad as me? Oh, hello, mate. You staying for tea?'

'Oh, do,' said Ellie. 'We could do with the company.'

'That would be nice,' said Dunn. 'But on the way over here I had another idea.'

'Go on,' said Skins.

'Well, no one's said anything official about Blanche.'

'No one at all?' said Ellie. 'Not even Blanche's brother? How is he – does anyone know? And what about poor Puddle? She and Blanche were close, weren't they?'

'They were. Tight as anything, those two. But as far as I know, no one's heard a dicky bird. So I was thinking we could ask Superintendent Sunderland.'

'I sent him a wire on Wednesday to let him know what had happened, but I've not heard anything back from him,' said Skins.

'What would he know about it?' said Ellie.

'Not much, I don't suppose,' said Dunn. 'But he'd know who to ask, wouldn't he?'

'He would. Why don't you call him?'

'Now?'

'Why not? It's obviously been on your mind. You know where the phone is. Go and call him.'

Dunn smiled and went out to the hall.

He returned a few moments later. 'This tea you offered me – is it anything as would spoil if we went out instead?'

'Just some sandwiches and cake,' said Ellie. 'The staff can eat them. Why? Where are we going?'

'Nowhere fancy. Sunderland wants to meet us at Lyons Corner House on the Strand in half an hour. His treat, apparently.'

'We'd better get our skates on, then,' said Ellie.

◆ ◆ ◆

The three friends hailed a cab and made it to the large café opposite Charing Cross station with a few minutes to spare. Sunderland was already waiting for them.

He greeted them warmly and, once the introductions were done, made no secret of the fact that he found the presence of a young American woman rather exotic. This entertained Ellie no end, and she managed to throw a few made-up American phrases into the polite chit-chat to help reinforce the impression that she and her home country were, indeed, somewhat exotic and mysterious.

Once the smartly uniformed Nippy (as the waitresses were affectionately known) had taken their order, Sunderland got down to business.

'Thank you for coming over,' he began. 'I'm most grateful for your reports from the Aristippus Club, and I was most terribly sorry to hear the news about your friend, Miss Adams.'

'Thank you,' said Dunn. 'Actually, that's why we wanted to speak to you. We've heard nothing from the police since it happened and we were wondering if you'd heard anything.'

Sunderland frowned. 'I'm afraid I have,' he said. 'I'm sorry to have to tell you that the news isn't good. Given the location of her passing and its connection to my case, I was able to pull some strings and get the post-mortem carried out urgently. Cases of obvious foul play take priority so there's usually a delay with other unexplained deaths, you see. Anyway, the results came through this morning and the police surgeon has confirmed that she was murdered.'

'Murdered?' they said together, slightly too loudly.

Diners at nearby tables turned to stare.

'Are you sure?' asked Dunn, much more quietly.

'Quite sure,' said Sunderland.

'But how?' said Skins. 'No one touched her.'

'Poison,' said Ellie. 'It must be poison.'

'I'm afraid it was,' said Sunderland. 'And a nasty one. Massive failure of all her internal organs. Never stood a chance, poor woman.'

'But how?' said Skins again. 'When? Was it at the club? We all ate the same sandwiches, drank beer poured from a jug.'

'The inspector in charge of the case will want to know all that,' said Sunderland. 'No idea who it is yet, but it'll be one of the C Division lads. Someone from Bow Street, I should think. We've only just had it confirmed as suspected murder so someone will be assigned today. He'll be calling on you all in due course, I'm sure.'

'Right you are,' said Skins.

'Make sure he brings a couple of uniformed coppers with him,' said Dunn. 'It'll give my neighbour a treat.'

Sunderland gave him a puzzled frown but decided not to ask. 'Given my interest in the club,' he said instead, 'I've asked if I can oversee the investigation, but you know what the politics of these things is like – everyone's got one eye on serving the public and the other eye on serving their career. But I'll definitely be poking my nose in.'

'Do you think they're connected?' said Ellie.

'The two cases? It's not obvious at the moment. Our man Grant isn't likely to want to draw attention to himself by murdering innocent musicians, but I'd be stupid to rule it out. I'd prefer to proceed as though it's possible and keep an open mind. It could be a coincidence, but I'm not keen on those.'

'But why Blanche?' said Skins. 'She didn't even know about us helping you out and she'd never done anything to anyone. Who would kill a saxophone player?'

'Who indeed?' said Sunderland. 'Look, are you two sure you want to carry on with all this? I'd quite understand if you didn't. You can't possibly be playing at the club any more, after all, not after that.'

'Actually, we are,' said Skins. 'We talked about it and we're sort of doing it for Blanche. The dance contest thing, I mean, not looking for your deserter. We said we'd see it through for her. She wouldn't want us to let them down. She was like that. Very professional.'

'The show must go on, and all that.'

'Something like that,' said Dunn. 'Get them through their contest for her.'

'Sounds like a nice tribute, as a matter of fact,' said Sunderland. 'How are you finding them?'

'The club members?' said Skins. 'It's difficult to convey it in a telegram, but . . . How can I put it? You never said – were you in the army?'

'Not I,' said Sunderland. 'I wanted to sign up, but the Bristol CID wouldn't release me. We'd lost too many youngsters to the war already and they insisted on us old hands staying behind to hold it all together.'

'Makes sense. But you've met young army officers in your time?'

'I have, yes,' said Sunderland. 'There were some fine men among them.'

'Undoubtedly. But there were some right idiots, too – rich as you like, more money than they knew what to do with, and not a chin nor an ounce of brains between them. It can be difficult not to think of this lot like that. One of them is a cunning thief – maybe even a murderer – but they all seem to enjoy playing the affable-idiot card. It can be hard to take the Alphabet Gang seriously sometimes.'

'The what?'

Skins explained the overly complicated system that had given the group of friends their name.

'So at least you've only got A, B, C, D, and E to remember. That must make it easier, surely?'

'You'd think so,' said Dunn, 'but I'm still trying to get to grips with it all. I've been too distracted watching them dance most of the time.'

'Good, are they?' said Sunderland.

Skins and Dunn both laughed.

'Probably not, then,' said Sunderland with a smile. 'But you're getting to know them a little? Finding out about them?'

'Bit by bit,' said Skins. 'And I'll be honest, they're not quite as dim as I like to paint them. They're not a bad bunch, really, and I don't like the idea that one of them's a wrong'un. We'll flush your man out.'

'Will we?' said Dunn.

'Course we will,' said Skins.

'How can you be so sure?'

'It's my detective instinct,' said Skins. 'I've got a nose for these things.'

'Who is it, then?' said Dunn. He was glad not to be thinking about Blanche for a while, and he was enjoying watching his friend squirm a little.

'Well, I mean, it could be . . . Well, there's . . . I mean . . .'

Ellie decided to bail him out. 'They haven't got a clue. But they'll be back and forth to the club a couple of times a week, maybe more, so I'm sure they'll trip him up at some point.'

'I see,' said Sunderland. 'And are you helping?'

'I'm certainly keen to get involved, especially now. So far I've only been offering moral support from the sidelines, but I'm intrigued by the secret vault. I've got Flo Armstrong in my corner, too, so I'm going to be following her advice on how to find it.'

The Nippy arrived with their tea and buns and Sunderland pressed the men for details about the Alphabets. They ran through more or less the same observations they'd made to each other at the Lamb and Flag after the first lesson. Sunderland made notes.

'Did you get any real names?' he asked when they'd finished.

'They did explain them to Millie Mitchell, but it wasn't fantastically easy to follow,' said Dunn. 'Alfie is something like Cornelius Something . . . No, it's gone. I just remember Millie saying he could have been Corny.'

'Charlie is Bob Something-beginning-with-C,' said Skins.

'Oh, and Ernie is Somebody Cashmore,' said Dunn. 'I liked the joke there. Earn-y. Probably the cleverest thing any of them has ever said.'

'I'll ask around, see if anyone has heard of any of them, but it's not much to go on,' said Sunderland. 'I'll check the deserters list, too, see if anything jumps out.'

'Sorry we can't be more help yet,' said Dunn.

'Don't be daft. Without you I'd not even have this much.' He waved his notebook.

The Nippy, thinking she'd been summoned, brought a fresh pot of tea and asked if they needed any more buns.

'Not for me, thank you, miss,' said Sunderland. 'But you three should feel free.'

The friends politely declined.

'We'd probably better let you get back to work,' said Skins.

'I better had,' said Sunderland. 'Thank you for coming down. And thank you for your efforts. I do appreciate what you're doing for us.'

'Think nothing of it,' said Dunn. 'Happy to help.'

'Well, thank you anyway. And my sympathies again for the loss of your friend. You should tell the others in the band that the case is under investigation so it's not a shock when the inspector turns up to question them.'

'They'll be fine,' said Skins. 'We'll set them straight.'

'I'm sure you will. Look, I know you have a lot to cope with, but please don't forget that time is against us. There are just two weeks to the dance contest and the possible theft – we need as much information as we can get.'

He paid the bill and they parted on the Strand.

◆ ◆ ◆

Ellie, Skins, and Dunn strolled back towards Trafalgar Square.

'You haven't got to rush back for anything, have you?' asked Skins.

'Mrs C's bottomless teapot and a new song I've been working on,' said Dunn. 'Got a better offer?'

'Let's go down the park and see the pelicans.'

They allowed their stroll to take them beneath Admiralty Arch and on to The Mall. St James's Park looked inviting in the late-spring sunshine, and the three friends followed one of the paths down to the lake. It was gone five and there were still one or two uniformed nannies pushing enormous prams, but most of the other people they saw were civil servants in their unofficial uniform of black jackets and grey trousers, scurrying home after a busy day spent running the country.

'You reckon any of them are spies?' said Skins as they found themselves a seat at the edge of the lake and sat down.

'Spies?' laughed Dunn. 'Really? Who for?'

'Could be anyone.'

'Don't be daft. No one does that any more. No need. The world is at peace, mate. They know what happens when they muck about with all that stuff.'

Ellie smiled and shook her head. 'You two idiots will be the death of me.'

The two idiots turned to look at her.

'One of your best friends has been murdered, and you're wittering on about bowler-hatted spies. Don't either of you actually feel anything?'

'About what?' said Skins.

'About Blanche. Murdered Blanche. Dear, sweet, talented Blanche.'

'She was talented, all right,' agreed Skins. 'She'd come a long way since we met her, and she was good even then. I'm surprised she stayed with us, to be honest.'

'Loyalty,' said Dunn quietly. 'I chatted to her one night after we'd played some awful club up the West End and she said she'd had an offer from some bloke who'd come over from New Orleans. She turned him down to stay with us. Or maybe because she had her eye on New York, but it certainly felt like loyalty.'

'There was that bloke from Berlin a couple of years ago, too,' said Skins.

'That wasn't loyalty, though, to be fair. That was just good sense. It was madness over there then. Remember that piano player? Dieter Something? He told us about getting his week's wages in the morning and it not being worth enough to buy a box of matches come teatime.'

'You see, you idiots,' said Ellie. 'She meant the world to you. And now she's gone. And you're twice as bad, Barty Dunn. Anyone could see she had her eye on you.'

'She never said.'

'Well, she wouldn't, would she? Not with you stepping out with a different doxy every other night. She didn't want to be made to look a fool.'

Dunn turned away to look at the ducks on the lake.

'We need to put things right,' said Skins. 'We need to find out who did this to her. It's more than just deserters and secret vaults. It's personal.'

'That's more like it,' said Ellie. 'I think we should ask Flo and Emily for help. They're in town this weekend and I'm having lunch with them on Monday.'

Skins smiled. 'That's a stroke of luck. How come you never said?'

'I did. You mumbled something like "That'll be nice" and then challenged Edward to a duel. I knew you weren't paying attention.'

'It was a matter of honour,' said Skins. 'He called me a "stinky weasel". I couldn't let that stand. But could we meet them tomorrow instead, do you reckon? All three of us? We can ask their advice. Do you think they'd mind?'

'I'm sure they'd be delighted to see you both. The worst that can happen is they tell us all to sit tight and let the gendarmes get on with it,' said Ellie.

Skins was distracted. 'There's one,' he said suddenly.

Out on the lake, a white pelican was ruffling its wings as it settled on to the water.

'Now, the pelicans might be spies,' said Dunn. 'They're definitely up to something.'

'Too big. Can't be sneaking into places looking like that. Draws too much attention. Your sparrow would make a good spy. Or a blackbird, if you want them to go somewhere fancy – they always look smart. But discreet.'

'You have the attention span of a small child, Ivor Maloney,' said Ellie. 'I've seen little Catherine concentrate on things for longer than you. But are you really going to stick at this investigation thing? Aren't you worried?'

'What about?' said Dunn.

'You've just found out Blanche was murdered. Any of you could be next.'

Skins looked up from his contemplation of the pelican. 'Actually,' he said, 'that never occurred to me. About the risk, I mean. Do you really reckon there's a chance we could be in danger?'

'If there's a mad poisoner on the loose at Tipsy Harry's, yes.'

Dunn laughed. 'Are you sure there's such a thing as a mad poisoner? And are they poisoning musicians? Or just sax players?'

Ellie frowned. 'It sounds dumb when you say it like that. But it's worth thinking about.'

'We'll be fine, love,' said Skins. 'Don't worry.'

'Just you be careful, that's all,' said Ellie. 'Both of you. Don't go taking any food and drink from strangers.'

He laughed again. 'You're starting to sound like my mum.'

'Sounds like she gave you good advice. You should follow it.'

'No one kills more than once, though, do they?' said Dunn. 'I mean, Jack the Ripper and all that, but killers kill and then that's it.'

'Sure, if there's a reason for it. But who would want to kill Blanche Adams? And from the way you describe it, how did they even single her out? Sounds like a random killing to me. And where there's one . . .'

'You're making too much of it,' said Skins, though in truth he was starting to doubt that she was. Now that she'd brought it up, he couldn't help thinking that maybe one of those weirdies at Tipsy Harry's really was killing musicians. Hadn't someone said something about one of the Finchley Foot-Tappers being ill? The sax player, wasn't it? And their sax player was a woman, too. He wasn't going to mention that to Ellie, though. Instead, he said, 'I don't think any of us knows enough about killers to be speculating like this.'

'Maybe not,' she said. 'But you know who would know? Emily Hardcastle. We'll stop at the Trafalgar Square Post Office on our way back and I'll wire Flo care of Emily's brother. Come on, let's get home.'

Chapter Six

Lady Hardcastle had telephoned the Maloneys on Friday evening, soon after receiving the telegram. She and Flo would be delighted to offer such advice as they were able, she had said, but not until Monday.

'I'm so terribly sorry,' she explained, 'but there are family obligations to be discharged – nieces and nephews to be taken to the zoo and so forth. You know how it is. But Monday is still fine. It'll be a pleasure to see the boys, too. One o'clock at The Ritz, as planned?'

Ellie had cheerfully agreed, and on Monday morning, she and Skins set out by taxi for Piccadilly via Wood Green. It was an extraordinarily long way out of their way, but they had arranged to call for Dunn. He had insisted it was a stupid waste of money, but in return they had insisted that it would be fun to arrive together. In the end, his fear of falling asleep on the tube and missing his stop had won the day. Although they'd had Sunday off, both Friday and Saturday night had been hectic and he was still weary by Monday morning.

They arrived at Coburg Road and waved at Mrs McGuffie as she peered round her net curtains to see who was calling at number 76. She scowled when she saw it was Skins, but neither he nor his American wife were worth opening her door to berate.

Dunn answered the door surprisingly swiftly.

'Come on in a minute,' he said as he let them in. 'I'm just putting my shoes on.' He held up a pair of freshly polished shoes.

'Cheers, mate,' said Skins. 'You're looking very dapper.'

'Got to make an effort for Lady H,' said Dunn.

Mrs Cordell popped her head out from the kitchen, where she'd been drinking tea with her friend Dolly.

'I thought I recognized that voice,' she said cheerfully. 'How are you, Skins, love? Oh, and Mrs Maloney, too. Hello, dear.'

'Hello, Mrs Cordell. Please call me Ellie.'

'Right you are, dear. Don't you all look smart, though? You going to The Ritz with Barty?'

'We are, Mrs C,' said Skins. 'Seeing an old friend.'

'So he said. What a treat that would be, eh?' said Mrs Cordell wistfully. 'Lunch at The Ritz. I hope she's paying for it, mind you. I can't hardly dream of such a thing on my widow's pension and I don't suppose you boys is much better off. Oh, come 'ere, Barty.' She pulled a small handkerchief from the sleeve of her housecoat and licked it, before bending down to where Dunn was lacing his shoes. She wiped a tiny smudge of shaving soap from below his ear. 'Can't have you going out looking a state.'

Skins smirked. 'Honestly, mate. Smarten yourself up a bit, there's a good lad. Letting the side down.'

'There, that's better,' said Mrs Cordell. 'You'll pass muster now. Can't have a lodger of mine being turned away by some snooty doorman because you didn't look your best.'

Dunn stood and kissed her cheek. 'Thanks, Mrs C. We'd best be on our way, though – don't want to keep Lady H waiting.'

'Ooh, "Lady H". Get you. You go and have a lovely time, dear.'

They trooped out the front door together and clambered into the waiting taxi.

'That's quite a landlady you've got there, Barty,' said Ellie.

'I know,' said Dunn. 'It's halfway between embarrassing and heartbreaking – I can never quite decide which. She misses her boys, though, that's the truth of it, so I just sort of let her get on with it.'

Ellie touched his arm. 'You're a much nicer man than you give yourself credit for, Bartholomew Dunn. I can't understand why you haven't been snapped up.'

'That's exactly what I keep saying,' he said. 'I'm a catch.'

'You are, honey. And don't let Ivor tell you any different.'

Skins had, indeed, been about to tell him different. Instead he said, 'Do they do nice cakes at The Ritz? Maybe we could get something to take back for her.'

Ellie leaned over and kissed his cheek. 'Oh, Ivor,' she said. 'You absolute sweetheart. You're a catch, too.'

Skins grinned.

The journey was an uneventful one and they arrived on Piccadilly at the front door of The Ritz at exactly one o'clock. A doorman in an inordinately smart uniform ushered them inside, and they stood for a moment, admiring the opulence.

'That's a lot of marble,' said Skins. 'It doesn't matter how many of these sorts of places we see, I'll never take it for granted.'

'I should think not,' said a woman in her late fifties wearing an extremely smart two-piece suit. She stood almost as tall as Dunn, and the dark hair peeping artfully from beneath her fashionable cloche hat was streaked with grey.

'Lady H,' said Skins delightedly. 'Wonderful to see you, old girl.' They kissed cheeks.

'And you, dear boy,' said Lady Hardcastle. 'And Eleanora, darling. You look simply marvellous.' Cheeks, once more, were kissed.

'And dear, dear Barty. It's been, what, a year?'

'Something like that,' said Dunn.

'We really should get to London more often, shouldn't we, dear?'

This last was addressed to the smaller woman standing, as ever, in her friend's shadow. This was Florence Armstrong, whose name in certain circles was often prefaced with 'the redoubtable . . .' She, too, was fashionably dressed, though her own dark hair showed a good deal less grey. Her smile was warm, and Skins could still see the mischievous light in her eyes that had attracted him when they first met nearly twenty years earlier.

'All right, Flo?' said Skins. 'I didn't see you down there.'

'Come here, you cheeky bugger,' she said, and hugged him. 'How are you? You missed my birthday party.'

'We were working,' he said. 'We tried to get out of the gig. Didn't we try?'

'They did try,' agreed Ellie. 'I was so sad to miss it.'

She hugged her old friend warmly. They had known each other for fifteen years, since Emily Hardcastle and Flo had saved her life at Weston-super-Mare when Ellie was just sixteen. Ellie and Flo had written at least once a month – often once a week – ever since, with only the same wartime restrictions that had slowed Ellie and Skins's correspondence getting in the way.

'Well, I shall entertain no such excuses for missing my sixtieth,' said Lady Hardcastle.

'You're never sixty,' said Skins. 'Really?'

'No,' said Flo, 'she's not. And she won't be for another two years, but she's already planning the party. The seventh of November, 1927. Put it in your diaries.'

'There's a three-line whip on that one,' said Lady Hardcastle. 'We've already agreed with the Farley-Strouds to use The Grange.'

'Is that where we played that time? The engagement party?' said Dunn.

'That's the place.'

'And it's still the same people who own it?' said Skins. 'They were ancient when we were there.'

'I've never been entirely certain how old they are, but I'd say they were well into their late seventies by now and still going strong,' said Lady Hardcastle. 'They've got years in them yet. But come, we haven't travelled all the way to this fine establishment to stand in the foyer and talk about birthday parties, no matter how much marble there is. There's a table in one of their splendid dining rooms with my name on it. We must eat.'

'I'll not argue with that,' said Skins, and they followed her as she strode off to find someone to take them to their table.

They were seated with some ceremony by a cloud of waiters. Lady Hardcastle, it seemed, was a regular and rather popular guest.

'That's enough fussing for the moment, dear,' she said, as she shooed the last of them away from rearranging her cutlery and glassware. 'I appreciate the attention, really I do, but consider my ego well and truly stroked for now. If you want to be properly useful you could be an absolute pet and bring us a couple of bottles of that champagne I like.'

'The '22, my lady?' said the waiter with a small bow.

'Good lord, no. The '21. Unless you have any of the 1915 left?'

'I shall see what the sommelier has to say, my lady. I'm sure he can find something extra-special for you and your . . . guests.' This last word was delivered with the tiniest hint of disdain as he inspected the rather-too-fashionable attire of the three strangers at the table.

'Cheeky little bleeder,' said Skins once the waiter had scurried away. 'My wife's a bloody millionairess, I'll have you know.'

'Not quite, dear,' said Ellie. 'And don't go running away with the idea that we'll be dining in places like this all the time when they finally release my inheritance.'

'I'd be happy with a saveloy and a ha'porth of chips if I was eating it with you, my sweet. But . . . I mean . . . really. Looking at us like we was nobodies.'

'I am a nobody,' said Dunn. 'And proud of it. But if you're going to carry on being soppy like that, I might have to send the pair of you out for your saveloy and chips while I stay here with the ladies.'

Skins harrumphed.

'He's right,' said Ellie. 'That was a bit saccharine even for you.'

'You're a miserable couple of bleeders as well,' said Skins. 'No romance in you, that's the trouble.'

'No saveloys for us,' said Lady Hardcastle. 'Unless you really want them, of course. It's entirely up to you. Feel free to indulge yourselves. It seems a shame to come to somewhere like this for lunch and not have whatever one wants.'

'That's very kind of you,' said Ellie.

'Nonsense, dear. If one can't treat one's friends, then what on earth is money for?'

After a minute or two of silence, during which everyone carefully examined their menus, Skins leaned over towards Ellie. 'What are you going to have?'

'None of your business,' she said.

'What do you think of the langoustines?'

'I haven't seen them yet.'

He pointed at her menu. 'There. Above the mussels.'

'So they are,' she said, distractedly.

'Or the chicken liver parfait?'

'What?'

'There,' he said. 'Right there. Look. Chicken liver parfait.'

'You're right,' she said. 'That definitely says chicken liver parfait.'

'So what are you going to have?'

'Ivor, for the love of all things holy, will you shut up for a minute. You do this every time. It doesn't matter what I'm going to have. Have whatever you want.'

'I'm just interested.'

'I don't know what I'm going to have. I can't read the menu because someone keeps asking me what I'm going to have and then pointing things out on another part of the page.'

'What are you going to have, Barty?' said Skins.

Dunn just looked at him and shook his head.

'We spoke to Inspector Sunderland this morning—' began Lady Hardcastle.

'Superintendent,' Flo interrupted.

'Yes, that's right. What did I say?'

'You know full well what you said.'

Lady Hardcastle sighed. '*Superintendent* Sunderland and I had a chat this morning. He's jolly grateful to you for helping him out with his deserter case.'

'Can't really say we've done very much,' said Skins.

'We've narrowed it down to a handful of possibilities,' agreed Dunn. 'But he could have done that himself in less time than it's taken us.'

'Well, he's grateful anyway,' she said. 'And I'm sorry to hear about your friend. And quite flattered that you thought to ask us two for help. Or that Eleanora did, at any rate.'

'Oh, they thought of it, all right,' said Ellie. 'But you know what they're like. They left it to me to send the cable.'

'And I'm jolly pleased you did. I know we have something of a reputation for this sort of thing, but I'm still surprised and delighted that you thought of us.'

'Well, it's not the first time we've had a bandmate bumped off,' said Skins. 'And you were the ones who worked it out last time.'

'With help from the police,' said Flo. 'But we have a certain knack.'

'So what do we do?' said Dunn.

'You leave it to the police,' said Lady Hardcastle. 'I know we've not got a frightfully good track record of leaving things to the rozzers ourselves, but they do know what they're doing for the most part. Are they doing anything?'

'We don't know yet. Sunderland said an inspector would probably pay us a visit, but we've seen no one.'

'When did she die?' asked Flo.

'Last Tuesday,' said Dunn.

Lady Hardcastle put down her menu. 'Almost a week and no one's spoken to you?'

'Well, Sunderland said they only found out for sure it was murder on Friday,' said Skins. 'When he spoke to us he wasn't even sure who was on the case.'

'But it's Monday now,' she continued. 'Time is everything in a murder inquiry. I know that much at least.'

'Maybe he just hasn't got round to us yet.'

'Perhaps. Ah, here comes our waiter. Is everyone ready to order?'

They were, and they did.

Conversation turned to more convivial things while the waiters fussed about them, bringing first the champagne (the 1915, as it turned out) and then their first courses.

Lady Hardcastle played the gracious hostess for a while, as she contemplated the best advice for her old pals.

'Who are your possible suspects?' said Lady Hardcastle when the conversation lulled after the next course had arrived.

'Suspects?' said Skins. 'That's the thing, isn't it. We don't know who to suspect.'

'Very well, then, let's look at it another way. Who could it possibly be? Who was at the club when it happened?'

'Well, there's the Alphabet Gang,' said Skins. 'And Millie Whatshername.'

'The entire staff of the club,' said Ellie. 'Don't forget them.'

'Blimey,' said Skins. 'All right, then, so we'd better include all the other club members as well.'

'And you,' said Flo.

'What?' said Skins. 'Me and Barty?'

'Technically, yes. But I actually meant the band.'

'You mean one of us could have killed her?' said Dunn. 'That can't be right. Not one of us.'

'The point is that anyone who was there could have killed her,' said Lady Hardcastle.

'Although, since it was poison,' said Flo, 'they didn't actually have to be there at all.'

'So you're saying we need to consider the entire population of London?' said Skins.

'Not quite,' said Lady Hardcastle. 'The people who were actually in the building will be enough to be getting on with. I find it's easier to start at the middle and work outwards. Work your way through the Alpha-Omega Conglomerate . . .' She grinned at Flo, waiting for the correction that never came. It was still one of her favourite things – deliberately getting some simple thing wrong and waiting for an exasperated Flo to correct her – but Flo was having none of it. '. . . the dance teacher, and the band. If you get nothing there, move on to the chap who brought in the food and drink, and the kitchen staff who prepared it. Then the other club members. Then food suppliers. Then, as you say, the rest of the population of London. Although if you've got nothing by the time you move on to suspecting people who weren't even in the club at the time, you're probably never going to catch them.'

'And when you say "work your way through" them,' said Dunn, 'what exactly do you mean?'

'Talk to them. Find out about them,' she said.

'You also need to work out a handful of other things,' said Flo. 'You need to know how she was killed—'

'Poison,' said Skins.

'Yes,' said Flo. 'But how was it administered? Once you know that, you might be able to work out when it was done. And when you know how and when, you might be able to rule some people out.'

'Alibis,' said Ellie.

'Exactly so,' said Lady Hardcastle. 'And while you're doing all that, you need to fathom out why someone wanted her dead. If we're assuming it was a deliberate act and not a terrible accident, then someone wanted to kill someone. Was it her they wanted to kill? Or did they just want to kill anybody who happened to be there at the time? And if it was her, then why? Why pick poor Blanche Adams?'

'Motive,' said Ellie.

'You're well up on the terminology,' said Flo with a smile.

'I learned from the best. I have a dear friend who solves mysteries for fun.'

'But there must be a million different motives for murder,' said Dunn. 'How do we even start?'

'You'd think so, wouldn't you?' said Lady Hardcastle. 'Although you can boil it down to three for most practical purposes: passion, money, and the need to cover up another crime. Outside those, you have the motiveless killings of the madman, but he's a last resort – most killers kill for a reason.'

'And we can find all this out by talking to people?' said Skins.

'That and a bit of poking about where you're not wanted,' said Flo. 'That's my favourite bit.'

'Talking of which,' said Ellie, 'have you had any luck with your newspaper contacts? Any new gen on the treasure?'

'Not yet. I've put out some feelers, but no responses so far.'

'What's all this?' said Skins.

'We know someone at the *Bristol News*,' said Flo. 'I asked if she wouldn't mind calling in some favours to get some of her London newspaper pals to have a look through their archives. You know – see if there was anything about the 1805 robbery. I told her what we already know and she had a few ideas for other things we could look for. General articles about the club, that sort of thing. There might be clues in there no one has ever noticed.'

'We appreciate you going to so much effort on our behalf,' said Ellie. 'Don't we, boys?'

'We do,' said the boys together.

'In the meantime,' said Dunn, 'it's just talking to people and "poking about"? Sounds like a lot of work.'

'It is, dear,' said Lady Hardcastle. 'That's why I suggested leaving it to the police. They have the patience and the manpower for all that sort of thing.'

'If they get round to it,' said Skins.

'Well, quite. We shall have to call at Scotland Yard before we leave and see if dear Insp— dear *Superintendent* Sunderland can shed any light on the identity of the investigating officer and why he might be dragging his feet.'

'Thank you,' said Ellie.

'You do have one advantage over them, though,' Lady Hardcastle said. 'You knew the victim well. You worked with her for . . . how long?'

'Band's been together since '23,' said Skins, 'but we bumped into her here and there before that. The jazz world is quite small. So two years of working together and a few odd days before that.'

'We only met her a couple of times, I think. She seemed nice enough. What was she really like?' asked Flo.

'She was a bit of a girl. Not anyone's idea of a shrinking violet. She never talked about her past much, but I know she was a Fanny in the war. Posh family, I always assumed. But she knew what she liked and wasn't afraid of going out and getting it, if you know what I mean.'

'I think I can remember,' said Lady Hardcastle.

'I think some people were a bit intimidated by her, to be honest,' said Dunn. 'She wasn't rude, but she didn't hold back.'

'So she could have upset someone,' said Flo.

'Maybe,' said Skins. 'But she wasn't that sort. She shocked a few people in her time, but she was never rude.'

'Sublime player,' said Dunn. 'It was like it came from somewhere deep inside her. Like you could hear her soul breathing out through her saxophone.'

'She sounds like a remarkable woman,' said Lady Hardcastle.

'She was,' said Skins.

It fell to Flo to break the contemplative silence that followed. 'Have we met all the other members of your band?'

'Do you really think it could be one of them?' said Skins.

'No idea. I'm just interested, that's all. We got the lowdown on the Alphabet Gang when we spoke to Sunderland, but I wanted to add the band to my mental list.'

'I think you probably have. There's me and him, obviously.'

'Best rhythm section in London,' she said with a smile.

'You better believe it. Then there's Elk – Jonathan Elkington – on banjo. We first met him in France in '17. His battalion had sent a few blokes to a big concert at the rear and we put together a scratch band. Nice bloke. Tiny bit . . . gormless, but he's all right. We bumped into him again when we were putting the band together and he's been with us ever since.'

'Could he kill?'

'We can all kill,' said Dunn. 'We learned that the hard way.'

'All right,' said Flo. 'Could he kill in cold blood?'

'No,' said Skins. 'Not Elk. Soft as puddin'. Hasn't got a nasty bone in his body.'

Flo smiled but said nothing.

'Eustace Taylor plays trumpet,' said Dunn. 'He's a snob, but he's harmless.'

'A snob?' said Lady Hardcastle.

'Classically trained, or so he says. He played with some symphony orchestra down on the coast, we know that much for sure. He thinks he understands jazz better than the rest of us because he knows a diminished ninth from a paradiddle. Puddle has forgotten more than he's ever learned, but that doesn't stop him lording it over her, an' all.'

'Puddle?' said Flo.

'Isabella Puddephatt.'

'Oh, I say,' said Lady Hardcastle gleefully. 'What an absolutely delightful name.'

'Delightful girl,' said Skins. 'Plays clarinet and alto sax. And she definitely is classically trained. Royal College of Music, if you please. Another posh girl. Posher than us, any rate.'

'And are either of them killers?' said Flo.

'Eustace is shy and insecure,' said Dunn. 'He might lash out if he'd finally had enough.'

'"Had enough"?' asked Lady Hardcastle. 'Did Blanche bully him? You said she was a forthright woman. Did she pick on him?'

'Everyone's had a go at him at some time or other,' said Skins. 'He's that sort of bloke. He provokes people.'

'Except you,' said Dunn. 'He doesn't seem to get to you.'

'Nothing much gets to Ivor,' said Ellie.

Skins laughed. 'Where's the profit in getting worked up over what other people do? I can't control it, so why let it bother me? But I don't think Blanche ever had a go at Eustace.'

'She backed down the other day, though, remember? I can't think what she said, but she apologized straight after. Maybe he'd warned her off after some other thing we never saw.'

'It can't be him, though,' said Skins. 'Doesn't make sense.'

'Can't be Benny Charles, either,' said Dunn. 'West Indian bloke. Plays trombone. He's too . . .'

'Kind,' said Skins.

'Yes, that's exactly it. Too kind. He's everyone's Uncle Benny. Pretty sure he could snap you in half if he had a mind to, but he's not that sort of bloke.'

'And then there's Mickey Kent,' said Skins. 'Dodgy as you like, but he's more likely to try to sell you a case of knocked-off scotch than poison you.'

'What does he do?' asked Flo.

'He's our *chanteur* – he prefers that to "singer". A bit of a charmer. Not in Barty's league, obviously, but he's no slouch with the ladies.'

'He's extremely dishy with it,' said Ellie. 'Although still not in Barty's league, obviously,' she added hurriedly.

'But not the murderous sort,' said Lady Hardcastle.

'Definitely not,' said Skins. 'Like Barty said, it can't be one of us.'

'Our own experience has shown that almost no one is the murderous sort until they actually find themselves committing murder. But unless you can think of any jealousies or resentments that might have hardened into cold homicidal fury, it's not especially likely to be any of your pals.'

'So they should start with the Alphabet Gang?' said Ellie.

'They should,' said Lady Hardcastle. 'And we should start wondering what to have for pudding. I see a waiter approaching with menus.'

◆ ◆ ◆

The boys were playing the Augmented Ninth as usual that evening, so Ellie had invited Dunn to spend the afternoon with them in Bloomsbury.

'You've no real reason to go home,' she'd said. 'Your suit will cut quite a dash at the club so there's no need to get changed. And Emily sent that box of cakes and treats to your landlady, so you don't even need to deliver that. Come back to our place and put your feet up for the afternoon. It'll look cute with you and Ivor snoozing in armchairs in the drawing room. It'll be like a gentlemen's club.'

He had accepted, but there seemed little chance of Ellie allowing him and Skins to have the promised snooze. Coffee had been called for, and she was sitting with her journal and pen.

'We need a proper plan,' she said once Lottie had delivered the coffee. 'We can't just keep bumbling on and hoping for the best.'

'We?' said Skins. 'You're involved now, then, are you?'

'You better believe it, buster. You two will just slouch about, making jokes, laughing at the posh boys and getting nowhere. And you'll get on the police's nerves while you're about it. I can add a little . . . structure. A little discipline.'

'I see just one tiny flaw, Mrs M,' said Dunn.

She raised her eyebrows.

'It's a gentlemen's club,' he continued. 'You're not allowed in.'

'How many times have you come home and whined about how you need a manager, Ivor?'

'I do it at least weekly,' said Skins. 'More often if I've been getting it in the neck about the lack of champagne in the green room, or there being no paper in the ladies' loo.'

'Meet the Dizzy Heights' new manager,' she said.

It was Skins and Dunn's turn to raise their eyebrows.

'Not for real,' she reassured them. 'I can't think of anything I want to do less than try to wrangle a herd of needy musicians. But the stuffy old fuddy-duddies of the Aristippus Club don't need to know that. I'll put on some natty duds, carry a briefcase. They'll splutter into their whisky and sodas and loudly ask what the world is coming to, but what are they going to do then? The youngsters have already staged their coup d'état and allowed a jazz band into the place with lady musicians. If another lady turns up and says she's the band's manager, what are they going to say?'

'They'll say, "Get out, madam",' said Dunn. 'I think they have a lot of experience of saying that.'

'We'll see,' she said. 'I can be quite persuasive.'

'She can,' said Skins with a nod. 'Very.'

'You'll have to let the band know,' she said. 'We don't want them "blowing the gaff", as you guys say. They'll have to go along with it.'

'We can manage that,' said Dunn. 'Benny and Puddle already know we're looking for Sunderland's deserter. Eustace, Elk, and Mickey won't mind. They all served. They'll get it.'

'But we'll be looking into Blanche's murder as well, don't forget.'

'Yeah, but they'll be all right with that, too.'

'They might be,' she said. 'But is it safe?'

'How do you mean?' asked Skins.

'Remember what Emily and Flo said? It could be one of them.'

'Theoretically,' said Dunn. 'But it's not, is it? We're going to be poking about asking questions, getting to know people. Our lot aren't anything to do with it and it's better to have them on our side.'

Ellie thought for a moment. 'Very well, then, let's get them involved.'

Throughout the conversation she'd been making notes in her journal. She finished her sentence, put the cap on her pen, and stood.

'If you two are going to maintain your reputation as the best rhythm section in London,' she said, 'you'd better try to get some rest before tonight. Your usual guest bedroom is made up if you want it, Barty. I'm going to my study to have a think.'

Chapter Seven

During one of the breaks at the Augmented Ninth, the Dizzy Heights had talked among themselves and had once again confirmed their commitment to playing for the dance classes at Tipsy Harry's. They would do it as a tribute to Blanche. Mickey had taken the opportunity to pass on a request from the club that they also play for a second lesson, on Wednesday evenings, and they agreed to that, too.

In an earlier discussion they had decided that it wouldn't be crass to replace Blanche – her parts were vital in some of the more complex arrangements – so Puddle had drafted in one of her old music-school friends to sit in on saxophone. He was keen to help out and he even said he would try to rearrange his Wednesday teaching obligations to fit around the extra dance lesson.

'Do it for Blanche' became the band's unofficial motto, replacing Skins's usual suggestions of 'Don't get your hopes up', 'Prepare to be disappointed', and 'Music for people who are too drunk to know any better'. He had wanted someone to translate them into Latin so they could put them on their calling cards, but they didn't know anyone posh enough to be able to.

Skins and Dunn arrived early for the Tuesday session, intending to use delivering the good news as an excuse for chatting to a few members of the Alphabet Gang. But when they finished carrying their instruments to the ballroom and went to the bar in search of their quarry, they discovered that the Alphabet Gang were busy. With the police.

Skins approached Alfie, who was sitting on his own in a slightly battered Chesterfield armchair. 'What's going on?'

Alfie looked up from his newspaper. 'I think it's an alpaca. Whiffy Wingrove brought some back from Peru. Says he's going to raise them for wool. Worth an absolute packet, apparently, alpaca wool.'

Skins frowned in puzzlement and looked at Dunn for help. Dunn simply nodded in the direction of the bar. A group of men were clustered round a pleasant-faced, middle-sized, docile animal that looked like a cross between a small humpless camel and a sheep. *That*, thought Skins, *must be the alpaca.*

'What did he bring it in here for?' he said.

'For a scotch and soda?' suggested Alfie. 'Spot of lunch? It would be nice to imagine so, don't you think? A chap going to his club and taking his alpaca for a drink and a bit of scran. But I think someone said it just followed him. Only lives round the corner – keeping them in the back garden of his London place until he can get them moved out to Norfolk. He has a massive pile in Norfolk. Acres of land. Perfect for alpacas, he says. They come from the mountains, d'you see?'

'Isn't Norfolk very flat?' said Skins.

'Is it?' said Alfie with a frown. 'Are you sure? I'm a bit of a duffer when it comes to geography.'

'Famous for it,' said Skins.

'Ah. Then I might have got that wrong.'

'Those blokes seem rather taken with it,' said Dunn.

'With Norfolk? Never been. Had an aunt who lived in Kettering, though.'

'That's in Northamptonshire,' said Skins.

Alfie smiled ruefully. 'Told you I was a duffer.'

'I meant they're taken with the alpaca,' said Dunn.

'Behaving like a bunch of kids if you ask me,' said Alfie. 'One of the masters at my school had a spaniel. Used to bring it to lessons sometimes. Boys went gaga over it.'

'But not you,' said Skins.

'No, not me. I was always wary of dogs. Got bitten on the backside when I was tiny. Never trusted them.'

'And that applies to all animals now?' said Dunn. 'Is that why you're not over there making a fuss of the alpaca?'

'No, not all. But that chap looks too much like a furry camel. Can't abide camels. Got bitten during the war.'

'You were in Egypt, then? Libya?'

'What?' said Alfie.

'In the war,' said Dunn. 'In the Middle East somewhere. When you were bitten by a camel.'

'Oh,' said Alfie, the penny finally dropping. 'I see what you mean. I was in Egypt for a time during the war, as it happens, but the camel incident occurred at London Zoo. Took a girl there when I was on leave. Thought it would be romantic. Camel pinched my hat and then bit my arm when I tried to get it back.'

Skins laughed. 'I'll be honest with you, though, Alfie – you don't mind if I call you Alfie?'

'Not at all, dear boy. Absolutely everyone does. Well, not Ma and Pa, obviously – they call me Cornelius. And Nanny always called me Corny. I miss her.'

'Thank you. The thing is, I wasn't actually talking about the alpaca. I was more interested in what's going on over the other side of the room there.'

'Ah,' said Alfie. 'Got you. The rozzers are here. Interviews. Talking to Charlie now, it seems. About your pal. Sympathies, by the way.'

'Thank you,' said Dunn. 'Who's the geezer in charge?'

'Inspector Something-or-other.'

Skins and Dunn rolled their eyes in unison.

'Oh. It's got a B in it,' said Alfie suddenly.

'Thanks, Alfie,' said Skins. 'I don't suppose you caught the names of the two uniformed blokes with him?'

'Not a clue, old bean. Sorry.'

The inspector, meanwhile, had stood up. He shook hands with Charlie, who ambled casually towards the bar. The inspector stretched and looked around the room. Catching sight of the two fashionably dressed musicians, he started purposefully towards them.

He held out his hand to Skins. 'Good afternoon. I'm Inspector Lavender.'

'See?' said Alfie triumphantly. 'Told you it had a bee in it.'

It was the inspector's turn to roll his eyes. 'I'm going to go out on a limb and guess you're the musicians Superintendent Sunderland told me about.'

'We are,' said Skins. 'What gave us away?'

The inspector beckoned them to follow him to a quieter part of the room. 'The cut of your suits. Very . . . à la mode. This lot's tailors haven't quite caught up with the latest fashions. Probably never will. I'm investigating the murder of your friend Blanche Adams, though – you have my sympathies. It must have been a terrible shock.'

'It was,' said Skins. 'She was a dear friend.'

'I understand,' said Lavender. 'I've had a fairly complete account of the evening's events from Mr Chandler.' He pointed across the room to where Charlie was ordering himself a drink from the bar. 'I'd like to hear from the two of you, see if you can add anything.'

'Of course,' said Skins. 'Well, it was last Tuesday night. We came to play for their dancing lesson.'

'You usually do that?' said the inspector.

'It was the second time. We got the job when the Finchley Foot-Tappers let them down.'

'Oh, we do like them, my wife and I. My wife is very keen.'

'Right,' said Skins. 'Well, we thought we were just filling in – nice easy job. Money for jam. Or for a jam session, you might say . . .'

The inspector looked at him blankly.

'So we were all set up to play by seven,' continued Skins. 'The lesson started. We played for about three-quarters of an hour, then stopped for a break.'

The inspector checked his notebook. 'Beer and sandwiches?'

'Yes, that's right.'

'And you all had the same?'

'We did.'

'No,' said Dunn. 'No, we didn't. The nervous one . . . Danny? Yes, Danny. He brought a couple of cocktails for the girls.'

'Did he now?' said the inspector, making a note. 'Danny, you say. I don't suppose you remember what these cocktails were?'

'One had gin in it,' said Dunn. 'I remember because Puddle wanted the gin. Likes a bit of gin, does our Puddle.'

'You're right,' said Skins. 'A Sidecar and a Gin Rickey. I'd completely forgotten that. I thought they both had beer.'

'No,' said Dunn, 'that was after the dance when they were complaining there was no champagne in our green room.'

'So Miss Adams had the Sidecar,' said the inspector.

'Yes, that's right,' said Skins.

'And it was this' – he looked down at his notebook – 'this "Puddle" who made the choice.'

'Isabella Puddephatt,' said Skins. 'Yes. Then we played a bit more, and suddenly everything stopped when Blanche collapsed on the floor.'

'Was she still breathing at this point?'

'Benny got to her first,' said Dunn. 'He said not.'

'Benny?'

'Benjamin Charles,' said Skins. 'Our trombonist.'

'I see,' said Inspector Lavender. 'So the men had the beer, the ladies had their cocktails, and you all ate the same sandwiches?'

'As far as I know,' said Skins.

'And it was this "Danny" who brought the cocktails.'

'It was,' said Dunn. 'He made a big thing of it. He said the sax player in the Foot-Tappers preferred a cocktail in the break. It seemed like a kindly gesture.'

'Kindly,' said the inspector. 'Yes. Very. And Miss Puddephatt made sure Miss Adams got the brandy. Strong flavour, brandy. What else is in a Sidecar, I wonder? No matter. It would all work together to hide the flavour of a poison. Did anyone keep the glasses?'

'What?' said Skins and Dunn together.

'So we can examine them for poison.'

'Wasn't that your man's job on the night?' said Dunn.

'He didn't know she'd been poisoned.'

'Nor did we,' said Skins. 'You reckon we'd just grab the glass and put it in a box on the off chance you might need it a week later?'

Inspector Lavender narrowed his eyes. 'All right, then. Did your Miss Puddephatt know this Danny character? Might they have been colluding?'

'You're not seriously suggesting—' began Dunn.

'My job is to keep an open mind, sir,' said the inspector.

'You're an idiot,' said Dunn.

'I should watch your tone if I were you, sir.'

'And I would most definitely do my job with a damn sight more compassion and sensitivity if I were unlucky enough to be you, Inspector.'

'I understand you're upset, sir, so we shall say no more about it.'

Dunn made a *pfft* noise and walked off.

'Did she have any enemies in the band, Mr . . .'

'Maloney. No.'

'So your pal is' – once again he leafed through his notebook – 'Mr Dunn?'

'That's right.'

'And had she fallen out with anyone at the club?'

'She didn't have time. None of us have. We come in, we play, we go home.'

'I see. And this Danny character – what do you know about him?'

'As much as we know about any of them – nothing.'

'Thank you,' said the inspector. 'You've certainly corroborated Mr Chandler's account, if nothing else. If you'd be good enough to let my constable have your address, we'll be in touch if we need anything further.'

'The band will be here every Tuesday and Wednesday evening until the dance contest, and every Friday night for the foreseeable. We're easy to find.'

'Dance contest? When is that exactly?'

'Friday the twelfth. But they'll need two lessons a week from now until it happens just to come in second.'

'Out of how many, sir?'

'Two.'

Inspector Lavender smiled, closed his notebook, and walked off to talk to one of the uniformed policemen.

'You've got to take it easy, mate,' said Skins as he caught up with his friend at the bar. 'We need that bloke on our side.'

'We need a decent copper on our side,' said Dunn, grumpily. 'Old Sunderland wouldn't be that much of a . . . of a . . .'

'Of a what, mate?'

'He's just so . . . I mean, starting to accuse Puddle. He can see how upset we are.'

'He can now. I've got to admit even I didn't know you were taking it so hard.'

Dunn looked directly at his oldest friend for the first time in the conversation. 'I asked her out.'

'Blanche?'

'Yes.'

'Bloody hell, mate. You never said. Even when we were talking to Ellie. You should have said. I didn't even know you were—'

'What was I going to say?' said Dunn quietly. 'I mean, I didn't love her or anything. Well, not yet. Maybe I could have, though. Maybe she was "the one". I don't know. But I've not lost any more than anyone else has.'

Skins put a comforting hand on Dunn's shoulder. 'You're an idiot,' he said.

'So your wife keeps telling me,' said Dunn. 'At least I'm not as much of an idiot as that Lavender.'

'No, he's hardly the Met's finest.'

'If he suspects the band, why did he interview us together? Should have split us up. Anyone knows that.'

'He didn't suspect anyone till it occurred to him that it could be the cocktail.'

'But it could, couldn't it?' said Dunn.

'I suppose so. Got to admit I didn't even remember they had different drinks from us.'

'Didn't strike me till just then, either.'

'But who would do it? And why?'

'There's definitely something not quite right about Danny. He doesn't seem to fit in. All the others are so brash and cocky, but he twitches and fidgets and makes shy offers of cocktails to the girls . . . I mean, it takes all sorts and all that, but birds of a feather.'

'What's this, Barty Dunn's Tired Old Saw Show? A smile, a song, and a worn-out cliché?'

'My lack of original phrasing doesn't make it any less true, does it? How come a timid bloke like Danny fell in with the Alfies and the Charlies of this world?'

'None of them fit, mate,' said Skins. 'That's why they fit. Who else would have them? They're mates because they're all a bit . . . you know . . . odd.'

'Perhaps.'

'Still doesn't explain why, though. Why kill Blanche? What had she done? Turned him down, maybe?'

'It's not something you kill for, though, is it? If I did that, half the birds in north London would be buried in Mrs C's backyard.'

'Unless he's one of Lady H's madmen,' said Skins. 'Motiveless murder, just for the sake of it.'

'You never know. There's that thing about Vera being ill, after all. The Foot-Tappers' sax player. Danny made her a cocktail, too. What if he's like Jack the Ripper, only he's going after lady sax players instead of prossies. Or that bloke in the war . . . in France . . . killed all those women . . .'

'I know who you mean. The Bluebird of Somewhere. But wasn't he nicking their money?'

'Bluebeard,' said Dunn. 'But what if Danny's got something against the saxophone? Maybe he was traumatized by one as a child. Or lady musicians? What if a lady musician broke his heart and he's taking it out on all of them?'

'Traumatized by a saxophone?'

'You never know. Stranger things have happened. There was that lad we met when we did that concert at GHQ in '17 – he was afraid of soup spoons.'

'As Ellie would say, "I remain unconvinced." But we do need to talk to him.'

'The soup spoon lad? I'm not sure where we'd find him now. He was probably laid low by a ladle in the mess and all his fears were realized.'

Skins shook his head. 'You're an idiot. Let's go and find Danny.'

◆　◆　◆

'I've got an idea,' said Skins. 'Why don't we have a bit of a nose-round "on the way"? See if we can see any sign of this treasure vault. If anyone challenges us, we can just say we're lost.'

Dunn smiled and shook his head. 'So you reckon the two of us can just walk round a corner and solve a puzzle that's baffled everyone for a hundred and twenty years?'

Skins frowned. 'At the very least, we could get a better idea of what the place looks like.'

'Come on then, Adventurer Jim. You reckon they've got some safari jackets and pith helmets we could borrow?'

They set off in the direction of the smoking room, as indicated by the signs on the wall, but turned off down another corridor before they got there.

'What are we looking for, then?' said Dunn.

'I don't know, do I?' said Skins. 'There's not going to be a big sign up saying "Hidden Treasure This Way", is there?'

'Exactly. And so why—'

'Just shut up moaning and keep your eyes open. It could be anything. Look at all this old tat on the walls, for a start. And all them paintings on the other side. What are they telling us?'

'That rich blokes like to have their portraits painted?'

'Well, that's a given. But who are they?'

Dunn looked at the tiny brass plaques on a couple of the pictures.

'Club presidents,' he said.

'Didn't Sunderland say the Mayfair Murderer was club president?'

'Something like that. Sir Dionisius Something-or-other.'

Skins scanned along the wall, travelling backwards in time through the club's history.

'Here you go,' he said. 'Sir Dionisius Fitzwarren-Garvie. That's a big old cravat if I ever saw one. He doesn't look like a murderer, though.'

'I think it's the same as with hidden treasure – they don't wear signs.'

'What's he got in his hand?' said Skins.

Dunn looked closely. 'A key?' he suggested. 'A big gold key? They've all got it, look.'

On closer inspection, the other club presidents were, indeed, holding the same golden key.

'The key to the secret vault,' said Skins.

'No one's ever thought of that, I bet,' said Dunn. 'Come on, you 'nana, let's go and see Danny like we planned.'

They turned back.

Eventually, they reached the smoking room. Tastefully decorated with green silk wallpaper on the walls and a luxurious Axminster rug on the floor, the smoking room was where the older members of the club went to doze away the afternoon. With a fug of pipe and cigar smoke hanging above them, and portraits of long-dead club members looking down from the walls, the old men sat in overstuffed armchairs of dark brown leather in silent companionship, and snoozed through the long hours between lunch and dinner. Bookshelves lined the walls, and tables were piled high with newspapers and periodicals of all types, but only one member was reading – Dudley 'Danny' Daniels.

Skins and Dunn looked uncertainly at each other. They had played manor houses and public houses, jazz clubs, gentlemen's clubs, and working men's clubs. They were at home anywhere, but despite their cheerful confidence, there were always one or two places where they knew they didn't belong. And the smoking room of the Aristippus Club in Mayfair was just such a place. Somehow neither of them could summon the will to step across the threshold and into the hallowed sanctum. It was as though the hand of some invisible guardian were pushing them back, telling them that their sort wasn't welcome here. Oiks.

Danny must have seen them out of the corner of his eye. He put down his book and waved at them to come in. Still they hesitated. He smiled. He waved them in again and mouthed, 'It's all right – come on in.'

Almost on tiptoes, the two musicians crept into the room. A sleeping man near the door – bald but for two unruly tufts of white hair above his ears – snored suddenly, making one of his neighbours wake with a start. The newly awakened man regarded them suspiciously.

'Who are you?' he demanded croakily. 'You the chaps from the War Office come to measure the horses for their ball gowns?'

'Don't worry, Sir Edgar,' said Danny. 'They're guests of mine.'

'Just you make sure they don't get any axle grease on the boiled mutton,' said the man, and he settled back to sleep.

'Good afternoon, gentlemen,' said Danny as they approached. 'Were you looking for me?'

'Actually, yes,' said Skins. He hadn't given any thought as to how they were going to approach this interview. Were they going to casually chat? Would there be any profit in a direct approach?

Should they construct an elaborate ruse? Or just come straight out and tell him what they were up to?

Dunn came to the rescue. 'We arrived early for this evening's lesson and we thought it would be nice to get to know a few of you blokes a bit better. Seems a shame to come here three times a week and not know anybody. Especially when we're so involved in helping you with your dance contest.'

'How very decent of you,' said Danny. 'Why don't we retire to the bar – leave the chaps in here to their rest?'

'We've just come from there,' said Skins. 'It's a bit lively. The police are asking questions about the night Blanche died.'

'Ah, yes, of course. Terrible business. How are you coping?'

'Well enough,' said Dunn.

'One can only imagine. Come on, I know a place.'

He stood up and led them out. They followed him back to the portrait corridor and on to a closed door, the sign upon which proclaimed it to be the 'Theodorus Room'. Danny opened it and ushered them inside.

It was a smallish committee room, with a table set for six attendees and with four armchairs arranged around a low table beside the unlit fire on the other side of the room. As elsewhere in the club, a marble bust on a plinth in the corner surveyed the proceedings.

'This room's almost never used,' said Danny. 'I often come in here when I want a bit of peace and quiet. Make yourselves comfortable. I was thinking of ordering a pot of tea just before you arrived. Would you care to join me? I can get you something stronger if you prefer.'

'Tea would be nice,' said Skins. 'Ta very much.'

Danny pressed the electric bell push beside the fireplace and sat in one of the armchairs opposite the musicians.

'It's really rather splendid of you to come and try to mix with the hoi polloi, you know,' said Danny. 'We look on in wonderment as musicians array themselves on our stage for our entertainment. What's the word you jazz types use? You're "cool", that's it. Stylish, fashionable – everything we duffers aren't. We're quite in awe of you, we really are.'

'I never thought of it like that,' said Skins. 'I thought members of clubs like this were all public-school confidence and "yah boo" to the rest of us.'

'Not a bit of it, old bean. We know enough to know when we're outclassed. We can get a table at the best restaurants with nonchalant ease. A seat in parliament? It's ours by divine right, don'tcha know? But we know talent and skill when we see it and it makes us feel just a little uneasy and small. We're well aware that we're an anachronism in these modern times.'

'Are you?' said Skins. He gave Dunn a wink. 'We might not get on, then.'

'How so?' asked Danny, clearly slightly disappointed.

'I'm arachnophobic.'

'That's a fear of spiders, you chimp,' said Dunn, cottoning on immediately. 'He said he was an anachronism.'

'What's that, then?' said Skins.

'Buggered if I know. It's a fear of open spaces or something, isn't it?'

'I thought that was angoraphobia.'

'No, that's a fear of woolly jumpers. You're probably thinking of aggrophobia.'

'No, mate,' said Skins. 'I know that one, that's a fear of punch-ups.'

'Ankaraphobia?'

'Fear of Turkey.'

'Could be agriphobia?'

'No, that's a fear of farm animals. You're probably thinking of agreephobia, anyway.'

'That's a fear of concordance. Aguephobia?'

'Medieval diseases.'

'Agraphobia?'

Skins grinned. 'That, my old mate, is an unnatural fear of the Taj Mahal.'

Danny was chuckling merrily. 'You can see why we find you intimidating.'

'Just a little bit we've been working on for our comedy act,' said Skins.

'You do comedy as well?'

'We're thinking about it. We sometimes do a bit in our music shows, but we've not got enough for a decent act yet. It's always handy to have another string to the old bow, though. We did a couple of comedy turns in the army, didn't we? Usually went down all right.'

Dunn nodded. 'Although, to be honest, the average Tommy was so desperate for a laugh we could have done anything and they'd still have lapped it up.'

'True, true,' said Skins. 'You must have had a different experience in the officers' mess, though, eh? We played a few dances for the officers and they were much more staid affairs. At first, at least. Get a few brandies in 'em and all soldiers are the same in the end, eh?'

Danny didn't respond. He was still smiling, but the joy had left him and the smile no longer seemed quite so genuine.

There was a knock at the door and a club servant came in.

'You rang, sir?'

'Ah, yes, Cuthbert. Thank you. Pot of tea for three, please.'

'Very good, sir.'

The servant withdrew.

'You know all the servants' names as well?' said Skins. 'You're not at all what we expected.'

The genuine smile returned. 'Ah, no, not really. Well, yes. In a way. I do know all the servants' names, because by club tradition all the servants are called Cuthbert. I've no idea when it started, but we just sort of go along with it. As it happens, I know that chap's real name is William, but he'd be mortified if I were ever to address him thus.'

'Different world,' said Skins, shaking his head. 'Different world.'

'Isn't it just? But what of you two? How did you come to be the coolest jazz musicians in town?'

'Right place at the right time, mostly,' said Dunn. 'We were playing ragtime before the war – got a bit of a reputation – but we met some doughboys near the end of the war and they changed everything. The blokes from the Harlem Hellfighters introduced us to proper jazz. It was a revelation, you might say. They had some blinding players – musical geniuses, some of them – and they taught us the ropes. Then it was just a case of finding the right people to help us out.'

'How wonderful. But how do you . . . you know . . . how do you get well known enough to secure engagements?'

'No idea,' said Dunn. 'How did we do that?'

'It's the old thing, isn't it,' said Skins. 'It ain't what you know, it's who you know. Like Barty says, we had a bit of a reputation before the war. So when the new clubs started opening up, they were pleased to see some familiar faces, especially familiar faces playing the most fashionable new music.'

'It all sounds a good deal more glamorous than my line of work, I must say.'

'And what's that?' said Skins.

'Notionally I run an art gallery. But as you can see from my almost-permanent presence here at the club, it rather runs itself. I leave day-to-day matters to my assistant, and he calls me in when he needs to impress someone.'

'You have a reputation of your own, then?' said Dunn.

'A modest one. I specialize in the avant-garde, and I seem to have become one of London's foremost experts on Dadaism, for my sins.' He grinned bashfully.

'We met some of them once, Bart, remember?' said Skins.

'I'm not likely to forget. That definitely counts as one of the weirder dates we've played. Can't honestly say I understood what they were trying to do, but they seemed like a nice bunch.'

'Dada was really quite exciting,' said Danny. 'That idea of making sense of things by not making sense. I became quite the enthusiast.'

'Do you . . . what is it they do? Paint? Draw? Sculpt?' said Skins.

'I dabble, but I never quite had the talent. Or the imagination. But it's why I'm drawn to jazz, I think. Some of the things you do – rejecting the old rules, playing with form, all that sort of thing – they might be said to be a little Dadaist.'

'Perhaps,' said Dunn. 'People certainly complain that we make an unmusical racket. But most of them don't really understand music, if you ask me. We might not sound like their favourite music-hall song, but deep down we play by the same rules of harmony. We're just a bit more . . . inventive sometimes. Like your Dada lot still stuck to the rules of shape and colour.'

'Hmm,' said Danny. 'Perhaps. Are you familiar with Cubism, at all? That takes—'

They never found out any more about Cubism. There was a loud knock at the door and a Cuthbert entered smartly.

'I'm sorry to interrupt, sirs,' he said, 'but is one of you gentlemen Mr Ivor Maloney?'

'I am,' said Skins. 'What can I do for you?'

'There's a . . . there's a lady' – he could hardly bring himself to say the word – 'at the porter's desk demanding entry. She says she's the band's . . . manager.' Again, the man's horror at the very idea seemed to make the words almost too difficult to say.

'Ah, that'll be my wife,' said Skins. 'Eleanora Maloney.'

'So she claimed, sir,' said Cuthbert. 'But she's . . . well, she's American.'

'Yes, that's our Ellie. Could you show her in, please?'

'I'm afraid club rules do not permit it, sir.'

'I don't imagine she's best pleased to hear that,' said Skins with a grin.

'No, sir. She's making rather a scene. Would you . . . Could you . . . ?'

'I'll see to it, Cuthbert,' said Danny. 'Come on, chaps. Let's go and meet this wife of yours.'

◆ ◆ ◆

They found Ellie glowering in the entrance hall. She caught sight of Skins and Dunn and, having checked that no one else was looking, gave them a grin and a wink before rearranging her face into an angry scowl.

'Now then, Cuthbert old chap, what seems to be the problem?' said Danny as he approached the porter's desk.

'It's this . . . lady, Mr Daniels. She's making a scene.'

'I am doing no such thing,' said Ellie. 'I am merely trying to do my job.'

'There you are, then, Cuthbert,' said Danny. 'The lady's just trying to do her job. Surely there's no need for all this fuss.'

'But she claims that she's the band's manager, sir.'

'And you dispute this claim?'

'Beg pardon, sir?'

'Do you doubt that Mrs Maloney is the manager of the Dizzy Heights?'

'Well, sir, not if you and the . . . musicians say she is. But she's . . .'

'She's what, Cuthbert? American? I can see how that might flummox you.'

'No, sir, not American. She's . . . It's just that they're not allowed in the club. Strict rules.'

'Rule seventeen, paragraph two, I believe, states that women shall be admitted to club premises for social events approved by the committee, and "when their presence has been previously agreed by the committee, provided that they be vouched for by a full member of the club". I vouch for Mrs Maloney.'

'But her presence hasn't been agreed by the committee,' said the porter with a note of triumph.

'Has not the committee approved the presence of all members of the jazz band known professionally as the Dizzy Heights?' said Danny. 'I believe I read that in the committee minutes. In which case Mrs Maloney, as a vital member of the band's organization, is a welcome guest. I'll sign her in, shall I?'

The porter reluctantly pushed the visitors' book across the counter and handed Danny a pen.

'Thank you, Cuthbert,' he said once he had entered the relevant details and signed his name with an extravagant flourish. 'You're doing a wonderful job.'

The porter scowled and took back his pen.

'Do come in, Mrs Maloney,' said Danny. 'I'm sure you'd like to check that the band's equipment has been set up properly for this evening's lesson.'

Ellie took his arm as he set off in the direction of the ballroom, with Skins and Dunn trailing behind.

Chapter Eight

Setting up in the ballroom at the Aristippus Club had become routine. It was still far too early for the rest of the band to have arrived, but Skins and Dunn had two willing helpers in Danny and Ellie and were able to get everything in place without even the slightest amount of fuss.

While 'the best rhythm section in London' were fastidiously tweaking their instruments, Ellie sat down with Danny.

'It's quite a place, this,' she said. 'Have you been a member long?'

'Not too long, no. Nominated by an old pal of my father's as part of some sort of recruitment drive. Trying to get some new blood in the place.'

'It must be lovely to have somewhere to go where you know you'll find some friendly faces. I have plenty of buddies but I haven't really had that feeling of "belonging" since I was a nurse in the war. I kinda miss it.'

'Fanny or Very Adorable Darling?'

'I was a Fanny – shut up, Ivor – they got me before I'd heard of the Voluntary Aid Detachment. Where did you serve?'

'I'm afraid I don't like to talk about the war. Prefer to put it all behind me.'

'I can understand that,' said Ellie. 'There's a lot more to be gained from looking forward than looking back. Although . . . well, I don't suppose you know anything about' – she looked around, as though checking that they couldn't be overheard – 'the Treasure of the Mayfair Murderer?'

Danny laughed. 'You've heard about that, too, eh? Before we got embroiled in this dance contest brouhaha it was all the Alphabet Gang could talk about some days. Secret vaults, club regalia. I swear they were all gaga.'

'You don't believe in it, then?'

'Not a word,' he said. 'It's exactly the sort of old nonsense some joker at a club like this would have made up a hundred years ago for a lark.' He laughed again. 'Secret treasure.' He shook his head.

'Ah, well,' said Ellie. 'That's my daydreams of wealth and glory shot down. How about the future, then? Are you looking forward to your dance contest?'

Danny smiled ruefully. 'Hardly. I honestly don't understand why we're putting ourselves through it. Someone at the Wags Club said something to one of our chaps about our dancing prowess one night. There followed a few minutes of ragging and manly chest-thumping, culminating in the throwing down of the gauntlet and the acceptance of this ludicrous challenge. None of us can dance. I don't think any of their lot can either, though, to be honest. Still, honour must be satisfied and all that. At least it didn't come to blows.'

It was Ellie's turn to laugh. 'When exactly is it? Ivor did say, but I can never remember.'

'A week on Friday at our regular Friday dance. The twelfth of June.'

'Just four more lessons to go after this one, then.'

'Don't remind me. It's a good thing we managed to secure the services of your husband and his pals for the extra lessons or it would just have been two. We're going to look like such fools.'

'There are worse things than looking like fools.'

'Many, many worse things. But there's something about dancing. I don't know. It's all a bit . . . personal. Do you know what I mean? Like singing in public.'

Ellie laughed again. 'I'm sure you'll all have a wonderful time.'

'Who'll have a wonderful time doing what?' Puddle had arrived with Benny. 'Hello, Ellie darling.'

'They'll have a wonderful time at their dance contest.'

'We'll all have a wonderful time, don't you worry.'

Danny stood. 'I'd better leave you to your preparations. I also feel the need for a good glug of scotch to calm the old nerves before this evening's ordeal. I'll see you all soon.'

'OK,' said Ellie. 'And thank you for looking after me.'

He waved over his shoulder as he left the room.

'Looking after you?' said Puddle.

'There was a bit of a kerfuffle with the doorman. He didn't want to let me in.'

'But you're our manager,' said Benny with a wink.

The band had been briefed about Ellie pretending to be their manager for the duration of the investigation.

'Such things count for little in the eyes of a Cuthbert,' said Ellie.

They looked blankly at her.

'The servants here are all called Cuthbert,' she said with a grin. 'I'd have thought you'd all know that by now. Score one for the Yank.'

'We knew,' said Skins.

'Oh,' said Ellie, somewhat deflated.

'But we only learned it this afternoon. Danny told us.'

'But why are they all called Cuthbert?' said Puddle.

'Tradition,' said Dunn. 'Got to respect the traditions.'

'They're all completely barmy if you ask me,' said Puddle. 'But never mind that. How's the snooping coming along?'

Ellie shrugged. 'I've only really spoken to Danny so far, and he was no more forthcoming than when I spoke to him at the dance the other week. There's definitely something odd about him, though. The boys might have had more luck with the others.'

'No,' said Skins. 'He's the only one we've spoken to as well. Nice bloke. Runs an art gallery.'

'There was something about the way . . . Oh, never mind, I'll tell you later.'

Charlie and Millie had come into the ballroom, closely followed by a few Alphabets and the remaining Dizzies. Discussion of Danny's oddness would have to wait.

◆　◆　◆

The lesson began with something similar to the usual uncoordinated chaos, but things were slowly improving. They were still some way from perfecting the old steps, but they were getting closer, and the new steps Millie was trying to teach them were coming more easily. For three of them, at least. Alfie and Ernie were still struggling.

Ellie watched from her seat on the stage with an uncomfortable mix of amusement, bafflement and pity. She didn't count herself one of Nature's most gifted dancers, but she was confident enough on a dance floor. More than that, she enjoyed it. It brought her genuine pleasure, and the only thing about Skins that had ever truly disappointed her was that he had absolutely no interest in dancing. He would get up and join in when pressed, but it was clear that he wasn't really enjoying himself so she never made him stay away from his seat for too long.

She decided to try to help one of the strugglers. She wondered if perhaps they might be able to get closer to something a little more like dancing if they had a partner. They were watching Millie, they were watching each other, they were watching their own stumbling feet. But it wasn't helping. Perhaps if they had someone to dance with, just one person to concentrate on, it might be less confusing. It couldn't hurt.

But which one should she choose? Ernie was most in need of someone's help – but was he, in fact, beyond help? He had no sense of timing, no feel for the music, no memory for the steps, and no real control over his limbs. It might be best for the gang if they tried to conceal him at the back during the contest and hope nobody noticed him. If he didn't actually fall over or injure someone, they might get away with it.

Alfie was a shambling mess, but at least his formless flailings were in time with the music. There was something to work with there. Ellie got up from her chair and jumped nimbly on to the floor. When Millie next called a halt, she made her way over to the dance students. She approached Millie and drew her to one side.

'Hi, honey,' she said quietly. 'We met at the dance a couple of weeks ago – the night you gashed your arm. How is it?'

Millie held up her arm, which was healing nicely. There was going to be a scar but, as Blanche had promised, it looked as though it would be a subtle one.

'It's not at all bad, thank you,' she said, just as quietly. 'I took the stitches out a couple of days ago and it all seems to be fine. But what can I do for you? Do please tell me you're a dance teacher and you're the relief column come to rescue me.'

Ellie laughed. 'Not quite. But I was wondering if I might be able to help a little anyway. I was wondering if one of them might benefit from having a partner. I was thinking—'

'Alfie,' interrupted Millie. 'Oh, yes please.' She lowered her voice still further. 'He's not . . . well, he's not terribly bright, is he?

My aunt had a Jack Russell who could do all sorts of tricks, but I'm not sure I could train poor Alfie to sit on command. If you could give him something to focus on, stop his mind wandering, perhaps he might start to get it.'

'That's exactly what I was thinking. Will the others mind?'

Millie sighed. 'They'll rag him silly, of course, but as long as you don't mind, I think it'll help. And as long as your husband doesn't mind, of course – dancing with another man and all that. He's the little drummer, yes?'

'I think he knows he's got nothing to worry about.'

'Then have at it, as they say. Do you know the dance?'

'Well enough. Better than Alfie does.'

They broke from their huddle.

'Alfie,' said Millie in her best colour-sergeant voice. 'We have a plan to help you out. Mrs Maloney has kindly agreed to play the role of your dance partner. I don't envy the poor woman, but she seems to think you're worth the effort.'

The Alphabets laughed.

'Jolly kind of you, Mrs M,' said Alfie.

'Please, call me Ellie.'

'Right you are, Elsie.'

The gang laughed again.

He looked baffled. 'What? What did I say?'

'Don't worry about those guys,' said Ellie, kindly. 'Just concentrate on me. You know these steps – you just have to stop thinking about them and start doing them.'

'It's always thinking that's the problem for me, old thing,' said Alfie. 'Never was much good at that. But we'll get there. I place myself in your capable hands.'

To everyone's astonishment, it worked. Sort of. Without the distraction of his fellow dance pupils, without worrying about what Millie might be thinking, and with only the beguilingly confident American woman to concentrate on, Alfie found himself remembering most of the steps. Or, rather, not so much remembering them as simply knowing what they were. He got a tiny bit lost in the middle eight, but Ellie steered him through it and they reached the end without major incident. This being only the second time since they'd started playing for the lessons that the Dizzies had made it all the way to the end of a number without being stopped, his achievement earned him a round of applause from the band.

'I say,' said Alfie, now slightly out of breath. 'You're a bally miracle-worker. Can we have you with us on the night?' He looked over at Millie. 'Can we, Miss Mitchell? I mean, it might make all the difference.'

'It's not up to me, darling,' said Millie. 'What are the rules of your silly contest, Bobby – Charlie, sorry.'

'Alphabet Gang versus five of the Wags. No partners. Sorry, old bean. They wanted to avoid the possibility of ringers.'

'She ain't a ringer,' said Alfie. 'She's my . . . She can be my nurse. Dodgy knee after the war and all that. Need to have her on hand in case it fails me. You don't mind pretendin' to be a nurse, do you, Mrs M?'

'I pretended to be one in France for three years. I'm pretty sure I still remember how.'

'See? She's one of us. D'you think we could get away with it?'

'We could put her in bags and a waistcoat and she could take my place,' said Ernie. 'I'm the one who's going to be letting the side down. She could be Eli. No one there has met me so they don't know who to look for. They'd never know.'

'I thought you were at school with Masher Watson?' said Bertie. 'He'd know at once she wasn't you.'

Ernie sighed dejectedly. 'I'd forgotten about him. Always was an absolute pill, that boy.'

'There'll be an audience, though, won't there?' said Ellie.

'It's the highlight of the Friday dance,' said Charlie. 'The Wags insisted it be in public to maximize our humiliation.'

'Then I shall be on the sidelines, dancing along. Just focus on me and you'll be fine.'

'That'll have to do,' said Alfie. 'Needs must when you're nodding and winking at a blind horse and all that.'

'That's that settled, then,' said Millie. 'Time for a break, I think. I could do with a drink. Fifteen minutes, everyone.'

The musicians downed their instruments and the gang formed up for a full-frontal assault on the beer table. Ellie pulled Alfie to one side.

'You really don't have anything to worry about, you know,' she said. 'You've got it.'

'You're very kind to say so,' he said. 'Always been a bit of a duffer, you know. Since I was a child. Ma and Pa despaired. Couldn't wait to send me away to school.'

'I'm sure you were never as bad as you think. You survived the war, after all. You were on the front line?'

'First Lieutenant, First Battalion, Essex Regiment. Gallipoli, Egypt, then France. Wasn't so bad as all that, really. Surrounded by good chaps. Camaraderie and all that.'

'I guess,' said Ellie. 'But something like three out of every twenty junior officers didn't make it. More than that, some say. But you did.'

'Well, when you put it like that . . .'

'If you can survive four years of war, you can survive four minutes of dancing.'

'Dash it all, m'dear, you're right. I bally well can. Were you like this in your what-do-you-call-it . . . aid station? You'd have built the boys right back up. I bet you broke a few hearts, what?'

'I couldn't say. I'd already given my own heart to another.'

'Yonder drummer chap, eh? Lucky fellow. You met during the festivities?'

'No, we first met years before the war, in Weston-super-Mare.'

Alfie laughed. 'Get away. Really? Had an aunt who lived near Weston-super-Mare. Ghastly place. Ghastly aunt. What the blue blazes were you doing there?'

'Travelling,' said Ellie. 'With my aunt.'

'Ghastly or otherwise?'

'Formidable. But quite lovely underneath it all.'

'You must have been terribly young.'

'I was sixteen. But the heart wants what the heart wants. Have you ever been in love, Mr . . . ?'

'Do please call me Alfie. No, never been lucky enough to find a gel who'll have me.'

'There's someone out there for you, I'm sure of it. But look, I'm sorry – I'm keeping you away from the beer. You'd better get back to it before your pals drink it all.'

She patted his arm and returned to the band.

'Is it him?' said Puddle, eagerly.

Ellie smiled. 'The deserter? I doubt it. He's either a fantastic actor or he's the sweetest guy ever to draw breath – my own dear husband excepted, of course. And Barty. But if he's a master criminal, I'll eat Ivor's bass drum.'

❖   ❖   ❖

The band packed up quickly after the lesson, and one or two expressed a desire for a chance to unwind at a local pub before retiring for an early night.

'Coach and Horses on Avery Row?' suggested Skins.

There were murmurs of agreement, though Puddle's pal reluctantly declined.

'I'd really love to,' he said, 'but I've got another engagement. Another night, definitely. And thanks for letting me sit in, by the way – you're a joy to play with.'

He left clutching his two instrument cases and the others finished their tidying up. To speed things along, they even pitched in and helped Skins carry his drums and traps to the storeroom – something they almost never did.

'Just think how quickly we could get everything done if you all helped like this every time,' said Skins as they piled up the last case.

'But then what would we moan about?' said Elk. 'Half the fun of setting up and tearing down is complaining about how long it takes the drummer to put all his mysterious gubbins together.'

Skins harrumphed.

The pub was a few minutes' walk away. It was busy for a Tuesday night, but they managed to find a spot where the seven members of the band and their pretend manager could sit or stand together.

'Let the ladies sit down, boys,' said Benny.

'Don't worry about us, darling,' said Puddle. 'We've got legs and we know how to use them.'

'Honestly, Benny dear, it's all right,' agreed Ellie. 'I rather like standing – makes me feel more like I'm part of the goings-on.'

'As you wish,' he said.

The drinks arrived and the toast, as had been customary over the past few days, was 'Blanche'.

'Gone too soon,' said Puddle.

'Great girl, great sax player,' said Elk.

'What are the police up to?' asked Eustace. 'Have they spoken to any of you? I've not seen a soul.'

'The investigating officer goes by the name of Inspector Lavender,' said Skins.

'We met him this afternoon,' said Dunn. 'Man's an idiot. He's decided it was Puddle and Danny working together.'

'What?' said Puddle loudly.

'Don't worry about it,' said Skins. 'He'll get nowhere with it. He's got no evidence, just a working whatsaname.'

'Hypothesis,' said Ellie.

'That's the fella. He got all worked up by the idea of the poison being in the cocktails and decided Danny was the killer, then thought you must have been in on it because you chose the gin.'

'But I always choose the gin. I didn't—'

'Of course you didn't,' said Dunn. 'He's an idiot.'

'What about Danny, though?' said Mickey. 'Is he an idiot?'

'Not sure about him,' said Skins. 'We had a chat with him. You did, an' all, didn't you, love?'

'I did,' said Ellie. 'He's quiet and thoughtful. He seems . . . gentle. The way he talked about their rivalry with the other club not coming to blows – like he disapproved of violence.'

'Could he be the deserter, then?' said Benny. 'Someone who didn't want to fight wouldn't want to hang around on the front line.'

'Perhaps,' said Ellie. 'He seems bright enough to steal the diamonds, too.'

'Wait a minute,' said Elk. 'Deserter? Diamonds?'

'Ah, sorry,' said Benny. 'Should I not have said anything?'

'No, it's all right, mate,' said Skins. 'We should probably have told everyone anyway.'

'Told us what?' said Mickey.

So for the next ten minutes, Skins, Ellie, and Dunn told the rest of the band about Superintendent Sunderland, Arthur Grant the deserter, twenty-five thousand pounds' worth of rough diamonds, and the rumoured resting place of the Treasure of the Mayfair Murderer.

'Twenty-five thou? Bleedin' 'ell,' said Mickey. 'You could live the life of Riley on that.'

'You could take it easy, join a gentlemen's club, horse around with your pals . . .' said Ellie.

'Murder lady sax players,' said Eustace.

They all looked at him.

'Oh, come on,' he said. 'Vera from the Finchley Foot-Tappers fell ill after working there. Now Blanche is dead. He clearly tried it out on Vera, realized he'd got the dose wrong, and had another go when Blanche and Puddle showed up. Didn't matter which one took the poison as long as it was a girl who played the saxophone. Probably even liked the randomness of it. A bit of godlike power, like tossing a coin to see which one died.'

'So you're backing Danny as the deserter and the murderer, then?' said Benny.

'Why not? Nobody said cowards can't be killers.'

'That's all well and good, like,' said Mickey. 'But what are we gonna do about it? And do we get a share of the diamonds?'

'The best thing we can do,' said Ellie, 'is keep our eyes and ears open. If you can go along with the fiction of me being your manager for a little longer, I can come and go at the club whenever you're there. I was going to carry on speaking to the Alphabet Gang one by one – seeing what I can find out – and if I ever get the chance I'm going to have a snoop round the rest of the club. I'll bet they have all sorts of nooks and crannies where folks can hide things.'

'We can chat, too,' said Elk. 'Everyone loves a musician. We might be riff-raff the rest of the time, but once we pick up an instrument we're royalty. We have a certain cachet.'

'Do we?' said Mickey. 'Is there an ointment for it?'

Elk looked momentarily doubtful. 'I think that's the right word. My wife said it the other day. Perhaps. Don't matter. Point is, we can all pal up with these blokes and they'll lap up the attention. We can root the bugger out.'

'Best play it cagey, though,' said Skins. 'If we all suddenly go in there, acting like we're all best mates and asking loads of questions, we're going to spook him. Probably be best if you leave it to us three.'

'Why you three?' said Eustace. 'Why not some other three?'

'No reason other than that we're the ones Sunderland asked to do it. It's not like there's any glory or reward we're cheating you out of.'

'He's right,' said Ellie. 'We all want to catch Blanche's killer and it doesn't much matter how we get it done. I'll be honest, I think the police will handle that just fine – but if we can help, then so much the better. But the deserter is only really of interest to Superintendent Sunderland, and if you can all just be aware of what we're trying to do and not give anything away, that would be . . . what is it you guys say? Spiffing?'

'I've never said "spiffing" in me life,' said Mickey. 'But I'll play along. Always happy to settle with a deserter. I hate them cowards.'

'Very well,' Eustace conceded. 'And what do you plan to do next?'

'I'll come along to the dance lesson tomorrow,' said Ellie, 'and see who I can talk to.'

◆ ◆ ◆

It was once again Ellie who saw an opportunity to talk to one of the Alphabet Gang the next evening. Having helped Alfie on Tuesday it was a natural move to offer the same support to Ernie. As before, she approached Millie shortly before the break and suggested she dance with Ernie. Millie agreed and the rest of the Alphabets ragged their dancing duffer.

'Couldn't we just erect some sort of screen for Alfie and Ernie to dance behind?' said Bertie. 'Like a windbreak on the beach, or a changing screen in a lady's boudoir.'

'And have them come out in different outfits,' said Charlie. 'I like it. Turn it into a comedy act. Distract the Wags from our collective ineptitude.'

'Oh, top-hole idea,' said Bertie. 'Have them come out dressed as gels – there's some choice outfits in the Ents Committee costume trunk.'

'Now look here,' said Alfie. 'More than happy to be the class duffer – been that all my life – but I draw the line at actually asking chaps to laugh at me.'

'That's the point, though, isn't it?' said Bertie. 'You come out dressed to make them laugh and you're in control of it. You're the one setting the pace, d'you see? They're not laughing because you're a duffer, they're laughing because you chose to do something funny. Completely different kettle of kippers.'

'Would you mind awfully if we concentrated on the dance steps for now and sorted out the finer details of the presentation some other time?' Millie was once again becoming impatient.

'Right you are, Miss M,' said Alfie. 'Lips buttoned. Dance on.'

Ellie joined Ernie, but quickly found that he was a hopeless case – an actual lost cause.

'I'm so sorry, m'dear,' he mumbled, as the number ended and Millie announced the break. 'I just can't seem to get the hang of it at all.'

Ellie squeezed his arm. 'We'll think of something.'

'Beginning to think Bertie's idea might not be so hare-brained after all,' he said. 'If we just come out from behind a screen dressed as fillies . . . or a . . . Actually, that's not a bad idea. That might work.'

'What might work?'

'Dressed as a filly. The both of us.' He turned towards the table by the wall, where everyone else was helping themselves to beer. 'I say, you chaps, know anywhere we can get a pantomime horse costume?'

The Alphabets looked blank.

'There's a couple of places in the West End would sort you out,' called Skins from the stage. 'Why?'

'Don't you see?' said Ernie. 'It's perfect.'

'What's perfect about it?' asked Bertie.

'D'you think it's easy or difficult to dance in a pantomime horse costume?'

'Rather tricky, I should imagine.'

'So if Alfie and I come out dressed as a horse, no one's expectations are going to be especially high. With me at the back just sort of shuffling about and trying to keep up, Alfie can Charleston at the front and the place will go bonkers. A horse doing the Charleston. It doesn't matter if we muff it up – we'll get points from the judges for the sheer hilarity of it. It's our way to win.'

There were murmurs of approval from the Alphabets, who raised their beer glasses in tribute to the best idea of the evening.

'That's certainly a . . . novel approach,' said Ellie as everyone else returned to their conversations.

Alfie came over with a glass of beer for Ernie.

'That's very much my game, d'you see?' said Ernie once Alfie had returned to the throng. 'Novel solutions.'

'How's that?'

'I'm an engineer. I design all sorts of weird and wonderful machines.'

'How fascinating,' said Ellie. 'Anything I might have heard of?'

Ernie laughed. 'Shouldn't think so. Industrial things mostly. We're building machines at the moment to make parts for other machines. If we could work out a way of having them operate themselves, we could have the machines make the machines, and free the factory workers from their chains.'

'What would they do then?'

'The workers? There, as they say, is the rub. What would they do, indeed? Still, it's a long way off, so no need to worry yet.'

'Do you enjoy it?'

'I suppose I do, really. Not got anything to compare it with, though, to be honest. Might be happier doing something else, but I've never done anything else. Straight from school to university to the offices of Cashmore Engineering Limited. Family firm, d'you see? Groomed for succession and all that.'

'Not even the army?'

'No. Wanted to, but Pater forbad it. We were making parts for the machines in the munitions factories and he was able to persuade the local military service tribunal that I was doing essential war work in the design office. I suppose I was in a way, but I always regretted not properly doing my bit.'

'But you *were* doing your bit.'

'Difficult to persuade myself of that at the time,' he said. 'And even harder to persuade people on the street. Had to make sure I never went out without my little brass "On War Service" badge pinned prominently on my lapel, or there'd be hell to pay.'

'I'll bet,' she said. 'No one likes a coward.'

'That they don't. And they were never slow to accuse an able-bodied young man of just that if they saw him out of uniform. Can't blame them, I suppose. Families losing sons, fathers, brothers, uncles left and right, and there's old muggins swanning about with nothing more than ink-stained fingers to attest to his efforts.'

'You were well out of it,' Ellie said.

'I know that now. I say, I'm sorry, was I being horribly crass? Did you lose someone?'

'No, no, don't worry, but I saw what war could do. I was in France. I was a nurse.'

'Good lord,' he said with some admiration. 'Well, I never. I thought nurses were all harridans. All the ones I've ever met have been. Spent some time in the hospital in '19. Spanish flu.'

'They sent all the pretty young ones to the Front,' she said with a smile. 'We were good for morale.'

Ernie laughed. 'I bet you were.' There was purposeful movement around the beer table. 'Hello. Looks like we're under starter's orders again. These breaks are getting shorter and shorter.'

'We'd better get back to it, then.'

'No need for you to put yourself through it,' he said. 'I'm rather taken with this pantomime horse idea – I think it might save me from having to get all this right. If you'd rather sit with your husband and his pals I'll quite understand.'

'I'll be honest with you, Ernie,' she said, 'I rather enjoy dancing. I'll join you if I may.'

Chapter Nine

Dunn spent most of Thursday doing odd jobs for Mrs Cordell. He changed a light bulb in the parlour, fixed a broken cupboard door in the kitchen, and replaced a washer in the cistern on the outside toilet. He was taking a break in the kitchen and drinking yet another cup of tea, while Mrs Cordell fussed about with the old biscuit tin that served as a first aid box.

'You've cut your hand, love,' she said. 'I'm so sorry. I should never have had you doing all those little jobs. I could have got a man in.'

'Don't worry about it, Mrs C,' he said. 'It's only a little scratch and I'm more than happy to help. You know that.'

'You're very kind. But you need those hands. A musician can't earn his livin' with damaged hands.'

'It's all right, Mrs C. Really.' He held up his right hand and waggled his fingers. 'See? It's my plucking hand. I only need the fingers to work.'

'Well, we'll still get some iodine on it and a nice sticking plaster. Don't want it getting infected – cuts on the hand like that can turn nasty.'

Dunn gave himself over to Mrs Cordell's motherly ministrations with a smile. 'Thank you, Mrs C.'

'Are you in for your tea this evening?' she said as she attached the plaster. 'Oh, no, it's Thursday, isn't it? You'll be off to see your pals in Bloomsbury, won't you.'

'I will. Ellie insists.'

'She's a nice girl, that Mrs Maloney. I never knew no Americans before, but if they're all like her it must be a lovely country.'

'I think they've got their fair share of rotters just like us, but Ellie is a wonderful woman.'

'You've got a bit of a soft spot for her, ain't you?'

'Of course. But not how you mean. She's not the one for me, but I've spent my whole life looking for someone who makes me feel how she makes Skins feel.'

Mrs Cordell touched his cheek. 'You'll find someone, my love. I know you will.'

He smiled. 'They've got a lot to live up to.'

'In the meantime, though, I need you to take a look at the mangle. It don't turn like it used to.'

'We none of us do,' he said, standing up. 'But it probably just needs a bit of a tweak and a touch of grease.'

'Don't we all,' she said with a wink.

Dunn laughed and picked up his toolbox.

◆ ◆ ◆

When Mrs Dalrymple opened the door for Dunn, the Maloney children were engaged in a noisy and energetic game whose principal objective seemed to be to hurtle around the house as fast as they could run while caroming off as many items of furniture as possible.

'You'll have to excuse the bairns,' she said. 'In my day, weans were to be seen and not heard, but times have changed, I suppose.'

'In my day, kids were shoved out on the street after breakfast and not seen again till bedtime. I like this modern way. It's nice to have a big house to run around in.'

She smiled and let him through to the drawing room, where Ellie was playing the piano while Skins busied himself with the children's building blocks. Mrs Dalrymple left just as Catherine and Edward exploded into the room.

Dunn watched for a few minutes in fascination as tiny children thudded into chairs, an occasional table, and the bookcase. A china figurine – a ballerina – tumbled from the table to the floor, but landed on the soft rug, undamaged. With Catherine taking the lead, they headed for the door.

Edward had reached that magical point in childhood where he was somehow moving faster than his legs could run, and he sprawled head first across the floor and into the impressively complex building-block construction his father had been working on. Bricks flew everywhere, but with no more than an 'Oof!' and a 'Sorry, Daddy', he was up and gone, following his little sister out of the room and up the stairs.

Ellie hadn't missed a beat.

'Is there a scoring system?' said Dunn.

'As far as I can make out, some credit seems to be given for knocking things over without breaking them,' said Skins. 'But I don't think there's a formal points system yet.'

'They seem to be having a lot of fun.'

Ellie came to the end of her piece. 'Did they break that stupid dancing girl?'

'Not yet,' said Skins with a grin.

'We're going to have to put it somewhere else. It keeps falling on the damn rug.'

'You want them to break it?' said Dunn.

'Wouldn't you?' she said. 'It's hideous.'

'You could just chuck it out,' he suggested.

'It was a gift from my aunt,' she said. 'Not the aunt I like – another aunt. I've never liked it – or her – but somehow I can't just throw it away. But if it were to break accidentally . . .'

'I'm sure I could bump into the table if you want something to happen to it.'

'Clumsy guest . . .' she mused. 'That might work, but I think she'll still be annoyed. She adores the children, though – if they shattered it into a million tiny pieces she'd just smile indulgently and tell me it's just one of those things.'

'And then buy us a new one,' said Skins.

'We'll have mastered the technique of accidentally breaking it by then. She'd give up eventually.'

Edward reappeared at the door. He had a serious expression and was clearly concentrating hard on remembering something.

'Nanny says,' he began. 'Nanny says . . . something about . . . Oh, I know. Does Mr Dunn want to read a story? Who's Mr Dunn?'

'That's Barty,' said Ellie.

'But Barty's name is Barty.'

'It is, but his other name is Dunn, just like your other name is Maloney.'

'So am I Mr Maloney?'

'Not yet. You're Master Maloney for now. But one day.'

'And will Mr Maloney read a story?' said Edward.

'Mr Dunn, dear.'

'Yes, that's it. Will Mr Dunn read a story?'

'I don't know. Why don't you ask him?'

'Mr Dunn?' said Edward earnestly.

'Yes, Master Maloney?' said Dunn.

'Would you like to read me and Stinky Catherine a story?'

'I'm pretty certain Nanny didn't ask you to say that, dear,' said Ellie.

'She would of have if her nose worked properly.'

'I'd love to,' said Dunn. 'Do you remember where we got to last time?'

'The evil Teddy Bear King had locked Bunny Rabbit and Rag Doll in the tower and the children were coming to the rescue,' said Edward proudly.

'Then we'd better see how they get on,' said Dunn. 'I'll be up in a minute.'

Ellie took Edward's hand and led him back upstairs.

'I always thought that teddy was a bit shifty, you know,' said Skins. 'Scotch while you wait for them to have their bath?'

Having forced a New World menu on her reluctant cook the last time Barty came round, Ellie had relented and allowed Mrs Ponton to cook something of her own choosing. She had opted for 'a nice roast leg of lamb', which Skins – who had discovered a love of wine as the years wore on and his budget had increasingly allowed it – had paired with a red wine from the northern Rhône.

'It's an impertinent little vintage,' he said as he poured Dunn a glass, 'and I think you'll enjoy the way its youthful fruitiness complements the robust flavours of a well-roasted leg of mutton.'

'Lamb, dear,' said Ellie. 'Don't let Mrs Ponton hear you calling it mutton.'

'And don't let me hear you talking such a load of old tosh again, either,' said Dunn. 'Coming the wine expert like that. I've seen you drinking plonk out of a tin cup in that village in France. It was one step up from vinegar and you were smacking your lips like it was the best thing you'd ever tasted.'

'I had to do something nice to keep the farmer sweet – if he'd seen the way you were looking at his daughter he'd have shot the pair of us.'

'That's as may be, son, but if I hear "impertinent little vintage" or "youthful fruitiness" again, we can't be friends.'

'Fair do's. Tastes lovely, though, doesn't it.'

'It does. And it goes nicely with the mutton.'

Ellie tutted. 'It's not Alfie or Ernie.'

The two musicians looked at each other and frowned.

'Either that's a sharp change of direction or you've taken to naming Skins's wine bottles. Or the sheep,' said Dunn.

'It's lamb, and it was a change of direction. I thought I might head off the wartime reminiscences before they got going if I talked about the club.'

'Ah, Tipsy Harry's,' said Skins. 'Twilight rest home for the posh and bewildered. So it's not Alfie or Ernie, then.'

'It is not,' said Ellie.

'What did you learn from your little tête-à-têtes with the brain trust, then?' asked Dunn.

'I learned that Alfie is charming and sensitive, and that Ernie is an engineer.'

'And that rules them out?'

'Not in itself,' said Ellie. 'But neither of them is your man. Alfie served in – hang on, it'll come to me – Gallipoli, Egypt, and France with the . . . Essex Regiment. He was there the whole time. No desertion.'

'So he says,' said Skins. 'I could claim I was on the beach at Margate all last week – doesn't make it so.'

'True. But it gives us something to tell Superintendent Sunderland. Something he can ask the War Office about. He's given us a story we can check. And he's adorable. Dumb as a barrel of beets, but so sweet with it.'

'Not sure being adorable is a defence allowed in law,' said Dunn, 'but I agree that he seems too easy-going to be nasty, and too dim to get away with nicking a bag of diamonds. And certainly no puzzle-solver. He'd never work out how to find the Lost Treasure of 1805.'

'He doesn't come across as a coward, either. I got the feeling he quite liked the army. He didn't seem to have noticed the horror and the carnage – he just remembers being surrounded by pals. I think a deserter might have a bit more to say about the horrors of war.'

'Too stupid to know how awful it was, you reckon?' said Skins.

'Maybe. Unless he's a terrific actor, like I said the other day. But he'd have to be really terrific, like why-isn't-this-guy-on-the-stage terrific.'

'And Ernie?' said Dunn. 'What rules him out?'

'He's an engineer,' she said. 'His father wangled some sort of "war work" exemption for him.'

'So he says,' said Skins.

'Sure,' said Ellie with a tiny hint of exasperation. 'But like I said, it's something Sunderland can check. It shouldn't be hard for him to track down records for Cashmore Engineering Limited with all his resources. He's got the War Office behind him, after all.'

'What's he like?' asked Dunn. 'As a bloke.'

'Nice enough. Funny how your impression of someone changes when you find out what they do for a living. I thought he was just another rich nincompoop, but then he told me he's an engineer and suddenly I saw him in a different light. He doesn't like cowards.'

'He mentioned cowards?'

'Or maybe I did. Either way, he didn't express any sympathy for them. And he was at pains to tell me all about his little brass badge.'

'I remember those,' said Skins. 'Like a regimental badge, with a crown on top and everything. They said something like "On War Service" round the outside. Do you remember we saw that bloke in

Lambeth that time, Bart? There was a bunch of old dears clustered round him, giving him what for.'

'Blimey, yes,' said Dunn. '"My Johnny's up the Front and you're swannin' about buyin' flowers for your fancy piece . . ." One of them was bashing him with her umbrella and he was scrabbling in his pocket trying to get his little badge out. "I'm on war work, you mad old bat," he kept saying.'

'That was it,' said Skins. 'It could get quite nasty once conscription started. If you wasn't in uniform everyone wanted to know why.'

'An easy lie to get caught in, though,' said Ellie.

'Assuming he really is Ernie Cashmore,' said Dunn.

'Edwin,' said Skins. 'But he's right. The real Edwin Cashmore might have been on war work, but we've only got this bloke's word for it that that's who he really is.'

'Agreed,' said Ellie. 'But it's a start.'

'So who's left?' said Dunn.

'Well, that's A and E,' she said, 'so I guess we've got B, C, and D to go.'

'We've already spoken to Danny,' said Skins. 'Remember?'

'You're right, sorry. Another nice guy.'

'They're all going to be "nice guys" around you, love.'

'He's right,' said Dunn. 'There's not many women in their world, are there? Then along comes a gorgeous American bird – they're all going to turn on the charm, aren't they?'

'You make me sound like a turkey.'

'You can be a chickadee or a bald eagle if you prefer, but it won't change the fact that they're all desperate to impress you.'

'I guess,' she said. 'What did you make of Danny?'

Dunn frowned. 'Like we said the other night at the Coach and Horses – coward.'

'When did we say that?'

'Yeah,' said Skins. 'When did anyone say that?'

'Oh, perhaps I just thought it. All that stuff about not wanting the rivalry to come to blows, the way he changed the subject whenever we tried to get him to talk about the war. He's hiding something.'

'Maybe,' said Skins. 'But a coward? That's a bit of a jump.'

'I don't know. Perhaps.'

'What about Blanche?' said Ellie. 'Do you think there's anything in Lavender's notions?'

Dunn laughed. 'I've said what I think of Lavender. I mean, it's possible Danny could have done it, but he'd have to be a certifiable nutcase. He had the opportunity, obviously. And if the Sidecar was poisoned he had the means. But what about motive? It's too . . . what's the word? Random?'

'So who else could it be? Who at the club could possibly have wanted Blanche dead?'

'Was she going out with anyone?' asked Skins.

'No,' said Dunn.

'That was quick, mate. You sure?'

'I told you I asked her out. She said yes straight away. There was no, "Well, I'm seeing someone else, but . . ." She didn't even um and ah. She just thought for a second and said yes. There was no one else, I'd bet my life on it.'

'I think we can rule out Alfie and Ernie for the same reasons we're ruling them out as the deserter,' said Ellie.

'They're too nice?' said Skins.

'Until Sunderland tell us they're liars, then yes, they're too nice.'

'Bertie?' said Dunn.

'He might have poisoned her accidentally,' said Skins. 'Gawd knows what he's got in his hair, but if she touched it . . . who knows? It might be toxic.'

The others laughed.

'Which only leaves Charlie,' said Ellie. 'I've not spoken to him.'

'He's very smooth,' said Skins. 'Remember that first dance lesson?'

'He was,' agreed Dunn. 'All suave charm and upper-class confidence.'

'Does that rule him in or out?' asked Ellie.

'Yes,' said Skins and Dunn together.

Ellie rolled her eyes.

Skins grinned. 'The deserter, this Grant bloke, was Other Ranks. Just a bloke off the streets like us. Whereas this Charlie is as posh as they come. On the other hand, look how much I've changed since you first met me. I used to be all "gorblimey", but now listen to me. If you didn't know me, could you even tell I was a Londoner?'

'Yes,' said Ellie and Dunn together.

'Yes, well,' said Skins, trying to sound a little more refined. 'It don't take much to put it on, do it? So his accent might rule him out as the deserter, but then again it might not – it's only an accent. And his swagger? It might be the natural swagger of the ruling classes. But it takes a lot of confidence to knock off a shipment of diamonds like you're Dick Turpin on a French holiday. So that doesn't mean anything, either. And the murder? Confident posh blokes can be insane killers, I reckon. Anyone can, if I understand it right.'

'But he doesn't have a motive for the killing,' said Dunn.

'Which is why I made sure to mention the "insane" bit.'

'What about Millie?' said Ellie.

'It's a bloody good disguise if she's Arthur Grant,' said Skins.

'She's gorgeous,' agreed Dunn.

'Not for the deserter, you chumps,' said Ellie. 'The murder.'

'No reason why not,' said Skins. 'But she went nowhere near the drinks or the food. She left just as it was all being brought in by the Cuthberts.'

'Where did she go?'

'She didn't say. But I'd bet you a tanner she went for a tiddle. Danny brought a tray straight over to us, though, and she never touched it before or after doing whatever it was she went to do. She can't have poisoned the drinks. She was at the House of Commons. Visiting Mrs Jones. Gone to look at the crops—'

'She was powdering her nose,' said Ellie. 'I get it. So she's out on both counts.'

'I should say so, yes,' said Dunn. 'Although I did see some blokes who made pretty convincing birds in the concert parties during the war. But not that good, I grant you, so she's definitely not the deserter. And the food and drink would all have been pre-pared during the first half of the lesson so she couldn't have got to any of it before she came in.'

'But Danny had access to it when it arrived.'

'He did,' said Skins. 'Actually, all the others did. They fell on the stuff like gannets before Danny wrenched one of the trays out to bring to us.'

'The tray with the cocktails on?' said Ellie.

'Yes.'

'So they all knew it was yours.'

'They must have.'

'Danny's even less of a sure bet now, then,' she said. 'Any of them could have slipped something into one of the cocktails.'

They were saved from more speculation by the arrival of Mrs Ponton's famous rice pudding. All conversation stopped while the delicious dish was eaten.

Dunn left to find a cab shortly before midnight but the Maloneys stayed up, sitting in the drawing room with a cup of cocoa each.

Skins luxuriated in a long sip of his bedtime drink. This was one of his favourite times of the day, sitting with Ellie and enjoying a moment of simple luxury.

'Do you really think we should be doing all this?'

'Drinking cocoa?' she said. 'Well, I suggested Horlicks but you don't like it.'

'Can't stand the stuff. Don't know why. But you know that's not what I meant. Should me and Barty be investigating jewel thieves, deserters, and murderers? I'm a musician – what do I know about it?'

'You know plenty – you're not as dumb as you like to pretend. And it doesn't matter how much we know – I want to do it. I want to help.'

'I know. And I've got to admit it does make a difference having you in the gang.'

'How, though? I mean, other than my general wonderfulness and the undiluted joy of having me around. I'm dismissed in the popular mind as "a lady of leisure", after all. What use can I be?'

'You're more than that. You've got a lot more going for you than me and Barty do, for a start. You were a military nurse, and your aunt's a spy, and one of your best mates . . . well, she's a spy, and a sleuth, and – as you like to put it – she can beat a man six ways from Sunday without messing up her hair.'

'Knowing Aunt Adelia and Flo Armstrong doesn't give me special abilities.'

'No, but it gives you more of a . . . what do you call it? An "insight" into how these things are done.'

'When you put it like that, I'm amazing. But there's a thrill in it, don't you think? Especially trying to avenge the death of a friend.'

'I suppose.'

'And it's got some intriguing elements. You know, with the secret treasure and all.'

'Old Sir Dynamite Fitzfiddlefaddle-Gumption? Did I tell you me and Barty found his portrait? Good-looking lad. Had a gold key in his hand.'

'A clue?' said Ellie, excitedly.

'Could be. He was on a wall of portraits of the club presidents and they were all holding it.'

'Oh. Probably not, then.'

'It's the talk of the club, though. Well, the Alphabet Gang, anyway. That Danny bloke says it was all they could talk about until the dance thing came along.'

'Really,' she said, slowly. 'And what else did he say?'

'That it was a load of old rubbish someone made up a hundred years ago for a laugh.'

'Trying to play it cool. Put you off the scent. Was it you who brought it up, or him?'

'Us, obviously – me and Barty. It was when we talked to him in the committee room before you turned up and did your "outraged manager" act for the porter.'

'Oh, then. But it's suspicious, no? You ask about the treasure, he says all the others are talking about it and laughs it off . . .'

'Or he really does think it's rubbish, and just said so,' said Skins.

'Well, I think you need to put it in your report to Sunderland anyway.'

'Well,' said Skins. 'Now . . . you see . . . the thing is . . . I'm not much good at reports . . . and . . . well . . .' He gave her his winningest smile. 'Perhaps we ought to call him.'

'Perhaps *you* ought to call him. You can do it in the morning while I write to Flo. It's Friday tomorrow, isn't it?'

Skins yawned. 'It is.'

'So you're playing at the dance at Tipsy Harry's as usual?'

'We are. It's not a bad night, actually. They're a lively bunch and they love their jazz. Not as much as the regular crowd at the Augmented Ninth, but I'm happy to play anywhere we're appreciated.'

'You should open your own club, you know. Then you could do what you wanted. Play when you wanted.'

'Pay rent and rates, hire staff, buy booze, deal with the council, advertise, book cantankerous bands . . . No thanks, love. I think I prefer the life of the wandering minstrel. And it has one huge advantage over owning a club . . .'

'Which is?'

'It irritates the bejesus out of your uncles back in Maryland.'

She laughed. 'They're still annoyed I married a penniless musician. What are we going to do about Barty?'

'He's all right. We make a good living, tell the truth. He's better off than he would be working at the sweet factory.'

'I'm not talking about money. I mean his love life.'

'None of our business.'

'Of course it is. You want your best friend in all the world to be happy, don't you?'

'You're my best friend in all the world.'

'OK, so do you want your second-best friend in all the world to be happy?'

'Of course I do. But there's no "do about" it to be done. A bloke doesn't interfere in another bloke's *affaires du cœur*.'

'Hark at you and your la-di-da French phrases.'

'I've travelled,' he said with another yawn. 'I know a thing or two.'

'But not about *affaires du cœur*. They always need a little help. A little nudge in the right direction.'

'Well, if you want to nudge Barty's "affaires" in the right direction, you'll have to do it without me. I'm not touching another bloke's affaires.'

'Men are idiots.'

'That's not in dispute. But we get by.'

'With our help.'

Skins yawned again. 'Seems like the perfect arrangement, then.'

'You'd better get to bed, honey.'

'I probably ought to. You coming?'

'No, I think I might play a little if it won't disturb you.'

'Play on, my love – one of the many advantages of this massive house is you could host a full rehearsal of the band in here and I'd not hear it in the bedroom.'

'I'll play quietly anyway.'

'Right you are. See you in the morning . . . Oh, fancy going out for lunch tomorrow?'

'That would be swell. And I'm coming to the club.'

'Of course. Wouldn't expect anything less of my wife the sleuth. Don't stay up too late.'

Bloomsbury
June 5, 1925

Dearest Flo

Just a brief one this time – I need some advice but I also need to get to a lunch date with some of the gals.

It was wonderful to see you both on Monday. You're looking so well . . . for a woman of your age. And thank you for steering the boys in the right direction.

I didn't want to say anything while we were all at lunch together, but Blanche's death has hit them harder than they let on. Barty especially. He asked her out just before she was killed, you know. I think they'd have made a wonderful couple.

The interviews are going well (or as well as can be expected, anyway) but we are running out of steam a little. We've learned quite a bit already and Ivor is passing it all on to Supt Sunderland, but I'm not at all certain what to do next. What happens when we've talked to everyone?

And have you heard anything from your newspaper contact? I do so hope it's not just another baseless myth.

Love to you both.

Your friend

Ellie

Chapter Ten

The room at the Aristippus Club that the band used as a green room had become, if not a second home, then certainly a favourite haunt. Everyone had claimed their own little bit of space, and they all settled in and helped themselves to the drinks set out for them by the liveried Cuthberts as they got themselves ready for the evening ahead. Instruments were warmed up and occasional impromptu "jam sessions" – as the new slang had it – would break out as other players joined in.

'Sometimes I wonder if we should let the audience in here, you know,' said Eustace after a particularly interesting exploration of Bach's *Wachet auf, ruft uns die Stimme* he'd instigated. 'Some of the stuff we do in here is better than our regular set.'

'It'd be a bit crowded,' said Skins. 'There's only just enough room for us as it is. But there's no reason we can't mess around at the Augmented Ninth. I bet they'd be happy to hear some experimental stuff. They're a good crowd.'

'I'd be happy with that,' said Benny. 'There's something . . . I don't know how to say it . . . Like you're floating away. Like the whole world has gone and all that's left is the music.'

'Sounds spiritual,' said Elk.

'Maybe it is.'

'What'll I do while you're all getting spiritual?' said Mickey.

'Same as always, Mickey boy,' said Dunn. 'You can sit on a bar stool and chat up the birds.'

'You've got to leave a few songs in the set, then. I can only impress the ladies if I've done a bit of the old singing.'

There was a knock at the door.

'Is everybody decent?' said Ellie as she poked her head round.

'Bit late if we weren't,' said Skins. 'You've already had a good look.'

'Oh, you know me, sweetie – I live to see musicians in their drawers. Oh, hi, Puddle. How are your drawers?'

'The elastic's seen better days, but they do the job,' said Puddle. 'Who are you going to quiz today?'

'Whomsoever falls into my cunningly woven web of . . . something or other. You know what I mean. We're getting closer, I just know we are. Has Inspector Lavender spoken to you, by the way?'

'Oh, yes, I forgot to say. Wednesday morning. He came to my digs and upset my landlady. She doesn't like her lodgers getting visits from the police and she wasn't shy about letting me know. I am, apparently, on my last chance.'

'How many times have you been visited by the coppers before?'

'He was the first. But one is too many.'

'And what did he say?'

'About my landlady? He gets stick from landladies all the time.'

Ellie sighed. 'Is this a band thing? Ivor does it and it drives me bananas. I meant, what did he say about Blanche?'

Puddle grinned. 'Only what one might expect. Well, mostly what one might expect. He asked me to describe the evening, so I did. Then he started asking me if I knew Dudley Daniels and if I had any particular grudge against Blanche. I told him I didn't even know who Dudley Daniels was, that Blanche and I were best chums, and he should mind how he talked to people about their recently murdered friends.'

'Dudley Daniels is Danny's real name.'

'I knew, really, but he was beginning to get on my nerves. He wasn't very forthcoming after that. Just kept asking me about the cocktails and whether I really do prefer gin.'

'He's still on about you being in it with Danny, then?' said Ellie.

'So it would appear. Am I the only one to have been graced with a visit?'

Eustace, Benny, Elk, and Mickey all confirmed that Inspector Lavender had called on them.

'I suppose we should be grateful he's doing something,' said Puddle. 'Even if he's stupid and wrong.'

'We'll just have to make sure we make up for his stupidity, then,' said Ellie. 'Eyes and ears open, Dizzies. Someone here knows something, and we can find it out.'

She kissed Skins on the cheek and slipped back out into the corridor.

'She'd make a pretty good manager, you know,' said Benny. 'She doesn't mind taking charge.'

'I'd not mess her about, certainly,' said Elk.

'You're probably not wrong,' said Skins, 'but I'd not wish you lot on my worst enemy, much less the love of my life.'

'That's sweet,' said Puddle. 'Apart from the part about us being a living nightmare. I, for one, am completely adorable.'

She was immediately pelted with cushions lobbed from all corners of the room.

◆ ◆ ◆

Ellie sauntered along the corridor without an enormous amount of enthusiasm. She didn't actually dislike the regular events at the Aristippus Club, but they were becoming a little routine. She tried to count up in her head how many other times she'd been there. Was it really just two lessons and a Friday night dance? It felt like she'd been coming to the place forever.

Charlie was walking towards her.

'Good evening, Mrs Maloney,' he said with a cheerful smile.

'Please, call me Ellie,' she said. 'I can hardly remember any of your real names and it feels decidedly odd to be calling you Charlie while you have to call me Mrs Maloney.'

'Right you are, Ellie,' he said. 'Looking forward to the dance?'

'I always look forward to hearing the Dizzy Heights,' she said.

He laughed. 'A properly diplomatic answer from the band's new manager. I can understand the reaction to this place, though. It's not exactly designed for ladies. To be honest, I don't think most of the members were designed for ladies. We find ourselves hopelessly attracted to them, but completely unable to figure them out. It's our upbringing, d'you see? The only women we ever meet are mothers, nannies, and school matrons. The war brought us into contact with nurses, too, I suppose, but for the rest of the time, women might as well be from another planet entirely.'

'Venus?' she suggested.

'A planet named for the goddess of love? Perhaps. But my point stands. We just don't know how to behave when there's a pretty girl around, and it makes us all seem a little . . . odd.'

'Perhaps I should dig out my old uniform.'

'That would confuse us even more. We already know you as the unapproachable beauty married to the cocky musician. An unapproachable beauty in a safe, familiar uniform would be too much of a contradiction for our poor little brains to cope with. Heads would explode.'

'You seem to be coping OK,' she said.

'Ah, yes. But I've already found love, d'you see? I've been immunized against the effects. And I'm slowly learning the mysterious art of dealing with a lady as though she were merely another human being. It's tough going, but I'm getting the hang of it.'

'Miss Mitchell must be a remarkably patient woman.'

'You don't know the half of it, old gel. And if we're to call you Ellie, you absolutely must call her Millie. I'm sure she'd insist on it.'

Ellie smiled.

'But I should leave you to your fun,' he said, giving her a tiny bow. 'I have to see a man about a dog, while you have a husband to admire and idiots to socialize with.'

'You're not idiots,' she said as he walked away.

'You've met Alfie, haven't you?' he said over his shoulder.

The dance got underway exactly on time and the Dizzy Heights were in fine form. The sound was subtly different without Blanche, but her temporary dep had arrived just as they were settling down to play and was an accomplished player and he added his own flavour to the blend.

The dancers, of course, were oblivious. They were the same club members, the same wives, the same sweethearts, and the same gaggle of unattached giggling socialites as always, but they had no idea there was a subtle change to the sound of the band. And why should they? They were there to drink and dance. As long as the band played familiar rhythms for familiar dances, who cared about the change in tone from the second saxophonist?

The Alphabet Gang certainly didn't. As usual, they were clustered together, laughing and chattering as though no one else was there. They were not, though, dancing. Ellie began to press her way through the expensively dressed crush of revellers to get to the only people she knew, but she didn't make it. Before she was halfway there, the Dizzies struck up a Charleston and, with whoops and cheers, the Alphabet Gang took to the floor and showed the club what they were made of. She stood back to watch.

The regulars made space around them and applauded the new moves. Ellie assumed they probably knew about the impending contest with the Wags Club, and they almost certainly knew the Alphabets well enough to be able to see the minimal progress they'd made in their lessons. Their enthusiasm seemed genuine rather than mocking. To a man, the Alphabets were still terrible, but they had a new-found confidence in their terribleness that Ellie found slightly endearing. It seemed their pals felt the same.

They were applauded off the floor when the number ended, and Ellie resumed her efforts to reach them. By the time she got there they were still congratulating each other heartily.

'Here comes our saviour,' said Alfie loudly. 'Welcome, Mrs M. What did you think?'

'You've come along in leaps and bounds since I first saw you.'

'It was the leaping and bounding that was causing the problems, according to Miss Mitchell. Much more control now, what?'

Ellie smiled. 'You and Ernie certainly look more comfortable.'

'All our worries have gone since Ernie came up with the pantomime horse wheeze.'

'All your worries? Or all everyone's worries?'

'Well, obviously Charlie thinks it's the stupidest thing he's ever heard. But he's a bit like that. Very strait-laced, our Charlie. Very proper. Looks down on our larking, I think. Looks down on us generally, to be truthful. Eton and Oxford, apparently. Cut above the likes of us. The others are agreed it'll be a proper hoot, mind you.'

'I've got to say I'm rather looking forward to it. Do you really think you'll do it?'

'Rather,' he said enthusiastically.

Bertie had turned round by this point. 'What will he really do?'

'He and Ernie are going ahead with the horse thing,' said Ellie.

'Of course they are. Wizard wheeze.'

'Wizard,' repeated Ellie sceptically.

Both men laughed.

Then the band struck up another tune they knew and their faces lit up.

'Talk to you in a few moments,' said Alfie.

And they were off. The dancing was still terrible.

◆　◆　◆

As it turned out, it was Puddle who next found an opportunity to talk to one of the Alphabet Gang. During the band's first break, at around ten o'clock, she was out in the corridor and on her way to the ladies' cloakroom when she espied Bertie sitting in one of the leather armchairs that were dotted about the corridors. In fact, she saw a head of Brilliantined hair, gleaming in the electric light like burnished anthracite, but who else could it be?

'Bertie,' she called. 'Hello.'

He looked up. 'I'm sorry, my dear, you seem to have the advantage of me.'

'I'm Isabella Puddephatt,' she said.

'Are you? Are you indeed?'

'From the band. I play saxophone and clarinet.' She held out her hand. 'And my friends call me Puddle.'

He shook the proffered hand. 'Charmed, I'm sure. Do sit down, won't you? Puddle, eh? Why Puddle? Why not something a little more endearing, like Pudding?'

She grinned and sat. 'Oh, that's easy. Anyone who called me Pudding would be found dead in a ditch, their mangled corpse eaten by foxes.'

'Duly noted,' he said with a smile. 'Puddle it is, then. But . . . well, you interest me strangely, Miss Puddle. There must be a story behind it?'

'Oh, there is,' she said.

He waited for more, but none came. He was going to ask again, but thought better of it. He'd already been assured of the fate that awaited anyone who got the soubriquet wrong – he didn't dare contemplate what might happen should he make the wrong guess as to the origin of what he presumed was a childhood nickname.

Instead he said, 'I'm sorry for not recognizing you. The honest truth is I have the most shockingly poor eyesight but refuse to wear my spectacles. Vanity, d'you see? A chap has to look his best, what?'

'Oh, don't worry about that. You always have other things to be thinking about while we're playing, after all. Those dance steps won't learn themselves.'

'Don't remind me. I do wish we hadn't agreed to that idiotic contest.'

'Whose idea was it?'

'I can no longer remember, to tell you the truth. Not mine, that's for sure. I'd rather have settled our petty rivalries any other way. Any way at all.'

'Pistols at dawn?'

'If it came to it – probably, yes. I'm almost certain I'd rather the threat of death or arrest to the humiliation of having to dance in front of judges. At least I know I'm a fairly decent shot.'

'You shoot, then?'

'What? Oh, I see what you mean. No. Family rides to hounds, of course. But I prefer to fish. We have fishing rights on the Scottish estate, d'you see? Salmon mostly. Trout, too, of course. I love it up there. I learned my shooting in the big show, I'm afraid.'

'So many did. But as I overheard Ellie saying to Alfie the other day, if you can survive four years of that hell, you can survive four minutes of the Charleston with a pantomime horse.'

'Best idea I've heard in years, that.' Skins had arrived.

'Pantomime horse?' said Bertie.

'Not half,' said Skins. 'How's everyone getting on this fine evening?'

'We're all having a cracking good time. You musician chaps are worth your weight in diamonds, you really are. I've no idea how you do it, you know. I had piano lessons as a lad, but I could never master anything beyond "Twinkle, Twinkle", and here you are, night after night, week after week, making musical magic for the masses.'

'You're too kind,' said Puddle. 'But now you've mentioned "Twinkle, Twinkle" I remember what I came out for. If you'll excuse me, gentlemen, I'll be about my business.'

'See you in a bit, Pudds,' said Skins.

'Fine filly, that,' said Bertie when she'd gone.

'She's a lovely woman,' agreed Skins. He indicated Puddle's recently vacated seat. 'May I?'

'Please do, dear boy. Is she attached? I think she might be interested.'

'You do? How's that?'

'Very encouraging about the contest, asked some personal questions. That's a sure sign, what?'

'It can be. What sort of personal questions?'

'All sorts. Hobbies and whatnot. Even asked about my war service.'

'You might be right, then. What did you tell her? Bit of advice there, mate – don't over-egg it when you're talking to Puddle. She can spot an empty boast a mile off.'

'Nothing to worry about there, old boy. I didn't say anything other than that I served. Didn't even say where.'

'And where did you serve, then? Out of interest, like.'

'All in France. Started out in 49 Brigade, RFA.'

'Howitzers, right?'

'Right you are,' said Bertie. 'Were we neighbours?'

'Noisy bleedin' neighbours if you were. No, I knew a bloke from your lot. Played the cornet.'

'Little chap? Lance Bombardier . . . memory's trying to make me say Tucker.'

'Davey Taylor?' said Skins.

'The very man. Used to play in a works band somewhere in the East Midlands.'

'Yes, that's the bloke. Nice fella.'

'He was. He came with me to the RTR but he copped it at Cambrai, I'm afraid.'

'The Tank Regiment? Blimey, that must have taken some guts.'

'It all seemed like such a lark at the time. We were young and brave and fighting for King and Country. And we had those mighty machines. Nothing could stop us. Bosch artillery stopped his mighty machine, though, poor blighter. But you must have lost pals.'

'More than I care to recount,' said Skins.

'Dark days. Dark days.'

They sat for a moment in contemplative silence before Bertie said, 'But we came to dance, old boy. And we can't do that if I keep you here gassing. I don't want to hold you up.'

'Not at all. It was nice to meet you properly. Enjoy the rest of the evening.'

'I shall. Thank you.'

'Well?' said Puddle as they were packing up. It was three in the morning, but she was still bubbling with energy.

'Well, what, Pudds?' said Skins. It was three in the morning and he most definitely was not.

'When are we going to arrest Bertie?'

Ellie was helping Skins put his temple blocks in the traps case. 'Why would we do that? And you know we can't, don't you?'

'Oh, I know we can't actually arrest him, silly. But he's our man. Definitely.'

Dunn, meanwhile, had made no progress on packing up and was distractedly plucking out a melancholy melody on his bass. 'How do you reckon that?'

'Diamonds,' said Puddle proudly. 'He has diamonds on the brain. He said that musicians are worth their weight in diamonds. Everyone knows it's supposed to be gold, but he's so fixated on his stolen Belgian diamonds that he dropped it in by accident. Like Dr Freud says. It's one of his slips.'

'He might just know more about how much things are worth,' said Dunn. 'I worked it out once.'

'You worked what out?' said Skins.

'I worked out how much I'd be worth if I were worth my weight in gold.'

'You worked it out?' said Ellie.

'I told you – I live on my own. I have lots of time on my hands.'

'And how much are you worth?' asked Skins.

'Ten thousand, two hundred and twenty-four pounds, ten shillings, eleven pence-ha'penny.'

'You're worth every farthing,' said Puddle.

'But if I were made of diamonds—' began Dunn.

'You didn't work that out as well?' said Skins.

'What did I just say about having time on my hands? If I were made of diamonds I'd be worth over five and a half million quid.'

Skins whistled.

'That's enormous fun,' said Puddle, 'and you really, *really* need a hobby, by the way – but what's it got to do with Bertie?'

'All I'm saying is that anyone who stopped to think about it would know that "worth your weight in diamonds" is a lot more impressive than "worth your weight in gold". I'm not saying you're wrong, I'm just suggesting it might not be the clue you think it is.'

'Well, maybe not. But I still think it's significant,' she said.

'I'm afraid I'm going to say you're wrong, though,' said Skins. 'Sorry.'

'Because you've worked out your value if you were rolled out, shredded, and woven into a Persian rug?'

'Two pound ten and a tanner,' he said. 'But no, that's not why. I carried on chatting after you'd gone off to powder your nose, and he never deserted from nowhere.'

Ellie sighed.

'He didn't desert from anywhere,' Skins said with a sigh of his own. 'He's pukka.'

'And how are you so certain of that?' said Puddle. 'Did he give you some sort of secret signal only men can understand?'

'In a way,' said Skins. 'You got him talking about the war, and I just encouraged him to carry on. He said he was in the Royal Field Artillery and the Royal Tank Regiment.'

'And you believe him?'

'I do. He knew a cornet player who Barty and I met at a concert party once. You remember Davey Taylor, Bart?'

'Tall fella with a limp?' said Dunn.

'Short fella with a silver cornet.'

'Oh, yes. Blimey, he was good. Came from Nottingham. Couldn't pronounce the letter R.'

'See?' said Skins. 'And Bertie knew about this bloke. Tried to call him Turner or Tucker or something, but when I reminded him, he definitely remembered.'

'And this Taylor was a cornet player. Good, you say?' said Puddle.

'Unbelievably good,' said Dunn. 'The purest, sweetest tone you've ever heard. I saw grown men cry when he played "Long, Long Trail".'

'I've seen grown men cry when they hear "Long, Long Trail" on an out-of-tune violin,' said Puddle, 'but I take your point. So if you'd seen and heard him, you'd never forget?'

'Once heard, never forgotten, definitely,' said Dunn.

'So, let's say you're Arthur Grant. The Third Disgusting Fusiliers or whatever lot he was in is behind the lines at a concert party. You hear this never-to-be-forgotten cornet player and you never forget him. Perhaps you meet him in a café later, share a bottle of wine. You get talking and you find out he's in the Tank Regiment, transferred from the Artillery. You file that little titbit away. Why wouldn't you? He's a fascinating fellow, and so very talented. Years later when you're on the run with a squirrel's weight in diamonds, you need to construct an alias for yourself. You remember Davey Taylor so you decide you'll be an officer in the Tank Regiment. If anyone starts asking questions you can casually remember the cornet player from the old days . . . What was his name? Tucker? Turner? Oh yes – Taylor, that was it. A trivial little detail that absolutely proves you were in the Tank Regiment.'

'She's got you there, darling,' said Ellie. 'Knowing a well-known person doesn't prove anything.'

'I brought up the cornet player,' said Skins.

'Even better. He was able to pass the test without having to clumsily bring an irrelevant cornet player into the story himself,' said Puddle.

Skins smiled. 'I admit defeat. Or at least I'm not so certain of victory. But we can add it all to the report we make to Sunderland.'

'I thought you were making regular reports by telegram or some such,' said Puddle. 'Are you seeing him in person?'

'We are,' said Skins. 'Monday. You coming, Barty?'

'Sounds good to me,' said Dunn. 'I'll stop off at your place and we can all go together.'

Chapter Eleven

Several minutes had passed since Superintendent Sunderland had sent a constable to fetch tea and biscuits for his guests, and he was growing agitated.

'I'm so sorry to be such a terrible host,' he said. 'It's not as though I've asked for anything exotic. Just a pot of tea and a few digestives. I swear the standard of our recruits is falling. It was never like this in my day.'

'Please don't fret, Superintendent,' said Ellie. 'We'll be fine without tea and biscuits.'

'But I like a digestive,' said Sunderland. 'Someone's for it, I can tell you. This isn't good enough.'

Ellie tried another tack. 'Have you tried the new chocolate-covered ones?'

'Chocolate-covered digestives?' he said incredulously. 'Whatever on earth have they done that for?'

'They're really quite delicious. You should give them a whirl.'

'I'll be fine, thank you. Unlike Constable—'

There was a knock at the door and the constable entered bearing a heavily laden tray.

'Sorry for the delay, sir,' said the young man. 'Sergeant Pennick had emptied the urn making tea for the big Flying Squad meeting so I had to wait for it to boil again.'

'All right, lad. Just set it down. Thank you.'

With the constable gone, Sunderland began fussing about, arranging cups and pouring the tea.

'Thirty-three sugars, wasn't it, Skins?'

'Six,' said Skins.

'He'll have two,' said Ellie. 'He's cutting down.'

'I'm cutting down,' said Skins. 'Probably better make it two.'

With tea finally served, and biscuits distributed, Sunderland returned to his desk and sat down behind it.

'So,' he said, 'what can I do for you three? Do you have news?'

'Of sorts,' said Ellie. 'We've been chatting to the Alphabet Gang. I'm not sure we can be too sure of very much of what we've learned, but we have some things for you to look into.'

'That *is* good news,' said Sunderland. 'Good news indeed.' He picked up his notebook and flipped to a new page, then dipped a pen in the inkwell and waited, smiling.

'Well,' began Ellie, opening her own pocket notebook. 'There's Alfie. Real name Cornelius Rawson . . .'

Skins looked surprised.

'I asked the nice Cuthbert on the front desk,' she continued. 'It turns out he's a lovely fellow, deep down. He was just doing his job when he tried to turf me out on to the street. Very obliging, as it turns out. Well, he was after I slipped him a few shillings. Anyway, Alfie claims to have served in the First Battalion of the Essex Regiment. He was in Gallipoli, Egypt, then France, he said. Somehow he managed to get through the whole thing having never risen above the rank of first lieutenant, so that must be quite rare.'

'Almost unheard of,' said Skins. 'They were handing out field promotions to officers like they'd won a load in the church raffle and didn't know what to do with them.'

'He is an idiot, though,' said Dunn. 'It's not too surprising.'

'I thought being an idiot was one of the main requirements for an officer. I mean—'

Ellie cut him off. 'So that should make him fairly easy to check. Then there's Bertie. Real name James Albert. He was an officer in the Royal Tank Regiment.' She described him briefly and went on to outline Skins's reasons for thinking he was the genuine article, along with Puddle's counterargument.

'You've got other members of the band involved?' said Sunderland.

'We thought it best,' she said. 'They're all keen to help. Then there's Charlie. Real name Robert Chandler. We've not managed to corner him properly yet, but Alfie says he comes from money. Educated at Eton and Oxford, he thinks.'

'That's a start. War record?'

'Not yet. But Alfie did say he's a bit snooty. Looks down on the others, he said.'

'So you think he's the real thing?'

'Well, if I were a farm labourer trying to pretend to be an officer and a gentleman, I'd be inclined to try to fit in as best I could,' Ellie said. 'Wouldn't you? I'd not set myself apart.'

'On the other hand,' said Skins, 'why not go the whole hog? Why not try to out-snoot all the other snooties with your super-charged snootiness?'

'I'll get someone to look in the War Office records for a Robert Chandler and see what we can find,' said Sunderland.

'Danny,' said Ellie. 'Real name Dudley Daniels. I've got a funny feeling about him. He's a nice enough fellow, but he's a bit cagey about his war record.'

'How so?'

'I talked about my own time in the First Aid Nursing Yeomanry—'

'Ah, you were a Fanny,' said Sunderland. 'Good for you. I had no idea.'

Ellie glared at Skins, but he was innocently inspecting the ceiling.

'But when I asked him about his own service,' she continued, 'he point-blank refused to answer. Said he doesn't talk about it.'

'A lot of chaps don't,' said Sunderland.

'He wouldn't talk to us about it, either,' said Dunn. 'But he did tell us he runs an art gallery.'

'Does he, indeed? Did you get the name?'

''Fraid not. He mentioned that he specializes in the avant-garde, though. Claims to be a leading expert on Dadaism.'

'Oh, that's helpful. I shouldn't imagine there are many of those. I wonder if Grant knew anything about art. It would be a great way to hide. And to explain his money – put a few fake art sales through the books to cover up the diamond sales.'

'Never thought of that,' said Dunn.

'You'd be surprised what the underworld sorts get up to.'

'And then there's Ernie. Real name Edwin Cashmore. He claims to be the scion of Cashmore Engineering and spent the war making machinery for the munitions factories.'

'Another easy one,' said Sunderland. 'You've done really rather well. Thank you. Is that all of them?'

'That's all the Alphabet Gang, yes,' said Ellie.

'There's Millie,' said Skins.

'Millie?' said Sunderland.

'Millie Mitchell. Dance teacher. Charlie's bird.'

'She's not terribly likely to be an army deserter called Arthur Grant, is she?'

'No,' admitted Skins. 'She's too tall for starters. Taller than all the blokes.'

'Actually, that's a point – how tall are these chaps?'

'Five foot seven,' said Skins and Dunn together.

'Every one of them,' added Dunn.

'Typical,' said Sunderland. 'Is that it?'

'That's everything,' said Ellie. 'Well, apart from the hidden treasure.'

'Go on.'

'I asked a Cuthbert about it. He was very cagey. Everyone is. But he did say I wasn't the first to ask.'

'And who was?'

'Every single member of the Alphabet Gang.'

The three men laughed.

'I suppose you'd have opened with that if it had been one of them in particular,' said Sunderland. 'Still, it's good to know it's something they're thinking about. Adds a little weight to the whole thing.'

'I guess,' said Ellie. 'I was hoping he'd say, "Oh, yes, madam. Young Mr So-and-so has been asking about that, too." Ah, well.'

Sunderland smiled as he made a few last notes on his sheet of paper, and slid it carefully into one of the many files piled up on his desk. 'I'm absolutely delighted with your efforts. Thank you so very much. This is all very useful.'

'You're quite welcome,' said Skins. 'Have you heard anything further about . . . you know, about Blanche?'

'I'm sorry, but I haven't. Remind me who's leading the investigation?'

'Inspector Lavender,' said Dunn.

Sunderland groaned. 'Oh lord.'

'Is that bad?' asked Ellie.

'I should say so. The man's an idiot.'

It was raining again on Tuesday afternoon as Skins and Dunn wheeled the instrument cart through the streets of Soho towards Mayfair.

'You're an idiot,' said Skins.

'What have I done now?'

'You said the next time you suggested we push this thing to the club in the rain, I was to tell you you're an idiot. Well, you're an idiot.'

'I'm beginning to think you might be right,' said Dunn. 'I honestly thought it was going to clear up before we could find a cab. And they get so bolshy about the gear. "I don't know about that, mate. That ain't never gonna fit in 'ere. What d'ya want all that tat for anyway? What is it? You nicked it?" I thought the rain would ease off and we'd have a lovely walk in the sunshine.'

The most direct route would have taken them along Shaftesbury Avenue and Piccadilly, but with London's traffic getting heavier by the day, they preferred to take the backstreets through Soho. The problem, of course, was that the backstreets were narrower and, in their own way, no less busy. They bustled with life as butchers, bakers, and at least one actual candlestick-maker plied their trade. Horse-drawn carts competed for road space with motor vans while handcarts zipped between them.

There was a clap of thunder.

'That'll be the rain easing off then,' said Skins.

'I never said I was a meteorologist.'

'A butcher?'

'A what? Oh, a meat-eorologist. Nice one. Can we get anything out of a hefty doctor specializing in downstairs?'

'A meaty urologist?' said Skins. 'Bit of a stretch, mate. But there might be something in "-ologists". I'll have a think.'

The traffic ahead had slowed to a standstill. Skins looked round. The narrow road behind them was completely jammed, too.

'Up on the pavement?' said Dunn.

Skins checked. 'Chocka, mate. We're stuck.'

Dunn leaned forward to let the rain run off the brim of his hat. 'What's the hold-up?'

Wearily, Skins clambered up on to the cart. 'I don't know why it's always me who has to look.'

'You're small and nimble.'

'Looks like a brewer's dray down the end of the street lost its load. Barrels everywhere.'

A portly man attempted to use the heavily laden sack truck he was pushing to shove Dunn out of his way.

'Steady on, mate,' said Dunn.

'Get out of the bleedin' way, then, why don'tcha?' said the portly porter.

'And where do you imagine I'm going to go?'

'Out of my bleedin' way, that's where. I've got to deliver this lot. I've got a livin' to make.'

'We've all got a living to make. There's been an accident at the end of the street. We're all stuck till they've got it cleared up.'

'Why don't you get down there and help 'em, then? I've got to deliver this lot.'

'Why don't you—'

'Everything all right down there, Barty?' said Skins from his vantage point atop the cart.

'This gentleman is just explaining that he's got to deliver that lot and that he has a living to make,' said Dunn.

'We've all got a living to make.'

'I told him that, but apparently his is more important. He wonders if we might go and help clear up so that he can more easily go about his business.'

'Did you tell him to get stuffed?'

'I was about to, but you interrupted.'

'Do you want me to tell him?'

'No, it's all right, I'll do it.'

'Right pair of bleedin' comedians, you two,' said the porter.

'Recognition at last,' said Dunn. He doffed his hat, allowing more of the rain collecting in the brim to tip on to the man's boots.

The porter scowled and started trying to push his way towards the pavement.

'I say. Steady on, old chap,' said a lazy, upper-class drawl.

'Get out of it,' said the porter. 'You want a smack in the chops?'

'Oh, do shut up, you silly little man,' said the drawl.

Dunn was struggling to see who the owner of the drawl was. He sounded familiar. 'Is that Charlie from the club?'

Skins gave him a thumbs up. 'Oi-oi, Charlie. Fancy seeing you here.'

'Skins?' said Charlie. 'What the devil are you doing up there?'

'Keeping an eye on things. Barty's down below.'

Charlie looked round the porter. 'Mr Dunn, too. How wonderful to see you both.'

'You gonna get out of my bleedin' way?' said the porter. 'Or am I gonna 'ave to give you a smack in the chops after all?'

'This fellow seems to have a thing about smacking people in the chops. Is it something we should be concerned about?' said Charlie.

'He's all talk as far as we can make out,' said Skins. 'Take no notice.'

'I'll show you who's all talk,' said the porter.

He took his hands from the handles of the truck and put them up in a boxer's stance. Charlie cocked his head and frowned. The porter took a swing but Charlie saw it coming and dodged aside. He saw the next one and dodged that, too. And the next.

'Oi, Jack Dempsey,' said Skins. 'Give it a rest, mate. You're never going to hit him. Just push your trolley over there and leave us alone before you get hurt.'

'And which one of you's gonna 'urt me?' he growled.

Skins shrugged. 'There's three of us, you idiot, we'd all join in. Seriously, mate – hop it.'

The porter muttered something none of them could quite hear. It sounded as though it might be another threat, but after a moment he dropped his guard and took hold of his hand truck once more. He managed to push it past Charlie and further towards the side of the road.

Skins climbed down and shook Charlie's hand. 'Nice to see you. You on your way to the club?'

'I am, as a matter of fact, yes. Got one or two matters to address before this evening's lesson. And you? I assumed from the pile of gubbins on your handcart there that you'd be heading in the same direction, but one never knows – you might have an afternoon . . . "gig", do you call them?'

'No, we thought we'd get there early,' said Dunn. He indicated the crush. 'That was the plan, anyway.'

'"No plan of operations extends with any certainty beyond the first contact with the main hostile force",' said Charlie.

'Does it not?'

'Not according to some German fellow, at least. Von Something. But then they all are, aren't they?'

'They do seem to be.'

Charlie looked up as though to indicate the rain. 'Look, I'm awfully sorry and all that, but I really do need to see a man about an alpaca. I hate to leave you chaps standing here in the rain, and on any other day I'd be happy to help you with your traps, but I do rather need to press on.'

'You go ahead,' said Skins. 'We'll see you later.'

'Look for me in the bar,' said Charlie. 'I'll stand you a warming toddy.'

By the time they reached the club, Skins and Dunn were drenched, but Cuthbert at the porter's desk had been briefed.

'Good afternoon, gentlemen,' he said. 'We've laid out dry clothes for you in the small committee room. Cuthbert will show you the way.'

'Thank you very much,' said Skins.

'Would Cuthbert be able to take our instruments to the ball-room for us?' asked Dunn. 'We've left them in the hall by the back door.'

'I think Cuthbert is busy,' said the porter. 'But I can ask Cuthbert to do it for you. Or perhaps Cuthbert. Leave it with me.'

Dunn shook his head and they followed the appointed Cuthbert to the small committee room.

'Is he taking the mike?' he said as they walked along.

'I used to think so,' said the young Cuthbert, 'but all the older ones do it. After a while I started to reckon it actually makes sense to them. I'm not sure some of them even notice what they're saying. They know which of us they're talking about and it doesn't occur to them that they're using the same name every time.'

'So what's your real name, then?'

'I'd honestly be more comfortable to remain as Cuthbert, thank you, sir.'

'Fair enough. Is Mr Chandler here?'

'Charlie, sir? In the bar. He asked if you'd meet him there when you'd dried off a bit.'

They changed quickly – putting on the correct trousers – and returned through the increasingly familiar corridors to the club bar. They found the customary mix of young and old, active and dozing, chatting and reading. They also found a scene they previously thought had been a one-off. In the corner, in the company of Charlie and a man they presumed from their last encounter to be known as Whiffy, were two alpacas.

Skins then noticed a club member he'd seen before. He was sitting on his own, so Skins approached and said, 'What's going on over there?'

The man looked up from his copy of *The Times*. 'They're alpacas.'

'I know,' said Skins. 'There was one in here the other week. But now there seem to be two.'

'Oh, sorry. See what you mean. I think Whiffy is selling them to Charlie. Brought a load over from South America. Been over there mining. Or raising cattle. I forget which. Was going to put them out to graze on the country estate in Norfolk, but the gaffer says no, apparently. "I'm not having those foreign beasts on my land," says Pa, so Whiffy has to get rid. Charlie's taking them off his hands. Wanted to inspect a couple before he sealed the deal.'

Skins leaped aside to avoid the croquet ball that was hurtling towards a hoop held up by two beer mugs under a nearby table. 'And they decided to do that here?'

'Commercial hubs, the gentlemen's clubs,' said the member. 'All sorts of business being done in rooms like this all over London at this very moment.' He folded his newspaper. 'You're those musician Johnnies, aren't you?'

Dunn had joined them. 'That's right.'

'Seen you at the Friday night dances. You're really rather good, you know. Wish I were musical. Had piano lessons as a boy. Complete duffer.'

'We're glad you enjoy what we do,' said Dunn. 'It's good to be appreciated.'

'Rather. I say, we could do with more chaps like you in the club. Liven the place up a bit to have some actual real-life jazz musicians about the place. You thought about joining? I'd be happy to nominate you.'

'Not sure I can afford the subs,' said Dunn. 'He might, though.' He nodded towards Skins.

'It's a tempting offer,' said Skins. 'Let me think about it.'

'Certainly, certainly,' said the club member. 'Didn't mean to embarrass you. But if you ever fancy it, just say the word. Place needs shaking up a bit and you seem like the chaps to do it.'

Skins smiled. 'Right you are.'

Charlie, his livestock transaction evidently completed, looked around the room. He saw Skins and Dunn, and sauntered over.

'You made it,' he said. 'Sorry about dashing off like that and leaving you in the rain. Let me get you that drink I promised you.'

'Thanks,' said Skins. 'And don't worry about leaving us behind. It's not like you lied to us, after all. You really did come to see a man about an alpaca.'

Charlie laughed. 'I really did. Charming creatures, aren't they?'

'Charming,' said Dunn. 'You might want to get a Cuthbert in to clear up after that one, though.' He nodded towards a boyish group who had gathered round the alpacas, but who were now leaping out of the way to avoid being splashed.

'Not my problem yet,' laughed Charlie. 'They're not mine till I hand over the cash – Whiffy was very insistent on that – so he can deal with it.'

He broke off for a moment to order a round of drinks from a passing Cuthbert.

'Tell me honestly, though, chaps,' he said once the flunkey had gone. 'How do you rate our chances in the dance contest? It's this coming Friday.'

'Well . . .' said Dunn.

'Now then . . .' said Skins.

'You see, the thing is . . .' said Dunn.

'It's not that we . . .' said Skins.

Charlie laughed again. 'Nuff said.'

'Seriously, though, mate,' said Skins, 'you're rubbish. And if you're honest, you know you are. Actually, you're better than the rest of them, but as a group, you're hopeless. But that's all right. I mean, we don't have a clue what the opposition's like – I'd be happy to put ten bob on them being hopeless, too. And you're much better than you were.'

'Your Millie has worked wonders,' agreed Dunn.

'Whose Millie?' said a woman's voice behind him. 'I'm very much my own Millie, don'tcha know.'

'Hello, darling,' said Charlie. 'I was just sounding the boys out about our chances on Friday.'

'Oh, you're absolutely useless,' said Millie. 'Truly terrible. Your one hope is that the Wags Club boys are even worse. I've never seen anything like it.'

'And you've got the comedy act to fall back on,' said Skins. 'Alfie and Ernie's pantomime horse act.'

'Don't remind me,' said Charlie.

'I think it could be the clincher, actually,' said Millie. 'If we can keep everyone's attention on how funny it is to see a pantomime horse doing the Charleston, they might not notice how badly it's doing it. You must thank your wife for us, Skins.'

Skins looked puzzled. 'Ellie?'

'Yes – wasn't it her idea?'

'I don't know. I thought it was Ernie's.'

'Oh, was it? Well, she gave the two of them the encouragement and confidence they needed. We owe her a great debt.'

'She'll take cash or cheque,' said Skins.

'Another canny one, eh?' said Charlie. 'I know what that's like. Can't get away with anything.' He reached out and touched Millie's arm affectionately.

'I've got your number, certainly,' she said. 'And talking of numbers, we'd better finalize the numbers you'll all be dancing to on Friday. Do you have any preferences?'

'I'm happy to let you decide,' said Charlie. 'It's between you and the band. As long as we can dance to them without looking like fools, it's up to you.'

'They're musicians, darling, not magicians. You'll look like fools whatever they play. But we'll settle on something.' She turned to Skins and Dunn. 'The chap from the Wags Club has sent a list of tunes they've been practising to. All on gramophone record, apparently. They say they're happy to dance to any of them and that, since we have a band, it depends on what you're able to play.'

'What we're able to play?' said Skins. 'Cheeky bleeders.'

'They can be a bit oafish like that,' she said, 'but they mean well. There's no malice in it – they just don't realize it's a little insulting. They're not used to dealing with anyone other than their servants and lawyers. Everyone else is a bit of a mystery.'

'It gives your lot even more of a home advantage,' said Dunn. 'Their own ballroom, their own home crowd, their own band, and their own versions of the tunes. I'd give you twenty-three to one we don't play them exactly like the versions they've got on their records.'

'Those are strangely specific odds.'

'All scientifically worked out.'

'Are they, indeed? Well, perhaps we can have a chat about the tunes on the way to the ballroom, and you can explain your method.'

'Certainly,' said Dunn.

Skins nodded. 'Lead on, Macduff.'

'Lay on,' said Dunn.

'What?'

'It's "lay on", not "lead on". Everyone gets that wrong.'

'Lay on, Macduff?'

'Exactly so.'

'Hence the name of that piano player. It all makes sense now.'

'That's where he got it – Léon Macduff.'

Skins turned to follow Millie, who had already walked off shaking her head.

'Did you ever see him?' he asked. 'He used to accompany that burlesque dancer, "No Time" Toulouse.'

'Although when we met him he was playing for Ma Blarch,' said Dunn. 'Great singer. She used to be part of a duo with her father-in-law, Billy Corner. But he had some trouble with the law so she had to hide Pa Corner, and the act wasn't the same without him.'

'She's not listening to us,' said Skins.

'Can't say I blame her. Perhaps we should do something with "-ologists" after all.'

◆ ◆ ◆

The rest of the band were already on the stage warming up, and Millie interrupted them for a few moments to agree the three songs they would play for the contest on Friday.

'Thank you,' she said. 'I'll let the Wags know as soon as possible so they have at least two practices with the proper tunes as well.'

The band was ready to begin. Millie was ready to begin. But only three-fifths of the Alphabet Gang were present. Alfie and Ernie were missing.

Elk started vamping some chords on his banjo. Dunn joined in, swiftly followed by Skins, who added a little swing to the proceedings and reined in Elk's tendency to let the tempo wander. Puddle picked up her saxophone and began to improvise a tune, with Benny and Eustace chipping in with perfectly timed brass stabs. After a few phrases, Puddle gave Eustace the nod and he took over the solo.

By the time Benny's turn had come around, Millie and the Alphabets were dancing. Without having to follow the formality of a recognized "dance", Bertie, Charlie, and Danny were making a pretty decent fist of moving in time with the music.

Puddle was about to take the lead again when there was a commotion at the door and a stag's head peered into the room. The Dizzies kept playing, but the Alphabets stopped to watch as the stag's head entered the room, with Alfie holding the wooden board upon which it was mounted. Behind him, bent double and with his hands on Alfie's waist, was Ernie. Or they assumed it was Ernie. It was difficult to tell with the old army blanket draped over him. They joined the group just as the band stopped playing.

'What do you think?' asked Alfie.

'You're going to be a pantomime stag now?' said Bertie.

'What? Oh, I see. No, this is a . . . What did you call it, Ernie?'

Ernie stood, and the blanket fell to the floor. 'A prototype,' he said. 'A mock-up. We thought it would demonstrate the concept and give us a chance to work out our moves before we got the proper costume. You see here? Alfie isn't going to be able to use his hands in the suit, so he's holding the stag's head from the smoking room. I'll not be able to see, so I'm draped in a blanket. It's how we design things down at the workshop.'

'By draping yourselves in blankets?' said Bertie.

'You're an ass, Bertie,' said Ernie.

'Better an ass than a pantomime horse.'

'Gentlemen, please,' said Millie. 'We have only two of these sessions before Friday. Let's not waste them.'

'He started it,' said Ernie.

Millie put her hands on her hips and glared.

'Sorry, ma'am,' he said. 'Positions, everyone?'

The lesson began.

◆ ◆ ◆

Ellie had timed her own journey so that she arrived at the Aristippus Club once the dance lesson was already underway. She approached Cuthbert the porter, who was behind the front desk.

'Good evening, madam,' he said with a smile. 'How wonderful to see you again. You'll be pleased to know I've cleared it with the committee and it's all right for you to sign yourself in now. I hope you understand I had to follow the rules the other day.'

'Of course . . . ?' She smiled encouragingly.

'Cuthbert, madam.'

'Ah, yes, my husband did tell me. Think nothing of it, Cuthbert. I'm very used to having to follow rules. We nurses were as bound by rules and regulations as any of the Tommies at the front.'

'You served in the war, madam?' He seemed impressed.

'I did. First Aid Nursing Yeomanry. I'm sure a lot of your members served. So many young men did. I think most of the dancers we're playing for were all soldiers. The Alphabet Gang, they call themselves now.'

'Not all, madam. I believe young Mr Cashmore – Ernie – was involved in important war work at his father's engineering firm.'

'Oh, do you know, I think you're right. I think Ivor told me something about that.'

'"Ivor", madam?'

'My husband.'

'The one they call Skins?'

'That's the fellow. He's a drummer, you see? Drum skins. A childhood nickname I've never persuaded him to abandon.'

'Ah, it makes sense now. I'd heard the gentlemen calling him Skins. I wondered if it was a middle name – Skinner, perhaps. Then I speculated that his family might have been tanners.'

'Nothing so romantic. He's been a drummer since he was a lad. I should have remembered about Ernie, though. But I'm sure the others were all soldiers.'

'That's my understanding, madam. Jolly proud of their service, the lot of them. And rightly so. I tried to join up, but they wouldn't have me. Caught a bullet in the leg in the Transvaal and they said I was unfit for service. Too old, too, they reckoned. I told 'em they needed some old sweats to show the youngsters the right way to do things, but they weren't having none of it.'

'I think you were well out of it, to be fair.' She leaned in conspiratorially. 'And I know it doesn't become one to talk about people behind their backs, but could you honestly imagine being led into battle by the Alphabet Gang? I think Charlie – Mr Chandler – might have had his wits about him, but the others . . .'

Cuthbert chuckled. 'I know what you mean,' he said. 'I heard tell that Mr Chandler was quite the hero, actually. Saw action all over. Decorated, they say. Field promotion to major, as well. I'd have been all right under him. He'd have looked after us.'

'I'm sure he would. He's a lovely chap.'

'Fine fellow, madam. Fine fellow. But they all are. In their own way.'

Ellie smiled. 'In their own way. I imagine Mr Daniels would have made a good leader, too. Thoughtful.'

'Don't know much about their Danny, madam. Never talks about his war service. Very private gentleman. Have you seen his paintings?'

'His paintings?'

'Yes, he runs an art gallery. Modern rubbish. Can't bear it meself – don't make no sense. But he did some lovely watercolours for the committee room. Pictures of the club and the street outside. Proper paintings, if you take my meaning. None of that . . . what do they call it? Abstract?'

'Abstract, yes,' said Ellie. 'Have I been in the committee room?'

'I couldn't say, madam, but I shouldn't think so. The members don't use it much – too big for anything other than committee meetings.'

'Then I shall prevail upon a member to show me the paintings one day. I should like to see them.'

'You definitely should, madam. Although now that your presence has been approved by the committee and you're officially signed in, you may come and go as you please. It's one of the club rules. Nothing is out of bounds.'

'That's good to know, Cuthbert, thank you.' She looked at her watch. 'Although I'd better get along to the ballroom and see the Dizzies. They should be taking a break now.'

'Right you are, madam. Enjoy your evening.'

'Thank you. And thank you for your time – it was nice talking to you.'

And with that, she set off.

Ellie followed a tray-bearing Cuthbert into the ballroom and stood by the door while the drinks and sandwiches were set out on the table. The band were mid-song and were 'hot', as Skins liked to say. Or were they cool? Ellie struggled to remember. They were good, anyway.

The dancers, meanwhile . . .

The dancers were still terrible, but they were terrible in a new and exciting way that Ellie really rather enjoyed. While the individuals hadn't managed to cast off their personal quirks and were still gawky and awkward, the group was now a coordinated dance ensemble who might just have a chance as long as the Wags were equally giftless. The Alphabets' training from Millie, and the comedy element added by Alfie and Ernie's animal antics, could conceivably give them the edge.

The song came to an end and Ellie clapped enthusiastically. To her surprise, the band put down their instruments and joined in the applause. The Alphabet Gang took a bow.

Ellie left them to their well-earned beer and joined the band on the stage. She sat down in the empty seat next to Puddle.

'Where's the deputy sax player?' she asked.

'He had a long-standing prior engagement. He'll be back tomorrow evening. And on Friday, obviously,' said Puddle.

'Have you found a permanent replacement yet?'

'We've not looked, to be honest. The word's gone out, though – the jazz world isn't so large as you might imagine. If there's someone out there who fancies the seat, they'll tell us soon enough.'

'Do you know when the funeral is yet?'

'No,' said Puddle with a sigh. 'The police still won't release the body until they know for certain how she was killed.'

'Still no closer, then? Have you heard anything from Lavender?'

'Not a dicky bird. Have you?'

Ellie frowned slightly in puzzlement. 'No,' she said hesitantly. 'Well, unless he's spoken to Ivor and he's not told me.'

Puddle glanced around conspiratorially. 'How's the' – she lowered her voice – 'you know . . . how's the "other matter" coming along?'

'We seem to have reached a dead end as far as I can see. We met Superintendent Sunderland yesterday and passed him a bunch of new information, but until he's had time to check it out we're kinda stuck.'

Skins had come to join them. 'She's not kidding. I'm beginning to wish we'd never agreed to help. It seemed like such a laugh when he first mentioned it, but I'm starting to feel like we've been taken for mugs. He's quite the charmer, old Sunderland. He's got that "just one of the boys" way about him, but he's an officer sort underneath it all. He knows how to manipulate people to get what he wants.'

'Should my ears be burning?' Charlie had arrived, unnoticed, at the stage.

Skins looked over and smiled. 'Not you, old son. Just someone we know.'

'Sounds like a piece of work.'

'He's all right, really,' said Skins. 'He's just a bit of a . . . a bit of a puppeteer, I think you might say.'

'Excellent quality in an officer, that. Always good to be able to get the best out of your men without shouting and bawling. Leave that to the NCOs, what?'

'Is that how you did it, then?'

'I should say so,' said Charlie with a laugh. 'You catch more flies with honey, and all that.'

'A motto to live by,' said Ellie. 'So where did you do all your fly-catching? You Alphabets have such fascinating stories.'

'Oh, you know,' said Charlie, breezily. 'Flanders, France – the usual.'

'Yeah,' said Skins. 'It was all the same in the end. Up to our armpits in mud and munitions – didn't really matter what the locals called it.'

'Quite so, quite so. But let's not talk about all that. I came over to thank you all once again for your wonderful work. You really have been quite tremendous.'

'Entirely our pleasure, old son,' said Skins. 'Just win and it'll make it all worth it.'

Charlie laughed. 'I'll get you some beers.'

Chapter Twelve

Next morning, Ellie and Skins were sitting together in the drawing room of their Bloomsbury home, sharing a pot of tea in the unaccustomed peace and quiet. The children's nanny had taken Catherine and Edward to Regent's Park to feed the ducks.

'What are you going to feed them to?' Skins had asked when they told him of the plan.

They had both looked at him blankly, but after a few seconds Skins was delighted to see a smile lighting up Edward's face as he worked out what the question meant.

'We're going to feed them to my dragon,' he said. 'He likes eating ducks.'

Catherine didn't quite understand what was going on, but it didn't sound good. She looked to her mother for reassurance.

'Don't worry, darling,' said Ellie. 'It's just the boys being silly. No one's feeding the ducks to anything, and certainly not to Edward's dragon. You're going to give them some lovely food.'

'Porridge isn't lovely,' said Edward. 'It's horrid.'

'He's got you there,' said Skins.

'If you were serving them a bowl of porridge, I'm sure they'd be most unhappy,' said Ellie. 'But Mrs Ponton has given you a bag of oats. They like oats.'

'I thought they liked bread,' said Skins.

'Mrs Pointy said she couldn't spare any bread,' said Edward. 'Are we poor?'

'Too poor to have bread?' said Skins.

'Yes. When people don't have enough money, they sometimes don't even have enough for bread. Nanny said. She said there are lots of poor people now.'

'Nanny's not wrong,' said Skins. 'But you don't have to worry. Mrs Ponton must have other plans for the bread.'

Eventually they had left, each clutching a tiny paper bag full of porridge oats, and their parents had retired to the drawing room.

Ellie took a sip of her tea. 'Did you mean what you said yesterday?'

'I said a lot of things yesterday,' said Skins. 'I meant at least half of them.'

'At the club. When we were talking to Puddle.'

'About wishing we'd never bothered?'

'Yes. It's not like you to be disheartened. You're one of the most determined people I've ever met, apart from Aunt Adelia. You don't know the meaning of the word "daunted".'

'True, but I never let my poor vocabulary put me off. But no, I was just venting my frustration. You've got to admit that all we've got going for us is a love of Blanche. We got into this to help a bloke we barely know on the say-so of your pal and her best mate, not because we're experts or anything. When it started it was a bit of a lark – deserters, uncut diamonds, hidden treasure. Then when Blanche was killed it all got very personal. I'm more determined than ever to see it through now . . . I was just getting a bit weary.'

'She's your pal, too,' said Ellie.

He laughed. 'That was the part you latched on to? Determination? Finding Blanche's killer? That's what it's about. We've got to do something ourselves, haven't we. The police are useless. Lavender's most creative thought was that it was Danny and

Puddle. Who were in it to . . . to what, exactly? To rid the world of all the other female sax players so Puddle could reign supreme? You know he thinks Danny poisoned Vera from the Finchley Foot-Tappers, too?'

'It was Barty who thought that. And Eustace.'

'Was it? Oh. Well, it's still bleedin' stupid.'

'Then we need to redouble our efforts. When's Barty getting here?'

'Not till four.'

'Why don't you send him a telegram and get him down here for lunch instead. We'll have a confab before we go back to Tipsy Harry's.'

Skins went out to the hall to telephone the telegram office.

Dunn, meanwhile, was sitting in Mrs Cordell's parlour, playing her piano. Against her repeated protests that he didn't ought to be wasting his money on frivolities like that, he paid to have it tuned at least twice a year. She thought it was a scandalous expense, but was secretly proud to have the best-sounding piano on the street.

He was working on a new song. He'd intended to try an upbeat dance number for the band, but his fingers had found their way to something more suited to a sentimental ballad. He shook his head and launched into his own interpretation of 'Daisy Bell'.

Mrs Cordell knocked on the door and came in bearing a cup and saucer.

'Here you are, love,' she said. 'I had the kettle on and I thought you might like a nice cup of Rosy Lee.'

'Ta, Mrs C.'

'I'll put it over here on the table.'

He carried on playing, taking the old familiar tune through some chord changes never envisaged by the music-hall artistes who had once sung about inviting Daisy on to their bicycle built for two.

'You're ever so talented, love,' said Mrs Cordell, 'but I do wish you wouldn't do all that jazz stuff with the old songs. Play me something I can sing along to.'

'What do you fancy?'

She put her hand on his shoulder. 'It's ten years ago today,' she said. 'Play me "Long, Long Trail".'

'Oh, Mrs C,' said Dunn. 'I'm so sorry. I'd completely forgotten. Are you sure?'

'They sung it to me the night before they left,' she said. 'It helps me remember.'

The Cordell brothers had been killed together on the tenth of June 1915, when an Ottoman shell hit their trench on Cape Helles. It had taken weeks for the news to make it back to London, and Phyllis Cordell had received both telegrams together. She was still coming to terms with the loss of her beloved husband, who had been a stoker on the *Lusitania* when it was sunk by a German U-boat that May.

Dunn began the introduction. He knew Mrs Cordell's range from playing for her regular sing-songs with her pals 'round the old Joanna', and he picked an appropriate key. He'd heard the song played often in the trenches as a jaunty march, but this wasn't the time for jaunty, and his fingers were in the mood for melancholy anyway. Mrs Cordell began confidently, her rich contralto voice singing about the lonely nights and wearyingly long days listening for their song. She made it as far as the nightingales singing in the white moonbeams in the chorus before her voice cracked and the tears began to fall.

She leaned against Dunn as she wept. He made to stop playing to comfort her, but she urged him to carry on and he picked up the melody himself, singing softly. He shuffled aside to let her sit next to him and she put her arm around his shoulders as he finished the song.

'I'm sorry, my love,' she said when he reached out to hold her. 'I don't know what come over me. I'm a silly old biddy. I ought to be used to it by now, but in ten years not a day goes by when I don't think about those three lummoxes.'

She blew her nose noisily into a handkerchief that had appeared as though by magic from the sleeve of her housecoat.

'It's only natural, Mrs C. I'm not sure I could have coped with it half as well as you have. I'm in a state over losing a friend – I can't imagine what it would be like to lose a husband and two sons in the space of a month.'

'We all muddle on, don't we?' she said, sniffing. 'Come on, let's have a cheerful one. What about "Tipperary"? And give it plenty of the old oompah. Make it a lively one.'

Dunn launched into an energetic rendition of "It's a Long Way to Tipperary", and was pleased to see Mrs Cordell laughing as he adopted a comic voice to sing a harmony part in the chorus.

He thought he could hear some sort of knocking sound as they began the last verse, but he was having too much fun to stop and find out what it was. As they launched into the naughty version of the final chorus, there was a sharp rap on the window.

They turned to see a red-faced telegram boy angrily beckoning them to open the door. They both laughed.

'I'd better go and see what he wants,' said Mrs Cordell. 'He don't look too happy to be kept waiting.'

Dunn arrived at the Maloneys' Bloomsbury house an hour later clutching the telegram.

'I'm being summoned by wire now?' he said with a grin. 'That makes me feel oddly important. Like some government official.'

'Make yourself at home, honey,' said Ellie. 'And if you had a telephone, we wouldn't have to cable you.'

Dunn sat in his usual armchair. 'You know that real people don't have telephones, don't you? Mrs C would be the only person on the street with one. The only one in the whole neighbourhood. People would queue up at her door for the chance to come in and admire it.'

'She'd be the talk of north London.'

'She would.'

'So she should get one. She seems like the sort who'd love the attention.'

'And how would she pay for it? Who would she call?'

'You'd pay for it – it's not like you've anything better to spend your money on. And you'd call us.'

'It seems like an expensive way of keeping in touch with you two. I think we'll stick with telegrams. There's talk of them installing one of the new telephone boxes near our place – I can use that to call here.'

Ellie harrumphed.

'Where's his lordship?' asked Dunn.

'Attending to matters of state.'

'With the luxury of indoor plumbing. I envy you.'

'You could live somewhere nicer if you wanted,' said Ellie. 'You don't have to live in a little two-up two-down in Wood Green. The band's doing well now – you can afford to move.'

'I like living with Mrs C,' he said. 'And what would she do without me?'

'She'd get another lodger.'

'Someone who messes her about and doesn't pay the rent. She's got no one to look after her.'

'You're an old softie, Bartholomew Dunn, and I love you for it.'

Dunn said nothing, but his face reddened ever so slightly.

Skins returned. 'There's the lad himself. You been offered tea yet?'

'No,' said Dunn. 'Mrs Maloney was too busy having a go at me for not having a telephone.'

'What can I say? She likes to be able to contact people. But do you want a cuppa?'

'Go on, then. Why not?'

Skins rang the bell. Mere moments later there were running footsteps in the hall and Lottie burst breathlessly into the room.

'Tea for three, please, Lottie,' said Ellie. 'And there's really no need to run.'

'Right you are, ma'am,' said Lottie. 'Although I do like to run. Good for the heart, me mum says.'

Ellie smiled. 'As long as you don't think you'll be in trouble if you don't. Just be careful you don't fall.'

'I takes care, ma'am, don't worry.' She hovered.

'Yes, dear?'

'Mrs Ponton says do you want lunch early, what with you havin' a guest an' everythin'?'

She smiled shyly at Dunn.

Dunn smiled back.

'No, thank you,' said Ellie. 'Two o'clock will be fine, as always.'

'Very good, ma'am.' Lottie curtsied and left.

'How are you feeling now?' said Ellie.

'Me?' asked Dunn. 'Right as rain. Why?'

'You lost someone you care about only a couple of weeks ago. I worry about you.'

'Oh, I'm fine,' he said, blithely. 'Tough as old boots, me.'

'I'm pleased to hear it. But don't . . . you know . . . overcompensate.'

'How do you mean?'

'She means leave our housemaid alone,' said Skins.

Dunn laughed. 'She's got to be half my age. Give me some credit.'

'You've got form when it comes to housemaids, matey boy.'

'I have? Oh, that one in Gloucestershire. I was younger then.'

'Well, just don't lead her on,' said Ellie. 'It might be flattering that she's taken a shine to you, but she's a good worker and I don't want to lose her over a broken heart.'

'She's safe around me,' said Dunn. 'I promise.'

Ellie frowned. 'Ivor and I were just talking about the police investigation.'

'Or the lack of it,' said Skins.

'No one's heard anything else, then?' said Dunn.

'As usual, not a tweety bird,' said Ellie.

'Dicky bird, love,' said Skins.

'Really? That's a real phrase? I just thought people kept getting it wrong. Puddle said it the other day and it was all I could do to stop myself correcting her.'

'No, it's your actual rhyming slang. Dicky bird – "word".'

'It's nonsense, that's what it is. What on earth's a dicky bird?'

'It's a bird. A little one. Barty?'

'Don't ask me, mate,' said Dunn. 'What do I know?'

'You live alone. You read books.'

'But not books about dicky birds.'

'The point is, though,' said Ellie, 'that no one's heard a word about the case. This Lavender guy doesn't seem to be doing anything that anyone can see.'

'He might just be playing his cards close to his chest,' said Dunn. 'It's not like he's got any obligation to tell any of us anything.'

'Close to his vest,' said Ellie.

'His what?' said Skins. 'His . . . oh, what do you lot call them? Undershirt?'

'No, his vest,' said Ellie. 'Like a . . . oh, what do you lot call them? Waistcoat?'

'We definitely say "chest",' said Dunn. 'No one wants to be talking about a bloke's string vest. But he might be, mightn't he? He might have solved it by now. We don't know anything about the investigation.'

'We could find out, though,' said Ellie. 'We could ask Sunderland.'

'We could, I suppose,' said Dunn. 'But I'd feel more comfortable about it if we had something to offer him in return.'

'Like what?' said Skins. 'We've got nothing.'

'We've got everything,' said Ellie. 'We've found our man.'

The two musicians looked at each other. Then at Ellie.

'Well, it's one of two. Which is better than one of five. And a heck of a lot better than one man somewhere in England.'

'And the two are . . . ?' said Dunn.

'It's obviously either Charlie or Danny.'

'Then let's talk to Sunderland and you can explain why,' said Skins. 'I'll call him and make an appointment.'

Superintendent Sunderland had asked them to come to Scotland Yard straight away. He offered to send a car but they decided a taxi would be quicker, and by half past one they were sitting in his office with yet more tea. This time, there were chocolate digestives to go with it.

'Thank you, Superintendent,' said Ellie as she took a biscuit from the tray. 'I thought you said you were opposed to the idea of putting chocolate on biscuits.'

'I was,' he said. 'And there's part of me that still is – it feels very much against the natural order to adulterate the perfect biscuit like that. But I have to concede that they're delicious.'

Ellie smiled and took another.

'I'm rather glad you contacted me today,' Sunderland said as he took a sip of his tea. 'I have news.'

'Blanche?' said Dunn.

'In a way, yes. I've taken over the murder inquiry. Lavender has been . . . well, one doesn't like to air the force's dirty laundry in public, but he's facing disciplinary action for . . . other matters. I can't say more, but his cases have been divvied up and I said I'd take this one, what with my team having an interest in the club. I convinced his superiors that the murder and my jewel theft are related.'

'You think they are?' said Skins.

'It's like I said before – I'm not keen on coincidences. I've still no proof of any connection, but I can't get past the idea that one serious crime is one too many, but two in the same place is even harder to swallow.'

'How were his enquiries progressing?' asked Ellie.

'Not well. He still hadn't figured out how the poison was administered. You remember he was convinced it was in the food or drink you were served at the club? Probably the drink, since the cocktail was the only thing that only one of you had.'

'The Sidecar,' said Skins.

'The Sidecar, yes. But the police surgeon said there was no trace of the poison in the stomach. If she'd drunk it, that's where it would have been, but he found none.'

'So how . . . ?' said Dunn.

'That's our problem in a nutshell – how? Until we know how she was given the poison, the surgeon can't even begin to speculate on the who, when, and where of it.'

'Was there any in her mouth?' asked Ellie. 'Or on her skin?'

'On her skin?' said Skins.

'Some poisons can kill you just by you touching them,' she said.

'Blimey.'

'The police surgeon is looking now,' said Sunderland. 'I'll let you know what he finds in case it jogs any memories.'

'And what about the diamond deserter?' said Dunn. 'Any news about him?'

'A little,' said Sunderland. 'I've had confirmation from the War Office about some of the chaps you told me about.'

'And they're not your deserter,' said Ellie.

'Probably not, no.' He opened one of the many files on his desk. 'Let me see,' he said. 'Ah, yes. Your man Cornelius Rawson—'

'Alfie,' interrupted Dunn.

'Alfie, yes. His official record confirms that he was in the Essex Regiment exactly as you said. Decorated at Gallipoli for safely leading his men out of a deadly ambush. Finished his war in France.'

'Still as a first lieutenant,' said Skins.

'Despite being decorated for gallantry,' said Dunn.

'Yes. It seems they thought about making him up to first lieutenant, and later straight up to captain when things got even dicier and they were short of suitable men to do the job, but officers in the field counselled against it. There's a confidential note from an Australian colonel who saw him during the action at Gallipoli, saying, "Nice enough bloke, and brave as they come, but he's not quite the full shilling. Give him the gong, but don't promote him too high or he'll start getting men killed." A major in Egypt said much the same.'

'He's a lovely man,' agreed Ellie. 'But they're right – he's not terribly bright.'

'Indeed. So, given that your assessment of his abilities matches theirs, I'm inclined to believe you've met the real Alfie,' said

Sunderland. 'So I don't think he's our man. Who's next? James Albert – Bertie. He's the fellow Skins thought was a real member of the tank regiment, and it seems he was. There was a Major James Albert of the Royal Tank Regiment, formerly of the Royal Field Artillery. Served with distinction.'

'And you're sure it was the same man?' said Ellie.

'His description matches, right down to the overuse of pomade. Who else have we got? Ah, yes, Edwin Cashmore of Cashmore Engineering. They're a very well-known firm up at the War Office and he's been personally vouched for by one of the bigwigs there.'

'Which leaves our two main suspects,' said Skins. 'Charlie and Danny.'

'Just so,' said Sunderland. 'And the main records aren't a great deal of help. There's no army record for a Dudley Daniels at all. Nothing for the navy, either. Not even the Royal Flying Corps.'

'What about the Secret Service Bureau?' said Ellie.

Sunderland frowned. 'The what, madam?'

'Oh, don't try that,' she said. 'Our mutual friend works for them. And my aunt has had dealings with them. You know exactly who I mean.'

He smiled. 'I'm afraid I'm unable to comment, but if it were possible to make enquiries of a non-existent government body, I'm sure we'd be making them.'

'But it could be him,' said Skins.

'It could,' said Sunderland. 'Just as it could be Robert Chandler.'

'Charlie,' said Dunn.

'Yes. There are a couple of records for Robert Chandlers. One was a lieutenant in the Royal Navy, the other was an infantry captain. The naval Chandler served in the North Atlantic; the infantry Chandler spent most of his time in France.'

'If it's our Chandler, it'll be the infantry one,' said Ellie. 'He mentioned Flanders and France. And don't forget Eton and Oxford. They must have records, too.'

'They do, but they're being unusually cagey. Or perhaps they're usually cagey – they're not the sort of people I tend to deal with so they might always be like that. But I'll get the infantry file sent over – that might lead us somewhere.'

'So it's one of those two?' said Skins.

'Well, that's the thing,' said Sunderland. 'Obviously we don't know for certain that Grant and his diamonds are at the Aristippus Club at all. Nor can we be certain that he's actually planning to steal the Treasure of the Mayfair Murderer on Friday. But yes, if Grant's there, then he's likely to be posing as Chandler or Daniels. And if we can thwart the theft of the treasure while we're at it, then so much the better.'

'If the treasure's real,' said Dunn.

'To be honest,' said Sunderland, 'it doesn't really matter. I'm relying on the legend of the treasure to act as bait to tempt Grant out of hiding. We might get him anyway, but he'll be a lot easier to nab while he's concentrating on finding some long-lost treasure.'

'If it even is Grant,' said Skins.

'You see my dilemma. This is precisely why I've not been able to devote resources to it. It's why I'm having to impose on the generosity of old acquaintances to get police work done.'

'And just to be clear – you're definitely working on the basis that the deserter is also the murderer now?' said Ellie.

'I am. If he thought Blanche Adams was on to him, he might have panicked.'

'She was a nurse,' said Dunn. 'Maybe he recognized her.'

'That's certainly a possibility. I'll get the War Office to send over her record as well and see if we can find any points of intersection once we get something for these last two chaps.'

'Very well,' said Ellie. 'What do you want us to do next?'

Sunderland thought for a moment. 'Just carry on as you are, I think. Keep chatting, keep scouting around the club – you're doing great work. Just try not to spook our man, that's all.'

'OK,' said Ellie. 'I think we can manage that.'

'And you'll let us know what the police surgeon says?' asked Dunn.

'I'll telephone the Maloneys as soon as I hear anything.'

They chatted inconsequentially as they finished their tea, and still managed to return to Bloomsbury less than half an hour late for lunch.

Littleton Cotterell
8 June 1925

Darling Ellie,
I ought to be brief, too (though I fear I shan't
be – there's a lot to tell you). I should at least
try, though. It seems Herself needs to go into
Chipping Bevington for 'essential supplies' (a
pound of tuppenny nails, two yards of blue silk
ribbon, and a jar of cold cream – don't ask). For
some reason, muggins here has to drive.

As for the case . . .

Dinah Caudle joined us for Sunday lunch
yesterday, bringing with her an impressive collection of clippings (well, transcripts of clippings,
anyway – newspapers are understandably precious
about letting their actual archived material out
of the building). There were contemporaneous
(that's one of your "fifty-cent words" right there)
reports of the robbery and the death of the jeweller, Gideon Kemp. Then the arrest of Sir Dionisius
Fitzwarren-Garvie at the Aristippus Club. There's

some stuff about the trial and a couple of pieces about the club.

Among the more sensational accounts are some absurdly breathless descriptions of the 'magnificent jewels' stolen from Mr Kemp. It seems he catered to the more luxurious (i.e., pointlessly extravagant) end of the market, and had in his possession some quite extraordinary items. To give you an example: there was a Ceylonese sapphire of 'some 347 carats' (I mean – really?) and 'about the size of a pheasant's egg' forming the centrepiece of a 'diamond-encrusted necklace'. The list goes on, of course, but it's hard to tell whether it's the truth, the lurid fantasies of newspapermen, or the exaggerations of a jeweller's brother hoping to bump up the value of the insurance claim on his dead sibling's shop.

It all goes cold for a year or two, then letters and other speculative pieces begin to appear in all manner of London publications about this 'secret vault' Supt Sunderland has been talking about.

It seems a good many extremely reputable individuals were convinced it was true, and there were calls for the authorities to mount a proper search. When no such search was forthcoming (reading between the lines, I suspect that powerful individuals within the club put the kibosh on it), several eager young men expressed their intentions to look for it themselves.

There was talk in one letter to *The Times* of a golden key. Another mentioned a 'staff or sceptre' and 'quasi-religious ritual', but, honestly, it all sounds a bit far-fetched and desperate.

Back at mundane reality, Dinah also brought news that one of her contacts (pals? – newspaper folk seem to collect 'contacts' in much the same way Lady Hardcastle and I do, so one can never be sure whether they're friends or merely useful people to know) – anyway, one of her contacts was surprised by her request for information on the Treasure of the Mayfair Murderer because it was the second time he'd been asked in less than twelve months.

Apparently he'd had a letter from a 'Mr John Smith', care of the Charing Cross Post Office, asking for almost exactly the same information as Dinah, but with one addition. This 'Mr Smith' wanted to know if there were any reports of alterations to the building, too. Obviously she asked him whether there had been, but the answer was no, it hadn't been covered.

She's put in a request to the London County Council to see if they have any historical records of requests for permission to make structural changes. I'll let you know how she gets on.

As for your next steps . . .

If the interviews are going well but you're still not getting anywhere, one of you has to bite the bullet and do some breaking and entering. People do rather tend to be a little careless when they're in places where they feel safe. The most fastidious criminal will leave things lying about his home – or his home away from home in this case – that he'd not want anyone to see, because . . . well, because it's his home. No one else would ever go into his home. Even housebreakers who make their living from going into other people's homes and helping themselves seem to imagine themselves safe from intrusion.

So someone has to start looking in your suspects' bedrooms in the club (you know that gentlemen's clubs have bedrooms, I presume). Get the keys if you can, pick the locks if you have to, but get inside and rummage through the things they think no one will ever see. I wish I could come down and help – I love a bit of burglary in the evening. It livens up the appetite.

So go. Burgle. Let me know how you get on.
Much love
Your friend
Flo

Chapter Thirteen

Ellie went along to the Aristippus Club with the band that evening. It was the last dance lesson before the contest on Friday so she felt a duty to show her support, but she couldn't face the thought of watching the Alphabet Gang galumphing about the ballroom again.

'Do you think they'll mind if I slip out?' she said to Skins as the band set up.

'Who, the band?' he said. 'Course not. Why would they?'

'No, I meant the Alphabets. I feel like I ought to be here, to . . . I don't know . . . lend my support or something. I'm supposed to be Alfie and Ernie's cheerleader, after all.'

'This is the dress rehearsal, though. They're going to be too wrapped up in trying to work their horse costume to notice who else is in the room.'

She shrugged. 'I guess.'

'Tell you the truth, I'm not completely sure they're even going to notice us.' He indicated the band. 'I predict chaos and hilarity, but not a lot of actual dancing.'

She smiled. 'In that case, I'll slope off quietly when I get a chance.'

'Good idea. Where are you off to? A bit of shopping?'

'It's seven o'clock, you goof. The shops are all closed.'

'Pub, then?'

'I'm going to snoop about the club. I heard from Flo the other day – it's what she'd do.'

'Would she, now? She's a bad influence, that Flo.'

She kissed his cheek. 'It's what attracted you to us both.'

'Put that drummer down,' said Dunn. 'You don't know where he's been.'

'Oh, I know exactly where he's been.' She gave Dunn a wink.

Dunn was still trying to think of some sort of response when the main doors opened and Bertie entered, pulling something on a rope. Something big.

As expected, the other end of the rope was attached to a comically oversized halter around the head of a pantomime horse. It was a bay, with a black mane, and it was moving extremely awkwardly.

Ernie's muffled voice came from within the belly of the horse. 'Are we there yet?'

'No idea, old bean,' said an equally muffled Alfie. 'These eyeholes are bloody useless.'

Danny and Charlie were bringing up the rear.

'Just a few more steps,' said Charlie, 'and you'll be bang in the centre of the room.'

The horse clumped on.

'Whoa, boy,' said Bertie, and patted the horse's neck.

'Ow!' said Alfie from within. 'Watch out, you idiot, that's my head. I'm not an actual horse, y'know.'

Ellie leaned in close to Skins. 'This has all the makings of a disaster. Part of me wants to watch as the chaos unfolds, but a much more insistent part wants to get the heck out. I'll be back before the class is over.'

'All right, my love,' he said. 'Mind how you go.'

Ellie slipped out through the small door near the stage that led to the band's green room.

◆   ◆   ◆

Ellie cast an eye around the room and quickly found what she was looking for. As she had known it would be, Skins's jacket was lying in a rumpled heap on the floor beside a chair. She picked it up and dusted it off as best she could. She put it on one of the coat hangers that had been thoughtfully provided by the club – and thoughtlessly ignored by her husband – and hooked it in the picture rail that ran round the room. Still tutting, she went out into the corridor.

It occurred to her that people tended to treat corridors in much the same way they treated roads. They were a useful way to get from one place to another, but they were never really worthy of anyone's full attention. Which, she decided, was a shame, because some corridors were fascinating in their own right. The ones in the Aristippus Club certainly were, and perhaps roads might be, too.

The walls were decorated not only with the portraits of past committee members that Skins had told her about, but with other curios and keepsakes he hadn't mentioned and which she had previously failed to notice.

One case contained the original club charter, signed in 1793 by men with some very impressive titles – including Sir Dionisius Fitzwarren-Garvie – alongside journals, notebooks, and letters from the time. One such letter had a note in the margin, presumably written by the recipient, which said, 'Don't be so stuffy!'

A little further on were the designs for the club's chinaware, commissioned by one of the founders and made by Wedgwood of Stoke-on-Trent, and some of the architect's original drawings of the building. Beside them were two swords. The accompanying card told her they had belonged to 'G Norman and J Hartshorn' and that they had been 'used in a duel to settle the matter of a ten-shilling debt, the rights of the grazing of a flock of twenty sheep, and the honour of Mr Hartshorn's sister'. There was no record of the outcome of the duel, nor whether the sheep were fed or Miss Hartshorn's honour had been restored.

There was a flight of stairs at the end of the corridor, broad and elegantly carpeted. There was no one around, so Ellie decided to ascend and see what she could see.

She saw another corridor. Running along the middle of this one, though, was the same elegant carpet as on the stairs, while the walls were free of mementoes. In place of the portraits and memorabilia were watercolours of London. One particularly pleasing sequence showed how the streets around Mayfair where the club had its home had changed over the preceding hundred years.

There were doors off the corridor at regular intervals and the place had the look and feel of a rather pleasant hotel. These must be the members' bedrooms that Flo had told her about. She was lost in thought, speculating as to what luxury might await on the other side of the doors when she heard a polite cough behind her. She turned to find a Cuthbert smiling at her.

'Might I be of assistance, madam?' he asked.

She smiled broadly. 'I rather think you might. I'm looking for the bathroom.'

'The bathroom?' he said with some puzzlement. 'Madam wishes to take a bath?'

'No, no,' she said quickly. 'The . . . umm . . . the can. The head.' She often found it helpful to play the confused American in situations like this, and misunderstandings of vocabulary were especially useful. 'The . . . oh, what do you guys call it? The WC?'

'The lavatory, madam?'

'The very place. You got one of those?'

'There is a ladies' cloakroom downstairs near the entrance hall.'

'There's not one up here?'

'No, madam, these are the members' bedrooms.'

'Bedrooms, eh? I'll bet you get all sorts of shenanigans going on up here.'

'I couldn't say, madam.'

'Mum's the word, eh? I like that. Discreet. So they each have a room of their own?'

'No, madam, there aren't nearly enough rooms for that. But members may book them as they require them.'

'Nice arrangement.' She raised her hand to point back towards the stairs. 'And the cloakroom's back that way? Down the stairs.'

'Down – as you say, madam – the stairs.'

'Swell. Thanks a bundle, buddy.' She didn't know anyone who spoke like that, but it always seemed to convince the English of her Dumb Yankee bona fides when she did, so she pandered to their prejudices and laid it on with a trowel whenever the need arose. She retraced her steps and headed downstairs again.

She found the ladies' cloakroom near the main entrance and went in, just in case Cuthbert had followed her. She waited for what she deemed an appropriate length of time and then re-emerged. Ellie looked around, but the coast was clear. She wasn't under surveillance after all. She set off for another attempt.

It seemed to Ellie that there was something about the portrait corridor that warranted another look. She retraced her steps and once more examined the row of portraits of the past one hundred and thirty-two years' worth of club presidents. They all had the gold key, but she already knew that.

Then, in the picture of Lord Eakins of Moreton Pinkney, the president from 1884–88, she saw something else. Flo had mentioned a 'staff or sceptre' in her letter, and there, leaning against the leg of Lord Eakins's chair, was an ornately carved wooden rod, a little over a foot long.

She took a closer look at the other portraits and, sure enough, there was the staff. Sometimes it was partly hidden by a fold of a coat, or peeping out from behind some other prop or item of furniture, but every portrait contained the same wooden staff.

It didn't prove anything, of course. The key and the staff were obviously part of the club regalia, so it seemed perfectly reasonable to include them in rumours about the hidden treasure, but it was interesting to confirm that they were real and not part of the elaborate fantasy.

She had turned her head to take a better look at the collection of artefacts on the opposite wall when she caught sight of something out of the corner of her eye. She turned back, but she couldn't work out what had attracted her attention. She tried again, trying not to look directly at whatever it was, but concentrating on her peripheral vision in case she could . . . And there it was. Running down beside the portrait of Lord Eakins was the tiniest hairline crack in the wallpaper. It went from floor to ceiling, and it was plumb straight. Now she saw it, she couldn't believe she hadn't noticed it before. It was so obvious. So, too, was the corresponding crack, two and a half feet further along the wall. A door.

She'd found it. Where a hundred and twenty years of men had failed, Ellie Maloney alone had succeeded. But how to open it? There was no sign of a handle, nor of anything that might control a hidden mechanism. She pushed hard against one side of the door. Somewhat disappointingly, nothing happened. Then she tried the other.

The catch released and the door opened outwards an inch. She looked round to check that the coast was clear, then pulled the door open just enough to slip inside.

Her first clue that her excitement had been misplaced was the electric light switch just inside the short corridor. She flicked it down and a single, unshaded bulb illuminated the top of a flight of stone stairs.

At the bottom, she found herself in a large wine cellar. It was clean and well stocked – this was not, she now knew, the location of the secret treasure. But there were treasures here, to be sure. She recognized a few of the labels on the wine bottles and knew they didn't come cheap. One wall was almost entirely filled with champagne of various vintages; another with green bottles of absinthe.

There wasn't much else to see apart from a ledger. She took a look, tutted to herself, and made her way back up to the corridor, switching the light off as she went.

She wondered briefly about going to look for Danny's watercolours to give herself a convincing story in case anyone asked her where she'd been, but all she knew was that they were in a 'committee room' and that could be anywhere. Reluctantly, she decided it was time to face the music. Well, almost time. If she hung around in the green room for a bit, she could wait until they broke for beer and sandwiches and sneak back in then.

◆ ◆ ◆

She timed her arrival to perfection. The Dizzies ended the number with an expansive flourish just as she opened the door, and she heard Millie say, 'Well done, chaps. Well done. Have a break and a beer. You deserve both.'

She slipped into the room and up on to the stage.

'Did you have fun?' asked Skins.

'Fun?' she said. 'I guess so, it's a fun place. Hey, guess what – I found a secret door.'

Skins started. 'You never. Where?'

She grinned. 'In that corridor with all the portraits. Don't get your hopes up, though – it was just a wine cellar. According to a ledger on one of the shelves it's the "Senior Members' Special Collection". They've got a fleetful of bottles of absinthe, but no treasure.'

'Well, you know what they say—'

'If the next words out of your mouth are "absinthe makes the heart grow fonder", you'll be sleeping alone in the guest room for the next week.'

Skins laughed. 'You know me too well. See anything else?'

'Just where the members' bedrooms are upstairs. I know Flo told me they had them but I wasn't sure she was right. I honestly didn't know gentlemen's clubs were just posh dosshouses – I thought they were for secretly running the country away from the tiresome scrutiny of parliament and the press.'

'Well, that as well, but mostly so that gentlemen can get puggled with their pals on the contents of some of the finest wine cellars in London, and then sleep it off without their wives knowing exactly what they're up to. Handy for . . . liaisons, too.' He winked.

'Or for husbands to discreetly give their wives a chance to have liaisons of their own while they're "away".'

'I'm sure there's a lot of that, too. Plenty of husbands and wives in the Great Families must be staying together for the sake of the dynasty rather than any mutual affection. A chance for a sly tumble must be welcome on both sides. Not everyone marries for love.'

She kissed his neck. 'I'm lucky to have you, even if you are an insufferably smug know-it-all.'

Dunn had joined them. 'Steady on – that's my game. I don't stay in night after night reading boring books just so someone else can come along and be the insufferably smug know-it-all. What did he know?'

'That gentlemen's clubs have rooms for the members to stay in,' said Ellie.

'Oh, everyone knows that,' said Dunn. 'Common knowledge round our way.'

'Well, I thought it was interesting,' she said. 'How did the rehearsal go?'

'Best yet,' said Dunn.

'That's encouraging.'

'Don't get your hopes up,' said Skins. 'They're still bloody awful, but that was definitely the best bloody-awful performance they've managed so far.'

'What did you guys think?' said Ellie to the rest of the band.

'I was thinkin' about me dinner,' said Mickey.

'I had my eyes shut,' said Eustace.

'Trying to decide on a birthday present for the missus,' said Elk.

'Drinkin' rum in my favourite bar in St John's,' said Benny.

Puddle's music-school pal smiled politely but said nothing. It belatedly occurred to Ellie that she had no idea what his name was.

'You're all dreadful,' said Puddle. 'They've all worked incredibly hard and I'm proud to have been part of it all.'

'Good for you,' said Ellie.

Puddle looked thoughtful, as though she were trying to decide whether to mention something. After a moment, she found her resolve. 'I've heard from Blanche's brother. He's in a bit of a state, as you can imagine. And he thinks it might help if he could have her instruments back. I said I'd take them round.'

'That makes sense,' said Ellie. 'They were so much a part of her. It might give him some comfort.'

'That's what I thought,' said Puddle. 'So can I pick them up from your chum's shop after we're done here?'

'Course you can,' said Skins. 'We can go over there together. Maybe stop at the Lamb and Flag for a pint?'

'Or back to our place for a nightcap in more salubrious surroundings,' said Ellie.

'Oh, that would be delightful,' said Puddle. 'I love your house. Thank you.'

'Can I come?' said Dunn.

'Of course you can, dear,' said Ellie. 'You never have to ask. Anyone else? We could make an evening of it.'

The rest of the band politely declined, all citing the usual mix of family obligations, other bookings, and difficult journeys.

'Places, everyone,' called Millie in her parade-ground voice. 'Full run-through. No stopping. No second chances. Contest conditions. Come on, Alfie, get your head on. Let's go.'

Ellie took that as her cue to slip out into the green room again. She'd brought a book.

The rain of the previous day had blown through and the weather had become a good deal more summery. It was a rather pleasant evening as the four friends made their way past the Royal Academy and eastwards, eventually towards Covent Garden.

'Why didn't we get a cab?' said Dunn.

'Because the exercise will do you good,' said Ellie. 'And I like it when we get to Leicester Square and St Martin's Lane. I love the theatres.'

'Do you go often?' asked Puddle.

'As often as I can. His lordship is always working when the good shows are on, but I get out with my pals. Lady Reasons can always get us good seats. Her husband is Sir Vivian Reasons, the producer.'

'It works out well. She gets to have fun with her mates and I'm saved from some of the worst excesses of the West End,' said Skins.

'I'd love it if you could come with us more often, though,' said Ellie.

'Fella has to earn a living,' said Skins. 'And I thought it was my musicianly allure that drew you to me in the first place, anyway.'

'I was only sixteen. And in England for the first time. Everything seemed exotic then, even a penniless drummer.'

'You met him when you were sixteen?' said Puddle. 'How romantic.'

'Surely he's told you that story.'

'There was something about a retired spy called Lady Something-or-other, and Weston-super-Mare, and a terrifying aunt. I didn't pay much attention, to be honest – I thought he was making it all up.'

'It's all true. Well, that's to say there's a true story involving retired spies and my terrifying aunt in Weston-super-Mare – I don't know if everything else he told you is true.'

'I stuck pretty much to the official narrative,' said Skins. 'I might have overstated the audience's reaction to our ragtime revels, though. I'm not sure the residents of the Arundel Hotel were quite as keen on our music as I made them out to be. But everything else was true. Including the beautiful American girl who came up to the stage in the break and stole my heart.'

'You're a soppy sod at times,' said Dunn.

'Shut up,' said Puddle. 'I think it's adorable. It must be a drag not being able to go out together in the evenings, though.'

'Oh, we get by,' said Ellie. 'I still get to go out and have fun with my buddies, just not with him. And he's hanging around the house most of the day so we probably see more of each other than most married couples.'

'Hanging about like a bad smell?' said Skins.

'Well, I didn't like to say anything, honey,' said Ellie. 'But since you brought it up . . .'

'Remind me why we walk through the backstreets,' said Dunn, indicating two drunken men ahead of them who were involved in an altercation, apparently about Arsenal and Tottenham's relative performances the previous season and their chances for the next.

'This is where we get to see the real London,' said Skins.

'I've seen the real London,' said Dunn. 'It's a dump. I grew up here. And Arsenal don't stand a chance.'

'What did you say?' said the Arsenal supporter belligerently.

'You heard,' said Dunn. 'And keep it down – there's ladies present.'

'Sorry, mate,' said the Tottenham fan.

They walked past the two men, who by this time had decided that they were best pals again.

They crossed Leicester Square and on to Charing Cross Road, then cut through St Martin's Court by the side of Wyndham's Theatre. They emerged on St Martin's Lane opposite New Row.

'Now that we've seen the real London,' said Dunn as he let them into his friend's shop, 'can we at least get a taxi to Bloomsbury?'

'If it'll shut you up, you miserable old bleeder,' said Skins, 'I'll get you a chauffeur-driven Rolls.'

'A black cab will do fine, thanks. Where did you put Blanche's stuff?'

'In the back there,' said Skins. 'Behind my old traps case.'

They picked up the two instrument cases and went back out on to St Martin's Lane to hail a cab.

◆ ◆ ◆

Skins let them in with his key and Ellie led the way to the drawing room.

'Drinks?' she said, indicating the well-stocked cabinet.

'I know I agreed to come for a nightcap,' said Puddle, 'but to tell you the truth I could murder a nice cup of tea.'

'Ivor's your man for tea,' said Ellie. 'Apparently I don't do it right.'

'She hasn't got a clue, bless her,' said Skins. Then, in a whisper, he said, 'She's American.'

'Darn tootin',' said Ellie. 'And don't you forget it, pardner.'

'Does that account for her obsession with the secret vault and the hidden treasure?' said Dunn with a wink. 'They love all that Olde Englande rubbish, the Yanks.'

'I'll be proven right,' said Ellie. 'You'll see. There's something in it – I can feel it in my Yankee bones.'

'And what gorgeous bones they are,' said Skins. 'I'll put the kettle on. Barty?'

'Not for me, thanks, mate. Mrs C is the best landlady I've ever had, but I do sometimes wonder if she's trying to drown me slowly in tea. I'll have a scotch.'

'You'll have one, love, won't you?' said Skins.

'I think I might join Barty, actually,' said Ellie. 'Can't let the poor boy drink alone.'

'Tea for two, then.' He set off for the kitchen.

The Maloneys' servants were used to their employers' unconventional hours, and although they had retired for the night they had made sure everything they might need for late-night drinks and snacks was ready in the kitchen. Skins filled the kettle and spent some time poking about in jars to find biscuits before performing the time-honoured ritual of warming the pot and spooning a precisely calculated amount of tea into it. At least, that's what he would have told anyone he was doing. In reality he absently sploshed some of the near-boiling water round the inside of the pot and chucked a few spoonfuls of tea leaves into it, hoping he'd counted right.

Back in the drawing room, he found Ellie and Dunn sipping scotch while Puddle examined a china ballerina.

'It's yours if you want it,' said Skins, as he put the tray down beside the figurine on the table.

'Oh,' said Puddle. 'Well, that's very kind . . .'

'But you'd rather smash it with a hammer?' suggested Ellie. 'Don't worry, honey, we all feel that way about it.'

'A present from a favourite aunt?' said Puddle with a smile.

'Something like that,' said Ellie.

'More like punishment from a hated one,' said Skins. 'Milk and sugar?'

'Oh, don't say that,' said Ellie.

'I always offer guests milk and sugar.'

'No, you goof, I meant don't say Aunt Martha is hated.'

'But you do hate her,' said Skins. 'We all do. She's a nasty piece of work.'

'She is, but you shouldn't say so.'

'As you wish,' said Skins.

'Milk and two, please,' said Puddle. She indicated the piano. 'Do you mind if I . . . ?'

'Please do,' said Ellie. 'I was going to suggest Ivor put the gramophone on, but the piano always sounds much better.'

'What would you have played?'

'On the gramophone? I've become absolutely obsessed with that George Gershwin tune from last year.'

'"Rhapsody in Blue"?' said Puddle. 'What's the chap's name? The bandleader. Paul Something.'

'Whiteman,' said Dunn.

'That's the fellow,' said Puddle. She settled herself at the piano and began to play. 'It sounds better with a full orchestra, but the piano arrangement is rather fun, too.'

'She can't come round any more,' said Ellie. 'She's far too good. I'm supposed to be the piano player in this house.'

Puddle laughed. 'I can talk at the same time, too.'

'Make her leave, Ivor.'

'At least let her finish her tea,' said Skins.

Puddle played on for a minute or two while the others sat quietly and listened. Suddenly, halfway through a phrase, she stopped.

'Why poison?' she said.

'Why poison what?' said Skins.

'Blanche. Why kill her with poison?'

'Why kill anyone with anything?' said Dunn. 'I've seen men killed. I could never see a good reason for it.'

'Fair enough,' said Puddle. 'But suppose you'd reached the point where you decided to off someone. You'd rationalized it and come to the conclusion that it was perfectly justified. Someone's friend, someone's daughter – another living, breathing, smiling, laughing, talented, beautiful person – had to die. Why poison?'

'It's easier to get away with, isn't it?' said Skins. 'You can slip them the poison and be nowhere near them when they go. Some poisons take ages to act. Hours sometimes. Days, even.'

Puddle contemplated this for a moment. 'So she could have been poisoned by someone in the café where she had lunch. Or her landlady could have put it in her breakfast tea. Or someone could have slipped her something the weekend before.'

'True,' said Skins. 'I reckon that's why the police aren't getting anywhere. They don't know what the poison was, so they don't even know where to start.'

'Oh, they know where to start,' she said. 'They started with me and Danny being in it together, remember?'

'That was Lavender,' said Dunn. 'He's an idiot. But he's not on the case now.'

'Who is, then?' Puddle said. She sighed. 'No, never mind. What am I going to tell Blanche's brother?'

'Why do you have to tell him anything?' said Ellie.

'He's going to ask, isn't he? I was there with her when she . . . you know. He's going to want to know what happened. We all want to know what happened. And I've got nothing to offer him apart from a sax and a clarinet.'

'Then do that,' said Ellie. 'Give him the instruments and tell him how much we all loved her. Talk about her work with the band.'

'You're right, of course. I shouldn't overthink these things. But it's horrible for us – the not-knowing, I mean. Imagine what it must be like for her brother.'

'We'll get to the bottom of it. Or Superintendent Sunderland will.'

'Who's he again?' said Puddle.

'He's the one who got the boys looking for the deserter, and now he's taken over the murder inquiry, too.'

'Once they know what the poison was, we might be able to fill in some of the blanks for them,' said Skins. 'Who was where, who saw what, all that kind of thing.'

'It would be a comfort to Bill, certainly,' said Puddle.

'Bill?' said Ellie.

'Blanche's brother. Sorry, I thought I'd said. William Henry Adams.'

'Ah. Yes, like you said, not knowing is horrible. Is he married?'

'With three children.'

'So he doesn't have to deal with it on his own,' said Ellie. 'But you shouldn't, either. Do you want me to come with you?'

'Oh, would you? I mean, I don't want to put you out, but I'd welcome the company.'

'It's no trouble at all. When are you going?'

'I said I'd pop in tomorrow around lunchtime. He's an accountant. Has his own practice. He said he'd nip home.'

'He's in Wimbledon, did you say?'

'He is, yes.'

'Then leave the instruments here and I'll pick you up in a cab at about, what, twelve?'

Puddle smiled broadly. 'That would be marvellous. Thank you.'

Chapter Fourteen

Ellie's taxi arrived at Puddle's digs in Balham at noon the next day. Instructing the cabbie to leave the meter running, Ellie hopped out and knocked sharply on the door to the bay-fronted semi-detached house.

A few moments passed before a well-dressed middle-aged woman opened it. Her face had either been set in an unwelcoming scowl for the purposes of answering the door to unexpected callers, or that was her natural expression. Either way, Ellie was unfazed and greeted the glower with her customary warm smile.

'Yes?' said the woman. 'Can I help you?'

'Hello,' said Ellie, brightly. 'I'm just—'

'We don't want any,' said the woman.

'I can understand how you wouldn't. Dreadful things. But—'

'And we don't want to join your religion, either.'

'Who would? It's a very personal thing, religion. But that's really—'

'And we're not going to vote for you.'

'I'm entirely sure I wouldn't vote for me, either. Is Miss Puddephatt at home?'

'Oh, her. Are you one of her . . . *musician* friends? I've told her I don't want your lot hanging round here. You lower the tone.'

'Well, I play the piano, but not professionally. She's expecting me. We're to go out for lunch together.'

'Are you, indeed? Wait here.'

She slammed the door.

Ellie turned round and waved at the cabbie to reassure him that she wouldn't be long. He was reading his newspaper and didn't see her.

The door opened again, this time to reveal Puddle. She was pulling on her coat and still had her hat in her hand.

'Sorry about that, darling,' she said as she put on the cloche hat and fastened it in place with a lethally long pin. 'She's not the warmest of individuals.'

Ellie held the door for her and they clambered into the back of the cab. She gave the driver an address in Wimbledon and settled back to talk to Puddle.

'Why the heck do you stay with her?'

'She's vile, and her husband can be a bit on the lecherous side, but their house is gorgeous. And the rent is so reasonable. I could get much less grief and have my bum ogled far less if I lived somewhere else, but my room is to die for. And they have an inside lav.'

'It certainly does seem like quite a posh place. What does he do for a living?'

'Something junior in the City, I think.'

'They don't seem like the sort of people who would need a lodger.'

'I've always wondered about that, but finding out would entail asking. And asking requires conversation and a little bit of . . . oh, I don't know . . . is "intimacy" too much of a word? But you know what I mean. I'd have to get to know them a good deal better than I'd like, just for the sake of sating my idle curiosity.'

Ellie laughed. 'Well, I hope I haven't caused any trouble.'

'I'd have been on yet another final warning if you'd been a musician, but she noticed your clobber and decided you were too well dressed to be one of us, so your unannounced visit was overlooked just this once.'

'Yet another final warning?'

'Oh, I get one a week, darling. She's never going to throw me out – I'm neat and tidy, I pay my rent on time, and I haven't yet strangled her husband to death for leering at me. I'm a model tenant.'

'It sounds like a perfect arrangement, then,' said Ellie. 'Apart from the bullying and the lechery.'

'It's amazing what one is prepared to put up with in return for a decent billet.'

The taxi headed up to Wandsworth and then turned south again to skirt Wimbledon Common before darting off into one of the many side streets. It pulled up outside an impressive Victorian villa. Ellie thanked the driver and paid the fare, adding a generous tip.

'Thank you very much, ma'am,' he said with an extremely happy smile. 'Do you want me to wait for you?'

'I don't think so,' said Ellie. 'I've no idea how long we'll be.'

'It's no trouble. I reckon you'll have a job getting a cab home if I don't wait. To be honest with you, I'm outside me area a bit. I only have to know the roads six miles from Charing Cross – this is no man's land as far as I'm concerned so I ain't keen on stickin' me flag up out here. Who knows where they'll want to go. I ain't even sure if I'm legal, like, so I'd only be headin' back over the river. You'd be doin' me a favour – it'll give me a fare back to town.'

'Well, if you're sure. I'll make it worth your while.'

'That's settled, then. It's me lunchtime, after all. I'm happy to sit here for a bit and eat me sarnies. My missus makes a lovely fish-paste sandwich.'

'Do you have tea?'

'Got me flask right here,' he said, and patted a holdall on the floor beside him.

'Thank you very much . . . ?'

'Tommy, ma'am. Tommy Butler. Though the lads all call me Tubs.' He patted his ample belly proudly.

'Well, thank you, Tommy. I'll send word if it seems like we'll be too long, and we'll just take our chances. We can get the District Railway from Wimbledon if it comes to it.'

'I'll be here, ma'am,' said Tommy. 'You need an 'and with them cases?'

'No, we're fine, thank you.'

'Right you are. See you in a tick.'

They left him to his fish-paste sandwiches and walked up the garden path to the gleaming front door of the house. Puddle knocked, and moments later the door was answered by a conserva tively dressed middle-aged woman. Puddle had met her before – this was the Adamses' housekeeper.

'Hello,' said Puddle. 'I'm Isabella Puddephatt and this is my friend, Mrs Maloney. Mr and Mrs Adams are expecting me.'

'They are, miss. Please come in.'

The housekeeper took their coats and led them to the drawing room.

◆ ◆ ◆

A tall man wearing a dark jacket and grey trousers leaped to his feet. Ellie had known Blanche long enough to be able to see a family resemblance immediately. There was no doubt that this was her brother.

'Puddle,' he said, holding open his arms for an embrace. 'Thank you for coming.'

Puddle hugged him awkwardly. 'Hello, Bill. This is Ellie Maloney.'

'Skins's wife? I've heard so much about you. Blanche talked about you all the time. Delighted to finally meet you.'

Ellie offered him her hand, but he embraced her, too.

'Please, sit. Grace has taken the children to the Common to give us some peace. I didn't know if you'd want to eat. To tell you the truth, I've not been eating well. I asked Mrs Green – that's our housekeeper, Hilda Green – I asked her to bring us some tea. I hope that's all right. I can get her to make you some sandwiches if you'd prefer. Or anything. I—'

'Bill,' said Puddle kindly. 'It's all right. We're fine. Tea will be lovely.'

'Righto, righto,' said Bill.

He began to pace nervously up and down the room.

'Have you . . . ah . . . have you brought the . . . ah . . . the doo-dah. The whatnot.'

'The sax and clarinet?' said Puddle. 'Yes.'

She took the two cases from Ellie and presented them to him. He took them both, almost reverentially, but didn't open either of them. He placed the smaller case carefully on a side table, and held out the larger one for Puddle.

'Would you do the honours? Would you mind? I understand if you'd rather not, but it would be a great comfort if you'd play a little for me.'

Puddle took the case and opened it up. She was reaching inside when Mrs Green arrived with the tea. The housekeeper fussed about for a few moments, setting cups in saucers and lifting the tea cosy to check the temperature of the pot.

'I'd give it another couple of minutes to steep,' she said. 'Will there be anything else?'

'No, Mrs Green, thank you,' said Bill. 'That's very kind.'

Puddle waited until the housekeeper had withdrawn before assembling the saxophone. She frowned at the mouthpiece as she adjusted the reed, then blew a few experimental notes. She thought for a moment.

'Ellie, darling, would you mind accompanying me on the piano?'

'Of course not,' said Ellie. 'Mr Adams? Would you mind if I . . . ?'

'Bill, please. And no, not at all. It's my wife's but she hardly plays these days. We keep it for the children – the older ones are having lessons. It's important, don't you think? A social skill. I wish I'd kept it up but Blanche was always the musical one in our family. I would be out climbing trees or playing with a rugger ball when I should have been practising. Funny, the things one regrets, isn't it? I had all that time, all those opportunities laid on for me, and I just thought it was a terrible imposition when I could have been having fun instead. And it would have meant spending time indoors with my stupid sister. I couldn't imagine anything more ghastly at the time. I'd give anything to be able to spend time indoors with my stupid sister now.'

He fell silent.

Puddle touched Ellie's arm and nodded towards the piano. 'Do you know "I'll Still Be Dreaming With You"?'

'Barty's song? It's beautiful. I heard it at the Augmented Ninth one night and made him teach me.'

Ellie sat at the piano. She had to think for a moment to remember the introduction, but her fingers knew it. She began to play, and as the verse began, Puddle joined in. Ellie was surprised to realize that she knew the band so well she was able to hear that Puddle wasn't playing her own instrument. It was still Puddle's style – always slightly more precise than Blanche – but the tone was different. The playing was Puddle's, but the tone was unmistakably

Blanche's. It was as though something of Blanche were with them. They all felt it.

When the song was finished, Puddle wordlessly returned the saxophone to its case and closed it. She propped it up beside Bill's chair.

'Thank you,' he said quietly as he wiped his eyes. 'That was rather more emotional than I'd expected. You must forgive me.'

Puddle touched his hand but still said nothing. Ellie poured three cups of tea.

'Have you heard anything from the police?' said Bill suddenly.

'No,' said Ellie. 'No one has. Not even our friend on the force.'

'You have a friend on the police force?'

'More of a recent acquaintance if I'm honest, but a friendly one. He's keeping an eye on things for us.'

'They won't even let us bury her,' he said.

'No, I know,' said Puddle. 'I'm sure it won't be long now.'

'I'm sure the police have already asked you,' said Ellie, 'but did Blanche have any enemies we didn't know of? We only knew her as a friend and a member of the band. I'm not sure any of us knows much about each other's lives outside work.'

'No,' said Bill. 'At least not that I was ever aware of. She was a kind girl. You know she was a nurse in the war? Ma and Pa were furious with her for putting herself in danger like that, but she insisted she had to go and help. That's the sort of girl she was, not the sort to have enemies and be poisoned in gentlemen's clubs.'

'We saw her nursing skills in action one day at the club. She stitched up the dance teacher's arm. It was quite a revelation,' said Puddle. 'She was so calm, so . . . well, so skilful. I'd never really thought about the realities of nursing before. I suppose I always thought it was kind words and cups of tea. Starched uniforms and a smiling face. But she cleaned the wound, stitched it up, and put

264

on a bandage, all the while chatting away about her time in France as though she were having tea with the vicar.'

Bill laughed for the first time. 'That's our Blanche. Are you sure I can't tempt you to some lunch? It really is no trouble. Grace and the progeny will be back soon and they'll be starving after playing on the Common.'

'I think we ought to be getting off,' said Puddle. 'I'm glad we were able to bring you some mementoes of Blanche, and I do so very much hope we can keep in touch, but . . .'

'Things to do, people to see,' he said with a smile. 'I ought to be getting back to the office myself, to tell you the truth. It really is jolly kind of you to have come all this way. Well, Balham's not that far, I don't suppose. But you, Mrs Maloney, you must have come quite a way. Didn't Blanche say you lived in Bloomsbury?'

'Not far from the British Museum, that's right,' said Ellie.

'I'd love to move back into town, but the practice is here so it's just more convenient to stay put. Do you have a car?'

'It's top of my husband's shopping list, but no, not yet. We have a cab waiting.'

'Oh, my goodness,' he said. 'Then you must away. It must be costing you a fortune to have him out there waiting for you. You should have said.'

'Nonsense,' said Ellie. 'We came to a mutually beneficial arrangement. But I would like to let the poor fella get back to his "manor", as I believe you guys say.'

'Quite right. Thank you so much for bringing Blanche's things. And do, please, keep in touch. I know how much she loved you all and it would be a comfort to hear of your successes.'

Following the English fashion, their goodbyes took another five minutes, but eventually Ellie and Puddle made it back to Tommy's cab. He was just putting the lid on his flask when they arrived.

'Perfect timing, ladies,' he said. 'Where to? Balham and Bloomsbury?'

Ellie turned to Puddle. 'Do you have anything to get back for?'

'No, just the usual bullying and lechery. Why?'

'Why not come back to our place. You can hang out there for the afternoon, then stay for dinner. Barty comes round on Thursday evenings and we all eat together. It'll be fun.'

'That sounds like a much better plan, if you're sure you don't mind.'

'Not at all. You get on well with the boys and it'll be nice to have another woman about the place.'

'Thank you very much, then. I'd love to. Oh.'

'Oh?'

'Am I dressed all right for dinner in Bloomsbury? I don't want to show myself up.'

'You goof,' said Ellie. 'We'll skip Balham and head straight for Bloomsbury, please.'

'Right you are, ma'am. Sit back and I'll have you there in a jiffy.'

'Thanks, Tommy,' said Ellie. 'That'll be swell.'

It really didn't hurt to turn up the Yankeeness from time to time – people genuinely seemed to enjoy it.

◆ ◆ ◆

Puddle was playing on the floor with Edward and Catherine when Dunn arrived. Vincent von Bear was hosting a tea party to which Catherine's doll – the inexplicably named Dodo Pickleknickers – had been invited, along with Charlie the Lion and Captain Pointy-Hat of the Household Cavalry. Puddle was having a whale of a time with the miniature tea set, but both children had long since grown bored of the party itself and were busying themselves delivering essential supplies using Edward's tin lorry.

'Looks like you over-ordered on the imaginary cakes there, Pudds,' said Dunn as he sat down to watch. 'That's the fourth lorryload to arrive since I got here.'

'I tried to cancel,' she said, 'but the girl on the other end of the phone just kept saying, "More cakes, more cakes." I don't think there's anything I can do.'

'More cakes,' said Catherine with a giggle, and drove the tin lorry forcefully into Puddle's leg.

'Come on, Maloney Monsters,' said Ellie. 'Time for your bath.'

'Can Isabella read us a story?' asked Edward.

'Isabella?' said Dunn. 'Who's Isabella?'

'She is,' said the children in unison, pointing at Puddle.

'Is she really?' he said. 'Well, I never. But *I* usually read you a story on Thursdays.'

'Oh,' said Edward, earnestly. 'That's a pickle.'

Dunn laughed. 'Isn't it just? I don't mind if you really want Isabella Puddle to read to you. She's not here as often as I am. What do you say, Pudds? Fancy reading a story?'

'I'm sure I'd be delighted,' said Puddle. 'But you have to choose. I want to make sure it's one you'll like.'

'All right,' said Edward. 'Uncle Barty tells us about the Teddy Bear King. We both like those stories.'

Puddle looked imploringly at Dunn for an explanation.

Dunn laughed again. 'She probably doesn't know those. But don't worry – I'll explain it all to her while you're in the bath. She'll be up to speed in no time.'

'You can say no if you want to,' said Ellie.

'Oh, but I'd love to,' said Puddle. 'I can't think of anything I'd enjoy more.'

'You're very lucky kids,' said Ellie. 'Off you go, then, or Nanny will be sending out a search party.'

The children raced out of the room and clattered up the stairs. Puddle began making neat piles of the toys.

'Don't worry about that,' said Ellie. 'Just hoick it all in the box any old how – they'll soon find what they want.'

Together they put the toys into a wooden chest that lived beside the piano.

Skins arrived with a bottle of gin.

'I wondered where you'd got to,' said Puddle. 'I thought you were just avoiding the tidying up.'

'I always avoid the tidying up,' he said. 'But we were also out of gin, so I went down to Mrs P's mysterious pantry to fetch a fresh bottle. What can I get you?'

'Do you have any lemons?' asked Puddle.

'Always.'

'Tom Collins, then, please.'

'Good choice. Ells Bells?'

'I'll have the same if you're making one.'

'Two Tom Collinses coming up. Mr Dunn?'

'Got any of that absinthe left?' said Dunn.

'Loads. You're the only one who drinks it.'

'Sazerac for me, then.'

'They're just showing off 'cause you're here, you know,' said Skins to Puddle with a wink. 'He makes do with a scotch and soda, and she drinks gin straight from the bottle. That's why we keep running out.'

He was a keen and knowledgeable barman, but a slow one. During the laborious mixing process, Dunn had ample opportunity to tell Puddle the story of the Evil Bear King, and by the time the drinks were ready Puddle had to leave to tell the children the next instalment.

By the time Puddle and Ellie returned, Lottie had brought the dinner up from the kitchen and they were able to sit down and eat straight away.

'So, how did it go with Blanche's brother?' said Dunn as he helped himself to potatoes. 'What's he like?'

'He's like a male version of Blanche,' said Ellie.

'Only sadder,' added Puddle.

'Was he pleased with the sax and clarinet?' asked Skins.

'Very,' said Ellie. 'Puddle played for him. It was rather touching.'

'What did you play?' asked Dunn.

'One of yours,' said Puddle. '"I'll Still Be Dreaming With You". With Ellie on piano. It was lovely, actually.'

'She always liked that one,' said Dunn. 'I'm glad it went well.'

'It did,' said Ellie. 'We didn't stay long, though. It wasn't a comfortable experience, to be honest, but I'm glad we were able to take him a memento of his sister. Those instruments were such an important part of her.'

'They were,' agreed Puddle. She tucked into her lamb chop, then frowned at a memory.

'Something wrong with the food, honey?' asked Ellie.

'No, no. Oh my goodness, no. It's delicious. I was just thinking about this afternoon. Did either of you boys mess about with the sax while it was in your pal's shop?'

'Mess about with it?' said Skins. 'What do you mean?'

'Open it up, put it together . . . anything at all.'

'Not us,' said Dunn. 'Why?'

'Oh, it's probably nothing. It's just . . . well, the ligature was on upside down.'

'The boys probably know what you're talking about,' said Ellie. 'But indulge me. What's a ligature?'

'Oh, sorry, darling,' said Puddle. 'Umm . . . you know the mouthpiece – the pointy black bit?'

'With you so far.'

'There's a flat reed on the underneath – that's what makes the noise.'

'You know, when I was a kid I used to think they hummed into them like a kazoo,' said Ellie.

'If only it were that simple. So, the reed is held in place with a band – the ligature. I like the metal cage ones, but Blanche had a fondness for an old leather one she picked up from a music shop in Paris. Anyway, it wraps around the mouthpiece and tightens up with a little screw so it can grip the reed. Mine can only go on one way round, and the screws are always on the right-hand side. Blanche's could go on either way, but out of habit, everyone always puts them on the same way, with the screw on the right.'

'Still with you,' said Ellie. 'Was there something wrong with it?'

'There was. The screw was on the left. It was on the wrong way round.'

'Maybe she was already feeling the effects of the poison,' said Skins. 'You know, a bit disorientated. Just put it on wrong without really thinking about it.'

'Maybe,' said Puddle. 'It's not the sort of thing you have to think about, though. I mean, when you pick up a pair of drumsticks, do you have to work out how to hold them every time? You just grab them and they fall into place without you giving it a second thought. Same with putting on a reed. We do it without thinking.'

'Well, we definitely didn't muck about with it in the shop,' said Skins. 'So it was like that when it went in. Which means it was like that when it left the club.'

'Did anyone touch it there?' asked Ellie.

'She fell on top of it,' said Dunn. 'When the ambulance men carried her off, it just sat there on the stage. We were all just sort of milling about the ballroom after that, while the police asked their questions. Anyone could have touched it. Why?'

'I don't know yet,' said Ellie. 'But it's out of the ordinary, isn't it? In the detective stories it would definitely be a clue.'

'Someone wanted us to look to the left?' said Skins. 'Someone knew who it was but couldn't say, so they left the adjustment screw on the mouthpiece pointing at the killer.'

'Don't be a goof, Ivor, it doesn't become you.'

'It's my most striking characteristic, I'll have you know. You can't take that away from me. All I've got is being a goof.'

Ellie shot him a look. 'Was everyone still there?'

'All the Alphabets?' said Dunn. 'Yes, all present and correct.'

'And Millie?'

'I don't remember. Skins?'

'I think so,' said Skins. 'To be honest I wasn't paying much attention. There was a lot of coming and going, but I think she was there most of the time.'

'Most of the time?' said Ellie.

'Well . . . you know. People were in and out of the room a lot. Calls of nature, private moments and whatnot. I wasn't keeping track, but I'm pretty sure I saw her in the room a couple of times when I looked round.'

'What are you thinking?' asked Puddle.

'I don't know yet,' said Ellie. 'I'm just trying to come at it from a different angle. We've only been thinking about the boys so far. We've never talked about Millie much.'

'Why would we?' said Dunn. 'We've been on the lookout for an army deserter. We ruled her out early on – it would be a bloody good disguise if old Arthur Grant was posing as Millie Mitchell the dance teacher.'

271

'What do we know about her?' said Ellie. 'What have you learned from three weeks of ogling?'

'I was not—' said Skins and Dunn together.

'I bloody was,' said Puddle. 'She's gorgeous. You know how some people just . . . I don't know . . . shine? Glow? She draws all eyes to her.'

'Other than her obvious physical charms, though, what do you actually know about the woman herself?' said Ellie.

'Definitely a professional dancer,' said Skins. 'She moves like she'd been training since she was a kid.'

'Apart from her limp,' said Dunn.

'Her limp what?' said Skins with a grin.

'Are you going to do that gag every time?' said Puddle. 'It's not getting any funnier.'

'It was Barty last time,' said Skins. 'But give it a chance. Fifth time you hear it, you'll not be able to stop yourself giggling.'

'I noticed her limping,' said Ellie. 'A dance injury?'

'We asked her about that,' said Blanche. 'She said she went over on her ankle and it never healed right. Damaged her AQMG or something.'

'Assistant Quartermaster-General?' said Dunn.

'Probably not,' said Puddle. 'But it was initials. And it started with A.'

'Oh, she's right,' said Skins. 'AT-something.'

'ATFL?' suggested Ellie. 'The anterior talofibular ligament is down there. You might tear it if you go over on your ankle.'

'She was a nurse, you know,' said Skins with a wink.

'Was she?' said Ellie.

'No, you chump – you. You were a nurse.'

'Oh, I was, yes. That's how I know what a torn ATFL is. Because I was a nurse . . .'

Chapter Fifteen

'I'm well aware that he's busy, Sergeant,' said Ellie with growing irritation. 'And I know what he's busy with. Which is precisely why we very much need to speak to him now. How much actual effort would it entail to call him and tell him we're here? What would it cost you? If he tells you to tell us to . . . to "bugger off" – which he won't, by the way, he's much too much of a gentleman for that – well, then, what's the worst that can happen? You'll get a flea in your ear for bothering him? You're afraid of someone being a bit tetchy with you? That's hardly the attitude that won us the war.'

'I'm quite sure "we" didn't win the war, madam. It had been going more than two and a half years before your lot turned up.'

'And yet you fought on without us all that time. If only the Bosch had known that all they needed to do was speak sternly to you and you'd fold like a broken umbrella, we'd not have had to turn up at all. And you'd be speaking German.'

'Now, you look here—'

'Just make the call, Sergeant,' said Puddle. 'You know she's right, and we all know she's not going to back down.'

Skins and Dunn just smiled.

The desk sergeant scowled, but picked up the telephone from his desk.

'Put me through to Superintendent Sunderland, would you, please, love?' he said while still scowling at the four friends. 'I know what he said, but can you put me through anyway?' He covered the mouthpiece with his hand. 'I told you.' He uncovered it again. 'It's Fenimore, sir. Front desk . . . Yes, I know, sir. I'm very sorry, sir. But there are four individuals here who insist I interrupt your important work.' He looked pointedly at them. Then he looked down at the paper on his desk. 'Mr and Mrs Maloney, Mr Dunn, and Miss Pontefract . . . It could be Puddephatt, sir, yes.' He laughed nervously. 'Can't read me own writing sometimes . . . Right you are, sir . . . Right away, sir.'

He replaced the telephone receiver in its cradle.

'Cooper!' he called loudly.

Constable Cooper arrived.

'Take this lot to Superintendent Sunderland's office, lad. Third floor.'

Without looking at the four friends, he returned to his work and left Cooper to conduct them up the stairs.

◆ ◆ ◆

Sunderland's voice drifted out from his open office door.

'. . . and put some of those new McVitie's biscuits out, too, please. The chocolate ones.'

An eager young constable scurried out.

'And put them on a plate this time,' called Sunderland.

The constable gave the friends an embarrassed smile as he set off down the corridor.

Cooper knocked on the open door and said, 'Your visitors, sir.'

He stood aside to let them in and Sunderland stood to greet them.

'Welcome, all,' he said, warmly. 'I'm glad you've come over. Perfect timing. Do sit down. There's tea on the way. And biscuits.'

'We heard,' said Skins.

'On a plate,' said Dunn.

'He just piled a handful on the tray last time. I mean, I ask you. Is it too much to ask for a plate?'

'Got to maintain standards,' said Dunn. 'Whole place'll go to pot.'

'You're teasing me now, and quite right, too,' said Sunderland. 'But all I wanted was a plate. Anyway, good to see you all again. Or see most of you again. We've not met . . . Miss Puddephatt, I presume? Oliver Sunderland.'

He held out his hand and Puddle shook it.

'They call me Puddle,' she said.

'Do they? Do they, indeed? And do you mind?'

She laughed. 'I rather like it.'

'Splendid. I have news about your friend. But you must have known that or you'd not be here.'

'No,' said Ellie, 'we've not heard a thing. Actually, we have news of our own.'

'Ah, I see,' he said. 'Well, I'll start, then you can tell me what you've learned. Mine is rather grim news, I'm afraid, but it does move things along. The police surgeon examined Miss Adams again at my insistence and discovered traces of an unknown substance in her mouth, mostly on her tongue. He'd missed it before, but when we spoke about her stomach being free of poison I insisted he take another look. He's not entirely sure what it is, but he's inclined to suppose it could well be some sort of toxin, absorbed through the' – he consulted the file on his desk – 'mucous membranes of the mouth. He lists a handful of possible agents. He said such a poison could take anything from a few seconds to an hour to have its effect, but when death came it would be sudden.' He pushed the file to one side. 'I'm terribly sorry – poison is all but confirmed, and it happened at the Aristippus Club.'

Puddle had gone white, but they had to wait for the young constable to finish fussing with the tea he'd brought in before they could ask her what was wrong.

'Are you OK, honey?' said Ellie when the young policeman had finally gone. 'You look dreadful.'

'It was the sax,' said Puddle. 'And it could have killed me.'

'The saxophone?' said Sunderland. 'Miss Adams's saxophone? How could it have killed you?'

'I played it yesterday. For her brother. He's still devastated.'

'Then it can't have been the sax,' said Ellie. 'You've been absolutely fine.'

'The killer swapped the reed,' said Puddle. 'Don't you see? You remember I told you the ligature was on the wrong way round? Someone swapped it after she died. The killer swapped it.'

'Slow down a moment, please,' said Sunderland. 'Actually, let's go back a step or two. You're saying the poison was on the saxophone's mouthpiece? What makes you think that?'

Puddle briefly told the story of their visit to Wimbledon the day before. She explained how the reed was attached to the mouthpiece, and about her momentary confusion at seeing the ligature on the wrong way round.

'The reed touches the tongue when we play,' she continued, 'and you said the poison was on her tongue. So, what if the killer poisoned the reed, then swapped it for an untainted one after she was dead so that no one would suspect how it was done?'

'That would be ingenious indeed,' said Sunderland. 'Though not without risk. He must have known that interfering with the instrument a second time would double his chances of being caught.'

'Perhaps the second time wasn't planned,' said Puddle. 'If he swapped the reed for a poisoned one but had the original reed in his pocket, he might have seen an opportunity to put things back to normal while everyone was milling about waiting for the police to finish their questions.'

'It's a starting point,' said Sunderland. He made some notes in the case file. 'I have other news,' he said when he'd finished. 'We finally managed to track down your Mr Daniels's record.'

'Is he our man?' said Dunn. 'Is that why he was being so cagey?'

'No,' said Sunderland. 'No, the reason for his reticence was that he was a conscientious objector.'

'A conchie?' said Skins. 'Danny? He doesn't come across as the type. I thought they were all religious sorts. "Thou shalt not kill" and all that.'

'Many were, it's true. His record doesn't give his reasons, but it does tell a remarkable story. He was an ambulance driver in the RAMC and he was awarded the Military Medal for carrying the wounded from no man's land under fire during a major offensive. He saved eight lives.'

'Blimey,' said Skins. 'And you're sure it's the same bloke?'

'He's known to the authorities,' said Sunderland. 'They kept tabs on him after the war – it makes me wonder if his objections were more political, actually, now I come to think of it. But it's definitely him.'

'A lot of conscientious objectors joined the medical corps,' said Ellie. 'I met a few.'

'Some did,' agreed Sunderland. 'Not as many as the stories suggest, but there were a few, as you say. And Dudley Daniels was a particularly brave one.'

'So that leaves Charlie,' said Dunn.

'It's looking very much like it,' said Sunderland. 'None of the Robert Chandlers we've looked at so far match the Alphabet Gang's

"Charlie", so I'm very much thinking of pulling him in and having a quiet word.'

'Before you do, though,' said Ellie, 'can you check one more thing for me?'

Sunderland frowned quizzically. 'You have something else?'

'Just a hunch,' she said. 'Can you look and see if there was a nurse called Millie Mitchell in the Fannies or the VAD?'

'I can ask. She's the dance teacher, yes?'

'She is.'

'And you think she might have been a nurse?'

'It was something she said to Puddle. She has a limp and said she got it when she tore her ATFL. She said exactly that. She didn't say "a ligament in my ankle", or even give it its full name. Just the initials, like a medic might.'

'You think they're in it together?' said Skins.

'I've no idea,' she said. 'But it's suspicious, don't you think? A military man whose records are difficult to track down and a dance teacher who uses medical jargon.'

'I'll make some calls and see what I can dig up,' said Sunderland. 'Any more bombshells before I order more biscuits?'

'No,' said Ellie. 'I think that's it for now.'

'Excellent. Just a word of warning – I'm about to shout very loudly. Please don't be alarmed.' He paused for a second before calling, 'Curtis! More biscuits, please!'

They left Scotland Yard and went their separate ways. It was Friday – the Friday of the dance contest, no less – and both Puddle and Dunn needed to get home for a rest and a change of clothes before the big night. It was a special night for the club, so the band had decided that best bib and tucker were in order.

Ellie and Skins went back to Bloomsbury with no real plans at all. Skins quite liked the going-back-to-bed option suggested by Dunn, but he was open to suggestions. Ellie didn't have any suggestions – she wanted to call her friend Flo to ask for some advice.

By the time they were ready to leave for the club, Skins had had his nap and a bath, and Ellie had spoken to Flo – so they were both content that things had worked out well.

'What do you reckon?' said Skins as he laced his dress shoes. 'Cab or Shanks's pony?'

'It's a lovely evening for a walk,' said Ellie. 'But maybe not in these shoes.'

She, too, had decided to dress up for the evening and was wearing an extravagantly embroidered cocktail dress of gold silk, set off with a pair of gold-coloured shoes decorated with velvet.

'You're probably right. These won't be much better.' He indicated his own two-tone brogues. 'They look the part, but they need a bit of breaking in before I'll be happy traipsing all the way to Mayfair in them. I'll go out and see if I can flag a cab.'

'Get Lottie to do it,' said Ellie as she adjusted her headdress. 'That's what we have servants for.'

'Poor kid doesn't want to be standing out on the street whistling at taxis. I'll do it.'

He left Ellie to finish getting ready.

He returned five minutes later. 'Got one. You all set?'

'Ready as I'll ever be,' she said.

'You make it sound like we're off to something awful. It's the dance contest. It'll be a laugh.'

Ellie said nothing as she followed him out to the cab. They clambered in and settled down in the back.

'What are you up to?' he said.

'Nothing. Why?'

'You look like you're up to something, that's all. I know you.'

'Just concentrate on keeping the band in time. I'll look after myself.'

'You're not doing anything to reassure me.'

'Ivor?'

'Yes, love?'

'Shut your trap, there's a good boy.'

'Right you are, my angel.'

Once they'd arrived, Ellie left Skins to join the band in the green room while she went to talk to Cuthbert the head porter.

'Good evening, madam,' he said. 'All set for the dance contest this evening? The club is fair buzzing with it.'

'All set, yes,' said Ellie. 'My boys and girls won't let you down.'

'Glad to hear it. Can I help you with something?'

She leaned conspiratorially across the counter. 'As a matter of fact,' she said quietly, 'I think you might.'

'Go on.'

'This club means everything to you, doesn't it? You'd be personally affronted if a member turned out to be . . . an impostor; if someone were to bring the club into disrepute.'

'I can't think of anything worse, madam,' said Cuthbert.

'I have a strong suspicion about one of the members.' She held up a hand to stay his questions. 'I can't say anything yet, but I might be able to settle matters if I could just take a look at the rooms register. Presumably you have such a thing? A record of which member is using which bedroom?'

'We do, madam, but it's strictly confidential. I couldn't possibly—'

'It's a dilemma, I know. Do you protect the privacy of the members, or do you protect the reputation and the secrets of the club itself? I don't know what I'd do, to be honest.'

Cuthbert thought about it for a moment. 'Come with me.'

He lifted the counter flap and led her through to a small office. He lifted a leather-bound ledger from a shelf and placed it on the cluttered desk.

'Oh, I'm so sorry, madam. I've just remembered I need to attend to something outside. That ledger's confidential, mind you, so I trust you not to look.'

When he had gone, Ellie flipped it open and riffled through the pages until she found the entry she needed. She took a key from one of the numbered hooks on a board on the office wall, closed the book, and stepped out to re-join him.

She touched his arm. 'I don't want to trouble you further,' she said. 'I'll get back to the band.'

'Good luck this evening, madam,' he said.

She smiled her thanks and headed for the stairs.

Ellie found the room she was looking for and, after casting a cautious glance up and down the corridor, knocked smartly on the door. She had no reason for being there other than snooping, and could think of no excuses she could offer the room's occupant if they happened to be inside, so she skipped stealthily away to hide in an alcove a few yards along the corridor.

She listened for nearly a minute but no one answered her knock. She walked back along the carpeted passageway and used the key to open the door.

She entered the stylishly appointed bedroom and looked around. It was neat and orderly, and if it weren't for two leather Gladstone bags on the floor at the foot of the bed, she would have assumed it to be unoccupied. There was a leather satchel and a make-up box on the writing desk by the window, and a few papers stacked neatly on the blotter.

She took a look through the papers. She found two passports and a pair of tickets for the boat train from London to Paris the following morning. Looking further, she found two tickets for the Simplon Orient Express from Paris to Istanbul leaving on Monday. They were about to make a run for it.

Superintendent Sunderland would have to be told about the tickets, but she couldn't leave yet. There was something else she hoped to find.

She began with the satchel. Personal papers. A journal. A novel by a writer she'd never heard of. A semi-automatic pistol. A soft leather drawstring bag about the size of her hand. A small, elegant case covered in red velvet.

Ellie had grown up around guns and considered herself competent in handling them. She took out the pistol and inspected it closely, even going so far as checking the fully loaded magazine. She replaced the gun in the satchel.

The prize, though, was the small leather bag. She took it out and pulled open the top. As she'd expected, it was full of shiny, yellowish pebbles of various sizes, some as big as raspberries. Or, at least, she'd expected it to contain raw, uncut diamonds, but she hadn't quite expected them to look like that. They looked more like glittery metal than the duller version of the sparkling gems she had expected. She was fascinated. She tipped some into her hand and rolled them about. Thousands of pounds' worth of uninspiring rocks in the palm of her hand.

She put the diamonds back in the leather pouch and returned it to the satchel exactly where it had lain.

She looked around.

She knew who they were. She knew where they were going. She knew what they were taking with them. She suspected she knew what they had done. But she couldn't prove it. Yet.

She needed to find something else. It would be small. It would be hidden. They may already have dumped it in the trash a long way from the club, but she doubted it. As far as they were concerned, no one knew what they had done. No one knew what to look for. They were safe. All they needed to do was to get away, then they could dispose of the evidence a hundred miles from the scene of the crime and no one would ever know.

She began a systematic search of the room. She started with the make-up case. It was full of the expected powders and brushes, several lipsticks in subtly different shades of dark red, a box of 'Maybelline Eyelash Beautifier', and assorted other cosmetic items, none of them cheap.

But she wouldn't keep it with her make-up. It was too dangerous to have it near things she'd be applying directly to her face, to her eyes.

Ellie moved on to the Gladstone bags on the floor. The first was his. Of course it was. With a choice of two near-identical bags, the one she went for first would obviously not be the one she wanted most to look at. Carefully, she took everything out and arranged it neatly on the floor. Clothes, underclothes, a sponge bag, a leather case containing shoe brushes and polish. A large bundle of cash. Nothing you wouldn't expect to find in a 'get the heck out' bag, as her Aunt Adelia had called them. Ellie put everything back exactly as she had found it.

The other bag seemed as though it was going to be equally disappointing. More clothes, more everyday personal items. She was beginning to think her reasoning had been faulty, that the evidence had already been carted away by the council dustmen. But then she came upon a small rectangular cigarette tin. She had never seen Millie smoke.

She used one of the silk scarves she had placed neatly on the floor to pick up the tin. Still holding it with the scarf, she prised off the lid and looked inside. Wrapped in tissue paper were the two things she had hoped to find. She replaced the lid and returned everything to the bag.

She took one last look around to make sure she had left no trace of her presence, then carefully opened the door and looked up and down the corridor to make sure the coast was clear.

Locking the door behind her, she hurried back to the porter's desk.

◆ ◆ ◆

Downstairs, Ellie thanked Cuthbert for all his help and then let herself quietly into the green room. The band had already gone out to the ballroom. She'd been hoping to have a word with Skins and Dunn before the dance to let them know what was going on, but that bird had sailed. Or the ship had flown. Either way, they'd have to watch things unfold with no forewarning. But they were jazz musicians – they were used to improvising. It would be fine.

She went out to the ballroom.

There was an older club member on the stage, talking to the band and handing out what looked like sheets of music. There were earnest nods from the musicians, and then a smile from the club member as he shook Mickey's hand and stepped down on to the dance floor.

The Dizzy Heights began to play Puddle's arrangement of 'Where Did You Get That Hat?' It had become a Friday night favourite with the club members, who had devised a new dance to go with it, complete with actions. Such was the excitement surrounding the dance contest that even the fustier members had found their way to the ballroom, and the familiarity of the song – even in its new, jazz style – had inspired several of them to attempt to join in the dance.

Ellie tried to attract Skins's attention, but he thought she was just saying hello and waved a cheery greeting in return. She rolled her eyes, shook her head, and went to look for Charlie and Millie. She wanted to make sure she knew where they were in case they did a bunk before Superintendent Sunderland and his men could get there.

She spotted them dancing together, surrounded by the rest of the Alphabet Gang. There were smiles and laughter. The two of them looked as though they hadn't a care in the world, and Ellie was confident they weren't going to draw attention to themselves by making a dash for it until after the dance contest. She relaxed and made her way to a table near the stage. She flagged down a passing Cuthbert and ordered herself a Tom Collins – she'd rather enjoyed the one Skins had made her the night before.

The room filled rapidly and split into two mutually friendly – but still very obvious – factions. At the far end of the hall were the members of Tipsy Harry's and their dates, with the Alphabets still at the centre of things. Or most of them, anyway. Of Alfie and Ernie there was no sign, but Ellie knew they'd be off in a side room somewhere getting themselves into their horse costume.

Towards the stage were the strangers, clearly the members of the Wags Club and their guests. They were more colourfully dressed than their competitors, and their behaviour was just a little more raucous. These were London's good-time boys and girls, without a doubt. But they were amiable enough, and Ellie was rather enjoying sitting in their midst as they larked about with the five men who obviously comprised their dance team. They were identically dressed in purple mess jackets, with matching purple bow ties. Their shoes were wingtip brogues in purple and white. They very much looked the part and Ellie had a momentary twinge of fear that the Alphabets were going to be hopelessly outclassed. But then they moved. They were every bit as uncoordinated and inept as her new pals, and she was able to relax and take a sip of her cocktail.

Eventually, the time for the contest had arrived.

There were three loud knocks on the ballroom door, as though it had been struck with something large and heavy. This was the signal for the Dizzies to play an elaborate fanfare from the sheet music that had been given to them when Ellie arrived.

The crowd fell silent and the band struck up a slow, ceremonial march as the club officials entered the room.

Dressed in heavy embroidered cloaks, the three men moved in solemn procession across the hall, the crowd parting before them.

They reached the stage and the band fell silent.

'With the key of keys,' intoned the first man, holding up a large golden key.

'And the tree of trees,' said the second, holding up an intricately carved wooden staff.

'And the knee of knees,' said the third, lifting his cloak to reveal that one of his legs was bare.

There was a cheer from the crowd.

The first official held up his hand for silence. 'We declare this dance contest . . . open.'

Another cheer.

The second official waved the staff, while the third – his knee now covered once more – unrolled a scroll and began to read.

As he outlined the rules and format of the contest, Ellie noticed some movement at the main door. Charlie and Millie had entered the ballroom – they must have left while she was watching the dancers. Slowly but purposefully, they were making their way towards the stage.

By the time the club official had finished reading the rules and regulations from his scroll, Charlie and Millie were right at the front; and as the officials processed from the ballroom, they left with them.

Ellie couldn't get to Charlie and Millie, nor did she have a firm idea of what she'd do if she managed to catch up. Once again she tried to attract Skins's attention, but he was too busy listening for jokes in the compère's speech and adding drum stings. He was in his element and was not to be distracted, not even by his wife.

Ellie made a snap decision and followed them.

◆ ◆ ◆

By the time Ellie made it through the crowd and out of the ballroom, Charlie and Millie were heading up the stairs.

She was confused. She'd assumed they were trailing after the club officials and that they had some plan to steal the club regalia before it was locked away. But now they were heading back upstairs, presumably to Charlie's bedroom to get their gear.

What could she do about it? If she challenged them before they did anything, they'd laugh in her face and tell her to scram. If she challenged them once they'd stolen the key and staff . . . well, then what? There was just one of her and two of them. Who knows what they might be prepared to do to her?

She decided she didn't really have a choice. She dashed to the porter's desk and spoke urgently to Cuthbert, then followed Charlie and Millie up the stairs.

As she reached the landing and looked at the closed bedroom door, she was forced to wonder once again what she had hoped to achieve by pursuing them. Did she think she could stop them? Not on her own, certainly.

Feeling immensely foolish, she turned and headed back towards the stairs. She was two steps down when she heard a bedroom door open and then close again. They'd left the room. Her instinct was to hurry back down the stairs, but what if they'd gone the other way? She peered round the wall at the top of the stairs and saw . . . an empty corridor.

There was another way down. Of course there was. They would have known that. They knew the Cuthberts were watching the front door, so they were using the back stairs. The back door. She hurried along the corridor in pursuit. Then she stopped. Again – what the heck was she doing? What did she imagine she was going to achieve if she caught up with them? Was she going to stop them? Persuade them to hand themselves in? Fight them?

She pressed on. She'd figure it out when it happened.

At the end of the corridor she turned a corner and saw the heel of Millie's shoe disappearing through another door. These must be the back stairs. She followed.

It was some sort of servants' staircase – plainly painted and uncarpeted. She could hear Charlie and Millie's footsteps clonking on the wooden stairs. She took off her own shoes and padded down on stockinged feet.

Another door opened below her and the footsteps were gone. She didn't want to lose them now, not after all this, but she didn't want to blunder into them, either. She gave them a few more moments and then hurried quietly down the rest of the stairs. Slowly and carefully, she opened the door at the bottom and peeped out.

She was at the far end of the portrait corridor and had taken slightly longer than she had imagined. Millie was already coming out of the side room and following Charlie towards the secret door to the senior members' wine cellar.

Ellie was still wary of following them – it might be weeks before anyone found her body in a secret wine cellar – but she had to know what was going on. Once the door had clicked shut behind them, she hurried down and opened it a crack, attempting to listen to what was going on inside.

'So the key goes in . . . here,' said Charlie's distant voice. 'And the staff fits in . . . here . . . and . . .'

'And nothing,' said Millie.

'But it's supposed to . . . I mean, the diary said . . .'

'I told you we were wasting our bloody time,' said Millie. 'All this preparation for nothing. I don't know why I ever believed you. Secret treasure, my Aunt Fanny. That bloke saw you coming. Sold you a fake diary and you bloody believed him. We could have been in Nice all this time, sipping cocktails. But no, Arthur bloody Grant has to get just one more big haul because he knows where the Treasure of the Mayfair Murderer is.'

'We've still got time. We can work this out.'

'We haven't got time. They're going to notice we're missing and then even those idiots are going to start putting two and two together and coming up with the murder of a musician. We've got to get out. Now. Let's take your diamonds and go to Istanbul like we planned. We can vanish and they'll never find us. We don't need your phantom treasure.'

'No, wait . . .'

'No, I'm going. Give me the bag.'

Charlie gave a frustrated grunt and Ellie heard footsteps on the stone steps. She hurried back along the corridor and hid once more behind the door to the servants' stairs.

She gave them time to get on their way down the portrait corridor, then peeped cautiously round the door again.

She was confronted by one of the most absurd sights she had ever beheld. And she was the wife of a mischievous musician and the mother of two frankly bonkers children, so it was up against some pretty stiff competition. As she emerged once more into the portrait corridor of the Aristippus Club of Mayfair, she found Charlie and Millie wrestling with a horse.

'Get out of the bloody way, Alfie, you idiot,' said Charlie.

A muffled voice from the horse's neck said, 'Charlie? Charlie, is that you? Thank god you're here. We were on our way to the ballroom but we got lost. No idea where we are at all. I can't see a blessed thing in here. And the fasteners are stuck so Ernie can't get out and help.'

'I couldn't give a tuppenny one what you and that idiot are up to. Just get out of the way.'

'But . . . the contest,' said Ernie plaintively.

Charlie tried to push past again but became even more tangled up with the two men and their horse costume.

'Leave it,' said Millie. 'We'll just have to go back the other way.'

'You could try,' said Ellie with a menacing calmness she didn't truly feel. 'But you'd have to get past me. The jig, as they say, is up. I know what you did.'

'You?' snarled Millie. 'And what the bloody hell do you imagine you're going to do?'

Charlie had the satchel slung over his shoulder. He was still struggling with Alfie and Ernie so Millie flipped open the cover and reached inside the bag. Her hand re-emerged holding the pistol Ellie had seen earlier.

'We've put up with that bunch of witless fools for longer than anyone should have to, and we're not staying another second. You aren't going to stop us.'

'I've called the police and they're on their way,' said Ellie.

'No, they're not,' said Millie.

'They've been on to you for weeks. Months probably,' said Ellie. 'I just confirmed a few things for them.'

'On to us? Don't make me laugh. How could they be on to us? No one knew what we were doing.'

'You were going to open the secret vault with the "Key of Keys" after the opening ceremony and make off with the Treasure of the Mayfair Murderer.'

Millie's mouth fell open. 'You knew about . . . How did she know about that . . . Bob . . . Charlie? Did you blab?'

Charlie was still trying to free himself from the horse costume. 'Bit busy at the moment, my sweet. You deal with it, there's a good girl.'

'The only thing we couldn't figure out,' said Ellie, 'is where the entrance is.'

Millie laughed. 'And I suppose you imagine I'm going to tell you while you threaten me with . . . Oh, no. Actually, I'm the one with the gun, aren't I? I think the location of the door to the vault will have to remain a secret. If we can't have it, no one can. Hands on head, on your knees, and face the wall.'

Ellie didn't move.

'Don't think I won't shoot you, you soppy Yank,' said Millie. She pulled back the gun's tiny hammer with her thumb and it clicked menacingly into place.

'Oh, I don't doubt you'll try,' said Ellie. 'Great weapon, the Colt M1911. Designed by John Browning, you know. Fires a .45 slug that can stop a full-grown man in his tracks.'

She took a step towards Millie.

There was another metallic click.

'But only if the gun is loaded,' said Ellie, holding out a handful of gleaming brass and lead cartridges. 'You idiot.' She let them cascade to the floor.

Millie let out a roar of rage and charged towards Ellie, swinging the empty pistol at her head.

Ellie stepped inside the swing and brought her open palm up into Millie's unprotected jaw. Millie went down – as Skins would have said, had he been there – like a sack of spuds.

Charlie, meanwhile, had managed to disentangle himself from the pantomime horse and had turned to follow Millie. He saw his lover's prostrate form and the savage glower on Ellie's face, and thought better of trying to take her on. Better, perhaps, just to charge straight past her and get away.

As he ran at her, Ellie dropped into a crouch, getting her body low. The corridor should have been wide enough for him to breeze past her without any trouble, but Ellie wasn't keen to let him pass. When he was almost level with her, she launched herself at his waist, wrapping her arms around him and bringing him down with an almighty 'Oof!' from the pair of them.

He caught his head on the wall as he fell, and by the time he hit the floor he was out cold.

'I say,' said Ernie's muffled voice. 'Is everyone all right? You couldn't get us out of here, could you? We've got a dance contest to get to.'

Chapter Sixteen

Superintendent Sunderland's men had arrived within minutes of Cuthbert's call, and had cleared the ballroom quickly and efficiently once Charlie and Millie were arrested. The names of all those in attendance had been taken, along with brief statements, and the majority had been given leave to return to their homes. Or, more likely, to find a nightclub where they could sink a few cocktails and talk about the extraordinary night they'd just had at Tipsy Harry's.

The only ones still there by the time Ellie had finished giving her account to Sunderland were the Dizzy Heights and what remained of the Alphabet Gang. Alfie and Ernie had been freed from their costume but had declined to get changed, preferring instead to sit in their vests, still wearing the horse's legs as trousers. They didn't want to miss anything.

The two groups were at opposite ends of the ballroom, with the band on the stage and the four remaining Alphabets sitting around a table in the far corner. Sunderland left Ellie with her friends and set off towards the centre of the hall, making a few more notes in his ever-present notebook as he went.

The Alphabet Gang huddled together slightly and then Danny leaned back.

'I think you owe us all an explanation,' he said. 'Just what exactly has been going on here?'

'I rather think you are owed an explanation, sir, yes,' said Sunderland. 'Might I prevail upon you to come down here by the stage so I don't have to shout?'

The four men stood. Alfie grabbed the open champagne bottle, which prompted the others to turn back for their glasses. Bertie took another two bottles, both unopened, from tables as they passed, while Danny and Ernie made an effort to gather enough glasses for the band. They settled themselves at a table by the stage and Mickey and Elk scampered down to get drinks for their colleagues.

'So, Charlie was a wrong'un, then?' said Alfie.

'As wrong as they come, sir, yes,' said Sunderland.

'And he did for that poor gel in the band?'

'No,' said Ellie. 'That was Millie.'

'Good lord,' said Alfie. 'Millie the dance teacher?'

'Yes, sir,' said Sunderland.

'But she was an angel,' said Alfie, still somewhat confused.

'Let him explain, Alfie,' said Danny. 'You can ask your questions afterwards.'

'Thank you, sir,' said Sunderland. 'A couple of members of the band already know most of the story. I don't want to burn anyone's bridges for them, but I always think honesty is the best policy. About a month ago I got in touch with two gentlemen I first met in a little village in Gloucestershire in 1908. They were your Mr Maloney and Mr Dunn. The . . . rhythm section of the band. Is that right? Rhythm section?'

There were nods and murmurs of agreement from the Dizzies.

'When I first met them I was a humble inspector in the Bristol CID, but now I'm a superintendent with the Metropolitan Police, attached to the War Office. And my current assignment is tracking down deserters.'

There were more murmurs, this time from the Alphabet Gang, and they weren't quite so approving.

Sunderland held up his hand and the muttering ceased. 'One particular deserter had popped into our line of sight – a man by the name of Arthur Grant. He was a farm labourer from Norfolk who was conscripted in 1916, and then disappeared a year later with something that wasn't in any way his to disappear with. Deserted his post, deserted his pals, and did a bunk with twenty-five thousand pounds' worth of uncut diamonds.'

There were appreciative whistles this time.

'Quite,' continued Sunderland. 'A very rich Belgian man was suddenly a very poor Belgian man, and Arthur Grant was on the run. Nobody knew what happened to him. Until now. Thanks to Messrs Maloney and Dunn, and especially to Mrs Maloney and Miss Puddephatt, we've been able to fill in the rest of the story.'

More murmurs of appreciation and a pat on the back for Puddle.

'We now know that Grant didn't escape alone. He went on the run in the company of a young nurse by the name of Annie Madigan. By all accounts she was a nasty piece of work, and I shan't be surprised if we learn that she was actually the brains behind everything. Grant was a lazy chancer according to his record, and I've always wondered how he managed to go from skiving sentry duty to masterminding a jewel theft in the space of a couple of months. Now I think I know – it was Madigan. Anyway, the pair of them vanished. They couldn't get home without papers, and even crossing France was a risk, but it seems they had a stroke of luck. Tired and hungry, they happened upon an Advanced Dressing Station – this is supposition, mind you, but they certainly ended up at such a place. I'd wager the plan was for Madigan to bring her "patient" in, get some food for them both and a bed for the night, and vanish again in the morning. Tragically – but to the immense good fortune of Grant and Madigan – a German plane crashed into the aid station. It had been shot down and witnesses said they could see the pilot was trying to get the aeroplane clear, but there was nothing he could do. Everyone was killed.'

'Good lord,' said Alfie.

'Madigan, it seems, wasn't quite as shocked as you, Mr Rawson,' said Sunderland. 'She saw only opportunity. They must have searched the wreckage of the aid station until they found what she was looking for – identity papers and records for two likely candidates – and came upon Captain Robert Chandler and Nurse Millie Mitchell. Once they had what they wanted, they went on their way, leaving the chaos behind them. I can't be certain how they managed to see out the last few months of the war and get home, but somehow they did. We had trouble tracing the whereabouts of the real Robert Chandler because his records were incomplete at the War Office. When we learned of the dressing station story I was able to see that that's where the Chandler trail ended. It made it seem possible that Grant had turned into Chandler and had then vanished again. With a small fortune in diamonds behind them, they were able to set themselves up in considerable luxury in London with genuine papers and no one aware that the real Chandler and Mitchell had died in France. Madigan had been a chorus girl before the war and it seems she went back to it before an injury put a stop to her ambitions for good. Then they fell in with you gentlemen. We knew nothing of their whereabouts until we had a couple of tip-offs from one of our informants.' Sunderland had no intention of revealing that the informant had been Cuthbert, the head porter – a reliable man inside a gentlemen's club was too good a resource to waste by revealing his identity. 'We learned that Grant had somehow been linked with a group of new recruits to the Aristippus Club. And we also heard that someone was planning to steal the legendary Treasure of the Mayfair Murderer. We reasoned it might very well be our man Grant.'

'Mayfair Murderer, indeed,' said Bertie. 'Are we still going on about that? Load of old tosh if you ask me. Ain't no such thing.'

'Charlie – or Grant, I suppose I should say – knew different,' said Ellie. 'Or he thought he did, anyway. He and Millie – Annie – were down in the senior members' wine cellar with the "Key of Keys" and the "Tree of Trees" thinking they could open the secret vault containing the lost treasure. It didn't work. I heard Millie saying something about a diary so my guess is that Charlie bought a diary from a man in a pub, believing it held the secret to the treasure. He was conned.'

'That's my assumption, too,' said Sunderland. 'So, thanks to Mrs Maloney, we caught Grant and Madigan before they could do a bunk to the Continent. It's a shame the diary was a fake in a way – I'd quite like to know if the treasure is real. But anyway, the rest of the story you know.'

'We bloody don't,' said Danny. 'What about Miss Adams? And how did you come to find all this out? What about the Dizzy Heights? How have they helped you?'

'Credit where it's due,' said Sunderland. 'I think Mrs Maloney ought to explain that.'

'Oh,' said Ellie. 'Umm, OK. Well, I only gave the superintendent an idea of where to look for the records and the story. It was Millie's ankle injury, you see. She referred to her torn ligament using a bit of medical jargon. I knew it because I was a Fanny – shut up, Ivor – but no one else would have.'

'Hardly conclusive, though, what?' said Bertie.

'No, you're right,' said Ellie. 'But later I remembered something about her arm as well. She gashed her arm at a dance one night and Blanche stitched her up. A couple of days later, she told me she'd removed the stitches herself. It didn't strike me as particularly odd at the time because I could remove my own stitches as well. But then, I'd been a nurse. Which suggested that she might have been one, too. And that, I suspect, was what got Blanche killed. When Blanche stitched her up in the green room she was chatting away and Blanche told a story about the war. She said she'd been home on leave and was on her way to her ADS but never made it because it was destroyed by a crashed aeroplane. Millie must have had kittens when she heard that. Fancy bumping into someone after all this time who had actually been on their way to the very same ADS. What if she knew people there? What if she remembered why she knew the name Millie Mitchell?'

'Oh,' said Puddle, 'of course. That first night we met Millie at the dance lesson. Blanche reacted to the name like she knew it but couldn't place it.'

'And Annie couldn't take the risk. Blanche would surely have remembered in the end,' said Ellie. 'Once she'd started reminiscing about the plane crash at the Advanced Dressing Station, Blanche's cheerful chatter sealed her fate. Millie decided she had to get rid of her – she couldn't be sure what she knew.'

'And how did she manage that?' asked Ernie. 'How did she poison her?'

'Her saxophone reed,' said Puddle. 'Before that second lesson she must have had time to put poison on the reed. The instruments were left in here while we all milled about the place. Then afterwards she swapped it for a clean one, but put it on wrong – I noticed when I played it.'

'More supposition?' asked Ernie.

'No,' said Sunderland. 'We found a bottle of poison and a discoloured saxophone reed in a tobacco tin in her bag.'

'Fast-acting poison?' said Ernie.

'Relatively,' said Sunderland.

'Then if she swapped the reed before the lesson, why didn't Miss Adams die until after the break?'

'Oh,' said Sunderland. 'Oh, that's a very good question indeed.'

There were murmurs of disappointment.

Puddle let out a little squeak as she realized the answer. 'It was the songs we were playing,' she said.

'The songs protected her from poison?' said Ernie.

'In a way, yes,' said Puddle. 'Before the break she'd been playing the clarinet. She didn't pick up her sax until we started again after our drinks.'

'Well, I'll be blowed,' said Alfie. 'So old Charlie wasn't Charlie at all. And Millie wasn't Millie. And the clarinet wasn't a saxophone. Just goes to show, what?'

'It definitely goes to show something,' said Sunderland. 'We're holding them both at the local nick. I'll let them sweat for the night and question them in the morning. If there's anything different in their stories I'll let you all know. I'll eat my hat first, but I'll let you know.'

It took a while for everyone to digest the news, but eventually the Alphabets and the Dizzies went their separate ways.

◆　◆　◆

Calm descended on the Maloney household for the weekend. The Dizzy Heights had played a private party on Saturday night but that was nothing new for Skins, and life continued around him while he snoozed through most of Sunday morning.

It was business as usual by Monday, though, and the entire family was happily engaged in the usual round of lunchtime shenanigans when the doorbell rang. Mrs Dalrymple knocked on the dining room door to announce a visitor just as Skins and Edward were putting the finishing touches to their mashed-potato model of a horse.

'There's a Mr Daniels to see you,' said Mrs Dalrymple. 'Are you at home?'

'To Danny?' said Skins. 'Definitely.'

'Show him in to the drawing room, would you?' said Ellie. 'Then fetch Nanny to take care of these two. I'll stay here, honey. You go and see to our guest.'

Skins beeped both Edward's and Catherine's noses and made his way through to the drawing room.

'All right, Danny?' he said, holding out his hand. 'Nice to see you. Make yourself at home.'

'Hello,' said Danny, shaking the proffered hand. 'I say, I've not interrupted your lunch, have I?'

'Not at all, mate. Not at all. Fancy some tea? Coffee?'

'Coffee would be wonderful, thank you.'

Skins rang the bell. Before he'd had a chance to sit down, Lottie arrived at a run.

'Yes, sir?' she said.

'Can you get us coffee for three, please, Lots? And check with Nanny in case the kids need anything else.'

'Of course, sir.'

She left as quickly as she'd arrived.

'Nice gaff you've got here,' said Danny. 'For some reason I never imagined you living in a place like this.'

'You'd have been right if I weren't married to Ellie,' said Skins. 'Family money.'

'Ah, I see. Well, it's all very charming.'

Ellie joined them and greeted Danny warmly.

'Do sit down,' she said. 'What's very charming?'

'Your home,' he said. 'And in a lovely area, too.'

'Thank you,' she said. 'We're very happy here.'

Danny smiled. 'I was just saying to Skins – I hope I'm not intruding. I just wanted to thank you.'

'Good heavens. Whatever for?'

'For keeping my war record to yourselves. I spoke to Superintendent Sunderland at the weekend and he told me how he'd delved into our backgrounds based on your conversations with us all. You know all about me now, and there's no need for you to keep mum, but you have anyway. And I greatly appreciate it. Thank you.'

'It's none of anyone's business, far as I'm concerned,' said Skins. 'You had your reasons for doing what you did, and you've got your reasons for keeping quiet about it. It's up to you.'

'It's funny, isn't it?' said Danny. 'At first I was afraid of being called a coward, then I was afraid of being called a hero. I think I just don't like being the centre of attention.'

'There's nothing cowardly about standing up for what you believe in,' said Ellie. 'The cowards were men like Grant who skulked away from their duty. It must have taken great strength to say no to fighting when you knew the whole country would be jeering at you. A coward would have faked a wound or hidden in the woods until it was all over.'

'Well, thank you, anyway. I'd rather my pals didn't know and I'm grateful to you all for not letting on.'

'We'll keep it between ourselves,' said Skins. 'And you can trust Barty and Puddle, too. It's not directly about him so he'll forget all about it by the end of the week, and she's . . . well, she's Puddle. Nothing to worry about.'

He smiled. 'Well, that's thing the first out of the way. On to thing the second. I mentioned my pals.'

'The Alphabet Gang,' said Ellie.

'Yes, indeed. The Alphabet Gang. You know, we either need to recruit a new C or change our name. Lord knows it was confusing enough as it was, what with Alfie's convoluted naming system, but with a missing C it makes even less sense.'

Skins thought for a moment. 'The Common Cold Cheese Boys,' he said after a while.

Danny and Ellie looked at him blankly.

'Well, you've lost your C, so you're A, B, D, E. You could be BADE, BEAD, or EDAB. Like the Dutch cheese, but said when you've got a cold with a bunged-up nose. Edab.'

Ellie rolled her eyes. 'Abed? The Sleepy Gang.'

Danny laughed. 'Let's not rush into anything just yet. At least not without the others. But whatever we're called, we worked dashed hard on those blessed dances and I've been co-opted to seek the assistance of the Dizzy Heights in accompanying the contest once more.'

'The Friday night booking is still in the diary,' said Skins. 'We're happy to play Tipsy Harry's until you get fed up with us.'

'That's what I thought, but it seemed like a sound idea to get your specific assent to do the contest. You have an agreed programme of songs and whatnot?'

'Don't you worry about us,' said Skins. 'We'll be there.'

Lottie arrived with the coffee.

'How are the rest of your buddies?' asked Ellie once they all had their drinks.

'Not wonderful,' said Danny. 'I'm not entirely sure the whole business with your Blanche had properly registered with them before. If it doesn't directly involve them, they don't really pay it much attention. But when it all suddenly turned out to be one of their pals and his girlfriend, it all got a great deal closer to home. There's been lots of agonizing and "Why didn't we spot he was a wrong'un?" Obviously, that comes with a hearty helping of "Of course, I knew there was something fishy about him from the start." Not to mention "A gel that pretty must have been up to no good." They feel betrayed, I think. No one likes finding out that someone in their midst isn't who they suppose him to be.'

He fell silent.

'You really must stop fretting about that,' said Ellie. 'They'll never find out about you. And if they did, I'd bet dollars to doughnuts they'd not think anything of it.'

'Ernie spent the whole time machining metal doodahs for military whatnots, after all. You saved lives. Eight families still have sons, brothers, husbands, fathers, because of you. I know your pals – they'd be proud if they knew.'

'Perhaps,' said Danny.

Skins leaned forward. 'While we're on the subject of the club, though . . . I don't suppose . . . well, has anyone said anything . . . ?'

'About the Treasure of the Mayfair Murderer? They've not stopped talking about it. Trouble is, no one knows anything. The club officials deny all knowledge; the staff haven't got a clue. None of the members, either. Seems the only one to have had even a vague idea was Charlie, and everyone says he was barking up the wrong tree. Other than assuming it has something to do with the "Key of Keys" and the "Tree of Trees", we're all just as much in the dark as always.'

'Probably for the best,' said Skins. 'There's likely some club rule about you all having equal shares in the club's riches, and no good ever comes of being fabulously wealthy.'

Danny laughed. 'You're very wise for a drummer. To be honest, I think it's much more interesting if we don't know. It's nice to have a mystery. But there's one mystery about to be solved: who are the best dancers, Tipsy Harry's or the Wags? How do you rate our chances?'

Ellie and Skins exchanged glances.

'Well . . .' said Skins. 'You've certainly got the best horse.'

Ellie decided she wanted to go along to the Augmented Ninth that night. She loved watching the band play, and even after all these years she still got a thrill from seeing Skins behind his drum set. She remembered that first time she'd seen him at the hotel in Weston as though it had happened fifteen minutes ago, not fifteen years.

She went to the Augmented Ninth often, but usually in the company of one or two of her more raucous friends. Tonight, though, she wanted to be with her other friends, the musicians she'd shared the past few weeks with. Most especially Puddle. She'd known the bubbly woodwind player for quite a while, but recent events had brought them closer together. Ellie wanted to check that she was all right.

Skins and Dunn had set off to collect their instruments from the shop on New Row, leaving Ellie and Nanny to get the monsters into bed with a story and, to Ellie's surprise, a few songs. Nanny Nora, it turned out, possessed not only an unusually pleasant singing voice but also a ukulele of which she was quite an accomplished player. Ellie helped out with the harmonies, and the children joined in the choruses. It was quite the jamboree.

Once everyone was settled, Ellie changed into a cocktail dress and poured herself a gin, which she drank while reading a magazine and listening to gramophone records. Eventually she decided it was time to go, and sent Lottie out to find a cab. By nine she was at her usual table by the stage in the Augmented Ninth.

The band, as Skins was later to say in the tiny green room when they were done, were on fire.

'I thought we were cool,' said Puddle.

'No, we were definitely hot,' rumbled Benny as he disassembled his trombone. 'Trust me, I know hot.'

'Well, I thought you were pretty good,' said Ellie. 'How's everybody holding up?'

'Not bad,' said Mickey. 'Pretty relieved, tell the truth. Glad it's all over, like.'

Elk was replacing a string on his banjo. 'Got that right. I don't half miss old Blanche, but . . . well, it was hard to settle, weren't it? I mean, not knowing. It feels like we can say a proper goodbye now.'

'Talking of which,' said Puddle. 'I heard from Bill this afternoon. The funeral is on Friday. Eleven o'clock at Richmond Cemetery. We're all welcome. He's her only family, so it would be nice if we were all there.'

Eustace looked up from applying a tiny amount of oil to the valves of his trumpet. 'That would be most appropriate. Would it be fitting to play one of her tunes at Tipsy Harry's afterwards, do you think?'

'Definitely,' said Dunn. 'How about something with a bit of oomph like "The Mayfair Stomp"? That always goes down a storm. She'd like to be remembered for making people dance.'

'I reckon she would,' said Elk. 'And . . . you know . . . we'll be in Mayfair an' all.'

'That we will,' said Dunn. 'That we will.'

'They're going ahead with the dance contest, yes?' said Benny.

'They are,' said Skins. 'They thought it would be good to carry on after they'd done all that work for it.'

'Can't disagree with that,' said Benny. 'Best bib and tucker again, then?'

'All the matching clobber,' said Skins. 'A send-off for Blanche, and look our best for the contest.'

'They're going to be a man short,' said Mickey.

'You offering?' said Skins.

'You've seen me dance, mate. What do you think?'

Skins laughed. 'Funny how we're the hottest—'

'Or coolest,' interrupted Puddle.

'You're not going to let that lie, are you? We're great musicians, but we can't dance for toffee.'

'Speak for yourself, darling,' she said. 'I'm a great little mover.'

'Their biggest problem,' said Ellie, 'is that they won't have a coach. Millie-Annie might have been an evil murdering witch, but she knew how to get those boys dancing.'

'You could do it,' said Dunn.

'I most certainly couldn't.'

'No, he's right,' said Skins. 'They know the steps – all they need is someone to gee them up a bit. Give 'em the old "Once more unto the breach" and let them take care of the rest.'

'I can do that, I guess,' she said.

'Course you can. Get them to stiffen the sinews and summon up the blood. They'll love a bit of that.'

'As long as the other lot don't take unkindly to the idea of the band's manager giving the opposition a pep talk,' said Dunn. 'You're supposed to be impartial.'

'It's not as though you actually are our manager, though, darling, is it?' said Puddle. 'We still don't have one.'

Ellie smiled. 'No, but they don't know that.'

'Well, I think I might have the solution to both problems. My sister—'

'Your sister again, Puddle?' said Mickey. 'Are you still on about that?'

'Hear me out. Katy is an absolute organizational wiz. We always rely on her for family parties and whatnot – she put on the most splendid do for Mummy and Daddy's silver wedding. And she keeps the books for her husband's business. She's the ideal candidate.'

'Yes, but what does she know about the entertainment business?' said Eustace. 'It's a cut-throat dog-eat-dog world, you know. It's no place for a woman.'

'Entertainment dogs armed with knives?' said Dunn. 'It does sound terrifying, you're right.'

Eustace just glared at him.

'What do any of us know?' said Puddle. 'We just muddle along as best we can at the moment. She's a wiz, I tell you. She'll get the hang of it in no time. She'll have London's club owners eating out of her hand.'

'I've no objections,' said Benny. 'We could do with someone taking care of the business side of things.'

'I'm all for it,' said Skins. 'Show of hands?'

Mickey, Benny, Elk, Skins, Dunn, and Puddle raised their hands.

'Against?' said Skins, though he knew there was only one objection.

Eustace raised his hand.

'The ayes have it, then,' said Skins. 'Sorry, mate.'

'It'll all end in tears,' said Eustace. 'You mark my words.'

'I've got another proposal, since we're all in a voting mood,' said Puddle.

'You're on a roll, after all,' said Dunn.

'That's what I thought. Some of the arrangements have struggled a bit without Blanche, and Mark isn't going to be able to sit in any more – he's got a chair in an orchestra in Manchester.'

'Who's Mark?' said Elk.

'Puddle's mate from college,' said Skins. 'Been sitting in on sax. Keep up.'

'I've been calling him Percy,' said Elk.

'He won't have taken it personally,' said Puddle. 'And it doesn't matter now anyway, because he's heading up north. So . . . umm . . . well, how do you feel about Vera?'

'From the Finchley Foot-Tappers?' said Mickey.

'Yes. She's fed up with them – they don't treat her at all well – and she's looking for a new seat. I said I'd ask.'

'Anyone heard her?' said Mickey.

'We saw her play at that place in Islington, didn't we, Barty?' said Skins. 'She's not half bad.'

'She's great,' agreed Dunn. 'She's no Blanche, but Pudds can show her the ropes.'

'Two blooming women in the band again,' said Eustace.

'Have I met her?' said Elk.

'You'd know if you had,' said Dunn. 'Short blonde hair. Laughs like a sea lion.'

'Oh, her,' said Elk. 'She's good fun. I vote "yes".'

'Show of hands again?' said Skins.

The vote went the same way, with only Eustace objecting.

'Motion carried,' said Skins. 'Give her the nod, Pudds. If she wants the job it's hers.'

'Thank you,' said Puddle.

'So does this mean I'm free to coach the Alphabet Gang now?' said Ellie.

'Looks that way,' said Skins. 'Can't see anyone having any objections if you're not our manager any more.'

'I bet Eustace could think of an objection, couldn't you, son?' said Dunn.

'What's the point of pretending we're a democracy if we don't get a chance to voice our opinions?' said Eustace. 'I was only saying what I thought.'

Dunn smiled but decided not to antagonize him any further.

'A good night's work, all in all, then,' said Benny. 'And we've got the rest of the week off. If anyone wants to meet for a drink, I'll be at Flapper Sam's on Wednesday night, otherwise I'll see you at the funeral on Friday.'

He picked up his trombone case and headed for the door.

'We'd better be off, too,' said Skins. 'I've got to get the cart back to Covent Garden before I turn into a pumpkin. Or the cart does. There's pumpkins involved, anyway. With drums on.'

The rest of the band agreed that it was time to go, and everyone headed out into early-morning London. Ellie managed to find a cab, while Skins and Dunn wearily pushed the instrument-laden cart back to New Row.

Bloomsbury
June 17, 1925

Dearest Flo
Well, that was bracing, as Emily might say.

I'm sure you'll have read in the newspapers that Arthur Grant and Annie Madigan were arrested last Friday, thanks, in no small part, to yours truly. And the boys. And the rest of the band. And Supt Sunderland. And, of course, you, my dearest friend. Thank you for all your help.

The newspaper reports are reasonably complete, and surprisingly accurate, though I did notice there has been no mention of where the ceremonial regalia (the 'Key of Keys' and the 'Tree of Trees') were found. I managed to slip down to the wine cellar that features so heavily in all the accounts before everything was squared away and found the key in a carved niche in the wall, and the staff inserted in a socket in the ground a few feet away. It could be just coincidence – maybe the holes were for something else entirely and whoever forged the diary thought they'd be just right for fooling a credulous and greedy man – or . . . You know, Flo, I can't give up on the thought that there's something in it.

The whole thing about the 'Key of Keys' and the 'Tree of Trees' and the . . . Oh, Flo, I've had a thought. The 'Knee of Knees'. Part of the ceremonial nonsense was a joke thing about one of the guys' knees. What if . . . But no. It's all bunkum. Of course it is. Shut up, Ellie.

It's been a thrilling few weeks, though, so thank you for mentioning the boys to Sunderland and getting us all involved.

In all the excitement, I completely forgot to tell you that we took Catherine and Edward to the Empire Exhibition in early May to see the London Defended show. It was quite a rousing affair, with horse displays, the fire brigade, and, Edward's favorite, what the advertisements called 'The breathless exploits of the Royal Air Force'. There were planes flying over the stadium, firing blank ammunition at the crowd. It was thrilling and Edward was utterly mesmerized. So . . . I was wondering . . . do you and Emily still have friends in the aeroplane business? Might you be able to show him a real plane close up? He desperately wants to fly and he can carry on dreaming about that, but I wouldn't mind him getting to touch a plane . . . maybe sit in one?

Perhaps we could talk about it the next time you're in town.

Thank you again for opening the door to your exciting world.

My love to you both.

Your friend

Ellie

Chapter Seventeen

Blanche's funeral was in equal measures heartbreaking and uplifting. The sadness of saying farewell to a sister and friend whose life had been tragically cut short by someone else's greed was offset to some extent by sharing stories of the joy and laughter that had followed her wherever she went.

Blanche had many more friends than her brother Bill had realized. The graveside service was so well attended by musicians, club owners, and even one or two jazz fans who had been following her career, that he worried they might not all fit into the function room he had hired at a local hotel for the funeral reception. As it turned out, it was crowded but comfortable.

Bill gave a moving speech about Blanche's childhood, and the scrapes they had got into together. Puddle told a few stories about her life as a working musician. And Skins regaled the assembled friends with a few of the racier tales of Blanche's exploits. Ellie winced at the inappropriateness of one of the stories, but she had badly misread the room. Instead of the tutting and disapproval she had feared, there was only warmth and laughter. The bit about the French waiter and the plate of oysters even earned a cheer and a round of applause.

Despite the competition among local bands for the limited number of bookings, there was no real rivalry between them and they were all pleased to be celebrating the life of one of their own. To Ellie's surprise, there wasn't even any friction between the Dizzy Heights and the Finchley Foot-Tappers when Vera announced her move.

'I think they're glad to be rid of me, to be honest,' said Vera when Ellie asked her about it. 'They never quite knew what to do about having a woman in the band.'

'How's your sight-reading?' said Dunn. 'Fancy coming along with us tonight? We're playing Tipsy Harry's – it's their dance contest.'

'Rather,' she said with a grin. 'I love it there – we played for the Alphabet Gang for a bit, don't forget. Shame about whatshisname. Charlie, wasn't it? He was rather a dish.'

'Kick-off's at nine,' said Skins. 'We set up about eight, but Barty and I will be there from about seven to get our gear in.'

'Lovely,' said Vera. 'I'll see you all there.'

◆ ◆ ◆

'Buy. A. Bloody. Car,' grunted Dunn as they heaved the handcart up a kerb in Soho later that day.

'Be cheaper to persuade Tipsy Harry's to buy a drum set,' said Skins.

'I don't much care how you do it, but there has to be a better way of carting this lot round London.'

'You can be a right miserable bleeder sometimes, you know.'

'What can I say? You bring out the worst in me.'

They arrived at Tipsy Harry's and started setting up on the stage. The Ents Committee had pulled out all the stops for the second attempt at the dance contest, and the ballroom was bedecked with banners, bunting, and streamers. In the week since the first abortive attempt, the committee had decided that it would definitely be an annual event and the banners proclaimed this to be 'The Aristippus Club Dance Contest 1925'.

The hall was full of Cuthberts arranging tables and organizing the temporary bar that had been set up at the far end. The club was keen to erase the memory of the previous week's scandal by making this the event of the year.

With everything set up, including the new embroidered music-stand banners, Skins and Dunn retired to the green room to wait for their friends.

Vera was the first to arrive.

'Hello, boys,' she said. 'Sorry if I'm early, only I didn't want to be late.'

'No one will ever moan at you for being early,' said Skins. 'Help yourself to tea if you want – that's a fresh pot.'

'There's stronger if you want it,' said Dunn.

'I'll get myself a tea in a minute,' she said. 'I don't mind a tipple, but I tend not to indulge before I play. You know that new law they're talking about? Don't want to be fined for being drunk in charge of a woodwind instrument.'

'I don't think it's in force yet,' said Dunn. 'And I think it'll apply more to drummers. Though ours never goes on stage with a snootful.'

'I always say if I'm not fit to drive a car, I'm not fit to play the drums,' said Skins.

'You can't drive a car.'

'Which rather proves my point – you've heard me play. But let me get you a cuppa, Vera. You just make yourself comfy.'

'Thank you,' she said. 'No one in the Foot-Tappers ever offered me tea – they expected me to make it for them.'

Puddle had entered the room. 'It's your first day, darling – they're trying to impress you. Give it a couple of weeks and they'll be getting you to darn their socks.'

'All right, Pudds?' said Skins. 'Do you want one?'

'Always, darling. Never been known to say no to a cup of tea before a show.'

They sat around one of the tables that had been left in the room for them.

'Do you want to run through the arrangements for tonight?' asked Puddle.

'I think I'll be all right,' said Vera. 'It all looks straightforward enough, and I've seen you play a few times so I should be able to keep up. It's not simple, mind you, but it makes sense. No wonder you chaps are so highly thought of – there's some clever stuff in there.'

'It's Puddle's work, mostly,' said Skins. 'Puddle and Benny – trombone player.'

'He's the handsome West Indian chap?' said Vera. 'I think he's the only one of your mob I've not properly met. All the others crop up on the circuit from time to time.'

'That's the bloke,' said Dunn. 'You'll like him. Everyone likes Benny.'

One by one, the other members of the band arrived. Instruments were tuned and warmed up. Skins worked through his own warm-up exercises by beating out complex rhythms on every available surface with a pair of drumsticks. Mickey's vocal warm-ups were supplemented by a cup of hot water with honey.

'Does that actually do you any good?' asked Elk, not for the first time.

'No idea, mate,' said Mickey. 'But it feels like it ought to. And that's half of it, ain't it?'

At half past eight, everyone was ready, so they decided to go out early and play while the guests were arriving.

As the time approached, the Dizzy Heights drew their overture to a graceful close and one of the club officials from the week before got up on stage, though this time without his ceremonial regalia. A hush descended and he made much the same speech as he had made seven days earlier.

There were to be three dances, he told them, with both clubs dancing at the same time. There had been much debate over whether to include partners so that they might dance something like a traditional waltz, or the new foxtrot, but it was decided to spare the ladies the embarrassment of having to dance with duffers, and to give the duffers no one to hide behind. They would dance alone.

The winner would be decided by a jury of instructors who had been enticed in from local dance schools with the promise of free booze and the chance to recruit fresh students from among the assembled revellers.

It had originally been intended that there should be five members of each team, but due to 'certain circumstances', the Alphabet Gang from Tipsy Harry's could only field four, and the Wags had graciously offered to leave their weakest dancer on the bench.

The prize would be a case of champagne for the winning team and an engraved plaque for their club.

Once the audience had retreated to the edges of the room and the dancers had paraded before them, the master of ceremonies introduced the Dizzy Heights. Everything, it seemed, was in place.

As promised, Ellie was on the dance floor as the Alphabets' coach. Once she was satisfied that her boys were ready, she gave Skins the nod and he counted the band in for the first number.

The dancing, as had been widely forecast, was a hilariously chaotic frenzy of arms and legs with very little actual skill in evidence, but with the addition of a pantomime horse. Alfie and Ernie had given the horse a policeman's helmet to wear in honour of its role in the capture of a notorious jewel thief and his murderous fiancée, and the crowd loved it.

The judges were less impressed, and between them awarded the Alphabets eighteen points out of a possible forty, while the Wigglers managed to scrape a slightly more respectable twenty-three.

The second dance was a straightforward Charleston, and was most definitely the Alphabets' strong suit. They'd worked out a tricksy routine involving doing the 'Bee's Knees' with the horse's legs. With Alfie and Ernie crouching slightly, Bertie and Danny reached across and put their hands on the 'horse's' knees to look as if the knees were moving through each other. Always a crowd-pleaser, and even better on a pantomime horse.

It got a massive laugh, and helped to boost their score for that dance to an impressive twenty-seven. With the Wigglers maintaining their mediocre standard and earning twenty-two points, the teams were tied going into the third and final dance at forty-five points apiece.

It was all to play for as Skins counted in the final number. The Wags started strongly, stepping neatly in unison and executing their turns with uncharacteristic precision. It looked as though they had it sewn up, but the Alphabets had one last trick up their collective sleeve. Unbeknown to everyone, including the band, Alfie and Ernie had been secretly working on a tap-dance routine. As the song reached the middle eight, Bertie and Danny stepped aside to give the horse room and off they went.

It was a massive hit. No one noticed that Ernie was out of time or that Alfie kept getting the sequence of steps wrong. It was a tap-dancing horse. The crowd went wild, the judges were on their feet, and the scores, when they came in, reflected everyone's enthusiasm for the dance. The Wigglers were awarded thirty-six points, with the head judge commenting especially on their synchronicity. But for sheer entertainment value, as well as the demonstration of a skill the other team didn't possess, they gave the Alphabets thirty-seven points and declared them the evening's overall winners by just one point.

The room went wild. Men cheered, ladies whooped, champagne corks popped, and the band played 'For He's a Jolly Good Fellow'.

It was all over bar the celebrations, and they continued into the small hours.

◆ ◆ ◆

Cuthbert, Cuthbert, and Cuthbert were sweeping up the streamers and mopping up the spilled champagne as the band packed away their instruments. They had been joined on stage by Ellie, who was helping Skins dismantle his drum set, and by an unknown woman who was talking to Puddle. There was definitely a family resemblance, though the newcomer had longer hair and wore a more expensive dress.

'Everyone?' said Puddle. 'This is my sister, Katy. I'm pleased to be able to announce that she's accepted the job, and is now the Dizzy Heights' new manager.'

The band applauded and offered their welcomes and congratulations. Eustace wasn't quite so enthusiastic as the others, but even he was secretly pleased that they finally had someone to make sure there were beer and towels in the green room.

'Thank you, everyone,' said Katy. 'I know you're taking an extraordinary gamble in taking me on as manager, but I won't let you down. And by way of demonstrating my commitment, I've already secured a new booking.'

The Dizzies reacted with some astonishment at this news.

'Next weekend,' she went on, grinning broadly, 'you'll be playing at the Midsummer Ball at Bilverton House in Oxfordshire. I've booked a charabanc to pick everyone and their instruments up on Friday morning.'

Above all the astonishment, the 'Yes, but what about . . . ?' and the 'Blimey, that was quick work . . .', one voice asked the most important question.

'How much are we getting?' asked Skins.

'Not much, I'm afraid,' said Katy. 'I could only manage to get you a hundred guineas.'

There were gasps.

'You, madam,' said Eustace, 'are most definitely hired. Welcome to the Dizzy Heights.'

Author's Note

The Aristippus Club (Tipsy Harry's) is entirely fictional, as are the Wags Club and the Augmented Ninth. The nineteenth-century jewellery theft is made-up, too.

The Lamb and Flag just round from New Row on Rose Street is real, though, and still exists. The Coach and Horses on Avery Row in Mayfair is now known as the Iron Duke.

There was a Barratt's sweet factory in Wood Green, and my mother grew up on Coburg Road just round the corner – in the house occupied in the story by Barty Dunn and his landlady Phyllis Cordell. The house no longer stands, but I do have vague memories of being taken along the street of Victorian terraced houses as a child and shown where my mother had once lived.

I have similarly vague memories of being shown an off-licence ('liquor store' for American readers) on New Row in Covent Garden, which my parents ran in the early 1960s before I was born. The shop still stands – though it's no longer an off-licence – and the street hasn't changed a great deal.

It's for these sentimental family reasons that both locations (Wood Green and New Row) appear in the book. I have no connection with Mayfair, though I have walked through its streets many times as a way of getting about while avoiding Oxford Street. To date I've never seen a nightingale in Berkeley Square, much less heard it sing, but that's probably because nightingales are now incredibly rare in central London, and there's not really anywhere suitable for them to live in Berkeley Square even if they do venture into town. No one in the story would think to mention this improbable bird, either, because the song 'A Nightingale Sang in Berkeley Square' was written in 1939.

The original headquarters of the Metropolitan Police was at Whitehall Place, with a rear entrance on Great Scotland Yard. This became the public entrance and the HQ became known simply as Scotland Yard. By the time of our story, New Scotland Yard had moved to the Norman Shaw Buildings on Victoria Embankment, just up the road from the Houses of Parliament. In 1967 it moved to a tower block on Broadway, and in 2013 moved back to Victoria Embankment in the Curtis Green Building, next door to Norman Shaw Buildings.

Superintendent Sunderland first met Skins and Dunn in the first Lady Hardcastle Mystery, *A Quiet Life in the Country*, which is set in 1908 when he was an inspector with the Bristol CID and they were the rhythm section in Roland Richman's Ragtime Revue.

The average height of a working-class British man in 1914 was 5'2", while aristocrats stood at 5'6". The British Army had a minimum height requirement of 5'3", though, which might account for the average height of a British soldier in WWI being 5'7". Incidentally, the minimum height requirement excluded many physically fit volunteers in 1914 and so 'Bantam Battalions' were quickly set up to accommodate them. At 4'9", Henry Thridgould was the shortest corporal in the British Army.

Lyons Corner Houses were three popular restaurants in central London from 1909 to 1977, offering a slightly less casual dining experience than Lyons cafés. They were also, according to my mother, famous for their quick service and fast turnaround. Whenever a waiter took her empty plate after what she considered too short an interval, she would declare, 'It's like a bleedin' Lyons Corner House in here.'

To this day, bands usually leave drummers to carry their own equipment, and often complain loudly about the amount of time it takes them to set up. I'm not bitter.

The alpacas appear at the Aristippus Club as the result of a challenge laid down in the bar at the Theakston Old Peculier Crime Writing Festival in 2019. The conversation had arrived at the subject of alpacas (I shan't trouble you with the tortured journey we took to get there) and someone suggested that we should all attempt to mention one of the adorable creatures in at least the first draft of our next books. Would our editors notice, we wondered? (Mine would – he was standing next to us while we giggled over it like schoolchildren.) I knew exactly how to go about it and agreed enthusiastically. If you see alpacas in any crime or thriller books published between the middle of 2020 and the middle of 2021, you'll know I wasn't the only one who managed it.

Lady Hardcastle makes a show of knowing which years produced the finest champagne. There's an argument to be made that there's no such thing as bad champagne, but she's right that 1921 and 1915 were declared 'vintage' years. So, as it happens, were 1914, 1919, and 1920, but she can't be expected to know everything.

The band's joke mottos – 'Don't get your hopes up', 'Prepare to be disappointed', and 'Music for people who are too drunk to know any better' – were all coined by my bass-playing friend Jim Randell, for the band in which we both play: Macaroni Penguins. We're not as bad as we like to make out, but it does help if the audience has had a glass or two before we start.

'The Bluebird of Somewhere' who Skins and Dunn vaguely remember was the French serial killer Henri Désiré Landru, 'The Bluebeard of Gambais', who murdered at least eleven people (possibly more) between 1915 and 1919. He was executed in 1922. Obviously they wouldn't have known him as a 'serial killer' – according to the Oxford English Dictionary, that term is first recorded in print in 1967.

It's inordinately difficult to work out the changing value of money over time. Many websites exist to make the conversion, and they use many different strategies based on inflation, purchasing power, average wages, etc. I got very bogged down in all this and ended up just plumping for one. The source I used has £25,000 in 1918 being equivalent to £1.4m in 2019 (the time of writing).

Barty Dunn's calculation of his own value in gold is based on the easily obtained value of gold bullion and the more-or-less fixed values of sterling and the US dollar in 1925. The diamond value is more of a fudge. Gemstone prices are less well recorded, but I did manage to find a reference in the US Geological Survey's archives to historical values. They have normalized the values to the value of the US dollar in 1998 so there was some wild, wild approximation on my part, but I still think the number he comes up with is reasonable.

Using the same calculation, I worked out that the amount of diamonds stolen by Grant in 1917 would, as Puddle suggests, have weighed as much as a squirrel.

'The Third Disgusting Fusiliers' is a reference to a regiment mentioned in the 1950s BBC radio series *The Goon Show*. I discovered the Goons as a child in the mid-1970s through LPs released by EMI and then the BBC. Spike Milligan's absurdist humour has always hit the spot for me and I often try to sneak in *Goon Show* references when I can.

The "phobias" bit in Chapter Seven came from an email exchange in the mid-1990s with my friend Henry Phillips, while we were working on a variety of comedy projects that never quite took off. I don't know how it started, but I still had the list in a file on my hard drive. No effort is ever wasted.

If you'd like to know more about the work of nurses during the First World War, I recommend *A Nurse at the Front: The First World War Diaries of Sister Edith Appleton* by Edith Elizabeth Appleton (Simon & Schuster), and *Women in the War Zone: Hospital Service in the First World War* by Anne Powell (The History Press).

In March 1916, all medically fit single men in Britain between the ages of eighteen and forty-one were automatically conscripted into the armed forces. In May this was extended to married men. There were exemptions for 'scheduled occupations' – clergymen, teachers, and some industrial workers producing essential supplies – but everyone else had to serve. Local tribunals would decide other applications for exemption from service on a case-by-case basis, and those men would be issued papers and a brass badge to prove their status. These exemptions were rare and it would have taken some string-pulling from some very influential people to ensure that Oliver Sunderland and Edwin Cashmore remained on the Home Front for the duration.

Charlie's quote about plans not surviving first contact with the enemy is usually attributed to Field Marshal Helmuth Karl Bernhard Graf von Moltke. It's no wonder none of them could remember his name.

They meet two men in Soho arguing about the Football League. Arsenal had finished third from bottom at the end of the 1924–25 season, narrowly avoiding relegation. Against Barty Dunn's partisan prediction, though, they finished the 1925–26 season in second place. His own team, Tottenham Hotspur, continued to prop up the middle of the table.

The idea of conscientious objectors serving as ambulance drivers in WWI is a popular one (it was even included in an episode of the popular British sitcom *Dad's Army*), but actually it was quite rare. Still, I liked the idea of Danny being an unsung hero, so I let him join the RAMC.

Vera mentions 'the new law' and talks about being 'drunk in charge of a woodwind instrument'. The law was the Criminal Justice Act 1925, which made it an offence to be found drunk in charge of a motor vehicle on any highway or in any other public place. It was the first UK law specifically prohibiting drinking and driving. It was not passed until December 1925, but, obviously, it had been discussed a great deal – and a clued-up person like Vera would have been well aware of it.

Using the same calculator as for the value of the uncut diamonds, their 100-guinea (£105) fee for the Midsummer Ball would be the equivalent of roughly £6,300 in 2019.

About the Author

T E Kinsey grew up in London and read history at Bristol University. He worked for a number of years as a magazine feature writer before falling into the glamorous world of the Internet, where he edited content for a very famous entertainment website for quite a few years more. After helping to raise three children, learning to scuba dive and to play the drums and the mandolin (though never, disappointingly, all at the same time), he decided the time was right to get back into writing. *The Deadly Mystery of the Missing Diamonds* is the first novel in a series of mysteries starring Skins and Dunn and their band, the Dizzy Heights. Tim is also responsible for the popular Lady Hardcastle Mysteries. His website is at tekinsey.uk and you can follow him on Twitter – @tekinsey – as well as on Facebook: www.facebook.com/tekinsey.

Photo © 2018 Clifton Photographic Company